# DEAD CALM

By
Jon Schafer

## Book Two of The Dead Series

Copyright© 2013 Jon Schafer

Cover art by David Reyes, but you know him on Fiverr as Bluecuore
Modification for the paperback edition by Jon Schafer

For Catface, Rocky, Kaiser, Kasey and Jaz.

Acknowledgments:
I want to thank my brother Steve and my friend Patti Mercier for all their hard work. Susan Herkness for deciphering my writing and putting it in a format that you all can read. If you're looking for a good editor, you can find her on Facebook at https://www.facebook.com/susan.herkness. Thanks to Orlando Fernandez for his first read of this book and a special thanks to Mac and Brat for their typing skills.

This book is a work of fiction. Names, characters, businesses, organizations, places, events and incidents are either the product of the author's imagination or are used fictitiously. Any resemblance to actual persons, living or dead, events, or locales is entirely coincidental.

Visit Jon Schafer's website at http://www.jonscatbooks.com/
or find him on Facebook at http://www.facebook.com/jon.schafer.94
Watch the promo video on YouTube at
http://www.youtube.com/watch?v=eOiSCF9QbWY

**Dead Calm**: A condition of no wind according to the Beaufort scale.

Chapter One

The Gulf of Mexico:

Steve Wendell woke with a start.

Jolting upward, he cursed as he banged his head against the low ceiling and fell back onto the mattress. Rubbing the knot already swelling on his forehead, he swung his legs out from under the blanket and placed them on the deck before cautiously trying again. Once upright, his eyes focused on the wall of the small cabin, memories of the dream that woke him rushing to the forefront of his mind.

Dead, decaying arms reached up from the depths of the clear blue waters of the Gulf of Mexico, grabbing and clawing at the hull of a sailboat. The hands dragged along its length, causing it to stop dead in the water. His sailboat, their sailboat, the sailboat named The Usual Suspects that he and his fellow survivors took after fleeing the city of Clearwater and the flesh eating dead that populated it. Shaking off the residual images of the nightmare, he pulled on a pair of cutoff jeans and his tennis shoes before slowly standing. Although the 48-foot sailboat they had taken was spacious enough for the seven people who had escaped the city of the dead, the cabin he and Heather shared in the bow had a slanted overhead which he always seemed to be hitting his head on.

Stooping slightly, he navigated around a cardboard box half filled with MRE's they had salvaged from a National Guard MRAP after its crew had been killed and eaten. Opening the door, not a door, he reminded himself, Tick-Tock told them to call it a hatch, he entered the main sleeping compartment. Bunk beds were set into the walls on each side of this area to create a corridor with a long table set in the middle. In the dim glow of a night-light, he could see that four of the beds were occupied.

Not wanting to wake anyone one and hear the ever-present questions, Steve quietly made his way past the sleeping forms and let himself through the hatch at the far end. Entering the next compartment, he glanced with longing at the small, enclosed shower. He would have liked nothing better than to sit under its spray and soap off the salt and grime caked on his body, but since water was at a premium this was not to be. Running along the left bulkhead was the galley. He approached the stove and removed the coffee pot from the brackets. He poured a mug and quickly downed the tepid brew. Grimacing at the hours old coffee, he muttered, "Not recommended to be taken internally except in an extreme caffeine emergency."

Glancing at his watch, he saw it was a little past five AM. Knowing the others would be awake soon, he poured more water from their dwindling supply into the container and added grounds to make a fresh pot. Re-securing it in its brackets, he adjusted the gas flame to the lowest setting before moving to the ladder leading to the cockpit. Above him, he could hear Tick-Tock say something and Heather laugh in reply. He paused as he considered the one good thing to come from having the dead walk the earth.

Heather.

A Pinellas County Sheriff's Deputy, she had been working part time at a bowling alley to help pay off her student loans when Steve met her. Although both were in a relationship at the time, they found themselves attracted to each other. They drew even closer when the HWNW virus loosed itself on the world, killing off its victims before bringing them back to life to feed on the living. It seemed like they'd just found each other though, when the disease split them apart.

On the night the dead rose up to challenge the living for possession of the Tampa Bay area, Steve went in search of his current girlfriend, Ginny, hoping he could bring her to the safe area he had prepared in the Garnett Bank Building where he managed a radio station. He had spent the previous days securing the high rise and had stockpiled supplies to help them survive the expected waves of walking dead. Ginny had not taken the growing threat of the HWNW virus seriously and had gone out bar hopping with friends in Tampa. After searching for her, and with no other way to find her, he had retreated to the safety of the bank building.

Meanwhile, Heather had been called to duty by the Sherriff's department to help repel the hordes of flesh eating dead that had clawed their way out of the sewers and storm drains running beneath Pinellas County. She fought side by side with her fellow law enforcement officers, but they were overwhelmed by the rapidly growing number of flesh eaters and pushed back into a small pocket near the St. Petersburg pier. When the Sheriff saw that the situation had deteriorated beyond anything his deputies could be expected to deal with, he released them from their duties so they might find shelter wherever they could. Although the pier itself was a safe area, to Heather, shelter meant joining up with Steve, four cities and dozens of miles away.

Since the living dead now populated the route overland, she had set out alone in a small, open boat.

After navigating her way around the peninsula that forms Pinellas County, Heather crept on foot through the city of Clearwater, now filled with tens of thousands of zombies. She made her way as far as a rooftop across from the Garnett Bank Building and managed to signal Steve. With the help of the other survivors holed up with him, he succeeded in getting her to the relative safety of the high rise. Once reunited, they rarely left each other's side. They might have failed in their individual endeavors, but not from lack of doing everything in their power.

Climbing the ladder, Steve poked his head up through the hatch and looked around the darkened cockpit of the sailboat. Heather spotted him and motioned for him to sit by her. Tick-Tock gave him a thumbs-up from where he lounged in a captain's chair behind the wheel.

The dark silence of the calm night made Heather speak just above a whisper as she said with a laugh, "Tick-Tock is one warped individual. Where did you ever dig him up?"

Steve smiled and shrugged as he settled into his seat. Tick-Tock had been working as one of the disc jockeys at the radio station he managed. Being in need of people with special skills, he invited the man to join him along with some of the others who worked there. As a former Marine and part-time adventure seeker, Tick-Tock quickly became his number two, making himself indispensable in helping to secure their position.

And trying to defend it.

The end had come when, after months of living in relative security, the dead breached their defenses and flooded the building. It had been Tick-Tock who slowed the initial assault and helped buy them time to evacuate. But even before that, when Marcia and Heather had discovered a ten year old girl hiding in the building, who appeared to be immune to the HWNW virus, it had been Tick-Tock's idea to use a sailboat to take her to one of the military bases that dotted the Florida coastline. It was everyone's hope that the child might hold the cure for the disease of the dead.

Looking at the endless expanse of flat, dark water around them, Steve asked, "Seen anything?"

"Couple of dolphins," Tick-Tock answered, "besides that, nothing. No boats, no planes, not even a mermaid to keep me company."

Heather spoke up, "I didn't see anything on my watch either. I crashed out for a while when Tick-Tock took over, and just came up here a few minutes ago to get some fresh air."

Steve found his unease at the situation growing. He had been hopeful that during the night, when lights stood out better, one of them would spot another craft. Their situation was getting desperate as their food and water was depleted. If something didn't happen soon, they would have to take drastic action.

The small group of survivors had set out over a week ago from Clearwater, their destination being the naval base in Key West. Everything was going smoothly until they reached a point just south of Fort Myers. Here, their original plan to follow the coast was frustrated by a late season storm that came up and blew them out into the Gulf. They were tossed around for two days before the storm passed, and then found themselves becalmed in its wake. For five days now there had barely been the slightest breeze to propel the sailboat or even cause a ripple on the water's surface.

Although they had a small engine in the stern of the sailboat, their fuel supply was limited to what they had on board. Until they could determine their position, they couldn't afford to waste it by heading in an arbitrary direction. If the storm had blown them too far to the south and they headed east to where there should be land, they might end up going through the Florida Straits and out into the Atlantic Ocean. Or, if they had been blown near the coast of Mexico or Texas, they would be heading in the wrong direction if they went east. Despite the mystery of their location, they decided to let the slight breeze that occasionally came up take them in an easterly direction in the hope they could reacquire the Florida coast.

"Still nothing on the GPS?" Steve asked Heather, whose job it was to monitor the device.

"It locks onto a signal every few hours but loses it before the coordinates come through," she replied. "Brain looked at it again and said it's not the electronics. Everything checks out. He thinks it's got to be a problem with the satellites, so there's nothing we can do about it."

Steve nodded. Brain had been an engineer at the radio station and was their tech guru.

Turning to Tick-Tock, he stated the obvious, "And still no wind."

Tick-Tock pointed to the slack sails in response. "Just barely making headway."

"Still heading east?" he asked.

Tick-Tock nodded in reply and then asked, "How are we doing on food and water?"

Steve sighed, "Food for another week, but we've only got enough water for three days if we stretch it. The inboard water tank is down to just a few gallons. Then all we have left is the water we brought with us. After we finish this pot of coffee, I'm going to put a restriction on who can drink it to only those on wheel watch. If we don't spot anything by tonight, we're going to have to crank up the engine and start heading east. It's a risk, but one we have to take. We can go without food for about three weeks if we have to, but without water, we won't last two or three days."

"When you caught Mary taking a shower, you should have thrown her worthless ass overboard," Tick-Tock said.

Steve nodded. His chief detractor was Mary Oliver. The former morning show host had only been included in Steve's plan to take refuge in the radio station because her brother owned it. In her quest for self-gratification, she ignored everyone's needs except her own. Now, like it or not, she was part of the group and was expected to pull her own weight. Steve had major doubts this would actually ever happen.

Heather laughed harshly. "I still can't believe what she said when you caught her." In a high-pitched mimic of Mary's voice she said, "But I'm not drinking it, I'm washing in it."

"If living, breathing human beings weren't in such short supply right now, I'd have cut her up and used her for shark bait," Steve replied.

A slight breeze rattled the sails, raising their hopes, but both deflated as quickly as they came up.

Noise from below caught their attention, so Heather bent down into the hatch to see who it was. Straightening, she said, "Susan and Cindy."

Susan had come along with Mary when Steve locked down the Garnett Bank Building. The two were a couple until Susan started to gravitate to Tick-Tock. Not wanting a jealous love triangle while they were living in such restricted quarters, Steve brought the situation out into the open the night they sailed. He made the three of them promise to back off from one another, no fucking or fighting, until they were once again on dry land.

A small voice called up through the open hatch to wish all of them a good morning.

This was Cindy, the group's hope for a cure. After her little brother, who was infected with the HWNW virus, bit her, Cindy's immune system fought off the disease. The day before the dead broke into the Garnett Bank Building, Heather and Marcia had come across the little girl hiding in some unused offices. After they saw the half-healed bite marks on her arm and came to the conclusion that she was immune, they laid plans to take her somewhere so that she could be studied and a cure found.

The three returned Cindy's greeting and then fell into a restless silence until Susan appeared carrying a tray with mugs of coffee on it. After passing these around, she took a seat on the far side of the cockpit from Tick-Tock. Since Steve's meeting about their back-and-forth relationship, she went out of her way to avoid both Tick-Tock and Mary.

False dawn came and went with the four of them sipping coffee as the boat drifted in an easterly direction. Steve, Heather and Tick-Tock tried to keep as much of the deteriorating situation to themselves as they could, but the group's state was readily apparent to Susan and Brain. Only Cindy and Mary seemed unaware of the danger they faced.

As dawn broke, Heather pointed to the northeast and said, "Cloud on the horizon, maybe we'll pick up some wind, or it'll rain and we can get some fresh water."

Steve squinted in that direction and felt his hopes rise when he spotted the faint smudge in the distance. In the days since the storm had passed, the sky had been cloudless and blue, so this was a very welcome sight. They desperately needed some wind. If it didn't kick in by nightfall, they would have to crank up the engine and take their chances heading east. He knew if they ran out of fuel before they reached land that they were in deep shit, but it seemed their options were getting more limited as time went by.

Feeling the discouraged mood of the group, Susan stood to go below and see what Cindy was up to. She had set the little girl to picking out breakfast MRE's from their dwindling supply and had promised to let her help put them together into some semblance of food.

As she moved to the hatch, she heard the sound of small feet pounding up the ladder. Stepping aside and turning to her left to give Cindy room to pass, her eyes locked on the small smudge in the distance. Remembering when she was little how she used to try and find shapes in the clouds, she asked Cindy what she thought it looked like.

Cindy studied the formless mass for a moment before saying, "Aw, that's not a cloud, Susan. It's a great big ship. You can see the smoke stack and everything."

Bored with the game, she turned to Heather to ask if they could go fishing later, but found herself ignored as everyone in the cockpit crowded the rail to look at something. Wedging herself between Steve and Heather, she couldn't figure out what was so exciting. It was just a big boat, and they already had a boat.

Wondering if Brain was awake, she went below to see if he wanted to play Monopoly before breakfast.

***

"That kid must have eyes like a hawk," Tick-Tock said as he steered the sailboat toward the vessel in the distance. "We all looked at that ship and thought it was a cloud. Shit, I could barely even tell what it was when I scoped it out with the binoculars."

Steve nodded in reply as the sailboat's small engine pushed them at a steady pace through the flat water. After days of barely making headway, he was enjoying the breeze brought on by the motion.

Heather agreed, "I must have looked at it a half dozen times and all I saw was a cloud."

Raising a pair of binoculars to his eyes, Steve commented, "Morning light is tricky. Sometimes it's hard to tell what you're looking at." To Tick-Tock, he asked, "How big do you think she is?"

Tick-Tock scrutinized the ship through his binoculars before replying, "Hard to tell. She's still a long way off and she was broadside to us when we first spotted her. Now we're looking at her bow on."

"Is it coming toward us?" Heather asked.

"I'll say no," Tick-Tock answered. "Looks dead in the water. I don't see any navigation lights, and it doesn't seem to be making any headway. It could be spinning on its anchor, but there's no wind. My guess is her rudder is turned and she's spinning in the current."

Steve let the binoculars drop to hang from the strap around his neck and asked, "How long until we're close?"

After judging the distance, Tick-Tock replied, "We're only making five or six knots, so I'd say it'll take over an hour."

"It seems like we're moving faster," Heather commented.

"That's because we've been sitting still for the past few days," Tick-Tock replied.

"If we've got an hour, then we've got enough time for a war council," Steve said. "We should go over our options." Leaning into the open hatch, he called out, "Brain, we need you up here."

The engineer appeared seconds later asking, "What's up? Are we close to that ship yet?"

Steve shook his head, "Not yet, I need you to steer the boat while we figure out how to handle this."

As Brain came on deck, Steve noticed how much weight the man had lost. Before Dead Day, Brain had been grossly overweight. This, combined with his arrogant attitude, made Steve reluctant to include him in his plan. Now he was glad he'd asked the young engineer to join them. After all they'd gone through since then, Brain had proven his worth countless times.

"Whatever you decide, count me in," The Tech said as he took the wheel.

Because of Brain's ego problem before Dead Day, or D-Day as they sometimes called it, Steve was reluctant to tell him that his engineering talents were too valuable to risk by allowing him to board the ship. He didn't want the young man's head to swell up so much it wouldn't fit through the door. While he didn't want to put any of the survivor's lives at risk, he knew that in the post dead world, Brain's knowledge was priceless in their struggle to survive.

"First, we have to figure out what kind of ship it is," Tick-Tock said. "From what I can see it looks like a tanker."

Brain shook his head, "It's not a tanker. It's a cruise ship. I could tell earlier when I looked at it through the binoculars. Every year on my Mom's birthday, I used to take her on a cruise."

"Cruise ship," Heather asked with excitement, "like in 'The Love Boat' cruise ship?"

Brain nodded, "It's so obvious, I didn't mention it."

Obvious to you maybe, Steve thought. Scrutinizing the craft in the distance, he said, "That little baby could have everything we need. Food, water and even gas for the engine."

"And showers," Heather added. "It's getting old trying to wash up with salt water."

"And shops for Mary to browse through, la-di-fucking-da," Tick-Tock wisecracked. Turning serious, he added, "But if their GPS is working, we can plot our position and figure out where in the hell we are. Even if it's out, we're not totally screwed. All we need to do is find a sextant, a nautical almanac and an accurate chronometer and I can plot our position and course by hand. On a ship that big, I'm sure one of the officers will have them."

"Do you know how to do that?" Brain asked. "Figure out where we are?"

"Haven't done it since I was a kid, but then again, I haven't sailed since then, and I seem to be doing a pretty good job so far."

No one could dispute this comment. During the storm, Tick-Tock had stayed on deck for its duration with Steve as his first mate. The two of them brought The Usual Suspects through twenty-foot troughs of water and battering winds with no loss of life or serious damage to the craft.

The conversation turned to the bounty the ship could provide, and their mood was charged with excitement, until Steve brought them back to earth by saying, "But first we have to figure out how to get on board."

\*\*\*

The four who would be in the boarding party, Steve, Heather, Tick-Tick and Susan, sat around the table in the forward cabin as they ran through the possibilities of who they might find on the cruise ship.

"It could be abandoned," Susan said hopefully.

"Abandoned by the living," Tick-Tock said. "That would leave us with a ship full of the dead to deal with."

"Or it might be full of the living," Heather added.

"In which case we'd be looked on as intruders," Steve pointed out. "Remember how we were prepared to kill anyone who tried to take what was ours at the bank building?"

"But this is different," Susan said.

Shaking his head, Tick-Tock spoke up, "No, it's not, we're just on the other side now."

The thought of being the bad guys didn't sit well with those gathered around the table. The label 'Looter' wasn't one they wanted to wear.

In their defense, Susan said, "But if someone had come to us peacefully, we wouldn't have turned them away. Look at that Harrison guy for example. You fed him and let him stay, and he was crazy as a loon." Looking directly at Steve she added, "And I'm sure we would have helped anyone else who asked. Hopefully, whoever's on board that ship will act as civilized as we did. I think it all hinges on how we approach them. If we go in with guns drawn, then they'll react in kind. If we signal them and ask for assistance, they might be more receptive to helping us."

Steve inwardly cringed at hearing Brian Harrison's name. The man had been found, half insane, holed up in an office on the twelfth floor of the Garnett Bank Building. They had come across him when they swept the building after losing one of their own to a zombie that emerged from its hiding place.

Donna was the first person lost under Steve's command and he took it hard. She had been bitten and infected, and he was the one who put a bullet in her heart to kill her before she died and came back. The two things that saved him that night from taking his own life were his overwhelming will to never give up, and the appearance of Heather.

Steve didn't know how the dead had breached the defenses of the building, but he had a suspicion that Harrison was involved somehow. The night the dead broke in, they lost three of their number. Jonny G, his girlfriend Marcia and Mary's morning show partner, Meat.

"We might want to seriously consider talking nice first," Tick-Tock decided. "If anyone's left alive on that cruise ship, and they're armed, we'd be hard pressed to mount any kind of assault against them. We'll take casualties."

"So, we'll try the soft approach first and ask to come aboard," Steve said.

"And if that doesn't work? If they tell us to go to hell?" Susan asked.

Steve said with determination, "Then we have no other option than to take that ship by force. I didn't make it this far to die at sea." Turning to Tick-Tock, he asked, "You were in the Marines, any ideas on how we can do this?"

His second in command thought about this for a second before saying, "A few. It depends on how many people we're going up against and how well armed they are. I remember reading that after 9/11 they removed all the shotguns used to shoot skeet from the cruise ships sailing out of U.S. ports. That'll at least cut down on any potential arsenal they might have. The ship's officers will have a few weapons. Maybe a couple rifles or a pistol or two. If this is a normal cruise that got interrupted by the HWNW virus, then we should be in good shape if we have to storm her. On the other hand, if that ship was taken by people fleeing the virus, then there's no telling what kind of firepower they have."

"I agree," Heather said. "Look at the weapons we've put together. M-4 automatic rifles, pistols, ammunition," turning to Tick-Tock, she added with a smile, "and that big old .50 caliber machine gun you insisted on bringing along. Why would you want that thing out here anyway?"

"To repel boarders," Tick-Tock answered in a matter of fact tone. "Let's just hope they don't have one too."

***

The cruise ship continued to spin around as they approached. When Steve went topside after the meeting ended, he saw that the stern was coming around to point in their direction. Now that the sailboat had closed in on the larger craft, its enormous size became more apparent. Looking at what he could see of its length, Tick-Tock estimated that the ship was around a thousand feet. As the rear of the vessel spun into view, they raised their binoculars and tried to make out the cruise liner's name painted on the stern.

"Calm of the Seas," Steve read aloud before lowering his binoculars.

Tick-Tock relieved Brain at the wheel, and after checking their position, said, "Now I'm sure she's dead in the water." Glancing at the brass gauges mounted above the steering station, he made a slight alteration in their course and added, "We've entered a current. I can feel the tug on the wheel and we've sped up by a couple knots. Current's moving in the same direction that ship's heading. This has got to be part of the Gulf Stream that loops south of the States before flowing out through the Florida straits. Since it's pulling us northeast, I'd say we're closer to the coast of Mexico or Texas than we are to Florida."

"The storm blew us that far?" Steve asked in disbelief.

"We were riding a wind out of the east for two days, so I'm surprised we didn't land in Mexico. I tried to keep us as close to Florida as I could, but without anything to navigate by except a compass, it was hit or miss." Pointing off to their left, he said, "If we were to power out of this current and head due west or northwest, we'd hit Mexico or Texas in two to three days. Maybe less. The wind can't stay down forever, and I'd feel more confident trying something like that now that I have a general idea of where we are."

"So are you saying you want to skip this and head for land?" Steve asked incredulously as he pointed to the cruise ship. He would have thought Tick-Tock to be the last person on the face of the Earth to miss an adventure like boarding a ship full of unknowns on the high seas.

"I just want everyone to know all the options," He replied.

Steve gave him an odd look before asking, "Don't you want to check it out?"

A broad grin split Tick-Tock's face as he said, "More than anything else in the world. If you all decide to head for land, I'm going to swim for that ship."

"I'm not too worried about anyone wanting to skip getting supplies, a hot meal of real food and showers," Steve said." And then considering what Tick-Tock had just told him, he added, "Besides, we don't know what we'll find when we hit land. We could make it to a coastal city, but as far as we know the dead have overrun them all. We could end up being in an even worse situation then we are now. HWNW was worldwide, so we can't count on Mexico being safe."

Switching subjects, Tick-Tock said, "Law states that if you find an abandoned boat at sea, you're entitled to the salvage rights."

Steve laughed. "I just want what's on it. What in the hell would we do with something that big?"

Tick-Tock shrugged, "Might be a good place to hole up for a while. That ship's got stronger radios than we have on the sailboat. If they're working, we might be able to contact the military and let them know we found someone who's immune to the virus. They could come and pull us off by helicopter."

"A lot of ifs in that statement," Steve pointed out. "Let's just get aboard her first."

Turning to go below, he added, "I'll let Heather know about being able to make land in a few days, but I think she's looking forward to a shower."

Steve found her in their cabin cleaning her CAR-15. After he let her know what Tick-Tock had told him, he watched for her reaction.

She frowned before saying, "I'll go along with what everyone decides, but I say we check the ship out first. It's a floating hotel with enough supplies on it that we won't have to head for Mexico or Texas. We can make it to Key West like we planned." She took a breath to continue, but Steve cut her off by saying, "That's what Tick-Tock and I decided too. I just wanted to see how you felt about it."

"I want a shower, preferably a hot one, but I'd settle for a cold one," Heather said stubbornly. "I'd also like to eat something besides MRE's and I want to shave my legs. I'm starting to look like a Sasquatch. That's how I feel about it."

Steve held up his hands in surrender and said, "Then we act like pirates. But if we hit any serious resistance, we back off and head for land."

With a half-smile that had come to be familiar to him, Heather said, "A pirate? You'd look cute with a cutlass and an eye patch."

Taking her in his arms, Steve reached around and gave her butt a squeeze while saying, "I'm only here for the booty, baby."

Chapter Two

The Dead Calm:

Brain throttled back to just above idle as they pulled broadside to the cruise liner.

"Keep this distance while we check it out," Tick-Tock ordered him. "I want to stay out of the range of any small arms fire."

Brain nodded as he concentrated on the sailboat's controls. At first, he'd been disappointed to find he was being left behind when they boarded the cruise ship, but now that they were near enough to see the tremendous size of the Calm of the Seas, he found himself a little relieved. He had been on numerous cruises and had always stayed close to his mother, who always stayed close to the casino, so he had only seen the outside of the ships when he was embarking and disembarking. Those ships had seemed gigantic, but as he approached one from the water, he was amazed at how it absolutely dwarfed their little 48-foot sailboat. The idea of searching a vessel that size made his stomach knot up in fear.

Tick-Tock tried to hail the cruise liner on the radio, but received no answer. Everyone crowded the port rail to help scan the decks and numerous balconies for any sign of the living or the dead. Tick-Tock took up a position behind Brain and raised his binoculars. The white painted hull reflected on the still water as the sun bounced off it to create a dazzling double image of the ship.

"Holy shit that thing's huge," Heather said with awe. "My eyes keep losing track of where I'm looking." Lowering her binoculars, she scanned the huge hull floating six hundred feet away before finding the area she had been assigned to search.

With only three pair of binoculars, Steve had split the ship into sections so that he, Tick-Tock and Heather could give it a good once over before deciding on their next course of action. With nine decks visible, and what seemed like hundreds of individual balconies, theirs was a daunting task. After letting everyone get their bearings, Steve turned to Susan, who had been given the job of taking notes, and said, "I can see that a few of the lifeboats are missing."

"And there's a lot of balcony doors open," Heather noted.

"Looks like an open hatch down near the water line," Steve added.

"Oh, this is too wild," Tick-Tock exclaimed. Leaning forward as if to get a better look at something, he was silent for so long that Susan finally asked, "What do you see?"

"A rock climbing wall," he said with excitement. "I've got to try that. Those things are cool as shit."

Susan smiled and punched him on the arm. "Be serious."

"I am serious, those things are a blast." Tick-Tock fell silent as he scanned the upper decks. Finally he said, "The Bridge has tinted windows so I can't see in. If anyone's up there, I'm sure they've seen us by now."

"Shit," Heather suddenly exclaimed. "I've got a couple of Z's."

"Where?" Steve asked.

"Go out to the bow and then pan back along that first deck. When you come to the superstructure, go up two decks. They're on the tenth balcony back," she replied.

Steve followed her directions and quickly found what he was looking for.

Focusing in on the balcony containing the zombies, what struck him first was that one of the dead was completely naked except for a baseball cap. Normally, this nudity wouldn't have bothered him as the dead were unaware of what they wore or didn't wear. What caught his attention though was that the man easily tipped the scales at three hundred plus pounds. It also didn't help that the dead thing's stomach had been ripped open and it had looped the fallen out strings of ropy intestines over its shoulder so that it didn't trip over them as it staggered around.

Switching his view to the second walking nightmare on the balcony, Steve decided that it was no prize either. Clad in the remnants of an evening gown that had once been white, but was now rust colored with dried bloodstains, fat man's companion was missing its arm from the elbow down and had part of its face ripped away to reveal gray bone around an empty eye socket.

Steve thought he had grown indifferent to the various sights of the tattered and ripped apart bodies of the dead, but after the brief respite of being away from them, he found himself revolted anew.

The two living dead stared hungrily while the people on the sailboat glided past out of their reach. As Steve watched, fat man extended his arms, reaching out as if to give a welcoming hug to the visitors and leaned too far across the top of the balcony railing. Gravity did its job and he fell about eight stories to hit the water with a huge splash.

Tick-Tock laughed, "That was one hell of a cannonball. Now we'll get to see if dead fat floats."

"It doesn't," Heather said. "Right before everything went to hell in St. Petersburg, we got a call that someone fell off a dock and didn't surface. A road unit went out but couldn't find anything, so they called in the divers. Two of them went down a few hours later to see if it was a false alarm or to recover the body if it wasn't. It was a Z and it killed one of them. The other diver got away and reported that the Z was tangled up in a net, just hanging out there on the bottom. As far as anyone knows, it's still down there."

To prove Heather's point, fat man's body went under and didn't resurface.

"Too bad they're not like lemmings," Steve commented. "Get the leader to jump and the rest would follow."

"Maybe we could try something to encourage them," Tick-Tock said.

He and Steve exchanged a nod to discuss the idea later.

They continued to scan the cruise ship for any sign of life as they paralleled its twisting course. Tick-Tock told Brain to circle around the massive liner to the port side, but the only thing there was more of the living dead. When they first pulled up alongside the ship, only a few zombies came out to look at them hungrily. As they stayed in view though, more and more crowded the balconies until there were hundreds of them stretching from bow to stern.

The low angle from where they were forced to look up restricted their view, but from what they could see, there didn't seem to be any of the dead crowding the rails on the open decks, just on the balconies. Eyestrain took its toll, so Tick-Tock and Steve handed their binoculars over to Susan and Brain. Mary said she was bored and wanted no part of the search.

Heather motioned Cindy over and helped her hold a pair up to her eyes. Within seconds, the little girl spotted the dead hanging on the balcony rails and quickly turned her head away. She stood silent for a moment before going below. Heather had not been trying to scare or shock her, but in a world mostly populated by the living dead, she needed to learn to accept their presence no matter how hideous they were.

After Cindy was gone, Susan gave Heather an encouraging smile. The two woman had talked earlier about helping the little girl come to grips with the sight of the dead since they didn't want her to freeze up if she came face to face with one of them. They explained to Cindy that she could outrun the creatures if she stayed calm and didn't let herself get cornered.

Although they had no intention of ever leaving Cindy alone or in a position where she might come into direct contact with a zombie, in the new dead world, it was better to be prepared. Cindy might be immune to the HWNW virus, but she could still be killed by one of the flesh eaters.

"She'll get used to the sight of them," Susan said.

Heather gave a dry laugh and replied, "She might, I just hope one day I do. It seems like every time I see one of those things, it's more horrible than the last one."

When Brain and Susan tired of scanning the cruise ship, they sat in the seats lining the cockpit to review what they'd seen and to decide what their next move should be.

"As far as I could tell, the open decks are empty or nearly empty," Steve started out. "And I could see on deck seven that most of the doors leading into the superstructure are wide open. I didn't see any of the dead using them to come out and look at us."

"And we definitely attracted their attention everywhere else, so I think it's safe to say that deck seven is clear," Heather added.

Susan wrote this down and said, "Deck seven appears clear," as a confirmation.

"The open decks on eleven and twelve didn't have any Z's rubber necking our drive-by," Tick-Tock said. "I spotted maybe a hundred on the balconies forward of them, but that was it."

Susan noted this and said, "The deck below that was swarming with them. That would be deck ten. The open deck at the rear of nine looked clear, but the balconies forward of that were full of the dead."

"The balconies at the front of deck eight looked like a Marilyn Manson concert," Brain said. "But I couldn't see anything at the rear because it's enclosed. Anyone else catch anything I might have missed?"

No one did, but before they could move on, Mary said, "I'm lost. How do you know which deck is which?" This was accompanied by a vacant look at the cruise ship in the distance.

Brain explained that they were numbering the decks by starting at the uppermost level that they had designated twelve. From there, they counted downward to deck four, which was the lowest visible deck on the hull. He went on to say that with most of the cruise ships he'd been on, the bottom three decks were used for mechanical equipment, storage and the crew's quarters. When this was met by another blank look from Mary, he tried to explain it again, finally giving up in frustration when she asked him to point out which deck the spa was on and going on and on about how she really needed a manicure and a pedicure.

"Like I was saying before," Steve interrupted her, "deck seven looks completely deserted. It appears there's no one on it at all. Below deck seven, the ship is mostly enclosed except for the rooms with balconies. I spotted Z's on almost all of those. We can't be sure about the areas we can't see, so we have to assume they're zombified."

"What about the open hatch on four, right next to the water line?" Susan asked.

Steve shrugged. They had attempted to try and see what was inside, but due to distance and the small size of the opening, none of them could make out any details. The question on everyone's mind was what would they face if they boarded the ship through that hatch?

"I've got a theory," Tick-Tock said. "Deck seven is where most of the life boats are, and I counted eight gone: three on the port side and five on the starboard. I'm going to hazard a guess here and say that the ship had an outbreak and was abandoned. We haven't seen any live people yet, so I think we can rule out the possibility of running into anyone if we go through the hatch on four."

"That leaves running into the dead," Steve pointed out.

"But they'll be easier to deal with than live people with weapons," Susan countered.

"I can come up with a few ideas on things you can check to see if the ship might be inhabited by the living," Brain volunteered. "The only problem is that you need to be on board."

"Before we get into all that," Tick-Tock said, "we need to figure out what's beyond that hatch. Living or dead, we'll find a way to deal with whatever we run into, but I'd like to know what the area inside is like." Turning to Brain, he added, "You're our resident cruise expert. You've been on eight different ships, so tell me what you know. What's in there?"

Knowing that what he said meant life and death to the four people boarding the ship, Brain thought hard before answering. "If it's laid out like the other cruise liners I've been on, I'd say it's storage for water craft. You can just make out the outline of a larger door next to the open hatch. You see, all the cruise lines have their own private islands where you can rent jet skis and kayaks and stuff. When they need to switch out the old equipment for new, they carry the stuff out with a cruise that's heading there. I remember coming back in the launch one day, and the crew was loading a bunch of old, beat up kayaks through a big hatch just about where that one is. There were also two brand new Sea-Doos tied up there waiting to go to the island."

When he finished, Susan asked, "What else is in that area?"

Brain shook his head, "I'm not sure, and I don't want to give you the wrong information. Because of the terrorist threat, the cruise lines quit giving tours of the bridge and mechanical sections, so I don't know most of the working areas of the ship. I managed to bribe one of the crew to let me see the engine room once, but that's on a lower deck."

"What about the common areas for the guests? What would be on that deck?" Heather prodded.

"Most of the cruise ships are laid out similarly, but not exactly the same," Brain said. "I've never been on the Calm of the Seas, but I've been on a couple like it. If I had to guess, I'd say it's one of the formal dining rooms and the first level of the main shopping area."

Mary, who had shown little more than bored indifference to the conversation since no one seemed to know where the spa was, suddenly perked up and said, "Shopping?"

"Yeah, it's a huge area anywhere from four to eight stories high with all the decks open to the inside. It's full of shops and clubs and coffee bars. They always have glass elevators in there too. It's really cool," Brain explained.

"What kind of shops?" Mary asked with excitement.

Brain opened his mouth to answer, but Steve cut him off. Speaking in a clear, firm voice, he said, "That's not our main concern right now, Mary. We have more important things to focus on."

Ignoring him, she leaned over and laid her hand on Brain's upper thigh. In a low voice, she said, "You and I will talk later, sweets." Then she gave the tech a wink and a smile.

Brain felt his face go hot and he knew it was turning bright red. He opened his mouth to speak, but not trusting his voice, he closed it with a snap.

Steve made a mental note to speak with Brain before Mary got hold of him. He needed to warn the tech that she would squeeze him for all she could, long before the engineer ever got close to getting in her pants.

Turning back to the matter at hand, he asked the group, "Anyone else ever been on a cruise?" Susan raised her hand, "I've gone twice. But only short little three day runs out of Port Canaveral."

Mary narrowed her eyes and asked suspiciously, "With who?" But Susan ignored her.

Steve said to Susan, "Then you get with Brain, and between the two of you sketch out a plan showing where everything is. If it's a guess, then put a question mark next to it. We only need it until we get somewhere that has a 'you are here' map."

"Those are always by the stairs and the elevators," Brain informed him.

Susan nodded in agreement, "It's really easy to get lost on one of those cruise ships. When we go in, we'll always have to keep in mind how to get out. You can get turned around real quick."

Steve remembered seeing a can of blue marine paint in the storage locker next to the shower. They could use this to mark their path out as they went in. That way, there'd be less confusion if they were trying to find their way out while being chased and hauling ass.

To Brain and Susan, he said, "Get going on that map."

"We'll have it in an hour," Brain promised.

"Take your time and get it as accurate as you can," he told him. "Besides, we have something we need to do first."

"What's that?"

"See if we can get the dead to commit suicide," Tick-Tock answered with a laugh.

\*\*\*

After they finished their first circuit of the ship, Heather said, "There's something I noticed."

"What's that?" Steve said before putting two fingers in his mouth and letting out a sharp, piercing whistle.

"I only see a few Z's on each balcony, and they seem to belong together," She told him.

Tick-Tock said, "Belong together. What do you mean?"

"Like those two right there." Heather pointed to a balcony containing a male zombie oozing black puss out of a dozen wounds on his chest and neck and a female zombie that slumped to its right from a large, crescent shaped gap chewed in her side. "They're both dressed in night clothes. He's wearing pajama bottoms and she's wearing a nightgown. And then, just one deck down are two Z's dressed in formal clothes."

"That goes along with what I guessed happened," Tick-Tock said. "They had an outbreak and first tried to deal with it by quarantining the sick in their rooms."

"Makes sense," Heather interjected. "And when the disease spread, they started closing off entire decks to contain it for as long as they could."

"But we know that doesn't work," Steve put in.

"So they bailed," Tick-Tock finished.

All three of them looked at the ship as if it expecting it to speak to them, to let them know that their theory was correct. Instead, they saw a zombie on deck ten climb up on the railing and reach out to them before falling to the water below.

"Got one," Tick-Tock commented.

"Only a thousand more to go," Steve said dryly.

"How deep is the water here?" Heather asked.

"Don't know," Tick-Tock replied. Tapping the depth finder mounted above the steering wheel, he added, "This only goes down to six-hundred feet and it's maxed out. My guess is that the pressure will crush them long before they reach bottom. But who knows how the dead react to atmospheres. They might end up walking around on the bottom for decades."

As they watched, two more of the dead fell overboard in their vain attempt to reach the living. Heather closed her eyes as the second one hit. It had been a child of about five or six.

Seeing her reaction, Steve said, "They're dead and they'll make you just like them if you hesitate. They're not people anymore, and we can't let ourselves think that they are or we're through."

Heather took a deep breath and let it out slowly before saying, "I know, I know. When they were coming at me in St. Petersburg and at the bank building, I never thought about the fact that they'd once been human beings with lives. I just took them out. It's just that, from this far away, they don't seem like such a threat."

"They will be when we go on board," Steve pointed out.

Heather locked eyes with him and said in a determined voice, "Then we better get rid of as many as we can while we have the chance." Turning to face the ship, she started waving her arms wildly in the air while shouting, "Over here you ugly bastards. Come and get it. Come to mama you freaks of nature."

Tick-Tock started hitting the horn button as Steve put two fingers in his mouth and let out a long, shrill whistle. Two hours later, Heather asked in a hoarse voice, "How many do you think we got so far?"

"A couple hundred at least," Steve answered, "Some of the ones who jumped from the upper decks landed on the lower ones, so we can't count them. If the fall doesn't destroy the brain, they'll be right back up again, dragging themselves by their hands if their legs are broken."

Susan and Brain had come up on deck after they finished the map and took turns zombie baiting. Steve wanted to get Mary up on deck to do her part, but when Tick-Tock said that even the dead wouldn't want her, he laughed and discarded the idea.

Let her do whatever she wants to for now, Steve thought. But when we hit land, she better pull her own weight or she might find herself left behind.

As the sun beat down and the day grew hotter, they became exhausted despite taking regular breaks. Finally, Steve suggested they pack it in. Checking his watch he said, "It's about noon thirty."

"Noon thirty?" Heather asked with a laugh.

"Twelve thirty," he corrected with a smile. "It gets dark around seven. If we go aboard the Calm of the Seas around four, it'll give us time to look around before it gets dark." Turning to Brain, he said, "Let's take a look at the deck plan you and Susan drew up."

They crowded around the sketch as Brain explained what he and Susan had come up with. "On the level where you'll be going in, we're almost certain you'll be right next to one of the main dining rooms and one of the kitchens. On every cruise I've been on they're always on the lower decks."

"Why?" Heather asked.

"Less back and forth motion than you get on the upper decks," Susan explained. She was about to add that if they ever booked a cruise they should reserve a stateroom on one of the lower decks to help prevent seasickness when it suddenly struck her that no one would ever book a cruise again in her lifetime. Or even Cindy's, she added as an afterthought. Depressed at this sudden awareness of how the world had changed, she stayed quiet for the rest of the meeting as her mind went over the hundreds of other things she would never be able to do again.

Brain continued the narrative by saying, "Past the formal dining room you should find the lowest level of the Centrum. When we were zombie baiting, I took a good look at the hull and saw the outline of another hatch forward of the open one. This is where you board the launch that ferries you to their private island. That will be on the far side of the Centrum."

"What's past that?" Tick-Tock asked. "Cabins?"

Brain and Susan exchanged a glance before Brain said with disappointment, "Neither of us is sure on that one. Susan stayed on the ship when she went out and I only took the launch once, and it was years ago on my first cruise. I keep trying to wrack my brain but I can't remember. Mom liked to hang around the casino and I mostly stayed with her."

Tick-Tock saw that Brain wore an expression like he'd just missed an easy field goal that would have won the Super Bowl, so he slapped him on the back and said, "Don't sweat it Pork Chop. You've given us way more info than we had before. Like you said, we'll find a map near the stairs or the elevators, so we should find one in the Centrum."

"If we go in that far," Steve said. After looking at the rough sketch again, he added, "When we first go aboard, we'll be right next to the dining room. This means the kitchen won't be too far away. That takes care of food and water. Since we'll be entering the area where they store the jet skis, then they should keep fuel somewhere around there. I think on our first excursion we keep it simple. Get in, take a quick look around, grab what we need and get out. We'll try to find a map so we can plan for any later foraging expeditions, but today we grab the necessities and haul ass. I don't want to get too far into that ship until we know what's what."

Tick-Tock agreed, but he pointed out that there were many other items they needed that wouldn't be found near the entrance.

"If everything goes good today, we'll plan on going back in tomorrow," Steve promised. "Then you can explore to your heart's content. If it looks secure enough when we check it out today, we might even be able to move aboard for a few days."

With the plan in place, Steve went over everyone's assigned positions. "Brain, you've got the wheel. Keep Cindy below with Mary. Once you drop us off, back up a hundred feet so none of those things drop down on you. Hold your position and listen for us to call you on the radio."

"Gotcha," he replied.

Indicating Susan, Heather and Tick-Tock, he said, "We move just like we did when we cleared the bank building, two people to a team. We can adjust our positions as the situation changes."

Remembering what happened the last time Tick-Tock and Susan were left alone when they searched the bank building, he added, "We all stay in sight of each other no matter what. Heather and I will be in the lead. If anyone does get separated and can't contact the others, then head directly for the hatch." Turning to Brain, he said, "Keep an eye out for anyone in case they lose radio contact. You'll have to come in and pick them up."

"What'll Mary be doing?" Susan asked.

"The usual," Steve replied.

"As little as fucking possible," Heather finished.

They all laughed as the sailboat passed around the stern of the cruise liner. Tick-Tock looked up and read its name aloud. "The Calm of the Seas." Turning to Steve, he said, "You know that once we take her, we can rename her whatever we want?"

Glancing at the zombies clustered on the balconies high above him, Steve said, "How about calling it The Dead Calm? From the looks of it, that seems appropriate."

Chapter Three

Russellville, Arkansas:

Jedidiah Cage looked in the mirror as he adjusted the double silver bars on his collar, still not used to the replacement of his single First Lieutenant's bar with the railroad tracks of a Captain. His promotion orders had come through while he was in the midst of rescuing civilians and trying to eradicate the walking dead infesting the city of Little Rock. In the confusion of those dark days, no one had passed the orders on to his commanding officer, so it was only recently he'd learned of his promotion.

Cage had been in one of the first units of the Arkansas National Guard called up after the HWNW virus reared its ugly head at a hospital in Little Rock. From there, it spread throughout the city, the nation and then across the entire world. Only a few people knew the actual cause of the disease, and in the carnage and terror that spread in its wake, most of those were either killed or turned into the walking dead themselves. Besides a small number of doctors and scientists who were transported to a research center set up in Russellville, along with himself when he and what was left of his men had been ordered to report to the facility to provide security, there were few people still alive who knew the beginnings of the virus.

When Cage and his unit were called up after the Governor of Arkansas declared martial law to keep order, Jedidiah's first posting was to provide security for the hospital where the HWNW virus had developed. Present at post-hurricane Katrina ravaged New Orleans, and having served in Afghanistan, he thought he was prepared for anything.

He was wrong.

Driving up to the hospital in his Humvee with a platoon of men accompanying him in two trucks, he was amazed to see sandbagged bunkers flanking the entrance to the emergency room. Manned by police officers carrying automatic weapons, the checkpoint created a choke point for anyone trying to get aid. The parking lot overflowed with hundreds of injured people, the wounded either sitting or lying on the ground, thrashing in agony, bleeding and vomiting onto the asphalt as two doctors moved among them. They were escorted by a Little Rock police officer that stood watching while the medics marked the wounded on the forehead with grease pencil to show the order in which they would be treated. Once triaged, the injured were then stripped of all their clothing by two orderlies who examined them from head to toe before allowing them to be admitted past the guards at the emergency room door.

After finally finding a spot for his Humvee on a grass strip far from the entrance, Cage started to collect his gear for the walk to the emergency room. Looking up when movement out of the corner of his eye caught his attention, he saw one of the physicians who had been examining a man lying on the asphalt suddenly back away from his patient as the man started going into convulsions. The police officer that accompanied the doctor drew his pistol and stood close by as seizures racked the prone man's body. People crowded the scene blocking his view, so Cage exited his vehicle and walked over to find out what was going on.

Seeing Cage's National Guard uniform, the cop looked relieved and said, "Thank God you all finally showed up. This is a fucking nightmare. We've only got maybe six guys left. Everyone else is out on road patrol trying to keep things under control. We've got looting all over the city and these things keep popping up." Pointing with his gun barrel at the man now lying motionless on the ground, the cop added, "You have to shoot them in the brain when they come back. Or hit them with a Taser. The electrical shock takes them out."

Cage didn't understand what the officer was talking about, but before he could ask for an explanation, the man on the ground twitched a few times and then lay still. After a few seconds, he jerkily rolled over onto his hands and knees before rising unsteadily to his feet and turning toward them. Jedidiah got a good look at his face as revulsion and fear battled for control of his emotions.

Tinged with a grayish-green skin color, and with its mouth pulled back in a snarl, the newly dead man's eyes stared in hunger at the crowd around him as saliva began to roll down his chin. Blood, mixed with a thick, black substance, leaked from what looked like a bite wound on his chest. A few people screamed and ran away, but most just backed up and continued to watch the show.

The Little Rock cop said, "You have to wait until you're sure they're dead before you kill them."

This contradiction was lost on Cage as he watched the cop take two steps forward, raise his pistol to aim it point-blank at the man's forehead and pull the trigger.

Chunks of skull, brains and a fine spray of black puss mixed with a small amount of blood flew from the back of the man's head to land on some of the onlookers. More screams, this time of disgust, met this volley of gore.

"Fucking rubberneckers," the cop said, "Serves them right. They're one of the reasons why we have to wait so long to shoot the ones who turn. Too many people complained about us shooting people who might still be alive, so now we got the ACLU on our ass about civil rights."

"What in the fuck is going on here?" Cage asked in amazement.

"You don't know?" The cop replied. Seeing the puzzled look on Cage's face, he explained, "Some guy had a disease of some kind. Something called Prader-Will or Willi-Prader or Darth Vader or something like that. It gave him an insatiable appetite for food.

Guy got into an accident and had a head injury. Word is, the hospital treated him with the wrong medicine or some shit, and his disease mutated into this virus. If you're infected, you get an appetite for a new kind of meat. Us."

"What virus?" Cage asked.

They're calling it the HWNW virus. What it does is it kills your ass off and you're dead, but then you get back up and try to eat people."

"Eat people?" Cage said with disbelief in his voice.

"Yeah, and that's how the virus gets spread too. It's transmitted by the bites."

Cage learned more details of how the virus came about by talking with hospital staff. They also warned him that any contact with infected body fluids on an open wound would transmit the disease. By then, it was too late for those already sprayed by the blood, puss or the saliva of the walking dead though.

In the first days after their arrival, his platoon of forty-two took heavy losses as they learned how to deal with the virus and those it infected. By the time they finally set up a system to keep themselves safe, the hospital was abandoned due to the attrition of its medical staff. Cage and his remaining twenty-nine men were reassigned to rescuing civilians trapped in their homes by the dead that had multiplied beyond anyone's imagination and now wandered freely through the streets of Little Rock. Eventually, there were no more living human beings left in the city, and the Guard was ordered to pull out. The once thriving metropolis gained the designation that was being given to all abandoned population centers. It was now referred to as a Dead City. Cage and his remaining twenty men were then sent to a newly constructed research facility outside of Russellville.

Checking his appearance again in the full length mirror hung on the back of the door of his cramped trailer, Cage decided he was sufficiently squared away to proceed with his daily duties. As he stepped out into the cool Arkansas afternoon, his eyes jumped to the fence that encircled the compound. He visually checked the wire ties holding the electrified mesh to the reinforced, eight foot high, chain link enclosure, and was reassured to hear the hum of the generator that sent a continuous charge through the barrier.

Remembering back to when what was left of his unit arrived at the research facility, he recalled that perimeter only consisted of some hastily strung coils of razor wire. Numerous bodies of the walking dead that had tried to breach the compound's defenses hung limply from this flimsy barrier. In one section, it was almost flattened by their weight. Cage had seen a Major coming toward him, and after exchanging salutes, the officer informed him that he and his men were needed for body disposal duty. They were to draw rubber gloves from the medical building and pull the bodies of the dead from the razor wire. Another detail would be coming along behind them to shore up the weak spots.

"Where is the medical building and what should we do with the bodies, sir," Cage asked.

Looking at him quizzically, the Major said, "I don't recognize you. Are you new here?"

Cage snapped to attention and rapped out, "First Lieutenant Jedidiah Cage reporting for duty with-."

The Major waved away the rest as he said, "You're one of the Little Rock crew that just arrived, aren't you?"

"Yes, sir," Cage answered.

The Major frowned and said, "I heard it was bad there."

"Pretty bad, sir," Cage replied.

The Major thought about this for a moment before saying, "I know you just got in, Lieutenant, and that you all just pulled out of Little Rock, but I need you and your men on disposal duty. I'm shorthanded right now."

"Yes, sir," Cage replied. "My men and I can do the job."

"We've got to maintain the integrity of the fence or we're totally screwed. The Army promised us an electric fence, but who knows when that'll show up. So far, the Z's are only coming at us in groups of four or five, so we've been able to deal with the assaults by engaging them with pistol fire once they get hung up on the fence. If that changes, your rifles will be needed to help defend the perimeter." Pointing to a three-story farmhouse, the only permanent structure in the compound, the Major said, "That's the research facility. Go and ask one of Professor Hawkins' people to give you some gloves."

"Yes, sir," Cage replied and said, "If I may ask sir, what are they researching?"

The Major broke eye contact and replied, "They're working on finding a cure for the HWNW virus." After a pause he added, "Among other things."

Cage nodded, not commenting on the Major's uneasiness at the question. "And the bodies of the dead?" He asked.

"Drag them downwind and burn them. You'll find diesel fuel at the motor pool."

"I do need to report in and let the C.O. know I'm here, sir," Cage said.

"You already did," The officer replied. "I'm Major Conway. I'm the ringmaster of this circus. When you're done with the bodies, get cleaned up and get you and your men something to eat. Come and find me, and I'll give you a full briefing on our position here. That'll also give me some time to find a place for you and your men to be quartered."

Since that day, Cage found himself working closely with Major Conway in building up the facility and its defenses. He was put in charge of security for the farmhouse itself and met twice with Doctor Lionel Hawkins, the head of research into the HWNW virus, but found the man distant and aloof. Cage was left with an uneasy feeling after both meetings and wasn't looking forward to a third.

It was a relief when, a week after he and his men took over security for the medical building, a platoon of regular Army soldiers had arrived and relieved them of this duty. Since then, Cage had little contact with the people at the farmhouse. After finding out the duties of this new platoon though, he was quite happy to keep it that way. Besides providing security, the regular Army unit was also charged with acquiring specimens for Doctor Hawkins and his staff to study.

Once a week, they went into the nearby town where the zombies congregated in large numbers and brought back ten or more of the living dead. Although Cage and his men regularly went into Russellville on scavenging missions, they tried to avoid the dead, while the Army unit sought them out.

One afternoon at lunch, Cage was sharing a table with Major Conway when he overheard the Lieutenant who commanded the Army unit explaining to another officer the process of how they trapped and brought the dead back to the base.

With bright, excited eyes, the Lieutenant said, "We take three of those four-by-four trucks with the big lift kits on them that make them sit up high and we cruise real slow-like through the streets of town. In no time at all, we got a whole slew of them things following us. We speed up a little so that the most beat up ones fall out, and then we only got the most intact ones staying with us. When we got about two or three of the best ones ahead of the rest of the herd, we stop. Six of our guys are in the bed of each of the pickups, but they sit so high up that them dead things can't reach them. Two of my guys are ropers, and they hang off each side of the pickup. They just drop a noose over the head of one of them and pull it up. Each roper has two handlers. When the roper hauls the Z up near the rail, the handlers throw a hood over its head and shackle its arms and legs. By this time, the other dead have caught up to them, so they drive off a ways and move the dead to the transport truck. Doc Hawkins tells us how many he needs, and when we fill our quota, we head back here."

"Where do they keep the Z's?" Cage asked. He was curious, since he had never seen any detention area for the walking dead at the facility.

Now that he had a larger audience, the Second Lieutenant sat up straighter in his seat and said with pride, "We just pull up behind the farmhouse and throw them down the old coal chute that drops into the basement. We got it all set up slick as shit, and we've only taken two casualties since we started."

Hearing this, Cage quickly put the basement of the farmhouse on the list of places he never ever wanted to fucking visit.

Looking at the farmhouse now, he shook off his feelings of unease. After finishing his walk of the compound perimeter, he went to the duty officer's trailer to read the reports from the previous evening. He, and what was left of the men he'd commanded in Little Rock, had guard duty that night so he wanted to know what kind of activity to expect.

After reading the reports, he asked the officer of the day, "Are these correct, Lieutenant? It says there was no attempt by the Z's to try and breach our defenses."

"That's correct, Captain," he replied.

"But last night's sentries reported a lot of activity in the woods beyond the fields surrounding us and over by the lake," Cage said.

"Correct again, Captain. The Z's seem to have learned that the fence takes them out, so they're keeping their distance."

"What do the patrols outside the compound report?"

"They estimate one hundred Z's are stumbling around in the woods, but they've been deemed no threat, so no action is planned against them."

"Has Major Conway seen these?" Cage asked, holding up the reports.

"I'm sure he has, Captain. We submit them to him at 0600 every morning."

Cage thanked the O.D. and went in search of Conway, eventually tracking him down in the communications trailer. As Cage entered, the Major was finishing up a call on the satellite phone. After disconnecting, he acknowledged Cage, but before the Captain could speak, he held up his hand and said abruptly, "My office, we've got new orders."

His question about the buildup of the dead outside the fence forgotten, Cage dutifully followed Conway while trying to guess what could be going on now. He didn't like to speculate on what the future had in store for him, especially when it was in the hands of the Arkansas National Guard, but he couldn't help but wonder.

When the two men were seated across from each other at the Major's desk, Conway said, "First, I need to inform you that you, along with every other reservist under my command have been placed on active duty and are now part of the regular Army of the United States of America."

"And that means what, sir?" Cage asked cautiously.

Conway leaned back in his chair before replying; "It means that of the two-hundred sixty three men and woman on this base, one hundred are to be transported to Fort Hood for redeployment. It seems that the Army has lost a lot of people while trying to retake New Orleans, and they need fresh bodies to fill the ranks."

Cage felt his stomach drop. He'd heard the stories and read reports about the units sent in to retake the Dead Cities. They searched every standing structure and crawled through the storm drains and sewers, seeking out and destroying the living dead. It was no wonder the Army needed more troops for what had come to be known as Dead Duty. The life expectancy of those engaged in the battle for the Dead Cities was measured in hours instead of days. Recalling the abandoned homes that littered the city of New Orleans after Katrina, and the maze that was the French Quarter, he started mentally making out his will.

The apprehension must have shown on his face because Major Conway said, "Not to worry Captain. You did your part in Little Rock. Besides, the Army has decided it needs you here."

Putting off his anxiety, Cage said, "If I'm needed elsewhere-."

"You're needed here Captain, and that's the end of it," Conway interrupted. "Besides, congratulations are in order, not condolences."

"Sir?" Cage asked, bewildered.

"You've been slated to take over command of this base and be promoted to the rank of Major," Conway told him.

"What about you, sir?" Cage asked, shocked by his promotion.

"I'm to go with the men to Fort Hood where I'll take over command of the training facility for the new recruits that are needed to offset the losses suffered in trying to retake the Dead Cities. Every man and woman who's capable of holding a rifle is being pressed into service."

Standing, Major Conway circled his desk with his hand outstretched and said, "Congratulations on your new post, Major Cage."

Cage stood awkwardly, trying to read the Major's mood about his own assignment. Should he return the congratulations? He settled for, "Thank you, sir," and fell silent.

"My orders are to report to Fort Hood within seventy-two hours, so we have a lot to go over in a short time," Conway said. "I need you to be here in my office at 0600 tomorrow morning so we can compile a list of who stays and who goes. We also need to review the additional duties you'll undertake as commanding officer of this facility." After hesitating, Conway said in a lower tone, "I will also be briefing you on some of the additional research that Doctor Hawkins is doing. Much of it is classified, but I'll relay to you the few things that I'm allowed to."

"How is it going over there, sir?" Cage asked. "Are they making any progress toward a cure?"

"It's complicated," Conway said evasively. "Finding a cure has become secondary to other considerations."

Cage was confused. He thought that the only reason for the existence of this facility was to find a cure for the HWNW virus.

Seeing that Cage was readying to ask more questions, and not being in the mood to open the can of worms that was the research being done at the farmhouse, Conway said crisply, "We'll discuss this tomorrow, Major."

By the tone of the Major's voice, Cage knew he was being dismissed. Coming to attention, he snapped out a perfect salute and took his leave.

As he exited the command trailer, he stopped and glanced over at the farmhouse. Smoke came from chimneys situated at each end of the white clapboard structure, which at any other time would have given the building a homey look. Today though, with Major Conway's evasiveness and Cage's own suspicions that something was going on behind the scenes, the farmhouse looked ominous.

'What in the hell are you up to over there?" Cage asked aloud.

Chapter Four

The Dead Calm:

Steve Wendell tried to discern any sign of life as he looked into the depths of the open hatch in the side of the Calm of the Seas. Without diverting his eyes, he said to Brain, "Keep the light centered."

Brain adjusted the controls next to the steering station, causing the spotlight mounted on the bow of the sailboat to yaw back and forth before shining directly into the dark cavity. Seeing nothing except some unidentifiable shapes in a large open area, Steve readied himself to jump into the relative unknown.

Armed with an M-4 as his primary weapon, he took a deep breath and slowly let it out as he chambered a round in the assault rifle. Switching the selector to full automatic fire, he watched as the distance between the bow of their sailboat and the open hatch on the side of the cruise ship dwindled. Directly behind him, Heather, Tick-Tock and Susan scanned the decks above them for any Z's who might try to jump down to land on their craft.

Originally they had planned to pull directly alongside the liner to gain access to the loading hatch. As they neared the ship though, Heather noticed that there would be a four-foot or more difference between the top of the gunwale on their boat and the bottom of the hatch. Since none of them wanted to board the Dead Calm empty handed as they hauled themselves up into the opening, they changed their plan to enter the liner from the bow of the sailboat which curved upward and would lessen the vertical gap.

Steve estimated that only a few yards remained between him and the hatch. He also judged that he would only have to jump upward about a foot from the bow. Much better than the four-foot gap if they had boarded from the side, he decided. Hearing Brain throw the engine of the sailboat into reverse to slow their approach, he crouched down. The bowsprit entered through the opening in the side of the ship and its underside started sliding along the bottom of the hatch as they thought it would, but then a problem arose. Seeing that the angled spar would stop their forward momentum before the bow of the sailboat came close enough to step up through the hatch, Steve took four steps back to give himself a running start. Dropping his sunglasses to hang from a string around his neck, he bolted forward and launched himself across the water. Landing on his feet inside the Calm of the Seas, he scanned the immediate area around him with his rifle at the ready, tracking back and forth with it as he searched for any threat.

After a moment of intense scrutiny, he saw that nothing was going to show itself or leap out at him, so he backed up to the hatch and removed his right hand from the fore grip of his rifle. Without turning or diverting his attention from the area in front of him, he waved for the rest of the boarding crew to join him.

One by one, Heather, Tick-Tock and Susan jumped through the hatch. Susan's feet had barely hit the deck before they heard the sound of the sailboat's motor rev as Brain backed rapidly away. Facing into the ship in an arc, the foursome split into two groups and moved to either side of the hatch so they didn't silhouette themselves against the sunlight streaming through it. They took a minute to survey their surroundings as they let their eyes adjust to the dim interior of the Dead Calm.

Heather was the first to speak. In a low voice, she said, "There are lights on."

"Emergency lights," Tick-Tock pointed out in an equally quiet voice.

"Battery?" Heather asked.

Not taking his eyes away from the area in front of him, Steve slowly crouched down and placed his hand flat on the metal deck as Brain had instructed him to. Feeling a slight vibration, he said, "Generator or some other equipment's running somewhere. I can feel it. And the floor's dry, so that hatch couldn't have been open very long."

They all considered this as they continued to look around the storage area. It had been months since the HWNW virus had swept across the world, so there was no way that something mechanical could have run this long without refueling or maintenance. Additionally, if the hatch had been open all that time, the floor should have been wet from water coming in.

"Someone's on board," Susan whispered nervously. Although she had no reservations about shooting one of the undead in the brain; living, breathing human beings were a different matter.

"Doesn't make a difference," Tick-Tock said. "We're here to get what we need. As long as whoever's here stays out of the way then there won't be any problems." Looking at a row of eight jet skis in front of him, and the numerous kayaks stored on racks to his left, he continued, "This is all water craft storage."

"Brain called that one right," Susan said.

A faint odor came to Steve and he said, "I smell gas."

"That was me," Heather said. "Sorry about that, but with all those MRE's I've been eating, it just happens."

All four of them laughed at the ridiculous bathroom humor, but the dumb joke had done as Heather had hoped and relaxed the tension a little. She knew it wasn't good for them to go into a situation like this so wired up that they started shooting at shadows.

"We clear this room first and then move on," Steve ordered. "Susan, Tick-Tock, check out the kayaks while Heather and I look behind the Sea-Doos. See if you can find where the gas smell is coming from."

Heather almost quipped; it's coming from my ass, but decided against it. One dumb joke was enough.

After a short search, they found the storage area clear of the living and the dead, so Tick-Tock and Steve ventured down a short hall they discovered behind the kayaks. The passage ended in a room stacked with a dozen, two wheeled gas caddies.

Inside the compartment to the right was a gas pump. When Tick-Tock tried to activate the equipment though, only a trickle of fuel came out of the nozzle.

"No power," Steve pointed out.

Indicating the lights, Tick-Tock replied, "There's power somewhere. When Brain gets on board, we'll get him to figure out how to reroute it."

Reminded at hearing Brain's name, Steve unclipped the radio from his belt and called the tech while they moved back into the main storage room. After telling him what they had found so far and promising to keep him posted, he walked to the hatch leading into the next compartment and said to the others, "Let's move out. We do it just like we planned."

After shouldering their weapons and setting up in a wide arc facing the door, Heather, Tick-Tock and Susan called out in turn that they were ready.

The heavy steel fire door opened effortlessly when Steve pushed down on the latch securing it. After pulling the portal open a few feet, he quickly backed out of the possible line of fire in case anything unfriendly came out. The area beyond was dark, and for just a second Steve's imagination ran away from him. He was sure there was about to be a rush of the dead pushing through the opening with their hands outstretched.

None appeared as in quick succession, the group turned on the flashlights they had earlier taped to the fore grips of their weapons. Heather carried the CAR-15 she had brought with her to the bank building, while the rest toted M-4's salvaged from the MRAP. Each member of the boarding party also carried a pistol and spare magazines for their weapons.

The beams of light that shot into the dark revealed a wide hallway with double doors set in its far wall directly across from them. Cautiously sticking his head inside the opening, Steve saw that the hall ended a few feet to his right and extended off to his left for a dozen yards before ending at another set of double doors. The scent of old and new cooked food reached his nostrils, giving him further proof that the living had recently inhabited the Dead Calm.

Stepping into the hall, he nodded to his left and said, "Watch the kitchen," before turning his attention to the doors directly in front of him.

Nudging one with the toe of his boot, it swung open at his touch. Steve pushed it further so he could look into the next compartment and saw that the same low-level lighting they had encountered in the watercraft storage area illuminated this area. In this more cavernous space though, the dim light left shadows everywhere.

Built on three tiers, the formal dining room was as wide as the ship and nearly as deep. Tables draped with white linen tablecloths were clustered on every available bit of floor space, creating hundreds of hiding places. Steve was surprised to see that they were set with dinnerware, cups and glasses, all of which was covered with a thin layer of dust.

With just a quick glance, he counted four bars and eight semi-enclosed serving stations for the staff. More hiding spots, he noted. Mirrors on the walls gave an impression of immense size, and multiple chandeliers reflected back to fool the eye as they gave a disco ball effect to the small amount of illumination thrown off by the emergency lights.

This'll be a nightmare to clear, he thought to himself. Shining his flashlight across the room, he noticed that the two sets of double fire doors, one on the port side, and one on the starboard that led into what he assumed were the next compartments, were shut. This gave him an idea. Ducking back into the hallway, he found Heather, Tick-Tock and Susan covering the doors that led into the kitchen.

"Here's what's up," he told them. "The formal dining room is fucking huge, and we could waste hours in there trying to clear it, and I don't even want to think about what a mess the kitchen's going to be when we check it out. The good news is that the doors leading into the next section beyond the dining room are metal, so they should be pretty sound proof. What we do is clear the kitchen first by standing at the doors and making noise to see what we can attract. One person stays here and keeps an eye on the dining room to make sure nothing comes up behind us and cuts us off. Once we're done with the kitchen, we do the same thing in the dining room. Almost like how we cleared the bank building. Draw them out and waste them if they show themselves."

Realizing it was the best way to clear the large, cluttered areas, they put the plan into effect.

With Susan watching the dining room for any signs of the living or the dead, Steve and Heather covered Tick-Tock in the kitchen as he banged pots and pans and smashed a dozen plates by flinging them like Frisbees against the walls. He added to this by calling out as loud as he could, "Here zombie, zombie, zombie" and "All-e-all-e-in-come-free." Echoing off the metal walls and floor, the noise was enough to wake the dead, but none appeared.

After ten minutes of this, the three of them rejoined Susan and moved into the dining room. Here the acoustics, muted by the heavy carpet, tablecloths and wall tapestries, were not as good and they found they had to yell louder. After Steve upended a few tables to send them crashing into their neighbors, they decided that the noise was enough that if any of the dead were around, they would have come out. Tick-Tock also pointed out that any humans hiding in ambush would have to be very disciplined not to show themselves. Satisfied they were alone, but still not letting down their guard, the foursome crossed the dining room without incident.

Standing in front of one of the fire doors on the starboard side of the ship, Steve placed his hand on its push bar and slowly, soundlessly eased it inward until he heard a click. Gripping his M-4 tightly in his right hand, he used his left to open the door just enough to look through. He starred so intently, and for so long, that Tick-Tock finally asked with anticipation, "What is it, what do you see?"

Without missing a beat, Steve replied, "It's a rock climbing wall."

Susan's hand flew to her mouth to stifle the laughter that bubbled up.

As Steve pushed the door open to give him a better view, the others were able to get a look. An almost perceptible thrill went through them at what lay ahead.

Without turning, Steve said, "Tick-Tock, grab a couple of chairs so we can prop these doors open. I don't want them closing and locking behind us." When he returned, Steve said, "We go through one at a time and spread out. There's plenty of open space just past the door, but there's also a lot of area to cover beyond that. Everyone take a good look before we move."

When they had each taken their turn, Heather held the door open while Steve went through. After checking the blind spot behind the door, he moved forward twenty paces and stopped. Rifle at the ready, he tried to take in as much as possible of the overwhelming sights around him.

Daylight, streaming in from skylights multiple stories above, lit the front of the shops, clubs and restaurants that stretched away from him in a neat row on the right side of the ship. The stores all appeared to have their glass panel and metal security doors shut and locked, but Steve made a mental note to check them anyway. They didn't want someone or something coming out after they passed by.

Perpendicular to his left sat a row of five elevators situated in their own hall with three glass elevators facing into the Centrum on the opposite side of their common wall. Beyond this, he could see more shops lining the port side of the ship. Although he was too far back from the opening to look straight up, due to the amount of light coming in, Steve assumed that the entire roof of the Centrum had to be glass.

Despite his vertical sight line being limited by the second floor walkway above him, he could look across the Centrum and see the top half of the restaurants lining the port side on the next deck above. Even from the small bit he could see, he was amazed at the detail.

There was a reproduction of an Italian sidewalk cafe right next to a Japanese sushi bar, both done up in exquisite detail. Turning his head to look back down the length of the deck, he could see the middle area was filled with kiosks, fountains and what appeared to be a miniature golf course. He noticed that, while grand in stature, the Centrum had a slightly eerie, unused look and feel to it. With everything intact, but with all of the storefronts closed, the fountains dry and chairs set around tables as if waiting for someone to sit down, it appeared the people had suddenly vanished. His mind wandered to thoughts of the Bermuda triangle and ships like the Mary Celeste, found abandoned but completely intact, right down to the tables set for diner. The dining room they just passed through came to mind, and he felt a shiver run up his spine.

Steve jumped slightly when he heard a sharp intake of breath next to him, but realized it was Heather when she said, "Oh my God, I've never seen anything like this in my life." Turning, he saw her standing a few feet away with mouth slightly agape as she tried to take in their posh surroundings.

Susan came up on Steve's left, and even though she had been on cruises before, she seemed awe struck by the sights of the Centrum. He could almost feel the excitement coming off her in waves.

Only Tick-Tock seemed less than impressed. He took in the area at a glance and then assumed the posture of a man waiting for his wife in a shoe store. While he appeared bored, Steve noticed that the former Marine's eyes never stopped moving as he searched for threats.

After giving everyone a chance to adjust to their surroundings, Steve asked Tick-Tock, "How do you want to do this?"

Without hesitation, he answered, "Diamond formation, you're on point, Heather's left handed so she's on the right. I'm on the left and Susan brings up the rear." Turning slightly toward Susan, he added, "You've got to walk backwards most of the time to cover our rear. You up for that?"

"No problem," she answered.

Nodding, Tick-Tock continued, "Everyone keep about a ten foot interval, and keep your eyes on the floors above us. If we stick close to the starboard row of shops, we should minimize our exposure from up top. Remember that if anyone fires on us to move toward them and unload with everything you've got. It's the only way to break up an ambush."

Steve put in his own thought. "Heather, since you'll be closest to the shops, make sure they're locked."

She nodded and added, "Like Tick-Tock said, we need to be careful so we don't bunch up. Right now, I'm not as worried about Z's as I am about getting shot."

"Words to live by," Susan said.

Grateful for Heather's experience in law enforcement, Tick-Tock's in the Marines and his own from his time in the Army, Steve stepped forward as the others fell into position behind him. Cautiously walking forward, they saw that the emergency lights were on in all the shops and they couldn't help but notice what was displayed in the glass storefronts. As they moved further into the Centrum without seeing anyone, living or dead, their confidence grew and they began to comment on what they saw.

"Duty free booze shop," Tick-Tock pointed out. "Maybe on the way back we can pick up something to celebrate with."

Heather tried the door, which only rattled in its casing, and said, "It's locked."

Hefting his M-4, Tick-Tock replied, "That's okay, I brought my key."

"Then you can open the door to the bath and body shop for me," Susan said.

"Or how about this one," Steve said as he pointed with his rifle at a shop with its facade done up in a nautical theme. "The Ship's Store."

Tacky tourist souvenirs cluttered its display racks, but lined up by the cash register were shelves full of bottled water, sodas, candy and snack foods.

"I'd kill for a bag of those Nacho Cheese Doritos," Susan said wistfully.

Tick-Tock brought the group back into focus by saying, "You might have to."

Silent again, they continued to move across the two hundred foot length of the Centrum. After passing numerous shops containing a variety of items from bedspreads to Waterford crystal, the opening to the upper floors ended at an ornate, curved, double staircase that Steve was almost tempted to use to explore the decks above. Looking in front of him though, he saw that the Centrum also ended a short ways past the stairs, and a long, angled registration desk of some type began that would funnel them to another set of the now familiar metal fire doors. This would be their turning around point, he decided. They had gone far enough on their first expedition and had come across the essentials, and some extravagances, they needed and wanted. They could grab a few things from the shops on their way back and explore the kitchen further to see if the coolers were still working. Steve suspected they were since he hadn't smelled anything rotten when they were in there. But even if the food had turned and the thick walls of the coolers had contained the smell, they could still raid the dry storage area.

He was even daydreaming about kicking back on the sailboat with a Bacardi and diet Coke, maybe with ice, when a familiar stink brought him to an abrupt halt.

"Z's," he hissed as he went into a half crouch. Without even looking, he knew that behind him the others had done the same and were now facing outward as they looked for targets.

"Where?" Tick-Tock asked as he searched the area.

"Don't know," Steve replied. "But I can smell them."

"I smell them too," Heather said, her voice thick with revulsion.

They had stopped just past the grand staircase and were in an open area, so any threat from the walking dead should be readily apparent. When nothing came at them, Steve decided to try and find the source of the stench. Heading toward the registration desk on his right, he made his way to within a few feet of the counter before stopping. Behind it was the only place where any of the dead could be hidden. Reaching out, he tapped the granite countertop with the barrel of his rifle and then drew back as he waited for any zombies to be attracted by the noise.

None of the dead popped up like a jack-in-the-box from hell, so he stepped forward and tapped louder. He knew he was close to something not still alive, because as he approached the desk, the smell had gotten stronger. Loathe to putting his head over the top to take a look, he moved further along the counter toward a pass-through a few feet away. Here he could move behind the desk without exposing himself too much. As he did, he noticed that the musky, rancid stink of the living dead became even more cloying, but now it seemed to be emanating from another direction. Suddenly realizing that the smell wasn't coming from behind the registration desk, he stopped and slowly turned around to see exactly where else it was coming from.

That was when he saw it. The double steel doors that led from the Centrum into the next compartment were chained together. Now he realized why they hadn't seen any of the dead, even though they could smell them. The Z's were locked away in the next section of the ship.

Not trusting any barrier that he hadn't erected himself, Steve cautiously approached the doors. He knew before they could turn their backs on them that he had to make sure they were secure.

Something he hadn't noticed at first in the low light became apparent as he drew closer. What he had originally thought was a decorative design on each of the doors was actually a five-foot high, ornately painted cross. Further proof of the religious graffiti was the discarded spray cans lying near-by on the rug. Stopping within arm's length of the barricade, he glanced over his shoulder at the others. All three of his friends stood with weapons ready to cover him. Turning back to the door, the stench of death became thick in his nostrils, telling him he had definitely found the source.

Cautiously reaching out to check the chain, and expecting at any second the doors would burst open to disgorge a horde of the dead, his hand was only inches away when it was stopped by a voice calling out loudly from behind him, "I wouldn't go in there if I were you."

Whirling around as his heart leapt to his throat, Steve brought his M-4 up to his shoulder and easily found his target. A boy, not even in his teens, stood at the foot of the grand staircase looking nervously down the barrels of the four automatic rifles pointed at him.

Steve's finger pulsed on the trigger as it started to squeeze the last half-ounce of pressure. Seeing no immediate threat in the kid, or anywhere else in the immediate vicinity, he eased off and said furiously, "That's a good way to get your shit sprayed all over the far wall, dumbass."

Not giving the youngster a chance to reply, and angry that someone, especially a kid, had been able to sneak up on him, Tick-Tock called out aggressively, "What the fuck are you doing creeping around down here? And who the fuck are you?"

Shocked and scared at the reaction from the four people, and amazed at how incredibly fast they had all spun around to point their guns at him, he answered in a squeaky voice, "My name's Tim." He cleared his throat and tried to put some bass in it as he added, "I'm the one who left the hatch open for you so you could get on board. I need your help."

"Is it zombies?" Heather asked as she looked around for any sign of the dead.

"They're part of the problem," he replied. "But mostly it's the living ones on the ship. They're crazy as hell."

Chapter Five

The Dead Calm:

After regaining his composure, Tim Lopez walked to the guest registration counter and jumped up to sit on it. His legs dangled over the edge and his heels thumped its face as he studied the four people he hoped could help him and his sister escape the madness they found themselves in.

The two siblings and their parents had boarded the Calm of the Seas almost three months earlier from Port Canaveral for what was supposed to be a seven day cruise to Mexico. Tim still remembered the fun and excitement of the first two days at sea, but after that, the trip had spiraled into a nightmare that continued to get worse. The first case of HWNW showed itself on the second day of the cruise when one of the attendants entered a cabin to clean it and to create an animal figure from rolled towels that he would leave for his guest's enjoyment. The room itself was empty, but when he opened the door to the bathroom, he found a bloody, half-naked woman lying on the floor. He summoned medical aid immediately, but before they could arrive, he saw the woman start to convulse and then lay still. Her body sagging as all its muscles relaxed.

Seeing that she had quit breathing, and fearing that she was dying, the attendant bent over her and started mouth-to-mouth resuscitation. The woman quickly came back, but not to life. Instead of giving her thanks to the attendant for his heroic efforts, she lunged up from the bathroom floor and bit off his right ear.

What the attendant didn't know was that earlier in the day when the ship had stopped in Miami, the woman and her husband had disembarked to tour the city and buy souvenirs. She brought back T-shirts, a coffee mug and a new sundress, while her husband brought back the HWNW virus after being attacked and bitten on the shoulder in a public restroom.

Thinking at first that the assault was nothing more than some freak getting his perverted kicks, this was Miami after all, and not wanting to ruin their vacation, the man kept the attack to himself. Although hours later when he started convulsing, died, came back to life and tried to eat his wife. His secret was out. She escaped her dead husband by locking herself in the bathroom. Here she fainted from shock and blood loss, lying unconscious on the floor until the cabin attendant found her. Hubby, in the meantime, having been denied his meal, went in search of other food.

Staggering down the passageway, the dead thing had barely gone ten yards when it found something to eat. A door to a cabin opened and an elderly man stepped out. Seeing food, the dead man turned and leapt at him, pushing him back into his room. The senior citizen's first impression was that he was being robbed. That thought was snuffed out, along with his life, when dead hubby tore his throat out and started to feed. In this manner, the zombie visited three more cabins over the next day before being discovered.

After the woman who had attacked the attendant was restrained, the Captain was summoned to deal with the bloody incident. Not wanting to alarm the passengers over what he suspected was a drug induced attack, he had the cabin sealed and the injured moved through the crew passageways to the ship's infirmary. The doctor who examined the woman had never seen a case like hers before, so he advised that she be airlifted to the nearest hospital. The Coast Guard was called and a helicopter dispatched, but before they could arrive, two more cases of passengers going crazy and attacking those around them were reported; one in the Sombrero lounge on deck ten near the bow and the other in the formal dining room on deck four near the stern.

The Captain, now thinking that since the three incidents were scattered throughout the Calm of the Seas that they could be related to some type of food poisoning, gave orders to have the ship's stores examined for any type of contamination. The reports came back negative, so he reverted to his initial theory that that the attacks were caused by some type of drug use. When no other cases were reported, and the three sick people were successfully airlifted, he felt justified in giving the order to continue on with the cruise schedule. All went well until early the next morning when the cabin attendant who had been bitten on the ear staggered into the crew's mess hall and attacked a sales girl who worked in one of the shops in the Centrum. Before three men from the engine room restrained him, he managed to infect them, the sales girl and four others.

Before the Captain could respond to this latest carnage, dozens of reports started coming in about other attacks on passengers and crew by maniacs who bit and clawed at their victims. Now fearing that whatever contaminates causing the outbreak were being spread by the water or air circulation systems, the Captain ordered that these be shut down and examined. No contaminants were found, but with the situation getting out of control, he ordered his First Officer to make for Cozumel.

Calling a general emergency, the Captain asked that all passengers return to, and remain in, their cabins. Using the excuse that the crew needed the passageways clear while they worked on the water and air systems, he left these off to support his lie. What he really wanted to do was to keep the decks clear so that the drug addled junkies could be restrained and locked up. Splitting his available crew into two person teams, the Captain ordered every square inch of the cruise liner searched for anyone acting aggressively. Once apprehended, these people were to be kept in the Sounds Lounge at the rear of deck eight. Although his intentions were good, and most of those carrying the virus were detained, the Captain's order caused a good portion of his crew to become infected when they came into contact with the dead.

After the sweep of the Calm of the Seas was completed and an all clear sounded, the Captain allowed the passengers to come out into the common areas of the ship. At first the mood was subdued, but as word leaked out about what was really going on, and that these incidents were connected to news reports about the spread of the HWNW virus, it started to get ugly.

Some passengers locked themselves in the relative security of their cabins, but many more besieged the crew with demands for protection. A large group banded together and initiated roving patrols that went in search of anyone who might be infected with the disease. The words 'plague ship' were used for the first time.

Over the course of the day, as the members of the crew who had been infected succumbed to their various bites and infected scratches, the Captain ordered them quarantined with the others in the Sounds Lounge. Finding himself shorthanded due to the attrition of his crew, he asked for volunteers from the passengers to fill the gaps in his staff.

Tim's dad had served in the navy on a cruiser, so he stepped forward to offer his skills. Assuring his wife and children they would be safe, he left to do what he thought was his duty. None of them ever saw him again.

Shortly after this, a passenger who had joined one of the roving patrols knocked on the door of the Lopez's cabin. Now better organized, the men of the patrol had taken to wearing crimson colored T-shirts so they could be more easily identified. The red shirt that came to the Lopez's cabin informed the family that they had to relocate since their deck was to be used to quarantine those suspected of being infected. After using the allotted ten minutes to pack their belongings, Tim and his family stepped out into the passageway to join the stream of other displaced passengers from deck four heading toward the exit.

Despite many people stopping and complaining to the red shirts stationed at twenty-foot intervals to make sure everything went smoothly, the exodus was moving along in a fairly orderly fashion as everyone filed toward the rear of the ship. Not liking the crowds and the noise, and wanting to keep her family together as more people flooded into the hallway from their cabins, Tim's mom had just finished telling him and his sister to stay close when, from behind them, they heard a blood curdling scream.

Since he couldn't see what was happening through the throng of people, Tim assumed it was an attack by one of the crazy people he had heard his mom and dad talking about. Not wanting to be separated from his family, he reached over to grab his sister's hand. Finding it, he locked it in a death grip. As he reached for his mom's behind him, a sudden press of people surged forward and separated them. Above the frightened screams and shouts that filled the passageway, Tim could hear his mother calling for him and his sister. No matter how hard he tried, he couldn't force his way back through the now panicked mob to reach her.

The forward momentum of the crowd pushed Tim and his sister out through the double doors of the cabin area and into the Centrum where Connie pulled Tim to the side of the flow. Here they could wait for their mom to appear. As they anxiously watched the exit, neither could find their mother in the throng, but they did see their first zombie.

When Tim spotted the thing, it appeared to be receiving a piggyback ride from a stocky man who looked like he had just stepped out of an ad for Muscle and Fitness magazine. As Muscle man stepped past the exit doors, it became clear that he was not willingly giving his hitchhiker a ride. Twisting and bending, he swung back and forth in an effort to dislodge the thing, but the zombie was not to be denied its meal. With its arms wrapped around Muscle man's neck, and its legs similarly wound around his waist, it clung to him like a remora as it repeatedly bit into the back of his head, ripping scalp from his skull in small flaps.

The crowd coming through the doors scattered at the bloody sight, and those still waiting to exit backed up into the cabin area's passageway. Two red shirts that had been standing by the doors jumped forward to try and remove the zombie from Muscle man's back but got nowhere for their efforts. Seeing they couldn't save the man, and knowing that anyone who was bitten would soon go crazy themselves and try to assault others, the two red shirts pushed Muscle man and his aggressor back into the cabin area and slammed the heavy, steel fire doors behind them with a resounding bang. Before any of the onlookers could step forward to point out that there were people trapped in the cabin area with the maniac, one of the red shirts produced a length of chain and a lock, using them to secure the doors.

Seeing this, Connie screamed and froze as Tim rushed forward to save his mother. A crowd formed around the red shirts, yelling at them to open the doors. Tim heard one of the men reply that he didn't have the key, someone named Reverend Ricky had it.

Hearing this sent fear and rage shooting through Tim and he threw himself against the barricade, tearing at the heavy links of chain that imprisoned his mother. Even above the noise of the crowd, he could hear screams of pain and terror coming from the other side of the door. As he tugged futilely at the lock, he never saw the red shirt step up behind him and raise the club in his hand.

Regaining consciousness, Tim's first sight was his sister leaning over him with tears streaming down her face. "Mom?" He asked groggily, but his sister couldn't speak. She shook her head and mouthed the word, "No."

Pain welled up in him. Looking around, he tried to focus on something besides his grief and hiding his tears, when he noticed that they were in a cabin. Connie finally got herself under control and explained what happened after he was knocked unconscious.

When the red shirt struck Tim down, the crowd surged forward in rage at seeing a small boy abused. Tim's attacker and his partner were outnumbered twenty to one, but they carried clubs while the passengers were unarmed. With their backs against the doors leading to the cabin area, the red shirts used these bludgeons to menace the mob and hold them at bay. Despite this, the angry crowd inched slowly forward until it looked like the two men would be pulled down anyway by sheer weight of numbers. Suddenly, screams erupted from the back of the group. Turning to what they thought was another crazed attacker, the people in the mob were astonished to see half a dozen men in red T-shirts knocking passengers to the left and right with an assortment of sawed off pool cues and broken off table legs. Seeing their rescuers coming to save them, the two red shirts at the door joined in by striking the passengers nearest them with their own clubs.

The crowd scattered under the assault, and Connie took advantage of the distraction to run toward her brother and pull him away from the melee. After dragging him a short distance, she covered his body with hers so no further harm would come to him.

When the noise of the short lived battle was over, Connie looked up to see the red shirts grouped in front of a man wearing a three-piece suit. Those clustered around this new arrival called him Reverend Ricky, and from what Connie could see, he appeared to be their leader.

When the red shirts finished explaining what had occurred, and how they even had to lock their own people in the cabin area to keep the infected contained, Reverend Ricky raised his hands in benediction as his followers bowed their heads. In a deep, bass voice, Ricky intoned, "Thy will be done Lord. Make me a tool of thy will and use me as you see fit on this Earth until you call me home at the rapture. My faithful Ushers have vowed their obedience to you, oh God, so I ask that you protect them as they go about your work, Amen."

The Ushers intoned, "Amen" and looked to their leader for further instructions. With a tight smile, Ricky ordered them to lock down the cabin areas on all the remaining decks, but not to clear them of the passengers first since they couldn't afford to risk losing any more of their people. Not questioning his orders, the red shirted Ushers went to do his bidding.

When they were gone, Reverend Ricky looked around with contempt at the few moaning, bloody people left behind. With venom in his voice, he warned them not to stand in the way of God's will again or they would risk an even more severe form of punishment. As he glowered at the beaten passengers, his eyes fell on Connie crouched next to her brother. Instantly in motion, the scowl on his face changed to a grin as he walked toward her and asked in a soft voice, "What's the matter child, do you need some assistance?"

Tim's friends were always telling him how beautiful his sister was, but he thought she was a pain in the ass. She was nineteen and still living at home, and had taken it upon herself since graduating high school to make sure her little brother didn't get into any trouble while their parents were at work. As far as Tim was concerned, she had ruined the past summer.

When he found out they were going on this cruise, he hoped she wouldn't ruin that too. Luckily, she had been distracted by all the attention she received from the guys her own age and hadn't tried to keep track of him. Tim had even heard one of the crew say that Connie was a hottie after she walked by in a swimsuit. He had almost thrown up. How anyone could call that warthog a hottie was beyond him.

Reverend Ricky gushed sympathy at Connie and deflected the blame onto others when she explained how their mother had been trapped in the cabin area and her brother knocked unconscious by the Reverend's men. Promising he would put the situation right, Ricky pulled out a walkie-talkie and spoke briefly into it. Within minutes, two of his Ushers appeared. Before ordering them to carry Tim to a safe place, Ricky promised Connie he would summon more of his people to extract her mother from the cabin area.

When Connie was done relating what had happened, Tim asked her where the Reverend was so he could thank him. At this, Connie shook her head and replied, "No, we have to get out of here. Ricky isn't doing this to be nice, he's after something else."

Confused, Tim asked, "What?"

"Me," Connie replied. "I've seen his type before, perverts that use religion to seduce their followers so they can have sex with the ones they lust after. Even though Ricky smiled, I could see the truth in his eyes. He's a pervert. The only reason I went along with his men was to get you somewhere safe."

"He said he'd rescue mom though," Tim pleaded.

"He lied," Connie said. "He'll say anything to get you on his side so he can use you. While you were unconscious, I snuck back down to deck four and saw that the doors leading into the cabin area are exactly the same as when we left, except someone spray painted crosses on them. No one tried to go back in there."

As Tim tried to absorb this, Connie asked, "Do you think you can walk? We've got to get out of here before Ricky comes back."

Motivated by the frightened tone in his sister's voice, Tim rose and stood a little unsteadily. He felt nauseous, but it passed quickly. Connie put a steadying hand on his shoulder. When he felt stable enough to move, he asked, "Where do we go?"

"Back down to deck four," she answered. "We need to be on the same floor as our old cabin in case dad comes looking for us. The shops there were all closed up and locked, but I know how to get in the back way. A steward gave me a tour of the ship yesterday and showed me the passageways that run behind the stores and cabins that the crew uses to get around."

Hearing they would be looking for their dad, Tim's expression grew determined as he shook off his sister's supporting hand and said, "Then let's gets to it. We're wasting time here."

At that moment, the lights flickered in the cabin and the familiar dull thrum of the engines slowly died off, leaving a heavy silence. Tim and Connie looked at each other in panic, then fled out the door and down a corridor now illuminated by only emergency lights. Thus the two went into hiding.

Tim noticed that no one paid any attention to a kid wandering the passageways, and he found that he could move around the Calm of the Seas without being noticed. Through listening in at doors and eavesdropping on conversations, he learned that Reverend Ricky now controlled the ship and that his followers numbered over two hundred. He also discovered the reason the engines had ceased operating. Three of the engine room crewman, those same men bitten and infected by the cabin attendant, had gone berserk and killed their fellow workers. Other crewmembers, not wishing to risk their lives in an attempted rescue, sealed the entrances to the engine room. Shortly after that, the huge motors that propelled the Calm of the Seas fell silent. The emergency generators kicked in, but they only provided electricity to the essential areas of the ship. After securing his position, Reverend Ricky had his Ushers start other generators to give more power to certain parts of the ship. Most of the decks had lights, but none had air conditioning or heat. Electricity was diverted to the huge coolers and freezers in the kitchens and the eateries on what was called restaurant row on deck five so the survivors wouldn't run out of food. With barely one twentieth of the passengers left alive, Ricky and his men calculated that their supplies would last for a long time.

This also worked out perfect for Tim and Connie, who survived off what was in the shops and food from the kitchen that serviced the formal dining room at the rear of deck four. Reverend Ricky and his followers had plenty of provisions on the upper decks; so only twice in as many months did Tim see anyone venture down as far as deck four, and then, only to take a quick look around before leaving.

Tim found an AM/FM radio early on in his wanderings and at night he and Connie could pick up a few stations broadcasting from Florida. They listened in as the world seemed to be coming to an end. The last radio station, KLAM out of Clearwater, Florida, had been broadcasting real time reports of what was going on in the Tampa Bay area and giving tips on how to stay alive in the new dead world. The signal slowly faded away when the range became too great as the Calm of the Seas drifted further into the Gulf of Mexico. Then the signal died, to be replaced by silence. When this happened, hope of being rescued also slowly faded in the Lopez siblings and their day-to-day life became more an act of just doing rather than living. That was until Tim saw the sailboat coming toward them.

After discussing it with Connie and explaining that it wasn't only men on board the small craft, but that he'd seen two women and a little girl, she agreed to let him open a hatch and allow the strangers on board.

Now, sitting on the counter looking at the armed foursome in front of him, Tim didn't feel afraid. He sensed no threat from the strangers as they stood a few feet away, studying him as he studied them. When the one that Tim took to be the leader said, "You've got nothing to be afraid of with us, kid," a feeling of relief washed over him and he believed the man. When the blonde woman asked what Tim meant about the people on board the Dead Calm being crazy, he told them.

After listening to Tim's story, Steve said unbelievingly, "The rapture? You mean to tell me that the people on this ship are waiting for Jesus to come down and carry them up to Heaven?"

Tim nodded, "They say it's the end times, so every night at dusk they gather on the pool deck and wait to be saved and ascend into Heaven."

With sarcastic amusement, Tick-Tock asked, "Anyone lift off yet?"

"No," Tim replied, "but I've seen a couple jump overboard when it doesn't happen and they lose hope."

"Jesus," Susan exclaimed.

"Has nothing to do with this," Connie called out loudly.

All four of the boarding party spun toward the voice as they raised their weapons, but quickly lowered them when they saw who spoke. Standing in the doorway of a clothes shop from where she had been listening to her brother tell the strangers their story, Connie looked anything but a threat.

Standing five foot three, with long, shiny black hair that fell to her waist and large dark eyes, Connie looked more like a model than the woman that Tim described as a warthog and a hag. Wearing shorts that showed off her legs and a t-shirt that couldn't begin to hide the rest of her shapely figure, she could only be described as a knockout.

Susan turned to say something to Tick-Tock, but when she saw the expression on his face, she instead whispered, "Put your eyes back in your head, pervert. You're old enough to be her father."

"Only if I was doing the wild thing when I was twelve," he replied as he continued to stare.

Heather looked at Steve to see his reaction, but he had already composed himself. She gave him a warning look on general principle before saying to Connie, "Thank you for deciding open the hatch and let us on board. I promise you, we mean no harm to you or your brother."

Connie only nodded as she walked forward to join them, still not sure if she had made the right decision. Tim hopped down from his perch and joined his sister as he said to her, "I was just about to tell them the rest."

"A boat load of Jesus freaks and zombies isn't enough?" Tick-Tock asked. "Who else is on board, Idi Amin?"

"They're not Jesus freaks," Connie corrected him. The people in control couldn't care less about religion. The leader formed a cult by playing on the survivors' hopes and fears." Looking at Tim as if not sure whether to continue, Connie shrugged and said, "They have orgies up on the pool deck every night after they fail to ascend into Heaven, and this includes the willing and the unwilling. But most of the Faithful, as Reverend Ricky calls his followers, worship him like he's the second coming and join right in. Tim's listened in on some of the conversations the rank and file Ushers have had, and they're so worked up with his false religion that they're ready to martyr themselves for their leader. The inner circle, Ricky calls them his Head Ushers, are in on the scam, and they use the regular Ushers to keep the Faithful in line."

"That's okay," Tick-Tock said nonchalantly. "I'll pop a cap in Ricky's ass and he can show his Head Ushers how easy it is to get to Heaven."

"His followers would turn on you," Connie warned. "Maybe not all of them, but over half are faithful to Ricky and the religion he's set up." Remembering how many survivors Tim had told him were left on the ship, Steve did the math as he considered the odds of assassinating their leader and getting away with it. Needing to know exactly what they were up against, he asked Tim, "Are they armed?"

"They've got three rifles and three pistols, but only the Head Ushers carry those," he answered. "But just about everyone carries a knife or a club or something in case they run into one of the dead."

"You've got Z's running around?" Heather asked. "I thought you told us that this ship was secured."

"I said that most of the dead were locked in the cabin areas," Tim replied.

"They show up from time to time," Connie interjected. "No one knows where they come from, but on a ship this big, with all the places they could hide, I'm sure there's a lot that didn't get locked in the cabin areas."

"They hide?" Susan asked.

"Look at what they did in San Francisco," Steve pointed out.

"And in Clearwater," Heather added. "Most of the dead hid in the storm drains and the sewers until there was a shitload of them, and then they came out to eat."

"So then we've got a couple things we need to consider," Steve said. "First off, we need to leave Reverend Ricky alone for the time being. As much as I'd like to kill his ass, I don't want a hundred religious nutcases making a suicide run at us."

Tick-Tock nodded, but looked slightly disappointed at Steve's decision.

"Cheer up," Steve told him. "They've got to know we're here. If they make any aggressive moves, we waste them. Now for the second issue, which also ties into the first one." Turning to Tim, he asked, "How many ways are there to get down onto this deck?"

"Only one," he answered, pointing to the grand staircase. "The doors to the stairs at the back of the kitchen are blocked off and none of these elevators have power. The only other way down to this level is the stairs back there."

They all looked to where he was pointing at the chained metal doors with the crosses painted on them.

"I don't think anyone's coming from that direction," Tick-Tock said. "So that leaves the stairs here in the Centrum, and we can cover them no problem." Looking at Steve, he asked, "You thinking what I'm thinking?"

"Maybe," Steve answered before turning to Heather and saying, "I'm thinking we can bring everyone on board." A cautious look crossed her face, so he added, "From what Tim and Connie told us, we're secure here as long as we keep the stairs covered. Reverend Ricky might be a threat, but I bet he already knows we're here. Since he hasn't made a move on us, I doubt he will." Heather still looked less than enthused at the idea, so Steve put in, "Besides, you said you wanted a shower and some real food, this is our chance."

"There's a shower in the locker room behind the kitchen," Connie volunteered. "We use it all the time. There's no hot water, but it's not too bad. I think the water tank is near the hull of the ship, so the sun heats it up pretty good."

Heather considered this before turning to walk the length of the Centrum as she surveyed their position. Coming back to study the grand staircase leading to the decks above, after a moment of thought, she said, "Okay, let's do it. I think we could all use a break from riding on the SS Minnow. Call Brain and tell him to get ready to come aboard and that we'll meet him at the hatch. We need to post someone to cover the stairs so we don't get any surprise visitors and we'll have to keep our guard up at all times. I want everyone to stay conscious of where they are and what the fastest route back to the sailboat is in case we have to evacuate."

Heather turned to Connie and said, "You and Tim are welcome to come with us when we leave, but first I think you need to know what the rest of the world is like. After you find out, you might want to stay here."

"I think we have a good idea of what it's like out there," Connie replied. "Before we lost the signal, we used to get radio broadcasts from KLAM in Florida-."

Tick-Tock laughed out loud, cutting Connie off.

"What's so funny?" She asked.

"Nothing," Tick-Tock replied with a big smile. "Go ahead with what you were saying."

Looking around, Connie noticed that all of them were smiling, but she didn't get the joke. Hoping that someone would eventually let her in on it, she continued, "So KLAM gave out reports of what was happening, and it sounded like things got bad, but I'd rather take my chances out there than stay here and live in hiding."

Heather shrugged, wondering if Connie would feel differently once she saw her first Dead City. Turning to Steve, she raised an eyebrow and said with a smile, "Looks like you're the new Captain of this ship, so what are your orders?"

Having mentally run through what needed to be done while Heather and Connie had been talking, he said, "Tick-Tock covers the stairs, Heather you stay with him. Susan, you, Connie and Tim go with me to meet Brain at the hatch."

"Bring back some tear gas canisters and extra ammo," Tick-Tock said. "They might come in handy."

"Gotcha," he replied.

"How many are with you?" Connie asked.

"Two other people and a Mary," Tick-Tock replied.

Looking at the rows of shops, Susan said, "She'll think she died and went to Heaven."

Unclipping the radio from his belt, Steve filled Brain in on what had happened and about their plan to move onto the Dead Calm. When he finished, he turned to Heather and said, "We're all set, but there are a few things that worry me. Why didn't Reverend Ricky or any of his followers show themselves when we circled the ship? And since he has rifles, he could have used them to keep us from boarding, but he didn't."

Tick-Tock, who was using his K-Bar knife to pry the Plexiglas cover off a diagram of the ship mounted near the stairs, said, "Maybe he wants us here."

Heather shook her head, "I don't think so. We pose too much of a threat of upsetting the balance in his little commune. There's got to be another reason."

"Maybe we have something he wants?" Susan proposed.

"Could be," Steve said thoughtfully, "but what?"

Chapter Six

The Dead Calm:

Richard Rosencrantz, known to his faithful followers as the Reverend Ricky Rose, looked out from the bridge of the Calm of the Seas at the sailboat holding position off the right side of his ship. Turning to his second in command, who in the pre-dead world had been a third-rate lawyer named Donald Parsons that worked out of a dilapidated double wide trailer set up in a strip mall parking lot, he asked, "How many came on board?"

"Four," Parsons replied. "My guys counted four that came on board and three more still on the sailboat. He said the ones on board move like they know what they're doing. Maybe former military. Altogether there are three women, three men and a little girl in their group. Two men and two women came onto the Calm and they were all carrying automatic weapons. A young woman and a kid met them down in the Centrum. That's who we think let them on the ship. They must have opened one of the hatches on deck four."

"Saved us from doing it," Ricky commented before asking, "Are the Faithful staying out of sight?"

Parsons nodded and said, "Except for one guy on deck five who's keeping an eye on the newcomers, I pulled the rest of the watchers back and herded the Faithful onto deck eleven. It's the only one that doesn't open up onto the Centrum. I don't want a bunch of people getting curious and hanging over the rail and gawking. I also tried to identify the girl and the kid, but I didn't recognize them as any of the followers. The kid looked familiar, like I've seen him hanging around, but I've never seen the chick before."

Ricky nodded at this. He and Don both knew that not everyone on board welcomed Ricky's leadership, and that a few passengers roamed the huge ship and didn't participate in the nightly sermon or the extra-curricular activities afterward. As long as these break-a-ways didn't interfere with Ricky or his Ushers, they were left alone. But if any did voice an objection to the way the ship was run, they were immediately silenced.

"Good work, Don," Ricky told his number two. "Make sure you keep your thumb on the Faithful and keep them under control."

Ricky turned and walked to a table covered with charts near the back of the bridge. After sifting through them, he unrolled one that showed the Gulf of Mexico, the Mexican coast and the Yucatan peninsula. Placing his forefinger on a red pencil mark, he asked, "Is this our position?"

"As of this morning it is," Parsons replied.

Ricky shook his head and made clucking sounds in his throat to show his displeasure.

"We're drifting further and further away every day," Parsons commented. "There's no way we could make it to Cozumel now, even if we tow three lifeboats full of fuel behind us. And then we'd have to tow another two for supplies."

With a heavy sigh, Ricky said, "I know Don, we're caught between Scylla and Charybdis."

Parsons gave Ricky a questioning look so he explained, "It means a rock and a hard place. We can't make it to safety, and time's running out if we stay here."

"Well, we didn't know the ship was going to sink when we made the decision to stay with it," Parsons replied.

"But we knew that Cozumel was free of the dead and taking in refugees if you brought your own supplies. We should have gone when we had the chance," Ricky countered.

Parsons nodded, but he knew that when they had first made radio contact with Cozumel and found out it was a safe haven, the Calm of the Seas was still in excellent condition. The booze was running freely and the orgies on the pool deck were going full tilt boogie. There was no way the people on board were going to give that all up to be farmers or fisherman on an island off the Mexican coast. It was live for the moment and to hell with the future. The only problem was that the future was here.

"How long did Brother Seth say we have until the pumps go out?" Ricky asked.

"Two weeks at most."

"Well, we had a good thing going here while it lasted, but I guess it's time to move on." Sighing, Ricky thought back over the past few months and the pure power he'd enjoyed.

And was about to lose.

When Richard Rosencrantz had boarded the Calm of the Seas months earlier, it had been to take a much-needed break from his business of promoting religious, tent revival meetings. Needing a breather from travelling from one end of the Bible Belt to the other while hawking an endless stream of snake handlers, people speaking in tongues and little girls in pretty, white dresses singing Jesus Loves Me, a seven day cruise seemed to be just what he needed. After decades in the business, he was starting to get burned out, and it seemed like he was doing too much for too little. Month after month he felt like he was working his ass off, and for what, he asked himself? Ten percent of the take when the plate was passed around at the end of the night. It just didn't seem to be worth it.

Despite making a decent living, Ricky's real problem stemmed from watching the preachers and charlatans over the years and how they lived off the other ninety percent. Jealousy and resentment ballooned as he watched the false prophets drive around in Jaguars, BMWs and Mercedes-Benzes while he was stuck with a Cadillac.

Last year's model, he often reminded himself. It just wasn't fair.

And the power that these so called men of God wielded, Richard often raged to himself. They could tell their flock to do damned near anything, claiming it was an order sent down from Jesus H. Christ himself, and the idiots would fall all over themselves to do it. Standing on the bridge of the Calm of the Seas, he remembered getting drunk with a Baptist minister one night after a rather profitable show, and what he had confided in him.

The minister explained how he used his ushers as spotters. They would watch the crowd for any mother and daughter combination that had come to the show unescorted. If the two females seemed to be taken in with the Holy Spirit during the service, an usher would approach them afterward and explain that the Minister had a private message to them from God. Once alone with his victims, the Minister would roll his eyes up and pretend to go into a trance. In an ethereal voice he would say that it was God speaking through him and that it was time for the little girl to become a woman. He would tell them that the vessel he was speaking through had been put on Earth to plant his seed that would grow into the Son of God. The Messiah.

Ricky remembered how the old pedophile had laughed and said, "I got more teenage pussy with that trick than you can shake a stick at. And that's not even counting the older broads who damn near threw themselves at me after every show." Proudly he added, "Eight to eighty, blind, crippled or crazy, I've had them all."

Ricky could only shake his head in disbelief and laugh. While craving the power these men had, he was not religious himself. He had seen early on in his life that the church was for suckers. Look at the suicide bombers killing themselves and everyone else around them in the name of Allah. There was no way a smart guy like Richard Rosencrantz was going to fall into a trap like that. The Christians, Jews and Muslims had been trying to wipe each other out for centuries and would keep on until one of them succeeded. He didn't get the upside to being a soldier of God and having someone dictate how he should live his life.

But then again, he didn't see any down side in profiting off other people's foolishness. Having grown up in the back woods of Georgia, he'd been forced to attend enough revival meetings as a kid to see they were so much bullshit, but he did recognize that there was a potential for profit to be made in an overlooked niche of the travelling religious organizations.

Promotion.

His entire childhood, he had watched as the preachers and ministers came to town on a Tuesday to start advertising their meetings with a few flyers and street corner sermons. They would tell the faithful to come out for service on Thursday, Friday and Saturday nights, which were ill attended at best, and culminating with the big show on Sunday, which was the best attended and the most profitable. What Ricky knew from being raised in an area where these revival meetings thrived, was that the people in these regions had work to do. Whether it was farming, running a store or working in a factory, they couldn't just take off with little or no warning to get closer to God. Besides being the Sabbath, this was why the Sunday sermon was the best attended. People had time to rearrange their schedules and plan ahead.

But, Ricky told himself, if these same people had more than a day or two of warning, like a week or two in which they were bombarded by constant reminders of the upcoming show, they would be more apt to put in an appearance for multiple meetings. And this meant the plate would be passed to more of the flock more of the time.

In 1994, armed with a computer, a printer and the idea that he could increase the profitability of any tent revival meeting, Richard approached three preachers working the same circuit a few weeks apart. After pitching his idea, he got all three to give him a chance. His idea ended up being so successful that by the following year, he'd contracted with twenty-two different travelling revival meetings to provide all their promotional needs. Expanding on his original idea to blanket an area with flyers two weeks before his client hit town, he turned his attention to the religious radio stations in the targeted vicinity and started getting himself booked on talk and morning shows to promote his patrons. Here he found he could spout the fire and brimstone just as well as, or better than, anyone he represented. He even toyed with the idea of hitting the circuit himself, but abandoned the plan when he realized how glutted the market was. It was better to continue profiting a little from each of the charlatans than risk it all by putting on a show himself.

But still, over the years, as he watched the power these preachers wielded, Richard craved what they had.

When the first cases of the HWNW virus were reported on the news, Richard saw his clients jump on the story and start calling it God's retribution for our sins. They had been spouting the same line for years about AIDS, herpes and the clap, but a little fear went a long way in convincing the masses of divine retribution. This in turn opened their wallets and purses in the hopes they could buy themselves into Heaven.

Although profits rose, Richard wasn't going to let business get in the way of his much needed vacation. Leaving things in the capable hands of his personal assistant, Rosencrantz Inc now had eight full time employees, he embarked on his planned vacation with a redhead named Sheila who he met in a dive bar in Tennessee. As the ship left Port Canaveral, he was secure in the knowledge that the additional money coming in, due to the latest virus spreading across the world, would be waiting for him when he returned.

After two days of sex, sun and self-indulgence, Richard woke on the third day to a knock at his cabin door. Answering it, he found one of the ship's officers standing nervously in the passageway. The man explained that because of some mechanical difficulties, temporary difficulties he stressed, all passengers needed to remain in their cabins until further notice.

Suspicious of the explanation and the jittery demeanor of the officer, Richard nonetheless agreed to remain in his room. As soon as the officer moved on though, he dressed quickly, grabbed his camera, and after making sure that the coast was clear, slipped out of his cabin. He'd heard horror stories of people on cruises being stuck at sea for days when their ship broke down, and if this was a similar case, he wanted pictures to back up the lawsuit he would slap the Cayman Cruise Lines with.

Looking for anything suspicious, while keeping his nose open for the smell of backed up sewage since this seemed to be one of the most reported causes of a cruise being disrupted, Richard hadn't gone far when he heard the sounds of cursing and fighting coming from a hallway ahead. Rushing forward, he found himself at one of the service corridors the crew used. Not quite knowing what to expect, he was completely unprepared and shocked at what he saw.

Two cabin attendants gripped the wrists of a middle-aged woman. She struggled and fought them with a rage that Ricky had never seen in a female before. Thinking he had walked in on a rape, he was preparing to back up and watch the festivities when the woman broke the grip of one of her attackers. Before the man could restrain her again, she lunged at his partner and sank her teeth into his forearm. Blood flew as the woman whipped her head back and forth and the attendant screamed for help.

While he was expecting to sit back and watch a sexual assault, Richard was shocked at this turn of events. He was even more surprised when he jumped forward and grabbed the crazy lady around the waist. Not sure whether he was helping her or the man she had bit, he dragged the woman backwards. The attendant screamed again, and this was when Ricky saw that the female fury wouldn't unclench her teeth from where they were clamped into the man's arm. He watched in fascination as the skin on the man's limb stretched further and further until it reached the breaking point. It let go with a wet plop, and Ricky saw more blood well up in the mouth-sized gap where a huge chunk of meat had been removed from the man's arm.

Rage and blinding pain overcame the attendant, making him forget the Captain's orders about not harming the passengers as he swung a roundhouse punch at the woman's head. It connected with her left temple, and Ricky felt her go limp in his arms.

Letting the dead weight drop to the deck, Richard quickly retrieved his camera and started taking pictures of the scene as he backed away. Both crewmembers seemed unconcerned with this, which Richard found curious. He stopped and watched as they wrapped the wounded man's arm in his shirt to staunch the flow of blood. When they were finished, the injured man said something in a thick brogue about seeing the ship's doctor and walked away. The remaining crewman then grabbed the inert woman by the legs and started dragging her across the carpet. Looking up from his burden to see Richard watching him, he said with a British accent, "Thanks for your help before, Gov, but I could use a bit more if you might."

Seeing that the woman had not regained consciousness, and believing that the Brit was now tampering with a crime scene, Richard decided that since he had already gotten involved in an attempted rape and assault, it was time to put some distance between himself and any liability.

Putting on an act of being an innocent bystander, in a loud, righteous tone, he said, "Just wait a minute, you can't move her. What do you think you're doing?" Looking closely at the lifeless body, he added in an incredulous voice, loud enough for any potential witnesses to hear, "What did you do? Oh my God, I think you killed her!"

Adjusting his grip on the woman's leg, the attendant seemed unconcerned as he replied, "Might have done just that, Gov, but she's still got to go with the others."

Richard was going to continue his charade by yelling for help, but the man's statement stopped the words in his mouth. Instead, he asked in a curious tone, "Others?"

"Lots of them, don't you know, Gov?" The man answered. Looking down at the body and then back up at Richard, he said, "It's an outbreak of some kind. At first the Captain thought it was drugs but...." The man's voice trailed off.

Richard quickly put together the reports on the news and in the papers he had seen before coming on this cruise with what he'd just witnessed and came up with the HWNW virus. Wanting to know more about what was going on, he reached down and grabbed the woman's arms and let the cabin attendant lead him through a maze of crew passageways to the Sounds Lounge.

Built on two levels, it really wasn't a lounge but a two-story theater complete with stage, orchestra pit and balcony. Entering through the doors leading to the balcony, the first thing Richard noticed was an unpleasant smell. It was a slightly rank odor, reminding him of the time he came across a raccoon that had crawled into a tin shed behind his house and died. No one discovered it until months later and it gave off the smell of old, musty death. The second thing he noticed was a strange sound that came and went. It was a high-pitched keening noise that seemed to dig for the center of his brain.

"What the hell is that?" He asked the Brit.

"You'll see in a minute, Gov," he answered and pointed with his elbow toward the edge of the balcony where two crewmembers were readying a rope.

After leaving the woman with the two men, Richard followed his guide as he ushered him to the rail and motioned for him to look. Leaning over cautiously, he only saw rows of plush seats with aisles cutting between them stretching away to the stage. At first noticing nothing unusual, he thought to himself, so what? It's a fucking theater.

A hissing noise made him look straight down. Jumping back slightly at what he saw, Ricky exclaimed, "Holy shit, what in the fuck is that?"

In just a brief glimpse, he had seen over two hundred former members of the passengers and crew clustered beneath the balcony in different stages of dress and undress, all of them with different types of grotesque, oozing wounds. Shaking off his initial shock, Richard leaned over the rail again for another look. Fascinated, he let his eyes scan the group below as he took in the different, gruesome aspects of the horror show.

One man's head flopped sideways, his neck muscles ripped away. A woman in shorts and a halter-top raised fingerless hands as if in supplication. A teenage boy dragged himself across the carpet by his hands, the muscles in his legs shredded to the point where they wouldn't support his body weight. He passed an older lady missing an ear and part of her scalp, revealing the gray white bone of her skull. A beautiful woman gawked up at Ricky. She was wearing nothing but bikini underwear bottoms as she stood with one ponderous breast half ripped away to hang limply from her chest. A college-aged man, who didn't appear to have a mark on him, but who had the same bluish-gray skin stretched across his face as the others, made a hissing noise when he noticed the two men above him. It went on and on. Feral, hungry eyes stared up at Richard as the whining noise he heard earlier rose to a crescendo. The sound had been coming from the things below.

Looking closer at the woman with only one breast, and then at the others, something that Richard had first thought was a trick of the light became apparent. A thick, black pussy substance had replaced the blood that should be leaking and spraying from their wounds.

Turning to his guide through Hell, Richard asked, "What's that stuff oozing out of their bodies?"

"Don't know, Gov, an infection of some sorts I'd guess," he answered with a shrug.

Another well-endowed woman, with her chest exposed through a torn Miami Dolphins jersey, caught Richard's attention. He watched her for a few minutes before turning away with a look of disgust on his face. He wanted it to appear like he was repulsed by the sight, but what he really wanted to do was hide the erection pressing against the crotch of his pants. He hadn't been this excited in years.

Richard's gaze settled on the two men who had taken custody of the woman he'd helped bring to the balcony, so he tried to take his mind off his growing lust by watching them. One held the woman's arms up while the other looped a rope around her chest and drew it tight. When he was finished, they picked her up and lowered her over the railing and down to the floor below. When she hit bottom, the man on the right gave the line a stiff jerk to release the slipknot he'd made and reeled the rope in.

Seeing Richard watching him, he called out, "I think that one's dead, but it's kind of hard to tell. They all kinda look dead."

Turning to look once more at the things below him, Richard had to agree. They did look dead. He'd just fixated on the breasts of the woman in the Miami Dolphins jersey again when a hand suddenly appeared out of the corner of his vision. At first flinching away, he felt embarrassment roll through him when he realized it was the Brit trying to shake his hand.

"Easy mate," the man said, "just wanted to thank you for your help. I'll escort you back to your cabin and then I need to get back to work. Idle hands are the devil's tools and all that."

Richard shook with the man and let the Brit lead him back to his room.

Sheila had woken in his absence, so after closing and locking the door behind him, Richard took out his lust for the woman in the torn jersey on her.

As he lay in bed afterward, his mind drifted to how he might gain from his present circumstances. Without question, a lawsuit would be forthcoming against the cruise line. With thousands of people on the Calm of the Seas though, the number of plaintiffs would lessen the payout. Richard racked his brain for the best way to profit from this disaster. Maybe blackmail, he thought. He had pictures of the crew assaulting a passenger, so that should be worth something.

Richard's thoughts were interrupted by a knock at the door and a voice calling out that the problem with the ship had been fixed. Remembering what he had seen that morning, he had a suspicion that the real problem was just beginning.

Wanting to find out more, he joined the passengers milling about in the Masthead Bar, listening to them speculate as to the cause of the temporary lockdown of the ship. Their theories sounded ludicrous to his ears, and he contented himself by feeling superior in his knowledge of what was really going on.

As he sat at the bar sipping one of the complimentary drinks being given out to assuage the ruffled feathers of the passengers, he thought of the people around him as being nothing but sheep. This led his mind to freely associate with the word flock. And from just that simple word, there bloomed an idea of such magnitude that he could barely contain himself. Taking a deep drink of his Mai Tai, he let the plan unfold. Not sure of all the details, but sure it would work if he played it right, he decided to begin right then and there.

Although he'd worked hard to lose his Georgia accent, Richard let it flow as he turned toward the two middle-aged ladies sitting next to him as he drawled, "I know what's going on, and all I can say is that it's an act of God."

Richard saw that the two women were instantly attentive, either cuing in on the word God or the fact that he claimed to know the reason for the disruption of the cruise. Laying it on thick, he reminded the two women of the HWNW virus before telling them they had an outbreak on the ship. He had seen it with his own eyes. Speaking loud enough to be heard by others sitting and standing nearby, he soon had a sizeable crowd gathered, hanging on his every word.

He started out by relating what he had seen in the Sounds Lounge, while throwing in any Bible verse that seemed appropriate for the situation, and then repeated the story a few times for the newcomers who congregated to hear his tale. When he had everyone's attention, he ad-libbed a story about ministering to a group of natives while working as a missionary in Africa. He told of how the heathens of the village he'd been sent to bring Christ to wouldn't give up their sinful ways. He related that the natives had run him off, and then finished his tale by saying that two weeks later, the entire community was wiped out by the Ebola virus. This brought gasps from some in his audience, so Richard added in a deep somber voice, "He who rejects the word of God and his messenger will be struck down in the coming plague."

A few in the crowd turned away at this prophecy and a few laughed at him before turning back to the bar. Richard noted the hecklers so they could be dealt with later. Despite this, most of the people seemed interested in what he had to say. An older woman laid her hand on his arm and asked, "What's your name, son?"

Without missing a beat, and raising his voice so all could hear, he said, "Brothers and sisters, I am the Reverend Ricky Rose, and I'm here to lead you to salvation."

With this declaration, the Reverend Ricky was born.

Ricky was amazed as he recalled how well his con job worked. Switching between the personas of a kind, caring, country preacher and a strongman dictator, he soon organized his faithful into groups that either prayed for salvation or went in search of anyone infected with the HWNW virus. By spreading the word that the end times were here and that only he, the Reverend Ricky Rose, could save the passengers on the Calm of the Seas, within hours he solidified his position as the spiritual and religious leader of the ship. By playing on the passengers' fears, and their willingness to grasp at any straw that might save them, he drew enough people to him to turn his attention to strengthening his physical hold over the ship.

Remembering what the Baptist minister had told him about how he had used his ushers, Ricky chose the most faithful from the groups that were searching for passengers infected with the virus. From these he formed a cadre that he could use. Giving them each a red T-shirt so they could be easily recognized, red to show the blood shed by Jesus Christ he told them, he named them his Ushers and set them to work relocating people to different decks since the Sounds Lounge was filling up fast. It was of no concern to Ricky that many of the passengers not infected with the disease were trapped with those who were when the plan fell apart and all the cabin areas were locked down. He already had over four hundred followers, so the loss of a few potential recruits was no big deal. When some of his flock approached Ricky to tell him that people were jumping into the sea to their death from the quarantine areas, he told them that God spoke to him and showed him a vision of this very thing coming to pass. God told him that the people were already infected and were simply saving themselves from the horror and ravages of the HWNW virus. They would be forgiven their sin of suicide and go to Heaven, after a brief stay in purgatory.

With the Bible as his reference, and a direct line to God, Ricky could find a vision, verse or a psalm to explain any of his actions. And if all else failed, he could always fall back on the greatest, empty justification that man had used since time began to excuse his actions.

It was God's will.

Reverend Ricky watched with interest out the side window of the bridge as the sailboat turned and headed toward the Calm of the Seas. "Contact your man and find out what they're doing," he told Parsons.

After pulling out a two-way radio, his number two held a brief conversation with the Usher posted to watch the newcomers from the second level of the Centrum. This was followed by a long pause in which neither man on the bridge spoke as they waited for an answer. Finally, the radio squawked, and the Usher informed them that it appeared the rest of the people from the sailboat were coming on board.

At this, a smile broke over Ricky's face as he said, "I told you they wouldn't be able to resist the temptation. Now you see why I wanted them to come on board unopposed. Let them get their fill of food and water. Let them get comfortable in the Centrum. Let them drop their guard and-."

Ricky was interrupted by Sheila, the redhead he had brought aboard as a play toy. Entering the bridge, she slammed the hatch behind her with a resounding bang. Swaying slightly, she called in an angry voice, "What the fuck do mean keeping me cooped up on deck eleven, Ricky? Someone said a boat was spotted and people were coming on board. What the fuck's going on?"

Looking at her with disgust, he replied, "You're drunk Sheila. Go sleep it off someplace."

Instead of letting herself be dismissed, the woman stuck out her hand and steadied herself against a wall. Squinting in Ricky's direction, she slurred, "Don't give me that shit. You may be the great and powerful Reverend Ricky to the rest of these idiots, but I know exactly who you are and where you came from."

This barb struck its mark, causing Ricky to sigh as he said in a gentler voice, "Alright, babe, I'll tell you what's going on. Yes, we spotted a boat, and yes, the people in it are coming on board. In fact, some of them are already on deck four."

Pushing off from the wall, Sheila took two unsteady steps forward and said, "Well then, let's go down and say hello. Make friends with them and get them to take us off this ship of the damned."

"It's not that easy," Ricky replied.

Anger flashed in Sheila's eyes. "We're on a sinking ship in the middle of the fucking ocean and-."

"Gulf of Mexico," Ricky corrected. "And we're not sinking yet."

"-and we need to get to Cozumel where it's safe," Sheila went on. "We've got maybe a hundred people left, and between the occasional zombie showing up out of nowhere to eat someone and the suicides, pretty soon there won't be anyone except you and your precious Ushers."

"I'm working on a plan right now," Ricky assured her.

Sheila snorted. "Planning on who you're gonna screw tonight. You and your big goddamn plans. I agreed to go along with you in the beginning, but now everything's falling apart and we're gonna die."

Moving close, Sheila pressed her body against Ricky's as she let her voice drop to an almost pleading tone as she said "Let's take one of the lifeboats and head for an oil rig. You and Don said we could make it that far. Just you and me, babe, just like in the beginning."

Ricky shook his head. "I explained why we couldn't do that. We'd be in even worse shape. We'd be stuck in the middle of the Gulf with fewer supplies than we have here."

"Then we need to go down and talk to the people who've got the sailboat. A sailboat doesn't need gas so it can get us to Cozumel," Sheila whined.

"A boat that size can only hold about ten or twelve people," Ricky said. "There are already seven of them on board, so that only leaves room for five of us. And that's if they even agree to take us. And on top of that, we don't know who they are or what they want yet. Plus, when we do go, we have to bring enough supplies to last us until we can get set up in Cozumel. It's the rule they have there. You heard them yourself when we talked to them on the radio. If you try to land on the island and you can't prove you're self-supporting, they run you off."

"So what are we gonna do?"

Ricky hesitated in telling her his plan. Although Sheila knew most of what was going on since she had backed him when he took control of the ship, she'd been drinking far too much lately. When she didn't get her way, she would threaten to expose him as a fraud to the Faithful. She told him that she would let them know that within a few weeks the pumps on the Calm of the Seas were going to fail and that the ship would sink... and... he couldn't have that.

And who was she to complain about whom I fuck, Ricky thought vehemently. It was her idea to have an orgy every night. And she was even the one who gave me the idea on how to rationalize it to his flock. She had told him to say, "If you are without sin, how then could you be saved?"

Ricky laughed his ass off at that one, but the Faithful ate it up.

Hell, he thought, before that they were all sneaking around jumping each other anyway. This just gave them an excuse to bring it out in the open. Now, every evening at sunset, the entire congregation moved up to the pool deck. After a quick sermon from Ricky, they waited for the rapture, for Jesus to lift his faithful up to Heaven. When it didn't happen, and Ricky would've shit one big brick if it ever did, the crowd moved to the pool bar and started drinking. Soon, threesomes, foursomes and full nude twister orgies would break out on mattresses dragged from the chairs scattered across the deck. The PA was turned on and music was blasted to the four corners of the earth while the Romanesque orgy went on until dawn. At this point, those few left standing staggered below to puke and pass out.

Looking at Sheila's face, Ricky saw the dark circles around her eyes and that the skin on her face had started to sag.

Along with her tits, he added.

With her constant threats to unmask him endangering what he had built, she had become a liability.

Holding Sheila close, Ricky stroked her hair and said, "Don't worry, babe. Don and I have an idea we're working on. Right now, we just need to lay low while we make sure the newcomers don't mean us any harm. In a few days, we'll approach them and make a deal to get us off the ship."

Pulling away from Ricky, Sheila said harshly, "Just make sure that I'm on that boat when it sails, or I'll make damn sure that no one is. Your Faithful will have your natural ass when I shout it out on every deck about how you conned them. How you've been keeping it secret about the ship sinking and how you wrecked the lifeboats to keep everyone here."

Pointing to some rust colored stains on the floor at the back of the bridge, she added, "I'll also let them know what you did to the Captain and the crew when they stood up to you. How you killed some and fed the rest to those things."

Like a light bulb being turned on, Ricky beamed a reassuring smile at Sheila and said, "Now there's no reason for any of that, honey. Of course you're going with me. You're my number one girl. Now, go get a drink at the Masthead and I'll be down to see you in a little bit. We'll spend some time together. Just you and me."

Slightly placated, Sheila turned to go as Ricky gave her an affectionate pat on the rear. When she was gone, Ricky turned to Parsons, his smile now gone, and in a cold voice, he said, "I'm through with her shit. Give her about an hour to get even more liquored up and then send two of the Head Ushers to grab her. Everyone else is on deck eleven, so she'll be alone."

"What do you want them to do with her?" Parsons asked. They had found numerous ways to dispose of anyone who threatened their control over the ship.

"Take her to the Sounds Lounge and dump her skanky ass off the balcony. Let those things take care of her." Ricky ordered.

"Do you want to watch again?" Parsons added with a sick smile.

Ricky thought about it for a minute before saying, "Yeah, I think I'd like that. Have the men radio me when they get ready to toss her in. They can do whatever they want to her until I get there. While we're waiting for that, you and I need to figure out how we're going to eliminate the intruders. They seem to have us outgunned, so we need to come up with a way to take them out without putting any of the core group at risk."

Looking out at the flat water, Ricky said in a low voice, "I want that sailboat."

Chapter Seven

The Dead Calm:

Steve toweled himself dry as he stepped from the shower in the corner of the locker room. Reaching for a new pair of jeans and the shirt that Heather had found in one of the shops in the Centrum, he stopped as an enticing aroma reached him from the nearby kitchen. It seemed like months, rather than just over a week, since he had eaten anything but MRE's, so the smell of broiling meat set his mouth watering.

Clipping the holster containing his pistol to his waistband, he picked up his M-4 and checked the safety before hanging the weapon over his shoulder by its sling. Exiting the locker room, he headed down a short hallway leading to the food preparation area. Set up to feed hundreds, it took Steve a few minutes to find Susan, Connie and Cindy in the huge kitchen. They had taken over a small corner of the serving line nearest the doors leading to the dining room where they had access to one of the coolers and a broiler the size of a full-sized pickup truck.

Everyone was still jumpy, those from the sailboat because they were in a possibly hostile environment, and Connie and Tim because they were still learning to trust the newcomers. Not wanting to startle anyone, he called out before approaching, "Whatever it is, it smells good,"

"We're cooking," Cindy yelled out excitedly. "Wait until you taste the garlicky potatoes I made."

"Connie's been a great help, too," Susan said. "I'd still be trying to figure out where everything is if it wasn't for her." The young woman gave a shy smile and said, "It's nice to cook for more than just Tim and me."

Looking around, Steve asked, "Where is everyone?"

"Tim's with Tick-Tock, they're watching the stairs," Susan said. Narrowing her eyes she asked, "What's Tick-Tock's real name anyway? He won't tell me, and I've been trying to find out for weeks now."

Steve smiled and shrugged. Lots of people had asked him that same question, and he always refused to answer. Even Heather had given up trying to get him to spill it. At one point, Heather and Susan had even tried to check the personnel records at the radio station, only to find Tick-Tock's file missing. He had gotten there before them.

Seeing that she wouldn't get anywhere with Steve, Susan gave him a dirty look and continued, "Heather's nesting and-."

Steve cut her off, "Nesting?"

"She's putting together a place for you and her in the Captain's Clothes store," she explained. "She dragged your mattress off the boat and set it up in there. There's a linen store where you can buy sheets and pillowcases, so we all raided it. Hope you like a nautical theme on your blanket."

Steve tried to remember where the Captain's Clothes store was and finally recalled that it was at a slight angle to the grand staircase, the perfect place to give covering fire if anyone tried to rush their deck from above.

You go Heather, he thought to himself; grateful he had her and Tick-Tock's help.

He recalled how after Brain, Mary and Cindy had come on board, Mary had headed straight for the nearest shoe store while Susan and Cindy went to shower. Trying to calculate how he would split the remainder of his people up to help secure their new environment, Steve was stymied when a few minutes later, Brain was struck with what he called motionless sickness. They all felt a little queasy standing on something stable after being on the sailboat for so long, but it seemed to hit Brain especially hard. Twenty minutes after his feet hit the deck of the Dead Calm, the tech found he couldn't stand up straight and he starting vomiting. Thus, it was Steve, Heather and Tick-Tock who went over every inch of the Centrum to make sure their position was secure. Once satisfied, they turned their attention to making certain that their means of egress were clearly marked in case they had to make a hasty exit. Using the paint Steve had carried with him on their initial exploration, the walls and floors of the Centrum and the dining room now sported blue arrows pointing toward the hatch where The Usual Suspects was tied up.

Tim had been assigned to kitchen duty, but grew bored and instead helped with the painting. When they were done, he showed them where to access the crew passageways that ran behind the stores. He provided a crowbar he'd found in one of the maintenance areas, and they used this to lever open the door of the shops they wanted something from. Although they all had a craving for fresh food, one of the first places they used the crowbar on was the Ship's Store so they could raid its snack counter. Then Steve went to relieve Heather at the stairs so she could grab something for herself before heading to the shower.

"Where's Brain?" Steve asked, watching with amusement as a blush crept up Connie's neck to bloom in her cheeks.

In a quiet voice, she replied, "He went to get us some water. The pump for the kitchen is out, so we have to bring it from the bathroom at the other end of the Centrum."

Susan added, "Actually, we didn't need any water, but he'd recovered from his love sickness-." Connie shot her a dirty look, so she amended, "Sorry, motionless sickness, and I got tired of walking around him every time he threw himself at Connie's feet, so I told him to get us some water to get him out of the way."

Steve smiled. The hot topic of gossip for the females was how Brain and Connie reacted to each other when they first met. After Brain had secured the sailboat next to the hatch, he helped Mary and Cindy aboard. Ignoring everything around him, he was talking excitedly to Steve about what they could get from the ship when his eyes settled on Connie. Stopping in mid-sentence, his mouth dropped open and he could only gawk. Later, he told Tick-Tock she was the most beautiful girl he had ever seen.

And it wasn't a one-way street either.

Susan had seen Connie watching Brain's every move as he tied up the sailboat and came on board. At first, she hadn't understood the attraction, and it was only when she stopped and took a good look at the tech that she no longer saw the overweight slob she had pegged him for when she first met him. He was still a little heavy but nothing compared to what he used to be. Additionally, where before he would only shower a few times a month, he'd started cleaning up every day, and even on the boat took pains to keep up his hygiene. Later, when she mentioned Connie and Brain to Tick-Tock, he sighed dramatically and commented, "Oh, to be young and in lust again."

Susan decided right then that Tick-Tock was something she needed to sort out. She had no doubt she was attracted to him, but she wasn't sure to what degree. Despite Steve's order, she had snuck up to the cockpit quite few nights while Tick-Tock was on wheel watch and everyone else was asleep. While she still had feelings for Mary, she had come to realize that her former flame was too shallow and selfish for her.

The HWNW virus and its aftermath seemed to bring out different qualities in everybody, she reasoned. As if reading her mind, and showing her the bottom end of the spectrum, Steve asked where Mary was.

Cindy spoke up, "She's looking for clothes. She said tomorrow she'd take me into the Centrum and teach me how to shop."

Steve thought about this for a minute and said, "We should put Mary's skills to use then. We'll make up a list of the things we need for the sailboat and have her find them in the stores. Cindy and Tim can go along and help."

Heather entered through the doors from the dining room with Tim in tow. After a quick look around, she asked, "Anything I can do?"

"We're almost finished, but thank you," Connie said.

"We're going to serve it buffet style from here," Susan told them as she flipped steaks in the broiler. "Everything's ready, so if you round up the rest of the crew we can eat."

Steve and Heather volunteered to go in search of the others, finding Brain first as he came toward them down the Centrum with a galvanized bucket of water in each hand and a lovesick look on his face.

Steve told him the food was ready. After he hurried off, Heather asked, "Why don't you look at me like that?"

"Like what?" He asked.

"A love sick puppy," she replied.

Moving around so he could put his left arm around her waist, and leave his right free in case he needed to un-sling his rifle, Steve let his mouth drop open and his tongue loll out. "Like this?" He asked and started panting like a dog.

Heather laughed, "Sounds more like you're in heat, but I guess that's close enough. Just don't let me catch you looking at Connie that way."

"I'm happily whatevered to you." Steve said.

"Whatevered?" She asked him with a raised eyebrow.

"Attached, coupled, devoted, enamored, tied, living in sin, pancaked-."

"Pancaked?" Heather cut in.

"It's something I saw in a porno movie once."

"Hmmmm, maybe we can try it tonight," she said with a half smile.

"Okay," Steve said, "but first we need to find a live chicken."

Heather covered her face with her hands. After catching her breath when her laughter subsided, she held up a hand and said, "Enough. No barnyard guests in bed. I have a rule about that."

"Prude," Steve said under his breath.

"What was that?" She asked accusingly.

Steve shrugged and mumbled just barely loud enough to be heard, "Tickle your ass with a feather?"

"What?" She exclaimed with a laugh.

Clearing his throat, Steve replied innocently, "I said, particularly nasty weather."

"I heard what you said the first time, and the answer is maybe. But no live chickens."

As they were approaching the end of the Centrum without seeing Mary, Steve said, "I'll try the shops on the other side. You can go tell Tick-Tock that I'll be by in a little bit to spell him on stair duty so he can eat and then get some sleep."

Heather nodded and veered to where Tick-Tock had set up his observation post behind a square of planters with seats built into them facing an ornate fountain. Steve headed toward the line of shops on the port side of the ship, but after taking only a few steps cut back to rejoin Heather.

In a low voice, he said, "We're being watched."

Out of the side of her mouth, she asked, "Where?"

"Near the top of the stairs. Looks like a woman maybe. She's set up in the entry to that 50's style diner. The one with all the chrome."

Heather nonchalantly gazed around as if taking in the sights before saying, "I see her. Just inside the doorway. You think it's one of Reverend Ricky's people down here spying on us?"

"Gotta be. If it was one of the dead, it'd be coming at us by now."

Stopping just short of Tick-Tock's position, Steve said in greeting, "Jehovah's Witnesses selling time shares and Avon. Is your husband home, ma'am? Beautiful cave you have here Mrs. Flintstone."

"You're only funny to you," Tick-Tock told him.

Steve said, "We've got a visitor upstairs."

"Yeah, I know. She's been there for about ten minutes," Tick-Tock replied. "I spotted another one earlier, but he's been keeping a low profile."

"Another one," Heather exclaimed. "Where?"

"Behind the tipped over tables at the sidewalk café to the right of the sushi restaurant. The tables look like they got knocked over by accident, but they're set up too neatly, and they're the only thing around that's out of place. Took me a while to spot him, but the chick's been pretty much in the open since she arrived."

"Setup?" Steve asked. "Get us to approach the woman and expose ourselves so the guy can snipe us?"

"I don't think so," Tick-Tock answered. "She hasn't been looking down here much, she's been checking out her own deck like she's worried about being spotted."

Steve thought about this before saying, "Do you think it might be someone like Connie and Tim who's trying to get away from Ricky?"

"Might be," Tick-Tock said. "It fits with the way she's acting."

"Then we need to help her," Heather said.

Steve considered their position and told Tick-Tock, "Draw a bead on the guy at the cafe. If he makes a move, take him out." To Heather, he said, "Cover our rear. I don't think it's a setup, but we don't know for sure."

Heather turned as if again taking in the sights of the Centrum spread out behind them and asked, "What are you going to do?"

With a shrug, Steve replied, "Invite her down."

Hoping he was making the right decision, he looked directly to where the woman was hiding and raised his hand, beckoning her to come to him. Her attention was so focused on the area around her that it took a minute for her to notice him. Even then, she didn't move, so Steve called out, "It's safe. No one will hurt you. Come down the stairs, but keep your hands in sight."

Hesitantly, the figure detached itself from the shadows and moved toward the stairs. The sun had set, and with the only illumination coming from the emergency lights, Steve could only tell it was a woman by the outline of her hair. Beyond that, he had a hard time determining if she was young, old or in between.

At the top of the staircase, the woman stopped and looked around again before suddenly uttering a small scream. Bolting forward, she took the steps two at a time in a headlong rush downward. Wondering what had set her off, Steve flipped off the safety on his rifle. Shouldering the weapon, he looked anxiously around for a target. When the woman reached the base of the stairs, he finally saw what had spooked her. Coming out of the shadows at the top of the grand staircase were a dozen shapes that moved in a staggering lope that was all too familiar to him.

"Z's," he called out loud enough to warn the others before setting his sights on the lead figure. Squeezing the trigger, he saw the outline of its head disintegrate as his bullet smashed into it. Switching targets, he heard two quick shots from behind him that almost sounded like one. In rapid succession, two of the dead dropped in their tracks. He knew it had to be Heather adding her firepower to his because no one else in the group could shoot that rapidly or with that kind of accuracy.

Steve shot another zombie, but before its body could hit the deck, more shapes materialized from behind it. Heather took down two of the newly arrived dead with head shots that painted the store fronts with black goo, while Steve hit one in the chest with a high velocity round. Not even fazed by this, the zombie kept coming. As it stepped into the glow of the emergency lights, Steve could see the damage his bullets had done. Bone splinters and rib ends protruded from gaping holes in its chest as black slime oozed from the wounds. It paid no mind to what would be a fatal injury if it were alive.

Adjusting his aim, Steve switched the selector on his M-4 to three-round burst and fired into the zombie's head. A chunk of skull and dead flesh flew upward and then dropped to the carpet with a wet plop. The dead thing staggered to its left and cart wheeled to land half way down the stairs.

The remaining dead started down as Steve and Heather moved forward to deal with them. With alternating shots, more of them fell in sprays of brain matter and black sludge. One tripped over its own feet and rolled down the stairs to land at its base as they both fired into its body, missing its head. Heather moved to within two feet of it and pulled the trigger of her CAR-15. She was rewarded by a click as the firing pin fell on a dud. The dead thing reached out with dirty hands to grab at her, its nails raking the denim of her jeans on her lower leg. Cursing, she took a step back and ejected the dead round as the thing scrambled onto its hands and feet to get at her.

Seeing she was in trouble, Steve drew a bead on the thing's head and squeezed the trigger. The bullet entered just above its ear and whipped its head to the side just as it was about to lunge forward to bite Heather. Distracted by this, he suddenly realized that two of the dead were almost within arm's reach. Too close to swing around and fire at the nearest one, he slammed the butt of his M-4 into the center of its face. This gave him the time and space to swing his rifle around and shoot it in the forehead while Heather brought her rifle back into the fight by putting a round into the forehead of the other.

Looking around wildly, Steve could only see the inert bodies of the dead scattered on the deck and stairs, and the haze of gun smoke hanging in the air.

Pounding and rattling noises drew Steve and Heather's attention to the secured double doors leading into the cabin area, and they zeroed in on them with their rifles. The sound of gunfire had attracted the zombies trapped inside and they were trying to break free. Steve watched the doors open slightly as the chain securing them was pulled taut. Dirty fingers clawed through the gap and groped around furtively to see what was restraining them. Remembering that he hadn't gotten the chance to check the chain securing the doors, Steve kept a close eye on the barricade to make sure it held.

After a moment, satisfied that the walking corpses couldn't break out of their confinement and that no more were coming from the deck above, he turned his attention to the woman. She had stopped a dozen feet away, gasping in fear as she tried to say something. Switching the aim of his rifle to her head, while out of the corner of his eye he watched Heather do the same, he asked in a harsh voice, "Are you bit?"

Seeing the rifles pointed at her, the woman raised her hands and screamed, "Don't shoot!"

"Are you bit?" Steve repeated louder.

"What?" She asked.

"Are - you - bit?" Steve enunciated each word.

Finally understanding, her fear turned to anger and she angrily retorted, "Fuck no! But I thought you were gonna shoot my ass when I came down those stairs." Looking back at the bodies of the zombies, she added in a more subdued tone, "I guess I should say thanks."

"If you have any weapons, you need to drop them," Heather ordered.

"I had a knife, but I left it in the chest of one of the assholes who tried to kill me," she replied.

Heather gave her a hard look, so the woman added, "I don't have a goddamn thing on me, so quit pointing those guns at me."

Not sure who she was, they lowered their rifles but kept them pointed in her general direction.

Turning his head, Steve called out to the still concealed Tick-Tock, "Where'd the guy who was watching us go?"

From his spot hidden behind a row of planters, he replied, "When the first Z showed up, he took off like a candy-assed baboon. Haven't seen anyone move that fast since I saw Mary heading for the shoe store."

"Oh, cool," Sheila said sarcastically, "a talking bush."

Already not liking the new arrival, Steve brought his attention back to her and asked, "Who are you?"

Flipping her red hair back over one shoulder, she replied, "My name's Sheila Keiser, and I need your help."

Tick-Tock said, "That's all we've been hearing since we came on this shit bucket."

After making sure that none of the dead were still lurking about and that they hadn't been sprayed by any infected fluids, Steve and Heather started toward the kitchen with Sheila in front of them. As they reached the entrance to the dining room, Brain and Susan met them. They hadn't heard the gunfire, but were worried because it was taking so long for them to come back. Steve mentally filed away how the metal bulkheads dampened noises. He had to make sure everyone stayed in contact by radio from now on.

Steve explained to them who Sheila was and how they'd come across her, and then said to Heather, "Take her in and give her something to eat. I'll go find Mary."

"She came back a few minutes after you left," Brain informed him. "She's in there right now whining about being hungry and asking when we're going to eat."

"Well, let's not keep her waiting then," Steve said.

Once seated in the dining room, Sheila declined to join them for dinner, but had no problem saying yes when some bottles of wine were passed around. Ignoring everyone's questions with a wave of her hand and an outstretched empty wine glass, she refilled it six times before asking, "How many people you got here?"

"Nine," Steve answered. "How many are there on the upper decks?"

Without hesitation, she answered, "About a hundred, give or take. We lose some to the … what did you call them?"

"Z's" Heather explained. "It's short for zombie."

Steve had asked his question to see if he could catch Sheila in a lie. He wasn't altogether trusting of her and wanted to see if her answer jibed with what Tim had told them. It did, but he still didn't trust her.

Sheila smiled at Heather and said, "We just call them the freaks or stinkers. We lose some people to the freaks every once in a while. And we also have some people who just can't handle it and open a vein or jump from the top deck."

"When God doesn't lift them into Heaven?" Steve asked.

This took Sheila aback for a second, but she recovered quickly as she said, "You seem to know a lot about what's going on for someone who just got here."

"God speaks to me," Steve said dryly.

"You and Reverend Ricky," she shot back. "But he's full of shit. What's your excuse?"

Seeing anger flash in Steve's eyes, Heather cut in and said, "Why don't you tell us everything from the beginning? You talk while we eat."

Seeing no sense in getting into a back and forth pissing contest with Sheila, Steve held his next comment about her dragging her sorry ass back upstairs to himself.

Knowing that the story would more than likely be obscene, since every other word out of Sheila's mouth seemed to be fuck, Connie had Tim and Cindy move to the other side of the dining room. While everyone was curious as to what Sheila had to say, Steve noticed that Mary seemed to be hanging on her every word.

Good, he thought. Maybe they'll hook up. Then she and Tick-Tock will quit being so pissy with each other.

Sheila explained how she came with Ricky on the cruise and how he had taken control of the ship. She then related what happened on the bridge between Ricky her. When she mentioned the fact that the ship would sink within the next few weeks, everyone around the table exchanged uneasy glances. Steve questioned her about the ship's position, and Sheila answered, "Fucked, completely fucked. That's our position." She then told them about leaving Ricky on the bridge and going to the Masthead Bar to wait for him.

"So, I'm sitting there minding my own business," she said before taking a drink of wine, "waiting for like an hour for Ricky to drag his fat ass down there, when two of his Head Ushers show up. I figure they came to tell me that Ricky changed his mind, or got distracted, or something and couldn't make it."

"How many Head Ushers are there?" Heather asked.

Sheila drained off the last of her wine and held out her glass for more. Brain looked at Steve who shrugged, so he refilled her glass.

"Thanks, toots," Sheila said before answering Heather, "Five. The two who showed up were Brother Seth and Brother Raymond. But anyway, back to my story. I knew I was in trouble the second they sat down on either side of me and started crowding in. I knew right away that I'd pushed Ricky too far and that the little shit was going to make me disappear just like the others."

"What others?" Steve asked.

Sheila toyed with her wineglass before answering, "A lot of others. Anyone who threatens Ricky or stands up to him disappears. The crew on the bridge were the first, and I don't know how many others there's been since."

Entranced by Sheila's story, Mary asked breathlessly, "What happened to the crew?"

"The Captain found out that Ricky's people had locked a whole bunch of passengers in with the freaks when they were shutting off the cabin areas to quarantine them," Sheila told her. "By this time, some of the ship's officers were carrying guns, so the Captain sent two of them to escort Ricky to the bridge. Then he sent another group to free the people trapped in the cabin areas and disband Ricky's band of merry assholes. Ricky found out what was going on from one of the crew he'd converted to God, so he had a couple of his guys ambush the two officers and take their pistols. Then Ricky used their pass card to get on the bridge and shot everyone down like they were rabid dogs or something. He just walked in, herded them to the back of the bridge, and opened fire, laughing like a loon the whole time."

Mary gave a gasp.

"That's not all. This was right in the beginning when all the bad shit was coming down and not everyone was in Ricky's corner. He wanted total control, so he called a few of his trusted Ushers up to the bridge. He picked the sneaky bastards who were just like him and laid it all out to them; how the religious shit was all a scam, but they could have the run of the ship if they followed him. All seven agreed and they became his Head Ushers."

"You said before that there were five Head Ushers," Susan pointed out.

Sheila shrugged and said, "Shit happened. A stinker bit one and another got too out of hand. He was drinking too much and raped a couple of the women, so Ricky had the others take him out." Sheila drained her glass of wine and held it out to Brain. Once he had filled it, she drank down half of it and continued, "So Ricky and his guys wait until it gets dark and there's no one around. They carry the bodies of the crew from the bridge and dump them in a couple of the lifeboats and let the tide take them away. He told me they disabled the rest of the lifeboats while they were up there so that no one could leave. The next morning, Ricky gets on the PA system and tells everyone that in the middle of the night, the crew abandoned ship and left them to fend for themselves, but he says that now he's in control and everything will be all right. God sent him to save them."

"And people believed him?" Susan asked incredulously.

Sheila thought about this for a moment before answering, "A lot of people believed him, but most just followed along because he got the generators up and running and his Head Ushers kept anyone from getting out of hand. He's a smooth son-of-a-bitch, and he talked the fence sitters over to his side, too. After that, he had the majority of the people behind him, so anyone who stood up to him got disappeared. I think everyone knows what's going on, but it's just better to go with the flow."

"Like the Jews did with Hitler in Germany," Susan pointed out.

"Don't know nothing about that, sweetheart," Sheila said with a smile.

"But you knew what was going on and you went with the flow," Steve said with disgust.

Acting as if this was of no concern to her, Sheila shrugged and replied, "I'm a survivor." Changing gears quickly, she brightened and said, "So, back to my story." Turning to Mary, she added, "You're gonna love this. So anyway, Seth and Raymond are crowding me at the bar, and I know I'm in deep shit. I act like I don't have a clue as to what they're there to do. I come onto them and offer to fuck them in a three-way."

Sheila laughed drunkenly, "They couldn't get their clothes off fast enough." Finishing the last of her wine, she reached over and took the bottle out of Brain's hand. Upending it in her mouth, she drained off the last few swallows and said, "I carry a knife, and I stuck it in Brother Raymond's chest while his pants were down around his knees and then pushed him into Seth. I took off like - what did the talking bush call it?" She laughed as she remembered, "A candy assed baboon."

Sheila was swaying and her eyes were unfocused as she mumbled, "Ran down here hoping you people would help me out, but then that bunch of stinkers came out of nowhere."

"Where do they come from?" Steve asked. Connie and Tim had both told him that it was rare to see any of the dead wandering the ship. Then all of the sudden, seven of them show up in the span of a few minutes.

The large amount of alcohol that Sheila had taken in that day had taken full effect, so she could only mumble something in reply before laying her head down on her arms. But what Steve thought he heard her say shocked him. Knowing her answer was vital to their survival, he picked up a pitcher of water, walked around to stand next to Sheila and unceremoniously dumped it over her head.

So drunk that she could barely raise up, Sheila nonetheless was aware enough to know what had happened. She started cursing, but was cut off when Steve slammed the flat of his hand down on the table next to her head, causing a loud boom to echo through the dining room and making her sit upright with a jerk.

"Where the fuck did those Z's come from?" He demanded.

"Sometimes a few of them just show up." Sheila screamed at Steve. Dropping her voice, she said, "No one knows where they come from. It's a big ship with lots of places to hide. But most of the time they show up because Ricky needs to keep the Faithful in line."

"That's what you said before. What the hell does that mean?" Steve asked harshly.

"Scared people stay in line and need someone to protect them. Every once in a while, he lets a couple of the freaks out from the quarantine area to stir up some fear. Ricky lets them out. They're his."

Steve and Heather locked eyes across the dining table before turning their gaze again to Sheila as she dropped her head back down on her arms. At first, Steve thought she might be crying until he realized she had passed out and was snoring softly. Mary surprised everyone by jumping up and almost running to Sheila's side. Stroking her hair gently, she said, "Poor baby." Turning on Steve she spit out, "All she's been through and you're interrogating her like she's a criminal or something."

Steve ignored this as he considered what he'd just heard. The only one to pay attention was Susan, who felt a flash of jealousy at the attention Mary was giving the redhead. She wanted to point out that Sheila was nothing but a drunken whore, but held herself in check as a thought came to her. *Maybe this is my out. If Mary's fawning all over Sheila, she'll lose interest in me.*

With a smile, Susan said to her semi-ex, "Why don't we find somewhere to lay her down? You can keep an eye on her and make sure she's okay."

"Make sure she doesn't puke in her sleep and choke on it," Steve added in an annoyed voice.

"But I don't even have a place set up for myself. Where can I take her?" Mary asked in a voice just begging for someone to come to her rescue.

Steve cringed inwardly. He was about to tell Mary that it was her own fault when Brain spoke up, "I grabbed your mattress when I brought mine in. I can go out to the boat and get another for Sheila."

Looking at Steve in triumph, Mary said, "At least there's one gentleman on this boat."

Steve was about to object and tell Mary to get the mattress herself when he decided that he didn't want to expend the energy arguing with her. With so many other things stacking up that needed his attention, he resolved it would be easier to just let it ride. "Go ahead Brain. Help her get Sheila out of here. Go and get the extra mattress and then get some sleep. You've got guard duty at the stairs in about four hours."

Brain and Mary each grabbed one of Sheila's arms and half-walked, half dragged her through the dining room. The last thing Steve heard as they went out the door into the Centrum was Mary saying, "It's so nice that you put my mattress by the T-shirt shop, Brain, but I really wanted to put it in the Birkenstock shoe store. I love the smell of all that leather. Be a dear and move it for me?"

Worried that he hadn't had a chance to talk to Brain about Mary yet, Steve was relieved to see Connie following them through the dining room. The dark haired beauty called out, "I'll give them a hand. I don't want Randy to get lost in the dark on his way back."

*Randy?* Steve asked himself. *Who in the hell is Randy?* Then it came to him, Randy was Brain's real name. Shaking his head rapidly to clear his overtaxed mind, he sank into his chair and reached for his wine glass. Remembering that he had to relieve Tick-Tock at the stairs, he let his hand drop to the table. He needed a clear mind for the next few hours.

"That little tidbit of info about Ricky using the dead to terrorize his people and keep them in line was kind of a shocker," Heather commented.

"Sounds like I should have let Tick-Tock track down and shoot that asshole when he first brought the idea up." Steve said bitterly.

"Bad move," Susan said. "Like you said before, we don't need a hundred of his fanatical followers coming down on us."

Steve nodded, but a growing dislike for Ricky welled up in him. All his life, he'd hated seeing the strong prey on the week or someone use and manipulate others for their own selfish needs. And to make it worse, there didn't seem to be anything he could do about it without putting his own people's lives at risk. Resolving that somehow Ricky would be dealt with before he left the ship, he turned his attention to Heather as she asked, "So, what's the plan?"

"Stay alive, get Cindy somewhere they can study her blood or spit, find a cure for the HWNW virus and live happily ever after," He answered. "But first we need to get off this ship with the supplies we'll need to get to Florida or Texas. Whichever's closer." Looking at his watch, he was surprised to see it was after eleven. "I've got to relieve Tick-Tock so he can get some sleep and food, but I think it would be a good idea to put distance between us and the Dead Calm as soon as possible. Tomorrow morning, bright and early, we start gathering supplies. If we bust ass, we can probably set sail by mid to late afternoon. In the meantime, we need to double the guard. I want two people on those stairs at all times and no one should be moving around alone. We can shut ourselves into the stores when we sleep."

Looking across the dining room to where the two youngest members of the group sat watching them, Steve called out, "Tim, are you tired?"

"Not at all."

"Good, then you're on watch with me. Go tell Tick-Tock I'll be there in a few minutes and that we'll clean up the bodies."

Excited at the prospect of being asked to participate like an adult, Tim bolted for the door.

"He's a little young for guard duty," Susan pointed out.

"No one's young anymore," Steve replied. "Don't worry though, he won't be shooting. I need him for a second pair of eyes to help keep watch. I also want to go over the floor plan of the ship with him and get him to show me the back ways he uses to get around. I want to know if he's seen a sextant or a nautical almanac. If he has, I want to know where, so we can grab it."

Rising, he said added, "You and Brain will take over the watch from me. Take one of the radios so I can call you when it's your turn. Before you do that, please feed Tick-Tock and then tuck him in. Make sure he gets some sleep tonight though. Don't wear him out. I need him fresh tomorrow."

Blushing, Susan asked, "What do you mean?"

"I'm a light sleeper," Steve replied with a smile. "Especially when I'm on a boat. I hear a noise at night and I get up to investigate." Turning to Heather, he said, "I'll walk you to your door. You need to get some sleep too."

Looking at the dirty plates and glasses scattered across the two tables, Susan asked, "What about the mess?"

Steve grabbed the four corners of the tablecloth and picked them up, dishware clanking as he made a neat bundle. Carrying it toward the kitchen, he said to Susan, "Grab the other one. We'll dump them in the trash."

With the thousands of place settings stored on the ship, he wasn't going to waste time washing dishes that no one would ever use again. Susan copied him, and in no time they had the dinner mess taken care of. Susan called Cindy over and told the little girl she had just volunteered to help clean up the kitchen. Even if they were leaving tomorrow, they still had a few meals to cook and she didn't want anyone getting food poisoning. Before leaving, Steve suggested she keep her rifle close by.

As he and Heather walked out of the dining room, she asked, "So what do you think about Sheila telling us the ship is going to sink?"

"In a couple weeks is what she said. We'll be long gone by then," he assured her.

"And the people left on board?" She asked. "We just leave them?"

Steve knew where this line of questioning was going and didn't want to follow it. Irritated, he said, "They've got lifeboats. All they have to do is load the first one with people and tow another full of gas. They can make it to land with no problem. I don't know why Ricky or one of his people didn't think of it."

"Sheila said that the Ushers disabled most of the lifeboats," Heather pointed out.

Steve stopped and faced her, trying but failing to keep the frustration out of his voice as he said, "I don't like what Ricky's doing to the people on this ship and it pisses me off, but I can't make myself responsible for them. I can warn them that the ship's sinking, but then it's in their hands. I'd like to save the world, but I can't. The best I can do is keep us alive."

Suddenly realizing how much pressure Steve was under from having to make decisions that might result in one of them, or all of them, becoming dead or undead, Heather regretted pushing him. They had enough going on without trying to save over a hundred people who put themselves in this situation, and, this wasn't even considering the fact that they would kill them all at the whim of a religious maniac. Although she knew she would do anything Steve asked of her, she saw that her responsibilities paled in comparison to his.

With downcast eyes, she said, "I'm sorry. I know you have a lot to deal with without adding more."

Feeling like an ass for losing it, Steve took her in his arms and said, "No, I'm sorry. I didn't mean to snap at you."

After a moment, Heather asked ruefully, "Did we just have out first fight?"

"Yeah, but the makeup sex is worth it," he said as he pulled her closer.

Heather laughed and pulled away. "Not right now though, you have guard duty."

"Responsibility blows," he said dejectedly.

Cutting across the miniature golf course to get to the starboard side of the Centrum, Heather was once again amazed at the variety of shops and activities on the cruise ship. Coming to a short, decorative wooden fence that separated the mini-golf course from the walkway, she noticed a warning sign on the barricade from the Astroturf onto a strip of real grass. As Steve stepped over it, Heather cleared her throat and pointed to the sign which read Please Keep Off Grass. In a mock angry tone, she asked, "Can't you read?"

Glancing at the sign, Steve responded, "I thought it was an anti-drug slogan." Looking again, he added, "Maybe I'll come back later and change it, so it says, Please Keep Off Grass. Smoke Crack."

Heather laughed and the residual tension between them evaporated as she said, "Your mind works in strange ways, Wendell."

Steve smiled, shrugged and continued on. As they neared the grand staircase, he unslung his rifle and held it at the ready. Although everything might seem peaceful and quiet, he knew that it didn't mean squat when you were aboard the Dead Calm. Reaching the planters, he called out softly for Tick-Tock. Fear rippled through him when there was no answer. Tightening his grip on the M-4, he looked around for any trace of his second in command or Tim, and was relieved when he heard Tick-Tock call out to him from behind the rolled down metal gate of a darkened jewelry store.

"Thought it might be best to find a new spot in case the guy watching from the deck above spotted my position before he hauled ass. You have to go back down to the access door next to the Sunglass Hut and come in through the rear to get in."

Steve and Heather did as instructed. Once they were in the passageway behind the shops, Heather said, "This is where we part company. I'm going to try and get some sleep. I'll keep the radio on though. Call if you need me, I'm just a few stores down." Stretching up to kiss him, she added, "Wake me up when you come in."

Steve found the back of the jewelry store and entered through the pried open door. Making his way through the darkened shop, he found Tick-Tock and Tim at its doorway facing in opposite directions so they could cover both the stairs and the length of the Centrum. He filled Tick-Tock in on what Sheila had revealed before she passed out and explained his decision to pack up and haul ass.

Tick-Tock nodded in agreement and said, "Then we've got a lot to do tomorrow. I'm gonna eat and get some sleep. It's too bad we have to leave, I've only seen a little bit of it, but I know I could spend a week checking this ship out."

Moving over to one of the showcases, he looked down and said, "Rolexes are on sale. I'm gonna get one before we go. You should grab one too."

After Tick-Tock left, Steve did a radio check to make sure he could contact the others. Heather, Brain and Susan replied instantly, letting him know they would be sleeping lightly and listening with one ear in case he called for help.

Despite being up since early that morning, Steve wasn't tired. He decided to let the others get some much-needed rest and stretched his shift out to five and a half hours. He spent most of the extra time going over the ship's diagram that Tick-Tock had pried off the wall, marking in red pen the routes Tim showed him that he used to move undetected through the Calm of the Seas.

Susan showed up shortly after Steve called, and told him Brain was right behind her. When Brain arrived, they dragged the bodies of the dead they had shot the night before behind the counter near the fire doors. Soon they would start to stink even more than they already did, but by then they should have set sail. Steve briefed Brain and Susan on the areas to watch and then headed for the Captain's Clothes store. He finally found it after two wrong turns, but stopped before entering. Heather had left a short note taped to the door, along with an object that made him laugh out loud.

The note read, Use this to wake me. Below it was a long, fluffy feather.

Chapter Eight

Quantico, Virginia:

The Chairman of the Joint Chiefs called the meeting to order over the speakerphone.

"The first order of business is the President, and it's not good news," he announced with mock severity. "I've been informed that he's issued federal warrants for our arrest."

This statement was met with laughter from the rest of the men listening in from different military bases scattered across the country.

After the fall of Washington D.C. to the living dead, the President had retreated to a secure base inside Cheyenne Mountain. Once ensconced in his new seat of power, he slipped into insanity by refusing to take the medication prescribed him for his bi-polar disorder. He started issuing commands that made no sense, while continuing to refuse to issue orders to combat the spread of the HWNW virus by declaring nation-wide martial law and releasing the military to deal with the dead. When it became apparent that the

United States was on the brink of falling into a chaotic state from which it might not ever recover, the Joint Chiefs took control of the country in a bloodless coup by simply cutting the President off from his lines of communication and issuing their own orders.

Sending designated units in to retake the Dead Cities, while at the same time having all available military units move out from their respective bases, forts and camps in order to retake the areas surrounding them from the dead. They soon gained a foothold that could be built on in the battle to eradicate anyone infected with the HWNW virus. After the initial push was over in mid-November, the Joint Chiefs called a halt to operations so they could resupply the front line troops and send in replacements for those who had fallen. These fresh recruits were enlisted from the newly cleared Dead Free Zones, otherwise known as DFZ's. Bolstered by the people from these areas who were eager to join up and fight the dead who besieged them, the volunteers swelled the ranks of the weakened military to pre-dead numbers. Basic training depots were expanded, and in no time the front line troops were back up to full strength. These were filled with men and women eager to take their country back from the hordes of dead that now freely roamed it.

The second push to expand the Dead Free Zones and to gain more ground in the cities deemed critical to the rebuilding of America started in mid-December... and ground to a halt after only one week. While the soldiers were willing, able and motivated, their supply lines had broken down and couldn't furnish them with the necessities to sustain the campaign. With no fuel for their tanks, and limited ammunition with which to fight, many became disillusioned. AWOL rates skyrocketed as soldiers headed back to the safety of the free zones or took their weapons and equipment to go in search of missing family and friends. The problem became so widespread that the military instituted a new set of laws. Simply put, the punishment for going AWOL was death by public hanging. This, and the fact that supplies were now reaching the front line troops stemmed the flood of desertions.

As the second campaign started up again, losses mounted in the battle for the cities. While the countryside and small towns were easy to take and hold, the major metropolitan areas were a nightmarish warren of hiding places from which the dead would emerge to attack the soldiers and Marines. Added to this were the logistical difficulties that arose from the lack of any battlefield intelligence. Communication breakdowns caused many platoons, and in one instance, an entire company to be cut off and wiped out when they ran out of ammunition. Another halt was called for until the infrastructure the military relied on was repaired and reactivated. They also needed real time intelligence so that losses could be cut down to acceptable levels.

After the laughter at the President's expense died down, the Chairman spoke again. "But I've also got some good news to share. I was informed early this morning that one of the main satellite relay stations located in Maryland has been retaken. Technicians from the NSA are getting the power back on and the equipment up and running. We should have real-time satellite photo capabilities and long-range communications back within two days. Once this happens, we can get some intelligence estimates and find the best way to move forward in the areas where we're bogged down."

"Thank the 82nd Airborne for that," the Army Chief interjected proudly. "They took some losses, but my boys got the job done."

"Which ties into the next bit of news," the Chairman said. "I've received reports that while we've taken high losses in our last push to retake the cities of Minneapolis, New Orleans, New York and San Diego, most of our front line units will be back up to full strength soon."

Calls of, "Good Job," and, "Way to go," met this announcement.

"In fact, I've been informed that the new recruiting drive is underway right now..."

Owens Grove, Louisiana:

A scene that had played itself out numerous times around the world was now coming to its conclusion in a small rural town in Louisiana. After barricading themselves inside any sturdy structure they could find when the living dead invaded, the residents of Owens Grove found themselves first cut off from the outside world and then slowly running out of food and water. In the end, their choice was simple, but the results equally hideous. Stay secure and die of starvation and thirst or leave their homes and offices to be attacked by the swarms of living dead that surrounded them.

It had started months earlier as the disease spread across the world. First, the television stations went off the air as the dead multiplied and overran entire cities. Although initially, the local and cable news stations glossed over the crisis, and even when they did start reporting on it fully only televised a long series of redundant images showing the dead wandering aimlessly about in search of food, it gave people hope. Hope that a turnaround in the progression of the disease would be announced at any minute. Hope that word would be broadcast that a cure had been found. Hope that a new weapon had been invented that would obliterate the dead.

It never happened.

Instead, only a few weeks after the initial infection, the final television station went off the air to be replaced by a screen filled with snow and speakers crackling with static. When this happened, many lost hope. But then radios were turned on and it was rekindled. The only problem being that while the television newscasts had long since ceased giving out any useful information on how to deal with the dead, the radio broadcasts were even worse. On most stations, the Emergency Broadcast System had taken over and continued to air the same looped tape. It advised those listening to stay indoors, avoid crowds, wash their hands with anti-bacterial soap and, if in dire need, try to make their way to one of the Red Cross aid stations set up around the state. A list of these was given, one of which was located on the outskirts of Owens Grove, Louisiana.

Upon hearing their town mentioned in the first broadcast, the men, women and children who had taken refuge days earlier on the roof of the three story Insurance building located in the heart of downtown Owens Grove knew firsthand the information was wrong.

"That just ain't so," Jessie McPherson drawled when he heard his hometown mentioned. "That place was overrun days ago. In fact, that danged Red Cross center's the reason we got so many of them dead things around us now. It attracted them like flies to a hog."

Jimmy McPherson, Jessie's brother, agreed. "And that's why we got stuck here in the first place."

Jo-Jo McPherson, sister to Jessie and Jimmy, said crossly, "It's your own fault Jimmy. You should be the last to be complaining. If you and daddy hadn't of let them Red Cross people set up on our north field, we could all be sitting home right now instead of being chased off our own land."

Hanging his head, Jimmy seethed inside. How was he to know that the dead would be attracted to where folks gathered? Hell, the television and the news people didn't even start warning folks until after the dead showed up. Besides, he was only doing his Christian duty by talking daddy into letting them medical people use the land out by the road leading into town.

Mumbling, "Things'll get better," he slunk away from his sister's accusing stare.

Unfortunately, things only got worse.

Now, the radio had long gone off the air and all was quiet except the sound of the dead pounding and scratching on the door leading to the roof. Wondering how it had come to this, he thought back to months before when the aide station was overrun by the flesh eating dead.

He recalled the cries of terror coming from the tent with the big Red Cross on it and couldn't see how he could have done anything different to change the events that led him, his brother and his sister to death's doorstep. Until the day the dead showed up in Owens Grove, no one in town had even seen one of them.

Jimmy, along with his brother Jason, God rest his soul, and his other brother Jack, God rest his soul also, had been working on the family's truck when they heard cries of disgust and horror come from the direction of the Red Cross tent. Startled, they looked in that direction to see what appeared to be the beginnings of a riot. People struggled with each other inside as some tried to flee, only to be dragged back into the melee or tackled and set upon with teeth and nails. Running toward the tent to break up the fight, the three brothers reached the mob scene only to find themselves confronted by hundreds of the living dead. They had come up the road from the direction of Baton Rouge and had flooded the aide center.

Although it had been reported that the people infected by the HWNW virus attacked anyone who came near them, the media hadn't released the information that being bitten by one of them spread the disease. Nor was it reported that those infected were actually dead beings who wanted nothing more than to eat human flesh. Not being aware of these key points, but soon to learn them firsthand, Jimmy and his brothers jumped into the middle of what they thought was a simple brawl. It didn't take long for the McPherson brothers to realize that this wasn't a simple set to. The invaders weren't fighting normal, they were clawing and biting at their victims and had already drawn blood from half the aid workers.

Jimmy realized too late that they had gotten themselves in over their heads as he called out a warning to his kin. Outnumbered three-to-one, and fighting with their bare hands as they tried to break out of the center of the mob to save themselves, the Macphersons made a good showing until the odds rose against them. More of the dead poured in off the road and into the tent. In seconds it became five-to-one and then seven-to-one. Jack was the first to be pulled down, dying under a mass of snarling creatures as they ripped him apart and started to feed on pieces torn from his body. Seeing this, Jimmy and Jason tried to join forces and come to their brother's aide but were blocked by a wedge of the dead who forced their way between them.

Screaming at Jason to run, Jimmy watched in horror as a dead woman dressed in a tattered meter maids outfit latched onto his brother's neck and ripped it open in a spray of blood. Knowing it was too late for his siblings, and that he too would fall under the teeth and nails of his assailants, Jimmy broke free and ran.

Once clear of the tent, he saw his sister Jo-Jo and his Brother Jessie bouncing across the field toward him in a pickup truck. Feeling his heart swell at the thought of reinforcements coming to help, he waved frantically for them to hurry. Looking past the truck, he saw that their house was now surrounded by the dead, most of which were banging on the doors and shuttered windows in an attempt to get in. With a sinking feeling, he realized that even with the whole family in on the battle there were too many dead to fight. Then it dawned on him that his brother and sister weren't coming to help him, but were fleeing the flesh eaters. As the truck came near and slowed, his sister waved and screamed at him to get in the back.

Jimmy jumped into the truck's bed and then nearly bounced back out when his brother drove through a drainage ditch and onto the road. From the truck bed he watched as more dead flooded across the field toward their home. Finding that he couldn't look at the scene anymore, he averted his eyes. Weaving back and forth, his brother Jessie ran over a few of the dead that blocked their way before coming to a clear stretch of road which led into town. Once in the open, he floored the accelerator.

Sliding open the pass-through window between the cab and the bed, Jo-Jo told him that their daddy had sent her and Jessie to get him and his brothers while he and their other brothers and sisters, John, Julian, Jackie and Joan helped him close all the storm shutters and block the doors. Knowing they wouldn't make it back to the house, their daddy told Jo-Jo and Jessie to make for town and lock themselves inside the insurance building. He assured them that they'd be safe since the building was made of brick, and he promised he'd come for them as soon as he could.

As they reached town, the trio roared down Main Street, honking the truck's horn and screaming warnings about what was coming up behind them.

Seeing and hearing this, most of the townspeople didn't take them seriously, and laughed at the McPherson kids antics. That family had always been full of hell raisers and practical jokers, they told each other. And wasn't that Jessie McPherson driving? The same Jessie McPherson who in his senior year had flushed dry ice down the commodes at school and made them explode? His daddy had tanned his hide for that little prank, but now it looked like he was at it again. This time he had even enlisted his older brother and sister to drive down Main Street screaming about the dead coming to life and eating the living.

As they pulled up in front of the insurance building, Jimmy realized why his daddy had sent them here. Built on a raised foundation, the bottoms of the first floor windows were an easy seven feet above the ground. A set of steps led up to the heavy wooden front entry, and Jimmy knew from making deliveries here when he worked at Dave's Fine Furniture that the rear doors were set up the same way. Racing up the steps, the three McPhersons burst inside and quickly slammed the door behind them. It was Sunday and the building was deserted, so they separated and went around shutting all the windows on the first floor and securing the rear entrance. As they met back in the foyer, the trio collapsed, panting from exertion and fear.

They sat this way in silence for the next twenty minutes, each lost in their own thoughts and worries. Then, they heard the first screams from outside. Looking out a window from an empty office located next to the foyer, the trio watched as first a few people ran down the street, looking furtively over their shoulders. Within seconds a flood of their friends and neighbors came rushing past, screaming and yelling in horror. A few gunshots rang out, but only a few. Although nearly everyone in Owens Grove owned some type of firearm, no one carried one around with them all the time except the Sheriff.

As Jo-Jo watched, one man sprinting down the street was so intent on watching his rear that he ran face first into a utility pole. He bounced off so hard she heard the boinging sound it made from inside the building. He hit the ground and lay still. Jo-Jo's attention was diverted from this by a group of refugees who came up the stairs and started pounding on the front door of the insurance building.

"We've got to help them," she called out to her brothers.

Jessie ran to the door and unlocked it, letting five people in as more of the citizens of Owens Grove ran by. Some, seeing the doors to the insurance building open and people going inside, followed them.

Shouted stories from the newcomers about being chased by maniacs, cultists and serial killers filled the foyer. By the time the first of the dead staggered into view on Main Street, thirty-five people of all ages crowded the foyer and surrounding offices to watch as the dead approached.

The first one to lope into view headed directly over to the man lying unconscious next to the pole. The zombie that was lucky enough to have its meal laid out before it was a bald, elderly reanimated corpse. Dressed in bright yellow pants and a sky blue shirt, its golf cleats clattered on the paved street as it rushed toward its free lunch.

Jo-Jo watched from the office window as the old man knelt down and lunged forward, biting into the unconscious man's cheek. As the dead golfer reared back to rip a piece of flesh loose, Jo-Jo's horror almost turned to laughter at the confused expression that crossed the zombie's face. Looking down, it took the dead thing a moment to see what Jo-Jo had seen right away. Its false teeth had been pulled out of its mouth and now lay on the ground next to its food. Frustrated, the elderly zombie squealed at its inability to eat. Jo-Jo felt hope for the man in the street, but it was short lived as the dead thing tore open the prostrate man's shirt and started tearing strips of flesh from his chest with its fingernails and stuffing them into its toothless mouth.

As hundreds of the dead crowded the streets of Owens Grove, many stumbled up the steps of the insurance building to claw and pound at its doors. The humans who had taken refuge inside ran for the upper floors, but Jo-Jo stayed where she was, transfixed by the scene outside the window. Jessie and Jimmy, sure that the building was secure, also remained on the first floor. They moved to either side of their sister and each put a reassuring hand on her shoulder.

"It can't last long," Jimmy said.

Picking up on his brother's tone, Jessie added, "Someone's bound to come and rescue us. Daddy knows we're here, so he'll come as soon as he can."

So they waited.

***

After three days of forced captivity with little water and no food, the McPherson brothers dug a hole through the common wall adjoining their building with the hardware store on their right. Using sharpened pieces of broken off table legs it took them two days. Once through, they armed themselves with a variety of tools that made it easy to breach the common wall on the left of their building which adjoined a beauty salon. Once inside QuickKuts, the urban miners were careful not to be spotted through its glass, storefront window by the dead who roamed freely in front of it. They then holed the next wall to reach their final destination.

Greene's Grocery Store.

Now, with provisions to last into the foreseeable future, the people in the insurance building settled in to await rescue. Offices were separated into sleeping quarters, and a lookout was posted on the roof to watch for any low flying aircraft they might signal.

When no one appeared over the following months, except for more of the dead, three of the survivors lost hope and committed suicide. One, an older lady who had seen her husband among the dead wandering in front of the building, spoke for two days about her darling Jacob calling out to her to join him. The others tried to convince her that it was her imagination, but she wouldn't believe them and ended up slitting her wrists. After natural selection took its course, those remaining formed a community that grew close and tried to help each other through the crisis. Faith that they would eventually be saved was the only thing that kept them going.

Their spirits remained high, until the large window at the front of the beauty salon broke when two of the dead got tangled up in each other's feet and fell through it. Other zombies, attracted by the strong scent of fresh flesh coming through the opening, followed their noses to the hole leading through the wall and into the insurance building. It was shortly before midnight when the first of the dead fell on the survivors staying in an office on the first floor. In the confusion and carnage that followed, eight people fell to the gnashing teeth of the dead.

Awakened by screams of terror to find their refuge invaded, everyone fled to the upper floors of the building. Creating a barricade out of office furniture in the stairwell, they managed to halt the advance of the dead just below the second floor. Safe for the moment, they turned their attention to the wounded.

Two people with bites were quarantined in an office while normal injuries were treated with the few medical supplies on hand.

Once settled into their now smaller quarters, they realized the cooking area they had been using was on the first floor at the back of the building. A quick inventory was taken, and it was found that the only food on hand was two ten-pound sacks of grits.

But this was just the beginning of their problems.

The furniture they had stacked on the stairs to stop the zombies was being cleared, albeit slowly and clumsily, by the dead as they frantically clawed at it in their attempt to reach the living. The survivors piled more desks and chairs onto the makeshift barricade, but with no way to secure them besides a couple rolls of scotch tape salvaged from an office, these were soon pulled away. The supply of office furniture on the second floor dwindled as the night went on, and by dawn, the second floor had to be abandoned. This pattern of retreat continued until the barrier to the third floor was pulled apart by the relentless dead and the last of the living humans in the building were forced to flee to the roof.

Looking at the heavy wooden access door that was the only obstacle remaining between them and death, Jimmy glanced at his stark surroundings and decided he would probably die of exposure, thirst or starvation long before the dead broke through it. That had been yesterday and nothing had changed, including the incessant pounding of the dead at the door leading from the third floor to the roof.

Jimmy now let his mind wander to take it off his obsessive thirst, and he daydreamed about saving everyone. Fantasizing about finding a rifle and shooting down the dead, his vision of killing the zombies surrounding them was so strong that he could actually hear the shots.

Feeling a kick to the bottom of his boot, Jimmy came out of his reverie to find Jo-Jo standing over him. Before she could speak, he became aware that it hadn't been a dream. He could hear gunfire. Lots of gunfire. And a strange whooshing sound he couldn't place.

With a huge grin on her face, his sister shouted in glee, "The Army's here. They're right on the edge of town and they're coming our way. They got guns and flamethrowers and everything. They're massacring them damned dead things."

Flamethrowers, Jimmy thought. That's what the whooshing noise is. I gotta get me one of them, he decided.

With a shout of triumph, he jumped up to join the throng of people standing at the parapet wall, cheering and shouting as the Army decimated the dead.

Perched on trucks, MRAPs and Humvees, and using automatic rifles, machine guns and flamethrowers, the first military unit swept through town leaving nothing but the inert bodies of the dead in their wake. The soldiers then came back and started a systematic search for survivors in the town while eradicating the few zombies they missed on their first pass. Seeing the people on top of the insurance building, a unit was detached to save them. They drove up to the front of the structure in armored cars. Dismounting, the soldiers broke down the front door and started clearing the building of the hundreds of dead which clogged its halls and offices.

Jimmy, Jessie and Jo-Jo ran to the access door to the third floor and waited. The noise of muted gunfire coming from inside the building grew louder. In minutes, the McPhersons had to back away from the door when stray bullets started coming through it.

The gunfire died down to be replaced by a voice that yelled, "Identify yourselves or we will open fire. This is your only warning."

Cries of relief greeted this announcement. The door was opened and a dozen heavily armed men wearing camouflaged utilities came onto the roof. After being hailed as saviors, the soldiers made sure that none of the people were infected before leading them down to the street. Here they huddled in a group, staring at the hundreds of dead bodies that littered the street. A Humvee, followed by a truck, roared up and disgorged more civilians, quickly recognized as fellow townsfolk. Reunions were common, and more were in the making as people shouted out that they had seen each other's family and friends.

More trucks arrived, and soon there were over three hundred citizens of Owens Grove crowding Main Street. Tears of joy were shed at reunions of family's that had been split apart, and tears of sadness were shed at the news that loved ones had been killed. Medics helped the wounded while soldiers moved through the crowd passing out bottled water, crackers and spam to the crowd. Despite the circumstances, a feeling of being at a festival soon prevailed.

They had made it. They were alive.

Darkness was falling when a Humvee with two speakers mounted on the roof approached and stopped a short distance from the edge of the crowd. Everyone fell silent as feedback whined when a PA system was turned on. The screeching stopped abruptly as a voice with a Cajun accent echoed across the downtown area saying, "My name is Major William H. Shurmann the Third. I'm the commander of the unit that rescued you. I would like to congratulate you for making it through, and I would also like to offer my condolences to those of you who lost family members in this tragedy."

Caught up in the spirit of having narrowly avoided death, the remaining citizens of Owens Grove roared their thanks to the soldiers who saved them and at the words of consolation. When the noise died down, Shurmann spoke again.

"I am seeking both male and female volunteers to join with us in our efforts to eradicate the plague of dead threatening our existence. For those of you who want to enlist for the duration of this crisis, please go to the post office three blocks down and give your name and vital statistics to the clerks on duty there. "

Nothing more needed to be said. Ready and eager to do their part, over fifty men and woman broke from the crowd and headed down the street, their excited chatter filled with shouted vows of, "Kill them dead things," and, "Take our country back."

Jo-Jo and Jessie joined this group, but when Jimmy tried to accompany them, Jo-Jo told him to wait. While they were worried about the rest of the family, the farmhouse was outside town and the soldiers hadn't advanced that far yet, so Jo-Jo decided that she and Jessie would sign up now and Jimmy would wait to see if they opened up the road heading to their house. If they hadn't cleared the way by the time she got back, then she and Jessie would wait while Jimmy signed up. Although they wanted to be reunited with their family, they felt sure that the resourceful McPherson clan would be all right. The farmhouse drew water from a well and had a pantry stocked with food.

When the noise of those going to enlist died down, Shurmann spoke again, "For those of you who remain I would like you to split up into two groups. The soldiers moving among you will assist you in an orderly separation. On the right side of the street, I want all men and women between the ages of sixteen and fifty. Everyone else needs to move to the left."

It was then Jimmy noticed that the soldiers who had been facing outward to guard the crowd against any stray zombies had attached bayonets to their rifles and were brusquely ordering people to the left or right of Main Street. People were confused at this new development, but since the soldiers had saved them, they went along without too much fuss. Once divided, a line of trucks pulled down Main Street and stopped between the two groups, further separating them. Now people started to feel uneasy, and shouted questions at the soldiers guarding them as well as to the unseen Major who had yet to step out from his Humvee.

"Quiet," a sharp, angry command boomed over the loudspeakers. The crowd fell silent as it continued, "You all had your chance to volunteer, but some of you didn't take it. Your country needs you in this time of crisis and you turned your backs on it. I am here to inform you that under orders from the Joint Chiefs of the United States of America, all men and women between the ages of sixteen and fifty are hereby conscripted into military service. While those people who volunteered will be given two days to get their affairs in order, those of you on my right who refused will be taken directly from here to Fort Hood, Texas. There, you will undergo basic training for a period of four weeks. After that, you will then be sent immediately to units working in the cities to rid us of the hordes of dead. Those who resist will be shot. Those who desert will be hanged upon their recapture. Any disobedience to any lawful order given by me or my men will be dealt with swiftly and harshly."

Shouted curses, including Jimmy's, filled the air as he protested that he was going to sign up. Everyone was silenced when a soldier fired a burst from his assault rifle into the air.

In the eerie quiet that followed, Shurmann said, "The next person to act out in disobedience will be shot where they stand. Everyone on the right needs to board the trucks and keep quiet."

In shock, no one moved until Shurmann's voice roared out, "Now!"

Slowly at first, and then quicker when prodded by the bayonet-wielding soldiers, the conscripts boarded the transports. Jimmy was the final person on the last truck in line and ended up sitting next to a guard who had positioned himself at the back. As the vehicle started to move, he realized that the road they were taking to Baton Rouge would lead them directly past the family's farmhouse. Sizing up the guard seated next to him, he knew he could easily knock the man out and jump from the truck when they went by his house. He needed to talk to his daddy about what was happening. He wanted to let everyone know that he'd been shanghaied. If he didn't do this, no one would find out for weeks what happened and might think him dead.

Right after I let the family know I'm safe, I'll go volunteer, Jimmy told himself. Thinking about the Major's punishment for deserting, he assured himself that this was America. He wasn't worried about being shot. Americans didn't do things like that to their own people.

Seeing the tattered remains of the Red Cross tent in the distance, he knew he was close. Readying himself to overpower the guard, he concentrated on the spot behind the man's ear where he would hit him. He was just getting ready to draw back his arm when he heard one of the other men in the truck ask, "Ain't that your place, Jimmy?"

Turning to look, Jimmy felt his heart drop to his stomach as despair washed through him. All hope fled at the sight of the wreckage that had once been his family's home. The only thing that wasn't burned down and scattered was an old outhouse. Bricks and wood were strewn in a huge arc across the front yard and he could see bodies lying on the front lawn. He hoped these were dead things and not his family, but looking closer at the scene of complete destruction, deep down inside he knew the bodies were his kin.

In shock, he whispered, "What happened?"

Hearing him, the guard replied, "They resisted. Happened about half an hour ago. Heard about it on the radio. The people inside shot one of the soldiers after he told them they were drafted. The old man who lived there was screaming about it being kidnapping and opened fire. The Major said he wanted an example set and called in a tank to level the building."

Completely lost in his misery, Jimmy sagged in his seat as the truck drove him to Baton Rouge, and whatever fate awaited him.

In such a way, the recruitment drive initiated by the Joint Chiefs of Staff swept across the country.

Chapter Nine

The Dead Calm:

The morning sun illuminated the bridge of The Calm of the Seas as Reverend Ricky looked at Brother Seth with disgust. After letting the man squirm for a full minute, he demanded, "What the hell happened? How did that bitch get away and kill Brother Raymond?"

Not wanting to tell Ricky how Sheila had caught him and Raymond with their pants down, literally with their pants down, Seth made up a story of how Sheila had ambushed them. About how she must have suspected they were coming for her and hid just inside the entrance to the lounge. When they walked in, she jumped out and slashed at him first before stabbing Brother Raymond in the chest. Hoping to turn Ricky's wrath further away from him and onto Sheila, he added to his lie by saying that as she ran off, she had yelled out that Ricky was a limp-dick who molested Border Collies.

Seth had to stifle his laughter when he saw the reaction this got. Ricky's face turned almost purple and he started shaking as he spit out, "That bitch," before falling silent.

After taking a moment to compose himself, Ricky finally gained enough composure to ask, "What happened on deck five then? I set a bunch of freaks loose when the spotter told us that Sheila was there."

Grateful to be out of the spotlight, and more than willing to throw someone else into it, Seth answered, "We had one of the Faithful keeping an eye on the newcomers. When he spotted the dead you set free, he panicked and ran. When we finally got another guy down there, he reported that a whole shit load of freaks were dead - or whatever the hell you call it when they don't get back up - and there was no sign of any other stinkers. We don't know how many were let loose, so there could still be a few walking around."

Ricky asked, "Did any of them make it down to deck four?"

"A couple," Seth answered. "He told me that six of them were lying near the top of the stairs and another one was halfway down, but the rest didn't make it much further. The six up top all had head wounds, but he couldn't see the other ones."

"So these people know how to shoot," Ricky stated.

"Apparently," Seth replied dryly.

Ricky considered this for a moment before turning to Parsons and saying, "This kind of throws a wrench into our plans. Doesn't it?"

Parsons nodded curtly as he pushed down at the anger bubbling up inside him. He and Ricky had come up with the perfect plan to draw the newcomers into the ship, and now it was worthless. Their plan hinged on everyone staying out of sight and letting the people from the sailboat feel comfortable in their new environment. They knew curiosity would overcome caution if someone were given what they thought was a safe environment to explore. Once scattered throughout its numerous compartments, they could be separated by locking down the watertight doors in front and behind them. This way, their combined firepower would be cut down and they could be killed from ambush without much risk.

But now, because of your snap decision to let some of the dead go, our plan isn't worth a shit, Don thought.

When Seth had radioed Parsons to let him know Sheila had escaped, he called for the rest of the Head Ushers to meet him at the Masthead. They split up to search for her, but couldn't find so much as one red hair. It was like she'd vanished. They were just about to give up when the spotter on deck five radioed that she had shown up there. Knowing she was trying to reach the people from the sailboat, he called Ricky to tell him the bad news.

Having retired to his cabin with two Hungarian sisters aged thirteen and fourteen, Ricky was annoyed at the interruption. When he found out the reason behind it though, he went totally ballistic. Wrapping a towel around his waist, he stormed to the bridge and threw the switch that opened a watertight hatch on deck five.

Although most of the doors keeping the dead secured in the cabin areas were simply fire doors that had been chained shut, a short distance beyond these were water-tight hatches that could be controlled from the bridge. After gaining control of the ship, Ricky shut the hatches and had the chains removed from the fire doors. This way, he could open these areas from the safety of the bridge and let the dead loose at will to terrorize his Faithful and reinforce their need for protection.

Normally, Ricky would only open one of these hatches for a few seconds, just enough time for one or two of the dead to escape. In his rage at Sheila though, he left the door open for a full fifteen count. Returning from the bridge, he called Parsons and told him he wanted Seth to report to him at nine the next morning. He wanted to know what the hell happened at the Masthead. Like a child throwing a temper tantrum, he screamed that short of the ship sinking, he wasn't to be disturbed for the rest of the night.

"So how do you want to do this?" Parsons asked, hoping Ricky didn't go off again and have a fit. This seemed to be happening more often and was distracting them from the real problem at hand.

To his relief, Ricky sighed and his anger dissipated. Turning to Brother Seth, he ordered him to personally check on what was happening on deck four. Once he was gone, Ricky sighed again and said in a regretful voice, "I guess I kind of blew it last night. Didn't I?"

Parsons gave a noncommittal nod, not wanting to rub Ricky's nose in the fact that his actions had trashed their plan. Now it might take weeks for the people from the sailboat to relax enough to feel free to explore the ship, and they didn't have weeks. Trying to assess how much damage Sheila's defection might have caused, he asked, "What does that red-headed bitch know?"

"She knows the ship's sinking and she knows how we operate," Ricky replied.

"So that means the people on deck four know."

"But at least she doesn't know that we plan to kill them and take their boat," Ricky countered.

"But she knows about Cozumel. If she tells them about that, they might make the connection. She's sure to tell them that we let the freaks go and why. That alone will keep them on edge. We need to find a way to take them out and get their boat," Parsons insisted.

"We've already decided we can't go head to head with them. They've got us outgunned and we're limited on ammunition. We need to split them up so we can pick them off one by one," Ricky said.

"We could let the freaks out on deck four and block the stairs leading up to five. Let the dead do our work for us," Parsons suggested.

Shaking his head, Ricky replied, "Won't work. Four is one of the decks where the doors are still chained shut. In fact, we never even bothered to shut the watertight door down there because the fire doors are strong enough to keep the dead contained."

"So we need to get the fire doors open," Parsons said forcefully.

"Would you like to do it?" Ricky challenged, his frustration and anger rising at their inability to come up with a useful plan. "I'll give you the key and you can run down the stairs and unlock them. Of course, that's if you can dodge four automatic weapons firing at your ass while you're trying to fit the fucking key in the lock."

Parsons was about to come back with an angry retort when the two-way radio clipped to his belt buzzed. Bringing it to his mouth, he said, "Brother Parsons here."

The voice coming through the speaker was rushed as it said, "It's Brother Seth. I thought you should know that there's a lot of activity going on down here. They're all moving around and loading stuff. It looks like they're getting ready to leave."

"Shit," Ricky said angrily. "We've got to stop them."

Holding up his hand to try and stem the tirade he knew was coming, Parsons pressed the transmit button and said, "Stay there and keep an eye on things. I'll call you back in ten minutes."

Turning to Ricky, he said, "I've got an idea, but it's a little risky. You'll need to back me on this one hundred percent or we might as well give up."

"Anything," Ricky said in desperation. "What's your idea?"

So Parsons told him.

***

Steve was stacking cases of plastic water bottles in the laundry cart they were using to transport supplies to the boat when Brain called him on the radio, saying in a rushed voice, "Steve, man. You've got to get over to the stairs right away."

Hearing the urgency in his tone, he grabbed his rifle with one hand while un-clipping the radio with the other and asked, "What is it?"

"Just get here right away," Brain urged.

"On the way," he replied. Wondering what was going on now.

Although reassured by the fact that he didn't hear any gunshots or screams, he still set off at a steady jog toward the stairs. He was half way down the Centrum when he spotted Heather in front of a designer sunglass shop, waving him over to her. She carried her CAR-15 and had her pistol holstered at her hip. Wearing a Kevlar vest, she held another one out to him as she said, "Brain sent Susan to get me as soon as she saw we had a visitor. I told him to call you, but not to say anything over the radio because I wanted to fill you in first."

Slipping into his vest, Steve said, "So fill me in. Who is it?"

After a pause, as if not believing it herself, she said, "it's the Reverend Ricky."

Stopping as he tried to take in this new turn of events, he couldn't have been more surprised if she'd just told him that the Keebler elves had dropped by. Instead of looking too much into the situation, he decided to concentrate on the logistics of the situation as opposed to the whys as he asked Heather, "Where is everyone?"

"After I sent Susan to tell Brain to call you, I woke Tick-Tock up and sent him to hole up in one of the shops on the port side. That way, we've got a good cross fire going if the shit hits the fan. He went through the back way so no one would see him. I don't even know which store he's in, but it's Tick-Tock, so I know he's there. He's wearing the other vest, and he took a couple tear gas grenades with him. Brain is with Ricky near the foot of the stairs. I had Susan fade back into the jewelry store to give him cover. I got Tim to find the others and tell them to stay where they are. Cindy's with Mary, Connie is in the ship's store and Sheila is still sleeping it off. Then I told Tim to set up at the far end of the Centrum to make sure no one dropped in behind us."

Steve gave her a wry smile and said, "Ruthlessly efficient are the words that come to mind."

"Well, I never told you this before, but I used to be a cop," she replied.

"As long as you only use your superpowers for good ..."

"So how do you want to do this?" She asked. "It doesn't smell like a setup since it's the Reverend Ricky's ass hanging out on the line."

That it was a setup had been the first thing to cross Steve's mind too, but Heather's reasoning made sense. Ricky wouldn't put his own life on the line, and he had to know he'd be the first one killed if any shooting started.

Unless he's crazier than I thought, Steve asked himself.

Knowing he could guess and second guess himself all morning and still not figure it out, he said to Heather, "The only way we can find out what the man wants is to ask him, so let's go."

As Steve grew closer to the stairs, he could see that Brain had his rifle pointed directly at Ricky's chest. From the menacing look on his face, he wondered if the tech would shoot him before they got there. Curious as to where this anger came from, it struck him that Connie must have told him how Ricky tried to get in her pants.

Steve stopped twenty feet away and called Brain over to him. In a low voice, he told him to find Tim and cover their rear. If anyone even looked like they were going to come down from the deck above, he was to open fire without hesitation.

Brain gave Ricky one final sneer before going into the jewelry store so he could access the back passageways. This way, no one could target him while he travelled the length of the Centrum.

You're learning fast, Brain, Heather thought.

Steve studied Ricky as his mind ran through a number of opening lines.

Hostile: What's to keep me from putting a bullet in your fat ass, fuck-boy?

Blunt: What do you want?

Friendly: Hi, my name is Steve Wendell. I've heard so much about you.

Sarcastic: If Jesus loves me, why doesn't he ever put money in my bank account?

Settling on blunt, he called out in a flat voice, "What do you want?"

Smiling and raising his hand in a wave, Ricky started to move forward and say, "You must be-," but was stopped in his tracks when both Steve and Heather raised their rifles to point at his chest.

"That's close enough," Heather warned in a cold voice.

Sweat popped out on Ricky's fat face as he slowly raised both hands. In a fearful voice, he said, "I'm unarmed. You wouldn't shoot an unarmed man, would you?"

"I wouldn't, but she might," Steve indicated Heather with a nod of his head, as she gave Ricky the hard look she reserved for the scumbags she'd run into in her previous career. More sweat popped on Ricky's face and he swallowed hard.

"What do you want?" Steve asked again.

"I come in peace, brother," Ricky said.

"That didn't answer my question," Steve said flatly.

"I've just come to tell you that neither I nor any of my followers mean you any harm," Ricky said, while thinking, if I get out of this, I'm going to have Parsons tossed to the stinkers. His great fucking idea for me to come down here and put these maniacs at ease and keep them on board is going to get me killed.

Forcing a smile, Ricky added, "Our religion is a non-violent one."

Heather snorted in disbelief as Steve said, "Is that why you let the dead out to walk around and terrorize people? Because that sounds kind of violent to me."

Indignantly, Ricky replied, "Whoever told you that is a liar. They're just trying to smear my name and stop the good works I'm doing on this ship. True, we have a problem with the frea-." Ricky caught himself before going on, "I mean, the poor souls trapped in purgatory that still wander the ship, but their occasional appearance has nothing to do with me."

"That's not how Sheila tells it," Heather said.

Ricky put on a thoughtful expression and said, "Ah, poor Sheila. I tried to bring her to the Lord, but her alcoholism and promiscuity kept getting in the way. I'd heard she'd run off again." Shaking his head sadly, he said, "That girl can sure tell some tales. I've urged her time and again to be truthful." Switching to a pious expression, he added, "You can lie to others, but the Lord knows the truth."

Heather and Steve exchanged a look that said, What a load of shit, before Steve asked, "What about the ship sinking. Is that a lie too?"

Hesitantly, Ricky replied, "We're having some trouble with a few of the pumps, but we're working on it." To avoid further questions, he put on a humble expression and said, "Now, the other reason I came down here, besides to welcome you to the Calm of the Seas, is to be a good neighbor and ask if I can be of any assistance to you while you stay on the ship. Is there anything you need?"

Steve was about to reply that they were leaving soon, but caught himself. He didn't want to give any information about their plans to this fat, bearded asshole. He oozed so much false sincerity that it made him feel physically ill. After a moment's thought though, he decided, what the hell? It's not like Ricky and his people can stop us.

"We need a sextant and a nautical almanac."

Ricky kept his joy at hearing this in check. He and Parsons had racked their brains for the reason behind the appearance of the sailboat. This request confirmed their suspicions that these people were fleeing the HWNW virus. This meant that they had nowhere to go and made it easier to convince them to stay on the ship.

At least until I throw them overboard, Ricky thought. Alive if possible.

This also confirmed his suspicion that it wasn't just their GPS that was malfunctioning, but it was a system wide failure. It had taken Brother Raymond weeks of studying the books they'd found in the Captain's quarters before he was able to figure out their position. Now that Brother Raymond was gone, one of the others would have to learn how to do it since it looked like GPS was going to be out of the picture for the next few generations.

Or, Ricky thought, I can find out who in this group knows how to plot a course by hand. Maybe in the upcoming slaughter I can spare them. At least until we reach Cozumel.

Putting on his thoughtful look again and pursing his lips, Ricky said, "I'm sure we could find those things for you. It might take some searching, but my Faithful have quite a bit of time on their hands."

Between the partying and orgies, I'd think they were pretty busy, Heather thought but didn't voice. If Ricky were going to give them the tools they needed to find their position, it probably wouldn't do to insult him. That didn't mean she was going to trust him though, since she knew he was scum. She'd heard the stories Sheila had told, and after meeting the Reverend Ricky in person, they didn't even seem to scratch the surface. There was something oily and slimy about him that left her feeling queasy.

Kind of like getting too close to a lawyer.

Not wanting to give up control of the conversation, Ricky continued on by saying, "Now that I've shown you my good intentions, I was hoping you'd reciprocate."

Thinking that Ricky would ask for Sheila back, Steve was prepared to cut him off with a flat 'No'.

Instead, Ricky beamed a smile at them and said, "I just want to know your names. Your Christian names of course."

Steve hesitated, wondering what he really wanted. Looking at Heather who only shrugged, he said, "Steve and Heather."

Heather didn't think it possible, but Ricky's smile got bigger. "Welcome to the Calm of the Seas, Brother Steve and Sister Heather," he cried out happily. "Please feel free to explore the ship and make yourselves at home. Even though we're running on reduced power, there are still a lot of activities that you can enjoy." With a wink, he added, "We even power up the casino every once in a while. I mean, we're not Baptists after all."

Steve gave a tight smile at this comment.

Not wanting to lay it on too thick at their first meeting, Ricky clapped his hands together and rubbed them back and forth while saying, "Well, I don't want to keep you any longer, so I'll take my leave. I'll get my people out searching for those items you need right away. What did you say they were again?"

"A sextant and a nautical almanac," Steve answered.

"Consider it done," he told them.

Ricky flashed them a peace sign and turned to go. As he walked to the stairs, he looked beyond to the double doors leading into the cabin area. One reason for coming down here was to put the newcomers at ease and keep them on board, the other was to get a good look at the chains keeping the dead in the cabin area. Letting the stinkers go was still an option if their first plan failed.

Satisfied at what he saw, Ricky headed for the bridge. His whole walk spent thinking of how he would kill the people he'd just met.

After he was gone, Steve said in a low voice, "Now that I've met Ricky, I can see what a scumbag he really is. Before this is all over, I'm going to kill him."

"Not if I get him first," Heather replied.

\*\*\*

Four hours later, Steve was called to the stairs again. When he arrived, he found Heather talking to a young girl. As he came closer, he heard the visitor speaking in a thick European accent. Seeing that she was carrying something in her hands, his first thought was of religious suicide bombers. Looking closer, he saw it was only a book, but this did little to ease his trepidation.

When he joined them, the girl asked with a bright smile, "You are Steve, yes?"

"I am."

"This is good then. The Reverend ask me to give this to you please," she said as she held out the book.

Glancing at the cover, he could read the words *Nautical Almanac*. Not believing Ricky had come through, he thanked the girl.

"But there is more," she said. "The Reverend say to tell you he look for other thing more or less now. Not find soon but he will find soon."

Steve was slightly confused by this, which was the reason Ricky sent the younger of the two sisters. Her English was barely passable. The obscure message, along with only giving one of the two things they'd asked for, had a dual purpose. Stall them while at the same time gaining their trust.

"Tell the Reverend, thank you," Steve said.

The girl turned to go, but Heather stopped her, saying she wanted to finish the conversation they were having. With a concerned look, Heather asked, "Does Ricky ever touch you or make you do things you don't want to? I want you to know it's wrong for adults to do this and that you can stay here if you want to. It's safe."

The girl gave Heather a big smile and said, "But it is the Reverend Ricky. He can do no wrong. He is a man of God's choosing."

With this, she turned and trotted up the stairs.

Steve gave Heather a curious look, so she told him, "I was talking to her while we waited for you to get here and I saw some signs that she might be abused. I used to be a cop and we were trained in what to look for."

"And?" Steve asked.

"I'm not sure, but if I find out he is messing around with her, all bets are off. Ricky's ass is all mine right there and then and fuck his Faithful."

With a nod, Steve said, "Then he's all yours and we take our chances with the Faithful. Until then, we need to keep a close eye on him though, because he's up to something. I had Tim sneak around the upper decks after Ricky left. Told him to do a little recon and see what was going on up there. He told me no one was looking for anything and that most of them were still sleeping off last night's drunken orgy."

"He's slow walking us then, but why?" Heather asked.

"I don't know, but I'm only going to play this game for a little while," Steve said.

"And then?" Heather asked.

"Then we take what we need," he replied.

Chapter Ten

The Dead Calm:

Sheila finally roused herself at two; an hour after Mary first woke her to see if she was feeling all right and to see if she might want something to eat. Nauseated and lost in her misery, Sheila could only shake her head as she tried to will herself back to sleep. When this didn't work, she shakily sat up on the mattress, wondering how she had gotten there the night before. Looking down at the disheveled clothes she'd slept in, she snorted in disgust. As she tried to smooth some of the wrinkles out of her blouse, her jangled nerves caused her to jump when she heard a female voice say from behind her, "I had to guess at your size, but I'm sure I got it close."

She turned to see Mary holding up a fashionable dress and tennis shoes as a shy look played across the woman's face.

Sheila gave a pained smile and said, "Thank you, but what I really need is a drink."

Setting down the clothing and reaching into a basket at her feet, Mary came out with a bottle of wine in each hand and asked mischievously, "Red or white?"

"Both," Sheila answered. Then laughed and said, "You and I are going to get along just fine. What's your name anyway?"

Mary deflated slightly at finding Sheila had forgotten her, and seeing this, Sheila racked her brain for the good-looking blonde woman's name. Suddenly it came to her and she said, "I'm sorry, I'm a little out of it. You're Mary." With a small, deprecating laugh, she added, "Now I wish I could remember who the hell I am. I really tied one on last night."

Mary giggled and forgave the good-looking redhead for her lapse in memory.

After Sheila had dressed in her new clothes, the two women had a few drinks while they got acquainted. As they sipped their drinks, Mary filled in some of the blanks of what happened the night before. Finally deciding they needed to put something in their stomachs besides wine, the two women window-shopped as they headed for the dining room. Entering, Mary stopped them short just inside the door when she spotted Steve and Tick-Tock sitting at a table eating sandwiches.

"Oh God, there's Doctor Buzzkill," Mary said in a low voice.

"Yeah, I know," Sheila agreed. "What's his problem anyway? One of the things I do remember from last night is him and some blonde chick running around looking like they just came back from a patrol in Afghanistan. I thought they were going to shoot me."

"Steve's got a John Wayne complex or something, and his girlfriend, Heather, is not much better," Mary told her. "They're on this mission to save the world from the dead, but the way I see it though, I think having zombies rise up from the grave is one of the best things that ever happened."

Sheila gave her new friend an odd look, so Mary explained, "Take for example everything here on this ship. It's the same way out there. All the shops and stores are just waiting for us to come along and take want we want. No hassling with rude sales people or fighting the crowds. No limit on my credit cards." She giggled and added, "No need for credit cards."

"But we heard on the radio that the dead overran all the cities. How can you shop when you're dodging the freaks?" Sheila asked.

Looking with slitted eyes at Steve and Tick-Tock, Mary replied, "Well, I guess the Neanderthals have some uses. They clear the area of the dead so I can shop, so that's something in their favor."

Steve noticed Mary and Sheila and waved them over to join them. Not seeing a way out of it, Mary led the way, pasting on the false smile she donned whenever she had to interact with Tick-Tock. When they reached the table, Steve said, "Connie and Brain made soup and sandwiches for lunch. You weren't here so they saved you some. They're in the kitchen." Looking directly at Sheila, he added, "Come back and join us after you grab something to eat. Now that Tick-Tock's here, I want to go over what you told us last night."

Sheila looked at Steve's number two and said, "Tick-Tock?"

"The talking bush," he replied.

Mary felt anger wash through her when Sheila giggled and batted her eyes at Tick-Tock. She wanted to scream at him, 'you're already fucking my Susan, so back off buddy.'

Instead, she said to Sheila in a sweet voice, "Let's grab something to eat, honey. I'm starved."

After the women went into the kitchen, Tick-Tock said, "Looks like Mary's got a new candidate for the tongue in groove club."

Steve laughed and said, "Crudely put, but true. I'm not too crazy about having two dead weights in the group, but it looks like we're stuck with them."

"Cut them loose," Tick-Tock suggested.

"Then I might as well put a bullet in Mary's brain," he replied. "She wouldn't last five minutes on her own. Cutting her loose is the same as murdering her. I don't know how Sheila would do, she might survive, but Mary..."

"So we're stuck with a drunken whore and a lipstick lesbian," Tick-Tock said with a slight smile.

Steve laughed and said, "Again, crudely put, but true. Right now, with the world the way it is though, I'm not throwing anyone to the wolves unless they're a direct threat to me or the group."

"Which means?" Tick-Tock asked.

"It means that I'll be the first to exile or shoot anyone who puts our lives in jeopardy. No hesitation. If I find out Sheila's setting us up, then at the very least she's getting her ass booted back onto the upper decks. That's if I don't just shoot her."

"What about the Faithful?" Tick-Tock asked.

"I consider them a threat, but not a direct threat," Steve replied. "I know I can't save them, especially since Ricky's probably convinced them that I'm the anti-Christ come to drag their souls screaming to Hell, and I can't even begin to sort out who to help and who to kill, but I still need to do something. If any of them become a threat, then they're dead, but the least I can do is let them know the truth about Ricky and the ship sinking. From there, they'll have to try and save themselves."

"It's more than I'd do," Tick-Tock said.

Steve shrugged, knowing this was one of the few points that he and Tick-Tock differed on. He had no doubt that his friend would put his life on the line for anyone in the group, except maybe Mary, but as for those who weren't with them or were apathetic toward improving their situation, they were on their own. Steve knew he wouldn't risk the lives of any of the others in the group to save the Faithful, but he would at least try to help those who couldn't help themselves. Those who could, but didn't, were on their own.

Mary and Sheila rejoined them, with Mary giving Tick-Tock a dirty look when he gave her new flame his most winning smile and offered to get her some coffee.

Steve let Sheila finish eating before asking her to repeat what she'd told them at dinner. He'd already relayed to Tick-Tock everything the redhead had said, but wanted the woman to tell her story again for a number of reasons, the most important being to see if he could catch her in any lies. Although it did appear Ricky wanted her dead, he still didn't trust her. The whole thing with the Z's coming out of nowhere could have easily been staged.

When Sheila was done, Steve had to admit that she seemed to be telling the truth. Her story was clearer than the night before, which Steve chalked up to a lessened blood alcohol content, and hadn't differed greatly on any points, so he decided that for now the redhead could stay.

When he mentioned that Ricky had paid them a visit that morning, Sheila grew white in the face and visibly trembled, further leading him to believe her story. Her reaction wasn't something she could fake. When he explained about the Reverend giving them the Nautical Almanac, Sheila leaned forward in her chair and said, "Don't trust him, he's after something. He wants…" But her words died out as she lost her train of thought.

Shaking her head at the alcohol fog that remained from the night before, and the one that she'd already started working on that morning, Sheila couldn't come up with the thought she was trying to voice. Although she knew Ricky needed a way to Cozumel, she couldn't make the connection between that and the people from the sailboat. Steve and Tick-Tock didn't make the connection to Ricky wanting the sailboat either, since Sheila hadn't thought it important enough to tell them about Cozumel. Besides, they all saw that the solution for the people stuck on the ship was simple; tow a lifeboat full of gas and supplies behind them so they could reach land.

Seeing Sheila's hesitation, Mary asked, "He wants what, Honey?"

Looking up morosely, she replied, "I'm not sure, I just don't trust him."

"Neither do we," Steve said. He wanted to add that the fake preacher's days were numbered, but didn't want to tell Sheila about the fate Heather planned for the Reverend Ricky Rose. Instead, he said to Mary, "Since we're waiting on the sextant, and for Brain to get the gas pump working, we're going to be here for another day at least. You can finish finding the rest of the items on the list in the morning. You've done a good job, so take the rest of the afternoon and do whatever you want. Just stay on this deck."

Ignoring the praise from Steve, Mary was concerned about Sheila as she seemed to be struggling with something.

Shaking her head, the redhead finally looked up at Mary and said, "I could use a drink, and since you have the rest of the day off, why don't we do some shopping."

Thinking about all the high-tension alcohol in the shops and clubs, Steve almost ordered them to stay away from the booze, but instead cautioned, "Take it easy on the liquor. If you get fucked up and something happens, we might not be able to help you."

With smiles and promises to be good, the two women got up to go. After they left, Steve said to Tick-Tock, "Do me a favor and please don't try to bang Sheila. I've got enough drama going on right now in my life and I don't need any more."

Tick-Tock laughed, "Don't worry. I'm just doing it to yank Mary's chain. I've got no interest in Sheila at all."

Relieved that he didn't have to deal with some kind of bizarre four-way emotional love triangle between Tick-Tock, Mary, Susan and Sheila on top of everything else, Steve said, "Last night I was talking to Tim and he showed me some of the crew passageways that run through the ship. He told me that most of the time he doesn't have to use them. He moves around by using the stairs and walkways because no one notices him. All they see is a kid wandering around. He also told me that the best time to go onto the upper decks is just after sundown. Ricky and his Faithful are partying on the top deck, so there's no one around."

"And you're telling me this because-?" Tick-Tock asked with an expectant smile.

"How'd you like to do a little recon tonight?" Steve asked.

"How do we get past the spotters on deck five?" Tick-Tock questioned.

"Elevator shaft," Steve answered. "Tim told me how he was getting chased by a couple Z's one time, so he climbed through the hatch on the top of the elevator car. There's a ladder that runs up and down each shaft."

"Sounds interesting," Tick-Tock said. "Just you and me?"

"Heather and Susan will stay here, which makes it a boy's night out. We'll take Brain along. He wants to try and get a look at the switching room or something," Steve said. "He's having trouble getting power to the pump that controls the fuel supply. He needs to switch over to another generator or another line. He says he'll know what to do when he sees the electrical room."

"What deck does he think this is on?" Tick-Tock asked.

"He's pretty sure it's on deck six, and I need to get onto seven to check out the lifeboat situation. After that, we can go wherever we want, but we need to stay together."

"Lifeboats?" Tick-Tock questioned.

Sheila says most of them are disabled, but that's just what she heard from Ricky. She never saw them herself. I want to take a look," Steve answered.

"To make sure Ricky's Faithful can get away safe?"

Steve nodded.

"Screw the Faithful and the horse they rode in on," Tick-Tock told his friend, "but I'm up for a little tour of the ship. I've got something I want to do anyway. What time do we go?"

"Seven o'clock, by then it'll be dark."

*\*\**

Located near the stern, and high above the Calm of the Seas, the Crow's Nest Lounge looked out over the length of the ship. Off limits to the Faithful and the regular Ushers, it was the private domain of Reverend Ricky and his Head Ushers. Enjoying the panoramic view enhanced by being hundreds of feet in the air, Don Parsons stood behind the bar mixing drinks for Ricky and himself. The remaining three Head Ushers sat with their leader as they watched the sun sink down to meet the horizon. Every afternoon, before joining the Faithful at their gathering for the rapture, Ricky and the Head Ushers met to go over what was happening on the ship and to brainstorm ideas on how to get to Cozumel. With the arrival of Steve's group, the main topic of discussion was how to get the sailboat without getting themselves killed in the process.

Finished with his bartending duties, Parsons brought Ricky a Black Russian, waiting for him to take a sip and nod his approval before settling into one of the overstuffed chairs pulled together in a half circle.

Ricky said, "I've managed to acquire an informant on deck four. Word is that three of the newcomers are planning to take a little tour of the ship tonight after it gets dark."

This announcement was met by excitement from the men gathered around.

"What are they looking for?" Parsons asked.

"We're not sure exactly, but it appears they're having trouble powering the gas pump down in the watercraft area. My person told me that they're also going to check out the lifeboats."

"Why the lifeboats?" Parsons asked.

"To see if they're really disabled. The one named Steve has a plan to tell the Faithful that the ship is sinking right before he and his people leave. He wants to tell them that if they take a lifeboat and tow another boat full of gas behind them, they can reach land."

"We can't let the Faithful find out we've been snowing them about the lifeboats," Brother Seth interjected.

Still mad at Seth, and sure that the man was lying about what had really happened at the Masthead, Ricky exploded, "No shit, but that's not the point. The point is, we can't reach Cozumel without that sailboat. That's what we need to focus on. I'm just relaying what my snitch told me about what the people on deck four are up to. I really couldn't give two shits what happens to the rest of the people on this ship. And another thing, if you hadn't let Sheila-."

Not wanting the meeting to turn into another one of Ricky's rants, Parsons leaned forward and interrupted by saying loudly, "Despite all that, our plan seems to be working. They seem to feel comfortable enough to explore the ship."

Ricky continued to glare at Seth, but nodded at Parsons' reasoning as he calmed himself. After giving Seth a last warning look, he said, "But we've still got to find some more things they need so we can keep them here long enough to feel comfortable going out in groups of one and two. There'll be three of them tonight with guns. Three people armed with automatic weapons are too many for us to take on." Giving Brother Seth a hard look he continued, "Especially now that we're down one man."

"They still need the sextant, so that should buy us a day or two," Parsons said. "We can crack the lens before we give it to them and hold back the spare to buy us another couple days while we tell them we're looking for it."

Brother William spoke up, "It's kind of hard to entice them with anything since they have damn near everything they need on deck four. Food, water and all those stores just sitting there waiting to be picked over. That's one of the decks we haven't raided for food and booze yet so it's pretty stocked." Turning to Ricky he asked, "Did your informant give you any idea about anything else they need?"

"Nothing yet," Ricky replied. "But you have to remember, our snitch just started telling us what's happening down there. We need more time, but time is what we don't have." Looking at the last Head Usher, Brother Cal, Ricky said to him, "Tell Don what you told me earlier."

"We're running out of water," Cal announced to the astonished looks from everybody except Ricky. "As you remember, our last desalination unit died a few weeks ago and I couldn't fix it. Even at less than one twentieth of passenger capacity, we still go through a hell of a lot of water. There's bottled water to drink, but when the Faithful find out that the tanks are empty and they can't shit, shower, or shave, we'll start to lose control over them. One of the main reasons most of them have followed us this long is because we've kept everything running."

"How long until were completely out?" Parsons asked.

"Three days at the most," Cal answered.

"Son of a bitch," Parsons exclaimed sharply. "Why didn't you tell us this earlier, Cal?"

Reverend Ricky cut in, "He told me when he first discovered the problem a few days ago. I saw there was nothing we could do about it, so I didn't see any need to pass the information along."

Parsons wondered what else Ricky was keeping to himself, like who his informant was, but dismissed the thought. Regardless of the situation with the water, their priority right now was still the same. They needed to get off this ship and get to safety. Thinking of the island they were trying to reach, he asked Seth, "Anything on the radio from Cozumel?"

"Nothing," he answered. "I'm picking up a signal out of Brownsville from a ham radio operator, and some distant military chatter that's probably from one of the military bases near Corpus Christi, but that's it. There could be a number of reasons we can't hear Cozumel though. Sunspots, distance or maybe their generator went out."

"If we hadn't gotten caught in the Gulf Stream, we'd be a hell of a lot closer to Cozumel than we are now," Brother

William pointed out. "At the rate we're going, we may have to try for Texas and take our chances going down the coast by land."

"And cross through five or six cities full of the dead?" Ricky asked. "No thanks. Everyone we've talked to on the radio since this shit started says that the stinkers are running around everywhere and eating up the living. People barricaded themselves inside because those things were roaming around every city and town across the country. We wouldn't make it two miles on land. Our only chance is to reach Cozumel by water."

"Maybe it's getting better," Brother William said. "We've had so little contact with anyone. Maybe the zombies ran out of food after they ate everyone. Maybe they died?"

"They can't die, William. They're already dead." Ricky pointed out as if explaining something to a child.

"Maybe they'll eat each other when they run out of food then," William proposed.

"That would be cannibalism," Seth pointed out.

"Isn't that what they're doing now?" William challenged, sounding like a five year old on a school play lot.

"Is not," Seth said.

"Is too."

Ricky shook his head sadly as he surmised that while both of them were loyal as dogs, they were so dumb their lips moved when they thought. Sometimes, when he'd been listening to them for too long, he got the feeling his IQ had dropped twenty points.

Ricky was about to break up the debate between his two Rhodes scholars when Don cut in and said sharply, "Enough about the dead. The ones we've had locked up in the cabin areas are still moving around and ready to take a bite out of your ass, so they're still out there in the cities too. We head to Cozumel like we planned. We only have a few days left, so we need to move our timetable up." Turning to Ricky, he said, "Our problem is that the newcomers need to be spread out so we can deal with them separately. Maybe what we need to do is give them more room."

"How so?" Ricky asked.

"We give them deck five. We pull the spotters back to six and let the newcomers move around. That might give us a chance to take them out. We'll just have to play it by ear and keep giving them enough rope to hang themselves. It should make them feel more comfortable, and maybe they'll split up and go off in different directions. Then we can isolate and kill them."

"What about having your snitch just cut the chain in the door and let the freaks loose?" William proposed.

"That's only going to be done as a last resort," Ricky said. "Don and I discussed it. We know there's a couple hundred stinkers locked in the cabin area on deck four, and that they could easily overwhelm and kill the people down there if we let them go, but then we'd have to deal with the dead to get to the weapons and the sailboat."

"So, do we let the three newcomers have the run of the ship tonight?" Brother Cal asked.

"I want no interference with any of them," Ricky ordered. "If we give them an inch, I hope they'll take a mile." Standing, he looked down onto deck twelve and saw that some of the Faithful had gathered for his evening sermon and their chance to ascend into heaven.

Dumbasses, he thought.

Turning back to his Head Ushers, he said, "After I finish with the magic show, I'm going to go down to deck four and tell Steve that he and his people should feel free to use the shops and restaurants on deck five. Then, we make a show of pulling the spotters out. I want them to see how trusting and generous we are."

With a big grin, Ricky added, "Maybe while I'm down there, I'll even get a chance to see Sheila again."

Chapter Eleven

The Dead Calm:

Tick-Tock pried the outer elevator doors apart and held them open, leaving the inner ones exposed for Brain to find and release the lever locking them in place. After a full minute of looking, he still couldn't spot the latch as he searched from top to bottom.

With an "Aha," Brain finally saw what he was looking for and reached forward to move a lever set flush with the inner panel. The doors parted with a soft click as both he and Tick-Tock jumped out of the line of fire. Steve was standing behind them with his rifle ready in case anything came out of the elevator. Just from the smell, or lack of it, they knew the car was clear of the dead, but they still they entered cautiously. On the Dead Calm, nothing could be taken for granted. After setting a chair under the maintenance hatch in the ceiling, Steve undid the fasteners that held it in place and eased it down to swing free on its hinges.

Tick-Tock looked at Brain and asked, "I need to know if your mind is a little preoccupied tonight, Pork Chop?"

With a cautious look on his face, he replied, "Why do you ask?"

"Because you spent all that time looking for the release catch for the elevator door and it was right in front of your eyes marked with the words, Emergency Release, Push Down."

Brain chuckled nervously and admitted, "I might have been thinking about Connie a little bit and my mind wandered."

"Put her out of your head," Steve ordered as he shined his flashlight through the access hatch into the darkened elevator shaft. "Keep focused, or you might end up dead. Or worse than that, undead."

"I can't help it, it's like she's invaded my brain," the tech said before asking, "Don't you ever think of Heather and get distracted?"

Looking down from his perch on top of the chair, Steve replied, "I think of her before I do something dangerous, but then I push her out of my head. If I'm thinking about Heather when I'm supposed to be concentrating on what I'm doing and get distracted and killed, it's no consolation to either of us that my last thoughts were of her. I'm still dead. If you keep thinking of Connie when you're supposed to be focusing on what you're doing, then that's how you'll end up, dead."

Brain nodded thoughtfully and replied, "Understood. My mind is now purged of Connie."

Laughing, Tick-Tock said, "You might want to do the same thing with Mary and Sheila. I've seen the way you've been looking at them."

"Steve already warned me about Mary," Brain replied. "But what's a lip-stick lesbian?"

Tick-Tock laughed again when Steve said, "You've lived a sheltered life, kid."

"A lip-stick lesbian is a lesbian who looks like a normal heterosexual woman," Tick-Tock explained. "You know, she dresses like one, does her hair nice and wears make up. She's not dyked out with a butch haircut or dresses like a guy."

Brain considered Mary's long blonde hair, feminine features and how she was attracted only to her own sex before nodded in understanding. Curious, he asked, "So what about Susan? She's like Mary, but she's with you, Tick-Tock."

"Susan's bi-sexual," Tick-Tock answered. "She goes both ways. Men and women."

"What about Sheila then?" Brain asked.

"She's try-sexual," Steve answered before pulling himself up onto the top of the elevator car. Sticking his head back into the opening, he added, "She'll try anything sexual."

Brain laughed, and in a mock serious tone Tick-Tock warned him, "You don't want to try tapping Sheila for a couple reasons, Pork Chop. One, is that Mary's on the trail of that and would cut your throat in your sleep, and two, is that you might come away with something incurable like gono-herpa-syphil-aids."

Brain chuckled, but from the look on his face, he seemed to take Tick-Tock's warning to heart.

Perched above them, Steve called down, "If we're done with tonight's lesson on alternative lifestyles, can we get going?"

Looking at Brain, Tick-Tock said, "Anything else you need to know, just ask me later."

After handing Steve's rifle up through the opening, Tick-Tock boosted himself on top of the elevator and reached down to give Brain a hand. Since the tech only had his holstered pistol, he waved him off and said, "I've got this," before jumping up and grabbing the lip of the opening and easily pulling himself up on top of the car.

"I've been working out," Brain explained once he'd settled himself with his legs dangling through the access hatch.

Giving him an appraising look, Tick-Tock said, "So I see."

Pointing to the rungs set in the metal side of the elevator shaft, Steve said, "Then you get to go first, Hercules."

Guided by a flashlight, Brain scaled the ladder until he was two floors above them. Tick-Tock and Steve waited while he listened, and sniffed, for the sound or smell of anyone or anything lurking outside the elevator doors. After a minute, he waved that it seemed clear. When the three men were stacked right below each other on the ladder, Brain stretched his arm out and undid the inside latch for the elevator doors on deck six. He eased the doors open to their stops and cautiously looked out into the short hall that ran in front of the elevators. After turning to give them a thumbs up, he motioned with his Colt .45 that he was going in. Swinging through the opening, he was quickly followed by Steve and Tick-Tock.

Brain crept to where the passageway T-boned into the main passageway running along the port side of the ship. Cautiously looking around the corner into the Centrum, he studied this area for any signs of life.

Or death.

Gone were the shops and restaurants of the lower decks. These were replaced with conference rooms for conventions, business service desks and small private rooms furnished with computers and office equipment so executives could use the facilities to keep track of their businesses while on vacation. Seeing the area was clear, Brain moved to the starboard side and repeated his performance, while Steve and Tick-Tock each covered an end of the hall from in front of the elevator. It had been agreed upon that Brain would lead them on the expedition into the upper decks since this was to give him more experience moving around in a hostile environment. It was a skill they all needed in the post-dead world.

After checking that the starboard side was clear, Brain led them in the opposite direction from the Centrum. Cautiously making his way down a short hall that dead-ended at a door marked Authorized Personnel Only, he stopped and took a quick look around before proceeding.

With Tick-Tock covering their rear, and Steve covering Brain, the tech tried the door in front of him only to find it locked. Extracting a large ring of keys that Tim had scrounged from somewhere, he tried the most likely ones first. On the fifth try, the lock turned. Steve shouldered his rifle as Brain eased down on the lever and opened the door, standing back while Steve searched the area beyond for anything living or dead.

Illuminated by emergency lights set twenty feet apart on alternate walls, Steve saw that the passageway stretched all the way to the stern of the ship. Besides the doors staggered every ten feet on both sides, he saw nothing that anyone or anything could hide in or behind. Waving Brain forward, he followed him through the opening. Seconds later, Tick-Tock backed into the passageway, closing the hatch behind them. Just in case they had to make a quick exit, he tested the door lever to make sure it would open without using the key. Turning to Brain and Steve, he nodded and looked down the passageway.

Since leaving the top of the elevator car, the men had moved in complete silence. Steve broke this by saying in a quiet voice, "Looks like you get to be Monty Hall, Brain."

"How's that?" He asked.

"You get to show us what's behind door number one," he replied.

"And door number two, three, four and five," Tick-Tock added. "We don't want to let anything come up behind us after we pass, so we need to check them all."

Brain took a deep breath and let it out before moving to the first door. Finding it locked, he went on to the next one. The undisturbed dust on the tile floor told them that no one had been this way in months, so they were more concerned with running into the dead than the living. They knew that Z's had a habit of milling around in one spot, and had difficulty opening locked doors, so they would only stop to check out the ones that were unlocked.

On his eighth try, Brain found one.

As the knob turned in his hand, Brain's eyes grew wide with surprise. Steve motioned him back against the far wall as he and Tick-Tock took up positions on either side of the door. Reaching forward, Steve turned the knob and gave it a slight push. As it opened to bang lightly against the inside wall, the three men saw the same thing through the entrance. A small room with two single beds, two dressers and another door set in the right side wall.

"Crew's quarters," Tick-Tock said in a low voice. Pointing to the door in the near wall, he added, "Gotta be a bathroom." Steve moved forward to check the area but Tick-Tock stopped him by saying, "I got this one."

Giving the beds a wide berth because they brought up childhood fears of the boogeyman reaching out from underneath and grabbing him, Tick-Tock checked the bathroom first and found it empty. After getting up his nerve, he used his rifle barrel to lift the blankets covering the beds so he could look under them. Relieved when he found no boogey men, he exited the room.

Steve looked at his watch and then at the remaining doors. Realizing that if even one in ten was open that it would take all night to clear the rooms, not to mention the exposure to possible attack in searching each one, he knew they needed to come up with a quicker way to by-pass this area.

Pulling the deck layout from his pocket, he saw the area where he was standing was grayed out except for the hallways crossing it. Knowing that these diagrams were for the passengers use, it made sense that they weren't going to show the crew's quarters and mechanical sections.

"We've got to figure out a way to secure these doors or we'll be here forever," Steve voiced his concern.

"We could use the keys," Brain proposed.

Tick-Tock and Steve both looked at him questioningly so Brain produced a second set of keys that Tim had given him. "These are the masters for deck six," he said.

"Masters?" Steve asked, "I thought you only had keys for the locks on the main doors. Don't you think you could have let us know that you had the masters a little sooner?"

Brain shrugged and replied, "You didn't ask."

Steve realized that he should have thought of asking about the keys, but this still didn't stop him from saying, "Okay then, you're back on point. Lock all the doors you find open."

Now moving at a much more rapid pace, they covered half the distance to the stern in minutes.

Stopping when they reached a passageway that dead-ended into theirs from the right, Tick-Tock pointed to footprints in the dust that went back and forth from that hallway into the one they were using.

Steve nodded and said, "Keep a close eye on our backs, Tick-Tock."

Now, with the additional threat of running into the living as well as the dead, the three men proceeded at a slightly slower pace. As they continued down the hall, they noticed that the doors in this section were spaced more widely apart and were labeled with their contents or function. Steve breathed a sigh of relief that they were finally out of the crew area and into the mechanical section.

Nearing the end of the passage, Brain suddenly called out, "I found it," as he stood and pointed at a steel door surrounded by a heavy jamb that protruded an inch past the wall.

Tick-Tock inspected the hatch, which to him looked like it would be more at home on a nuclear submarine, and said, "If we open this and Captain Nemo comes out, I'm gonna cap his ass."

"If anything comes out I want you to cap its ass," Steve advised.

Seeing that the footprints in the dust ended at the hatch, Brain was sure he had found the switching room. With a simple sign over the door reading Electrical D214, and with all the traffic in and out, it had to be the control room where power from the generators could be shunted to different parts of the ship.

Six large, round, locking bolts activated by hand levers were spaced equally around the hatch, of which five were unsecured. After glancing at Steve, who nodded at him to go ahead, Brain twisted the last one and pulled on it before jumping out of the line of fire.

Cool air wafted out from the opening. Steve was happy to see that the room was deserted and surprised that it was just a twelve by twelve room with three computer work stations lined up on the far wall. He had expected something larger and more complex since the area dealt with controlling the emergency power on the Dead Calm. Shrugging it off, he realized that with everything being computerized now, it was a wonder the entire ship wasn't controlled from a laptop.

"A/C is on," Tick-Tock noted.

Brain pointed to the computers and said, "They need it. It's shut down everywhere else on the ship except for areas like this."

Even though the Dead Calm's main air conditioning system was off, the ship didn't to heat up to the point of being uncomfortable because the weather was mild. Despite this, the men found it refreshing to feel the cool air blowing on them.

Brain entered the room and made for the center computer. After moving the mouse around, the screen saver depicting the logo for the Cayman Cruise Lines dissolved to reveal a standard windows desktop. Sitting in the chair in front of this screen, he indicated the empty chairs on either side of him and said, "It'll take a few minutes while I find my way around the system so you might as well get comfortable."

Pointing to the computer on the right, Tick-Tock asked, "Think this thing has Spider Solitaire?"

Already lost in his own world, Brain didn't answer, so Tick-Tuck clicked the start button and was pleased to find it did.

Forty minutes later, Brain leaned back in his chair and said, "That's it. I rerouted power from the disco on deck ten down to the water craft storage area on deck four."

"Good choice," Tick-Tock said. "Disco sucks."

"Well, my reasoning is a little deeper than that," Brain explained. "I didn't want to cut power to anything vital that Ricky's people might use on a regular basis. If something they're using goes out, they'll suspect we've been here and they'll just come down and switch it back and cut us off."

"To be on the safe side, we'll fill the gas caddies as soon as we get back," Steve said. "We can use them to top off The Usual Suspects and then refill them so we can store them on board."

Making sure they left everything as they found it, the trio started down the passageway until they came to where it branched off to the port side of the ship. Steve suggested they go out a different way in case someone had seen them come in and was waiting in ambush. Brain made the turn with the others following a few steps behind. They had only gone a dozen yard in this new direction when a clanking noise from their rear made them spin around and raise their weapons as they searched for a threat. Although the ship made all kinds of creaks and groans, this sound was one they hadn't heard before. It sounded like something had fallen or been dropped on the deck.

Motioning for Brain to stay where he was, Steve signaled Tick-Tock that they go back and investigate. Brain watched as Tick-Tock dropped into a half crouch and cautiously made his way down the passageway with Steve following a few feet behind.

Watching his friends' progress down the hall, Brain was suddenly distracted when he heard a familiar sound coming from the other side of the door he was standing in front of. Curious and excited at what he thought he'd heard, he forgot all about covering his friends as he stepped closer to the hatch and listened.

The mewing noise came again, and Brain was sure of it. On the other side of the door was a cat. Remembering how Connie had told him she loved cats, he decided this could be his chance to make major points with the girl of his dreams by bringing her a furry little companion.

Turning his attention back to the end of the hall, he saw Tick-Tock cautiously look both ways down the passage they had just come from. Shrugging, he turned to Steve and said, "Nothing there."

Brain heard the mewing noise from beyond the door again, excitement coursing through him at his find.

YES, he thought to himself. Connie's going to love me when I give her a cat. With his eyes on Tick-Tock and Steve, he reached out with his right hand and grasped the doorknob. As he turned it, he called out, "Hey guys, I think someone locked a cat in here. Help me catch him for Connie."

Tick-Tock looked beyond Steve and saw what the tech was about to do. At the top of his voice he screamed, "No Brain!"

But it was too late. The door swung open...

And the dead thing standing there made a mewing noise as it lurched forward with outstretched arms.

\*\*\*

Heather tried not to show her nervousness as Reverend Ricky made his way down the stairs. Still twenty feet from where she stood, she called out, "That's far enough. Hold it right there."

Smiling as he held his hands out to show he was unarmed, Ricky said, "No need to fear me Sister Heather, I come in peace."

Since Steve, Tick-Tock and Brain were out exploring, it left only Susan and herself to hold down the fort. With their diminished firepower, Heather wanted to get rid of Ricky as fast as possible. Although Susan had a rifle, of the rest of the group, only Sheila had ever handled a firearm. Steve didn't want anyone who was unfamiliar with a weapon, or in Sheila's case, couldn't be trusted with one yet, walking around armed. If Ricky found out that the group was split up and under gunned, he might try something.

Wanting to put Ricky off by being rude, Heather asked bluntly, "What the fuck do you want?"

"I've come to talk to you and Brother Steve," Ricky said.

"Steve's asleep," Heather replied. "Tell me what you want and I'll tell him when he wakes up."

Ricky smiled at the woman's lie, knowing from his informant that Steve and two others named Randy and Tick-Tock had left on their little tour an hour and a half earlier. He was tempted to call Heather's bluff by insisting he talk to Steve, but restrained himself. The urge to feel superior pushed back up, and he was almost overwhelmed by the wild urge to blurt out, 'I know where they are' and then tell her, so he could show how smart he was. Pushing these feelings down again by reassuring himself that the people from the sailboat would soon realize how much more intelligent he was than them as they lay dying, choking on their own blood, he turned his attention back to the task at hand. Giving Heather an appraising eye, he decided that while she wasn't bad looking, she was too old for him. Considering how things might play out, he decided that if she was taken alive, he would give the little blonde to his Head Ushers to use before having her thrown into the Sound's Lounge.

Alive of course.

With that settled, Ricky turned to business by saying, "I've got good news for you, Sister Heather. If you'll look up to deck five, you'll see that the three people I've got watching you are packing up and moving out."

Not wanting to turn her back on Ricky to confirm this, she replied, "So what?"

Ricky's smile faltered for a second at the woman's insolent tone, and he wondered if it was possible to have her raped by one of the dead.

Why not, he thought. I've had a few of the woman.

Deciding it was something to look into, he said, "It's a sign of my trust by pulling those people back. At first I didn't know if you meant us any ill will, but now that I've seen you're not a threat, I've decided to let you have the run of restaurant row."

Instead of saying thank you, Heather gave a curt nod and asked, "Is that all?"

Ricky had planned on spending some time giving this woman the details of how the power had been kept on for the coolers in the restaurants on deck five, and how they should feel free to explore the rest of the ship at their leisure, but he was stopped in his tracks by the woman's insolent replies. Feeling increasingly uneasy at the blank stare he received from her, he instead gave Heather the abbreviated version of his speech before bidding her good evening and making his way up the stairs.

Heather risked a quick glance over her shoulder, and saw two men and a woman making their way along deck five to join Ricky at the top of the staircase. After losing sight of them as they ascended onto deck six, she breathed a sigh of relief.

\*\*\*

"Get him off me," Brain screamed weakly from flat on his back.

When the Zombie had appeared in the doorway and reached for him, he had reacted like a civilian as opposed to a hunter. Dropping his pistol, he reached forward and grabbed the dead man's outstretched hands with his own, and while he may have been working out, he was no match for the strength born of the need to feed on human flesh that the dead possessed. Pushing forward as it lunged toward him, the zombie stepped on Brain's right foot, tripping him and causing him to fall backwards.

Thinking that if he could get his foot into the zombie's chest that he could flip it over him, Brain tried to raise his leg. He moved fast, but not fast enough, only putting his knee into the zombie's solar plexus as they both went down onto the deck. Holding tightly onto the creature's wrists and bracing his knee as he fell, Brain felt the wind knocked out of him as he landed hard on the tile. In a small voice, he called out for someone to get the dead thing off, feeling the strength flow out of his body along with the last of his breath. Every muscle in his body went weak. His knee slipped from its position down to the dead man's stomach. Now with nothing to hold the dead thing back, Brain knew it would be over in seconds. The thing would lunge forward and bite him. Not wanting to see it coming, he screwed his eyes shut.

Expecting to feel a wet gnashing mouth on his cheek or neck, Brain felt nothing. Thinking he was in shock and that his body wasn't registering the pain, he hoped it didn't register the feeling of the bullet that either Steve or Tick-Tock would fire into his head now that he was infected. As if from a distance, he heard a voice saying his name, and wondered if it was Jesus calling him home.

His mind cleared when he realized it wasn't Jesus calling him, but Tick-Tock. Opening one eye, he saw his role model straddling the zombie from behind. Tick-Tock had one hand dug into the dead things hair and the other grasping the collar of its shirt to keep it from rearing back at him or lunging forward. Steve stood to the left with his rifle aimed at the abomination's head.

Tick-Tock saw that Brain had opened one eye, so he changed from calling his name to saying calmly but firmly, "You've got to let go, Brain. I can't pull him off you because you've still got hold of his hands."

Opening his other eye, Brain glanced down to see that he still had a death grip on both of the zombie's wrists. Revulsion at what he was touching shot through him as he felt the leathery skin and the dead thing's wrist bones grinding as they worked back and forth under this grip. Forcing down the bile that rose in his throat at the smell of the zombie, he croaked out, "Tell me when."

As if in answer, the dead thing made a mewing noise. When it did, Brain saw that part of its throat that had been ripped away, causing it to sound like a cat.

I'm such a dumbass, he thought.

"On three, let go and roll to your right." Tick-Tock said in a calm voice and then started counting, "One, two, three, NOW."

Brain let go and rolled.

Tick-Tock braced himself with his feet and lifted the zombie up while pivoting his body. Using his momentum and the weight of the dead thing, he spun it around and half threw it back through the door it had come out of.

Seeing that their plan had worked, Steve moved forward and sighted in. Before the zombie could regain its feet, he shot it once through the forehead. Ready to fire again, he saw that neither the south, nor the Z, was ever going to rise again.

Steve spun around and saw that Brain had made it onto his hands and knees and was vomiting onto the floor. Tick-Tock leaned against the wall with his rifle at the ready for any other threats. Once he saw that the danger was over, he his second in command slid down to sit on the floor and laid his M-4 across his knees.

Brain had recovered enough to sputter out, "Fuck me running."

Tick-Tock snorted and replied, "Fuck me running doesn't even begin to cover that."

Chapter Twelve

Woman's Lake, Minnesota:

The bonfire in front of the lodge melted the snow around it in a wide circle. Clustered on the half frozen ground was an assorted collection of slat, camp and folding lawn chairs that were as varied as the people occupying them. Some were refugees who fled from the HWNW virus when it swept through the big cities, but most were residents of the nearby small town of Woman's Lake. Even before the call for tonight's emergency meeting, they came out most evenings to enjoy the company of Carl Hibbing, owner of the lodge and the cabins that surrounded it. Having lived his entire life in the small town, Carl was well known to its inhabitants as were his father and grandfather. For three generations, one Hibbing or another had served as mayor to Woman's Lake, which, after the last census, could brag a full-time population of six hundred seventy-nine.

Scattered among the townies around the fire were a dozen summer residents who owned cabins near the lodge. Among them were also a few refugees who had moved into some of the unused fishing camps scattered around the lake. They had shown up in October and November after being forced from their homes in the cities, but before the town quarantined itself to outsiders.

These refugees were at first met with the inherent friendliness that the people of northern Minnesota were known for, but soon distrust built up in the locals and they kept their distance. This suspicions and exclusion came about as the newcomers told horrendous stories about bodies infected with the HWNW virus being burned by the thousands in the streets of Minneapolis, Fargo and Duluth, and of armed National Guardsmen shooting down anyone acting strange or aggressive.

The most horrendous story they told though, was that people were dying and coming back to life to feed on the living.

The citizens of Woman's Lake watched the news, and although it was reported that some isolated incidents of death had occurred as a result of the spreading virus, they had been reassured that the government had the situation under control. Since this didn't jibe with what was being related to them by the refugees; there was just no way that their story could be true. Thus, the people of Woman's Lake discarded what they considered tall tales, and a schism was created between the townies and the refugees.

This changed however, when the first case of HWNW cropped up in a local man named Otis Trevor who had recently returned from a trip to the State Capitol. On a sales trip to sell his homemade fishing lures in the big city, Otis had been bitten and infected after propositioning the wrong prostitute. The people of Woman's Lake quickly became believers after Otis had to be beaten down and killed by a frying pan wielding cook at Gram's Diner. This was after he entered and attacked a waitress and one of the patrons during the lunchtime rush, tearing bloody chucks of skin and muscle off and swallowing them. The incident was witnessed by thirty of the townsfolk, so there could no longer be any denying that the disease was just as the refugees claimed.

Further proof came about when the Constable tried to contact Otis' wife to tell her about the unfortunate incident. Failing to reach Linda on the phone, Constable Nielsen went out to the Trevor residence on the edge of town. Here, he found the entire family butchered and torn apart as if by a pack of wolves. The Constable also found Sally Trevor, the youngest in the family, feeding on her mother's dead body.

That evening, the town council convened the first of many emergency meetings. With hat in hand, they asked some of the refugees to come and relate what they had witnessed before they fled the cities.

Word about the attack and the meeting spread quickly, and the number of people showing up at the town hall got to be so great that it had to be moved to the High School gym. Despite this, it was standing room only an hour before the meeting was to begin.

By the time the first three people were finished telling their tale of people killing and eating each other in Minneapolis, you could have heard the proverbial pin drop in the gymnasium. There were still a few doubters in the crowd, but a majority believed the city folks. Carl Hibbing took the microphone and asked that no decisions be made on how to proceed with the defense of the town against the HWNW virus. He called for the council to table any motions they were considering until they had a chance to look more deeply into the crisis. As a situation like this was beyond the scope or imagination of any of the board members, this was seconded and approved to give everyone time to grasp the reality of the dead coming back to life.

The meeting was then adjourned.

As people filtered out of the gym and into the parking lot, a few naysayers who had kept silent during the meeting decided to voice their point of view about how civilization couldn't be breaking down because everything was still working. One man orated for a full ten minutes on how America was too strong to be pulled down. At the end of his speech, as if in a dissention to his view, the power went out all through town.

A second emergency meeting was immediately called for right there in the parking lot. This time, there would be no waiting and no tabling of motions. Something needed to be done tonight. Cars were pulled into a circle facing inward and headlights were turned on so the council could immediately reconvene. Emergency measures such as rationing the available supplies in town were passed, and an immediate quarantine was voted on and unanimously approved. To add to their small force, twenty-six new officers were deputized to support the village constable in enforcing the quarantine.

The following morning, after guards were posted at the grocery store, the quarantine was implemented. Two groups of the newly sworn-in deputies went three miles past the outskirts of Woman's Lake in opposite directions along the only road through town. Here, they found the biggest trees they could and dropped them across the roadway, effectively isolating the town. Hiking trails were also similarly blocked, and armed men in boats patrolled the lakeshore to make sure no one tried to get into what was now a Dead Free Zone. Two person teams were assigned to each of the roadblocks created by the fallen trees, and anyone driving or walking up to the blockades was approached by one of the men on guard duty. Unless you were from the town or could prove you owned one of the cabins that dotted the area, you were asked politely to turn around and go back the way you had come. Most did, but a few of the more hard headed cases tried to bull their way past the sentries.

These gate crashers never knew what hit them when the second guard shot them with a scope equipped deer rifle from a concealed position. Most of the citizens of Woman's Lake had grown up hunting deer, bear and moose in order to eat, so a one hundred foot shot into the center of the chest of someone trying to run their blockade was nothing compared to some of the shots they had made to put meat on the table. Either way, it came down to the same thing. Survival.

Although the traffic at the roadblocks was sparse, at least once a day, someone approached and was either allowed to pass if they belonged, turned around if they didn't, or shot if they tried to break through. This continued until the first heavy snow fall. With the throughways soon blocked by twelve inches of unplowed powder, no one tried to brave the road or trails that led to Woman's Lake.

Already a close-knit community, once further isolated from the rest of the world, the citizens and refugees turned to their fellow man, going out of their way to help each other survive. Food was shared with the needy, and those with the know-how taught others who didn't know how to hunt and fish. Luckily, with the outbreak of HWNW coming in the fall, the residents of Woman's Lake had already filled their heating oil tanks, so freezing to death wasn't an immediate threat. Most houses had a fireplace, and for those that didn't, they were put up at the High School until the weather warmed and an alternate heating source could be built for their home. A feeling of self-sufficiency prevailed, and already, spring gardens were planned. The citizens of Woman's Lake were survivors.

At the bonfire this night though, those good vibrations were missing.

Earlier that day, a man by the name of Derrick Olsen, whose ex-wife lived across the lake in a neighboring town, had gone to visit her and drop off some venison. As Derrick approached the town of Hanson, after driving his snowmobile eleven miles across the frozen lake, he noticed what seemed to be all the citizens of this small village roaming around on the streets. At first, he wondered if they were having some type of winter carnival, but on closer inspection, he saw large mobs circled around some of the houses and shops that lined Main Street. Feeling that something wasn't quite right, he stopped a quarter mile from shore and pulled out his rifle. Using its scope, it took him only seconds to confirm his sense of dread.

The HWNW virus had arrived at Woman's Lake.

Oblivious to the cold, Derrick watched as the dead staggered through the thoroughfares of Hanson in a variety of dress and undress. He was amazed to see one man, naked except for a pair of brown socks on which the feet had worn away leaving nothing but the tops wrapped around his ankles, wade unflinchingly through a waist high snow drift before finding a section of walkway that someone had shoveled. Continuing on in the ten degree below temperature as if taking a slightly unsteady stroll across a nude beach on a Caribbean Island, the zombie staggered along until it joined a group of the dead banging on the doors and windows of a small house.

Switching his view, Derrick saw there was a large crowd of the dead clustered around the brick building that served as the town's City Hall. He started searching their faces, or what was left of their faces, for anyone he knew. In reality, he was hoping desperately he wouldn't see one face in particular. That of his is ex-wife.

Relieved when he didn't find her in the grotesque group, Derrick suddenly realized as he scanned the faces that he could only recognize one in twenty of the nightmares lurching through town. Looking closer at the clothing of the zombies, he saw that some were wearing ragged suits and ties, while others wore light casual dress that you'd be more likely to see if you worked in an office. This was when he noticed something else. It was the number of people on the streets of Hanson. Although the population of the tiny burg was just over three hundred, there appeared to be twice that many figures wandering around the main drag with more showing up from side streets every minute. Quickly, he came to the conclusion that these weren't the citizens of Hanson.

Although Derrick did spot a few distorted faces he recognized, these were few and far between. It seemed like the dead had come from somewhere else. How they ended up out here in what was almost the middle of nowhere, he couldn't even begin to fathom.

Slightly elated that he hadn't seen his former wife among the dead besieging the town, he turned to look further down the shore where she had her trailer at the end of Main Street. Zooming in with the scope, his elation turned to dismay when he saw that the front door of her doublewide had been torn free and now hung crookedly by a single hinge.

Although they had parted on bad terms, in the four years since the divorce, he and Mary had actually grown closer than they ever had been as husband and wife. Almost certain that his former spouse was dead due to the trashed door, a flicker of hope sparked the idea that maybe she had seen the zombies coming and had taken shelter in one of the sturdier buildings in town. If that were the case, he would do whatever was in his power to save her.

Realizing that he couldn't do anything on his own, he pushed aside his emotions and prepared to focus on another section of town so he could describe everything he saw to the Constable and his men. He knew that once he reported the sacking of Hanson, the people of Woman's lake would band together to help their neighbors. Within hours, they would put together a team to try and rescue anyone holed up in any of the buildings. Derrick knew he would have to lead the group back here in order to find Mary, but to do this, he needed to gather all the information he could so they weren't going in blind.

Giving one last, longing look at his ex-wife's trailer before focusing elsewhere, Derrick's heart suddenly leapt with joy when he saw a figure wearing a yellow dress enter the doorway. Remembering with rising excitement that Mary loved this color, he zoomed in on the familiar shape as it exited the trailer and moved into the light.

She's alive, he thought gleefully.

Looking intently as he adjusted the focus on his scope, Derrick's hopes were shattered when he saw that while he was correct in that it was Mary, she wasn't alive.

With fluttering hands, the thing that Derrick had once shared a bed with felt its way to the rail next to the stairs and descended to the walkway. He noticed with sadness that it was the walkway he had cleared of snow on his last visit. Blind, fish white eyes set in a shattered half eaten face stared blindly out at the world as the thing turned its head back and forth as if looking for something it would never see. Dried blood spotted the yellow of the dress and disheveled blonde hair that he instantly recognized as Mary's.

Lowering the rifle, Derrick wept openly at his loss. In his grief, his mind alternately raced with thoughts and then stopped dead and went blank. After fifteen minutes of this, his sorrow lessened enough that he could think clearly again.

He knew what he had to do.

Raising his rifle, he sighted in on the side of the blonde head as his finger moved to the trigger. Hesitating, as he thought back on all the good times they had shared, he steeled his resolve by rationalizing that he wasn't killing someone he loved. He was shooting a blind, wounded animal that needed to be put down.

As Derrick took up the slack on the trigger, the zombie turned as if it sensed his presence. It seemed to stare directly through the scope at him with sightless eyes.

The rifle jumped in Derrick's hands.

A second later, a quarter mile away, the blonde head exploded in a spray of black pus.

The emotional pain gripped Derrick again, so he set the rifle down across his thighs and lowered his head. Tears streamed from his eyes to freeze on his face in the below zero temperature. After allowing himself to grieve a few minutes, he once again raised his rifle to check out the town. The more information he could gather, the better they could prepare for what he hoped would be a slaughter of the dead.

Shouldering his rifle and looking through the scope, the first thing he saw sent fear shooting through his body. His shot had alerted the dead and they had zeroed in on his location. Hundreds of them were staggering and sliding across the ice in his direction.

Not that I'm too hard to miss, he thought sardonically. I'm on a black snowmobile, wearing a bright red snowsuit, sitting on a field of white.

Putting the rifle back in its case, Derrick thumbed the throttle on the snowmobile and turned it in a narrow arc before gunning the engine. As he started the trip back to Woman's Lake, he realized that he was moving into a strong wind.

That's why we didn't hear any shots or noise when Hanson got overrun, he thought sadly. The whole town had been wiped out, and no one knew it was happening because the wind was blowing in the wrong direction.

Returning to Woman's Lake shortly before sunset, Derrick went immediately to the Constable's office and reported what he had seen to the deputy on duty. The Deputy used the shortwave radio to call Carl Hibbing and inform him of this new development. Carl ordered him to send Derrick over to his place immediately and to call or send messages to the rest of the town council that they were to meet at the lodge in one hour. He also told the deputy not to let anyone know about this recent development since he didn't want to start a panic.

But secrets are hard to keep in a small town.

With so many people showing up after hearing about the meeting through the grapevine, an hour after sunset, Carl decided it would be too crowded to gather in the main room of the lodge and suggested they move it outside. Besides the ten men and women on the town council, over sixty others had shown up when they heard of the disaster that had befallen Hanson. More wood was added to what was already set in the fire pit, and soon a good-sized blaze was going.

Once everyone was settled, Carl had Derrick stand in front of the fire and relate what he had seen. Embarrassed at being the center of attention, Derrick lowered his head and, leaving out the part about his ex-wife since that was no one's business but his own, related how it appeared that the town had been overrun by what looked like a thousand dead with few survivors. Finishing his story about how he went three miles out of his way so that the dead couldn't follow him back to Woman's Lake, he expected to be overwhelmed with questions when he was done. Instead, he was surprised to hear only the crackling of the fire behind him. Looking up in curiosity as to why everyone was so quiet, all he could see were shocked faces staring back at him. The crowd was speechless. At first he didn't understand, but then it dawned on him. The people of Woman's Lake had been insulated for so long that it was hard for them to comprehend that the HWNW virus, and the dead, were only a few miles away and would be soon heading in their direction.

Finally a woman spoke up, breaking the silence as she said, "My sister lives in Hanson, and a lot of you have friends and relatives there. We have to organize a rescue party. Even if there's only one person left alive, we have to try and save them. People might be dying as we sit here."

This statement was met by others agreeing that this was what they needed to do. Immediate action was called for. When the initial clamor died down, Carl Hibbing stood and raised his hand for silence. He reminded those gathered that Derrick had seen thousands of the dead in Hanson and that it would be foolish to go off half-cocked in the dark with only a small number of men and women. He suggested they get better organized and set out at first light when there would be more volunteers and the rescue party could see better. It would also cut down on the risk of them shooting each other or any of the survivors by accident.

While many calls of, "Strike while the iron's hot," and "People might not make it until the morning," rang out, the wisdom of Carl's suggestion prevailed. Soon, those gathered around the fire settled back into their chairs or roved around to talk about the hell they would send the dead back to in the morning. Small groups formed and broke up to reform as plans were laid, and a few bottles were passed around to lubricate the thought process.

The moon rose, reflecting its light against the snow and ice on the lake and causing it to glow a bluish-magenta that created a surreal landscape. Covering hundreds of square miles, Woman's Lake was one of the bigger bodies of water in the area and it was easy to get lost on it in the winter, or the summer, unless you had a landmark to navigate by. Before Dead Day, finding your way had been fairly easy since the lights of the resorts and small towns dotting its shores each had their own characteristics. Now, with the power out, the dark mass of the trees surrounding the water made finding any single point of reference difficult if not impossible.

This being the case, the hundreds of dead who tried to follow Derrick Olson across the ice might have wandered around all night until they were spotted the following day when the rescue party came across them on their way to Hanson. With the dead scattered all over the ice, it would have been like shooting fish in a barrel.

Except for three things.

The first was the bonfire in front of the Hibbing Lodge. Seen for miles across the ice, it acted like a beacon in the night for the dead to follow.

The second was the wind. Even though some smells are frozen out in cold weather, the overwhelming stench of the dead would have given those at the Hibbing Lodge some sign of their imminent appearance. Since the wind was still blowing from the shore out over the frozen lake though, the musky rancid odor of the zombies was picked up and sent in the wrong direction.

And third was the lack of warning. Since the first snowfall and freeze, the populace of Woman's Lake had received no visitors except a few people from neighboring towns that stopped by to barter. Thinking they were safe, the citizens voted to temporarily discontinue the roadblocks, and halted the patrols along the lake's shore until the snow melted and the ice broke up. With no sentries to raise the warning, and being deep in discussion about the rescue mission to Hanson the next morning, no one around the bonfire saw the dead until they were among them.

Pandemonium broke out as dark loping shapes appeared in the flickering firelight to grab at people and drag them screaming to the ground. A few men and women managed to raise their weapons and fire off a quick shot or two before being pulled down by six, seven, or even eight of the zombies that flooded off the frozen lake. But, even if more people had managed to open fire, it would have been useless as there were too many dead and they had gotten too close.

In minutes, the killing was over. Leaving only the feeding. The dead tore at the clothes of their victims to get to the still warm meat underneath. They had been roaming the frozen north for months now in search of food and had learned that if they didn't eat quickly, the meat would freeze.

The dead who hadn't been quick enough to grab food stumbled past their bloody brethren and followed the very visible trail used by snowmobiles to get back and forth between the town and the Hibbing Lodge. Within an hour, they had spread out and started smashing their way into homes, pulling the residents down in flurry of screams, teeth and fingernails.

By the time the sun rose, the town of Woman's Lake, Minnesota had been almost wiped out. A few human holdouts that living in sturdy dwellings, or those who barricaded their homes against a possible invasion of the dead, looked out through peepholes at the devastation wrought on their community. Although some of dead remained to try to get into these few remaining outposts of humanity, a majority of the zombies had moved on once the food that could be easily accessed was depleted. One of the few learned behaviors in the dead was that it was futile to try and bust into these strongholds unless they had an overwhelming number. Instead, they found that if they went in search of food, they might come across something easier to get.

Thus, the majority moved on.

Many small groups, banding together over the past months, had formed the horde of living dead that assaulted Woman's Lake. Coming from as far away as Duluth to the north and Des Moines to the south, their number fluctuated between seven and twelve hundred. Although some of the dead didn't stay with the mob and stopped to outwait their food when it was barricaded inside a structure, the main mass found and absorbed into its group many new smaller packs of zombies. This kept their numbers high.

All throughout the country, this scene was repeated as the dead used up their food sources in the cities and towns and went in search of more. In California, one group numbered over thirty thousand walking dead that moved like an army of ants as they devoured any living flesh they came across. Where in the beginning, the zombies preferred to eat human flesh, now nothing was safe as dogs, cats, birds and livestock were fair game. If it weren't for a biological barrier that prevented the disease from jumping to animals, the infected beasts would have soon overrun the Earth.

Early on in the war against the dead, when a large group of zombies had been spotted and their location pinpointed by the military, helicopter gunships were sent in to deal with them. As parts and fuel became scarcer, the number of air missions against the zombies dropped dramatically until they were almost non-existent. Now, it was left to the ground troops in the immediate area to deal with the problem.

Search and destroy missions quickly declined and soon became of secondary importance as the local military unit's numbers were depleted when men were taken from them and assigned to units tasked with driving the dead out of the cities. With multiple buildings, and miles of underground sewers and drainage tunnels to hide in, this had become a deadly game of cat and mouse. The kill ratio stood at one dead soldier for every two destroyed zombies. In most rural areas, the troops garrisoned there were doing their best to just hold onto the ground they had taken in the initial push that had been ordered weeks earlier by the Joint Chiefs.

Although they didn't know about these events, the dead now moving through the snowdrifts piled on the road leading out of town could sense it.

They had an almost uncontested free reign of the countryside.

Chapter Thirteen

The Dead Calm:

Having recovered from his fight with the zombie, Brain slowly got to his feet and started checking himself to make sure he hadn't been bitten. Stripping off his shirt, he turned his back toward Tick-Tock so his friend could make sure the dead thing's fingernails hadn't scratched him.

"You got a gouge on your side, but it doesn't look like it came from the Z, Tick-Tock observed. Looking closer he said, "It's a pretty good scrape, but it's stopped bleeding. You must've landed on your pistol after you dropped it." Straightening up, he added with derision, "And by the way, the next time a Z comes at you, just shoot the son-of-a-bitch and don't try and wrestle his ass."

Brain looked apologetic as he put his shirt back on. "I forgot I had the gun in my hand. That thing was so close that all I could think of was trying to keep its hands and teeth away from me." After a moment's thought, he asked, "Why didn't you shoot it when it was on top of me?"'

Tick-Tock pointed to Steve, "I was going to but he stopped me."

"You would have gotten sprayed by that black shit those things have for blood," Steve explained. "It would have gone in your mouth and eyes and up your nose. Then we would have had to shoot you."

Brain shivered as he remembered lying helpless beneath the zombie, knowing what would happen to him if he got infected, and wondering if he would feel it when the bullet fired into it cleaved his head. Instead, Steve had saved his life by not firing. His mouth dry, Brain croaked out a thank you. Swallowing hard, he asked Tick-Took, "How did you know it wasn't a cat behind that door?"

"Without food or water, it would have died months ago. Anytime you hear anything moving around in a room on this ship and you can't figure out what it is, it's bound to be something dead moving around."

Brain lowered his head at his near fatal mistake and said, "I wasn't thinking."

"Oh, you were thinking all right," Steve said harshly.

When Brain gave him a questioning look, he added, "You were thinking about Connie." He then gave Brain a none too gentle cuff on the back of his head as he growled, "What did I tell you about that shit?"

"You need to keep your head and your ass wired together if we're gonna do this," Tick-Tock warned Brain.

"Or I'll send your ass back downstairs and Tick-Tock and I will finish up," Steve tacked on.

This threat got Brain's undivided attention. In fact, it frightened him more than if he had to face a legion of the dead armed with only a feather duster. All his life, he'd been an outcast. Even though he knew that much of it was brought on by the condescending way that he treated people, he didn't feel like it was his fault. People were just idiots. They always started it, making him feel alienated. Since attending elementary school, he wanted to fit in, but just didn't know how or wasn't allowed to since he was overweight and not very athletic. After being excluded for so many years, he found it was easier to treat others with contempt and be a loner. He claimed he didn't need others in his life, but it was a lonely world he'd created.

When the dead started coming to life, and Steve told him he could lock down inside the bank building with him and some other people - actually after Brain begged to be let in to escape the coming onslaught of the living dead - the main condition was that he quit being such a pompous ass and get along with everyone. Despite his initial reaction that it wasn't his fault and that it was other people constantly trying to put him down that caused him to look at them with contempt, he agreed. This capitulation was brought about by the fact that the thought of being killed and eaten by the dead appealed to him less than getting along with people.

Barely.

Despite his promise, at first he was hesitant since he didn't want to have to kiss up to a bunch of people he knew were going to treat him like shit on their shoe. The alternative was certain death, so he went along despite his reservations. It wasn't easy, since most of the people seeking shelter in the radio station knew him and didn't believe he was actually going to change, but he stuck with his end of the deal. He worked hard at his social skills, cleaned himself up and in just a short time was amazed that he was accepted for who he was. For the first time in his life, he felt like he belonged. He even felt like he had become friends with Tick-Tock, a man who he actually despised when they had worked together at the radio station before Dead Day. After that, Brain decided he never wanted to go back to being the person he had been. It was too lonely.

With the threat of being sent below hanging over him and fearing that this would be the first step back into exile, Brain almost pleaded when he said, "No, no, I promise I'll pay attention. I won't think of Connie and I'll do exactly what you say." Seeing Steve hesitate, he added, "Please. I promise."

With a doubtful expression, Steve seemed to think about it for a few seconds before reluctantly saying, "Okay, start checking doors."

Not believing he was being given a second chance so easily, and sure that he was going to be sent back downstairs, Brain could only stare dumbly at him. Not trusting what he thought he had heard, he shook his head and said, "What?"

"The - doors - Brain - start - checking - them," Steve enunciated each word.

Snapping out of his trance, Brain pulled his pistol out of its holster and picked up the ring of keys from where he had dropped them on the floor. Cautious of his newly returned status, he asked tentatively, "You guys ready?" Receiving a curt nod in return from Steve, he turned and started off.

He came across another unlocked door a short distance down the hall. Exaggerating his movements to show that he was paying attention to what he was doing, he secured it.

Finished, he turned to his two solemn faced friends with a raised eyebrow. Steve motioned with his rifle to move on and Tick-Tock nodded. Relieved he had received at least that much recognition, he turned and continued down the passageway.

He'd only taken a few steps though, when he swore that he heard both Steve and Tick-Tock making purring noises. Thinking all was forgiven, he turned around to smile at them but was met with hard stares. Without a word, Steve gave him a stern look and motioned for him to move on. As soon as his attention was back on the task in front of him though, he heard the purring again. This time he also heard a meow. Whirling around, he found both Steve and Tick-Tock smiling at him. Relieved that his two heroes had forgiven his screw-up enough to make light of it, he gave a warbling meow in return and went back to checking doors.

Coming to the passageway that paralleled the one they had used to enter the starboard side crew's quarters, Steve halted them.

Brain pointed to the last few doors at the end of the corridor and said, "Got a couple more to check."

"We'll get to them in a minute," Steve replied. "Take a break."

Unlike the crew area where they had first entered, most of the doors they came across on the access corridor had been unlocked. Having to deal with each one as a potential threat, Steve wanted to take a break to let some of the adrenalin that was pumping through them dissipate before moving on.

He was just about to explain this to Brain and Tick-Tock when the banging of a door and voices coming from the passageway they were about to enter interrupted him. Steve's first thought was that someone had heard the shot he'd fired and come to investigate. When he heard the conversation though, he realized it was just bad luck.

"- and that's why the fuck we have to come down here and switch full power back on to deck five," an angry male voice answered an unheard question.

"This sucks," a second man's voice commented. "Now all the good looking broads will be taken. By the time we get back up to the party, we'll be left with a bunch of Stank Ho's."

The voices grew louder as the two men fed into their anger and continued to complain that while everyone else was up on the pool deck stripping off their clothes and getting ready to get down, they were stuck with shit duty.

Steve lowered himself into a crouch to minimize being seen at eye level and risked a quick peek around the corner. He saw two men coming toward him, both armed with bolt-action rifles. Even as he pulled his head back, dozens of options started running lightning fast through his brain on how to deal with the situation.

Kill them?

They're carrying weapons, he reasoned, so chances are they're two of the Head Ushers Tim told us about. If we kill them, they'll definitely be missed. That means Ricky will have to do something about it. It wouldn't take a genius to figure out we had something to do with it. The question is, what will Ricky do? Attack?

Not wanting to start a war before he was ready to start it, Steve dismissed the idea of killing the Head Ushers.

Take the two men hostage? Same result as killing them.

Show ourselves?

Then Ricky will know we've been down here, and the first place he'll check is the electrical switching room. It's too obvious that's the reason we're here. They might not shut off the power to the gas pump when they find we switched it, but it'll let him know what we're doing.

Ricky's up to something, Steve decided, so the less he knows about what we're up to the better.

Hide?

He considered this as he looked at the numerous doors in the corridor. Anything could be behind them. The one compartment they were sure was clear was the one with the dead Z in it, but that was at the far end of the hall. He knew they'd never make it before the two bozos heading in their direction came around the corner and spotted them.

Then, he noticed a familiar sign above the door directly on his left. Making a snap decision, he motioned for the others to go through it. Of his limited choices, this one seemed the best. They had come across two similar rooms so they would know the layout of what they were walking into. He was aware they were taking a huge risk since they hadn't searched this particular space yet, but they didn't have a choice. The two Head Ushers would be on them in seconds. It suddenly flashed through his mind that the downside of his chosen hiding spot was that the door couldn't be locked.

He followed Tick-Tock and Brain. Once inside, he saw that only a single emergency light burning at its far end to illuminate the bathroom. Dark shadows were cast over everything in the narrow compartment, making him squint to see in the low light. Motioning Brain to cover their rear, since they didn't know what else might be in there with them, and Tick-Tock to cover the entryway from behind him, he put his foot against the base of the door to keep anyone from getting in. It wasn't the best solution, but it was all they had.

The voices in the passageway grew louder as the two men turned the corner. One man was extolling the physical attributes of a certain female passenger he wanted to get with, while the other kept interrupting him to say the woman in question was a dog, flat-chested and had the clap. Hearing their voices fade as they went further down the corridor, Steve let loose the breath he'd been holding. He waited a full minute without hearing anything, and was about to crack open the door to take a look, when he heard a voice which sounded like it was right outside "I won't be a minute, so hold on."

Shit, Steve thought as adrenalin surged through his body. One of the Ushers decided he needed to take a piss and came back. Now he's going to come in and I'll have to take him out.

Steve readied himself for the door to be pushed against his foot, then changed his mind and moved it out of the way. He decided he was going to let the door swing open instead of stopping it. He would shoot the first man in the chest before jumping out into the passageway and killing his buddy. He just hoped he had a clear shot at the second man and it didn't turn into a standoff.

Seconds passed as he waited in anticipation for the door to swing open. Instead, he heard a familiar clicking noise from beyond the door.

A faint voice called from down the corridor, "Hurry the fuck up."

"Screw you and the horse you rode in on," the man outside the door replied. "You know I can't smoke in the electrical room. It'll set off the smoke detector again." He laughed abruptly and added, "Last time that thing went off, you almost shit one big brick. You thought the ship was sinking."

"Screw you, too," came the terse reply from his partner. Then in a conciliatory voice, he added, "At least you moved down there so I don't have to smell that stink. You're gonna die from those things. They smell rancid."

Steve exhaled a quiet sigh of relief at these words. Now he knew what was happening in the corridor. The clicking noise was the man outside the door using a lighter to fire up a cigarette. He wasn't down here to use the facilities, he was taking a smoke break. Realizing that if the Head Usher were coming in that he would have done it by now, he relaxed slightly.

We just have to give him a few minutes to finish his butt and then he'll haul ass and we can go, Steve thought. Patience. All we have to do is stay cool and we're home free. We're doing good.

He'd just convinced himself that they would come out of the situation unscathed when Tick-Tock leaned forward and whispered in his ear, "We're not alone in here."

Instantly on alert, Steve's eyes narrowed as he spun and looked for any potential threat. He gave the bathroom a once over and noted the simple layout. Sinks lined the wall on his left with stalls on the right. No row of urinals since it was the women's room. Nowhere to hide except...

"Which stall?" He asked in a voice barely above a whisper.

"Second from the last," Tick-Tock replied in an equally quiet voice.

Then, he heard the all too familiar high-pitched keening noise the dead made. It was quiet enough that it might not be heard outside the toilet, but he knew that would change. Once the dead smelled fresh meat, they got louder and louder until whatever incited them went away or they got to eat it. He could see Brain with his pistol held at arm's length, pointing it at the second stall. He knew the Z was covered since there was no way the tech could miss from that distance, and then though, as long as he didn't drop his gun again.

The zombie in the stall made a slightly louder whine. Any second, the man in the passageway would hear the noise and open the door to investigate.

Now we have no options, Steve thought. We'll have to kill the two men and hide their bodies. This'll be a bitch since the two Head Ushers will be alerted by the sound the Z's making and be ready for something to go down when they come in. The only thing going in our favor is that they won't expect to be confronted by something like us. Still, the element of surprise was gone.

Deciding to take the initiative, he whispered to Tick-Tock, "I'm going to pull the door open. I want you to waste the guy in the corridor. Make it two quick shots to the chest because I'm going to be moving out in the hallway to nail his partner. Let Brain deal with the Z when it comes out."

Tick-Tock stepped back and shouldered his rifle, aiming it at the door just as the zombie in the toilet stall let out a long, loud whine. Steve grabbed the door handle and prepared to yank it open. With the sound of the Z echoing off the metal walls, there was no way the Ushers could miss it.

And they didn't.

A harsh voice from the other side of the door called out saying, "Shut the fuck up Delores or I'm going to come in there and braid your tits." This was followed by harsh laughter.

A faint laugh came from the man down the corridor before he said, "Someone should go in there and shoot that old bag in the head. Put her out of her misery. She's been locked in that crapper for months now."

The voice from outside the door grew distant as the man standing there walked toward his partner saying, "Fuck that dead bitch."

The other man answered, "I wouldn't, but Ricky might." This was followed by more laughter that faded to silence.

Steve drew a deep breath and let it out. That was too close. Wondering why Brain hadn't fired at the Z, he looked at the line of toilet stalls and saw the reason. There was only a five-inch gap at the bottom of the cubicle so it wasn't big enough for anything to squeeze through. He also noticed that the sides and front of the stalls went all the way up to the ceiling. The zombie was trapped in a sheet metal cube.

Either the door is jammed or it can't figure out how to open it, Steve thought. It can't get out and that's why it didn't attack. It must know it's trapped since it isn't even trying to tear the door down. These things can learn simple things so it knows it's screwed.

Then an idea struck him, but it would have to wait a little while.

Glancing at Brain, Steve saw he still had his pistol pointed at the door to the second stall and that his hands were shaking slightly, either from fear or from holding the .45 extended for too long. He needed to get Brain to stand down before he squeezed off a shot by accident.

Even though the two Ushers were gone, he kept his voice low so he didn't startle the tech as he said, "Relax Brain. It's only Delores."

Tick-Tock laughed, "Delores, meet Brain. Brain, meet Delores."

After making their way down the port side passageway to a door leading back to the Centrum, Steve told Brain to go lock the door they'd used to access the crew area on the other side of the ship while he went back to the bathroom to take care of something.

Tick-Tock gave him a knowing smile and asked, "Need any help?"

Steve only grinned and said, "Nope, I got this, but I need to borrow your K-bar."

Hurrying back to the bathroom, Steve used a trashcan to prop the door open. Moving to the second stall from the end, he studied the lock on it for a moment as the zombie inside whined at his presence.

Extracting the K-bar from its sheath, he said, "Take a big bite out of one of those assholes when they come back, Delores."

Using the knife, he popped the lock and ran from the bathroom, leaving the door propped open behind him and not stopping until he rejoined his friends. Tick-Tock had filled Brain in on what was going on, and as soon as Steve cleared the door it was locked behind him. Steve hoped that neither of the Head Ushers had a key. Let Delores fuck with them for a while.

Moving down the hall that held the elevators, the three men had to stifle their laughter. While open warfare didn't exist between them and Ricky's people, they all knew it would only be a matter of time.

Tick-Tock asked, "Do you want to stay and watch?"

"Not this time," Steve replied. "We've still got things to do." Eyeing the elevator, he added, "And like the Captain of the Titanic said, To the lifeboats."

\*\*\*

Brain poked his head out from under the canvas cover and told Steve, "This is the fourth one I've checked. Short of firing one of the engines up, I'd say that there's nothing wrong with any of these boats. The safety seals are still on the engine covers, so no one's been in there, and no one's screwed around with the steering that I can tell. The zincs are missing on a couple-."

"Tick-Took cut him off by asking, "Sinks? Do these things have a bathroom in them? Cause I gotta throw a piss like a racehorse."

Brain went into serious mode and said, "No, Tick-Tock. A zinc is a-."

This time it was Steve who cut him off by saying, "Lighten up Brain, he's screwing with you. Button that thing back up, so we can get the hell out of here." Turning to Tick-Tock, he said, "Alright, Brain did his thing and I did mine, now what do you want to do?"

Tick-Tock only smiled.

\*\*\*

Holding onto the safety rope, Brain said nervously, "I don't think this is such a good idea."

"What?" Both Steve and Tick-Tock shouted back at him.

Straining to be heard over the thumping bass of the techno-dance beat booming out from a pair of five-foot high amps set on the deck thirty feet away, Brain repeated his statement.

"Don't worry," Tick-Tock assured him as he buckled on a safety harness. "This'll be a blast. You'll love it."

"I'm next," Steve yelled out.

"Then it's your turn," Tick-Tock told Brain.

Looking up at the rock-climbing wall towering above him, Brain shuddered at the thought of having to scale it. That's if the rope held.

Doubtfully, he yelled, "I don't know, I think I'm having flashbacks to our escape from the bank building."

"That was rappelling down, this is climbing up," Tick-Tock pointed out. "There's a big difference." After thinking about it he added, "Besides, that was kind of fun."

Turning to the wall, Tick-Tock found hand and footholds on the small protrusions jutting from it and rapidly started up, moving with ease.

Under his breath, Steve kept saying, "Miss, miss."

When Tick-Tock was halfway, his foot slipped and he started to drop. Brain gasped in fear and tightened his grip on the safety rope, arresting his friend's fall and lowering Tick-Tock gently to the deck.

Smiling, Steve yelled, "You missed and you owe me one-hundred pushups and a bottle of Jamaican rum. You said you could climb all the way to the top on your first try and you blew it."

Holding up the broken handhold he'd brought down with him, Tick-Tock shouted, "Not fair. This is a mechanical failure. That's not my fault."

"Like rocks don't break off on a real cliff?" Steve shot back with a triumphant smile on his face. "You lost and now you owe."

The two men argued loudly, not in the least concerned they would give themselves away to the Faithful since the music playing over the PA system on the pool deck was so loud it would cover the sound of a jet taking off.

After leaving the lifeboats, the three men made their way to the stern of the ship where an exterior stairway ran from deck seven all the way up to deck twelve. As soon as they went outside to check the lifeboats, they heard the music coming from above, but they just didn't realize how loud it was until they reached deck nine. By the time they reached the pool deck, the noise was deafening. Taking a few minutes at each landing for a quick reconnaissance, they found all the decks empty. Their destination was deck twelve so they didn't spend too much time exploring the other areas.

Remembering what Tim had told them about the nightly party on the pool deck, Steve and Tick-Tock weren't too concerned about being spotted by the Faithful since they would be occupied with each other. Besides, with the noise of the music for cover, and the upper decks only lit by low wattage light bulbs strung on wires like Christmas lights from the bow of the ship to its stern, they would just be three figures in the distance.

Seeing how close they were to the Faithful, Brain grew nervous when they broke cover on deck twelve to cross over to get to the rock-climbing wall and he wouldn't calm down even after they were once again hidden from view. Noticing that the tech was uneasy, Steve did little to reassure him when he said, "Don't worry. If anyone sees us, we'll just kill them all."

Although deck eleven actually held the pools, hot tubs and most of the bars, deck twelve had a wide jogging track and tanning area that circled this area and looked down on it. With easy access to both decks via multiple stairways, it became one large party zone.

Even though the Faithful gathered on deck twelve each night as they waited for the rapture, it was deck eleven they went to first when they failed to ascend into Heaven. The bar was always open, and the drinks were free, so everyone indulged. Many did make their way back to deck twelve later to use the deck chairs scattered about since they found they could be folded into different positions that could make for some interesting sexual positions. Thus, when Steve, Tick-Tock and Brain arrived, they found themselves within a few dozen yards of people engaged in a variety of sexual practices. On the pool deck below was the balance of the Faithful doing the same.

Before moving to the rock-climbing wall, Steve stopped to look over deck twelve and the pool deck below. Satisfied that no one had seen them and raised the alarm, he called out to move on. Now he found he had to literally pull Brain away from the area as he gazed in wonder at two women and a man having three-way sex. Reaching the base of the Crow's Nest Lounge towering above them, the trio circled it and found themselves at the stern of the ship. With the wall and the tower between them and the rest of the ship, no one could see them. Tick-Tock discovered a storage locker containing the climbing gear, and after untangling the safety ropes, he was the first one to attempt the wall.

Brain looked on as the two men finally ended their disagreement by making the contest the best two out of three. Although nervous about being so close to Reverend Ricky's people, some of his jumpiness had faded now that he saw the safety ropes did their job. As his mind wandered, he started dwelling on the sight of the three-way he'd witnessed earlier. While he didn't particularly get off on watching a naked guy, he did enjoy watching naked women. Seeing them live was much better than watching clips on the Internet like he'd been doing for years. Thinking of what Connie would look like naked, he was brought out of his reverie by Tick-Tock snapping his fingers in front of his face.

"Steve's ready, Pork Chop." With an evil smile, he added, "And if the rope slips through your hands and he crashes to the deck, we'll just write it off as a training accident."

Steve gave Tick-Tock the finger and started to climb.

After each man scaled the wall two times to the same height, they were too exhausted to try again and declared their bet off. When they told Brain it was his turn, it took them ten minutes to persuade him.

The first time, Brain made it a quarter of the way to the top before he fell. On his second try, he passed that mark and was nearly halfway when suddenly he stopped.

After calling up to the tech and receiving no answer, Tick-Tock was worried he was frozen in fear. He was about to put his gear back on and climb up to talk him down when he saw Brain push off from the wall and let himself be lowered while he frantically waved and pointed toward the rear of the ship.

When his feet were once again on the deck, Brain yelled out excitedly, "Don't you feel it?"

Steve's mind spun. Feel what? He asked himself. Are we sinking?

Seeing the quizzical looks he was getting, Brain pointed to the multi-colored banners attached to the guide wires that secured the climbing wall to the base of the Crow's Nest Lounge and screamed, "Look."

It took them a moment to understand what he was trying to show them. Suddenly, it hit them both at the same time and they whooped with joy.

The banners were fluttering and snapping in the breeze. The wind had come up.

Chapter Fourteen

The Dead Calm:

When Steve told the rest of the group that the wind was up and they had all the more reason to depart the Dead Calm, he was met by a less than enthusiastic response. He could understand Mary not wanting to leave the shopping Mecca she had fallen into, but even Heather seemed depressed at the news.

When he asked her why, she replied, "I know there's a million reasons to go, the most important being that we get Cindy somewhere to see if she holds the cure for HWNW virus, but ..." Her voice trailed off.

"But what?" He asked.

"I may sound selfish, but screw it, I'm saying it anyway. I've just gotten comfortable here, and now we've got to leave. That sucks. I knew this was only temporary when we decided to come on board, and even more temporary when we found out the ship was sinking, but I want to enjoy it while I can."

Steve considered his reply before saying, "I'm not telling you that we've got to leave this very minute, but I'd like to try to get going as soon as possible. We have to stay here for the next day anyway while we load up the supplies and see if Ricky can come up with a sextant so ..." Now Steve's voice trailed off as he looked at Heather's crestfallen expression. He knew she would go if he said go, but would be disappointed at having to leave the Calm of the Seas. After a second, he continued, "So I guess it's no big deal if we take a couple extra days and relax."

Heather gave him a smile and asked, "Really?"

Steve smiled back and said, "Really. We can get everything loaded up and then take a break and relax. You told me about Ricky letting us have deck five with all the restaurants, so we'll fill up on some good food before we go. The extra time will also give Tick-Tock the chance to figure out our position if we get that sextant from Ricky."

Heather threw her arms around him and said, "Don't worry, babe, I'm not breaking weak on you. It's just that it's so nice here, and it's kind of hard to leave it knowing what we're heading out into."

"I never thought you were going soft," Steve assured her. "But remember, we also have to deal with Ricky and his people before we go."

After kissing him, she said, "I'll take care of Ricky. Don't worry about that. And as for his Faithful, they can take their chances in the lifeboats."

\*\*\*

Reverend Ricky opened the lid of the case containing the sextant. After picking up and removing its lens, he threw the circle of glass against the wall. Examining it and seeing it sufficiently cracked so as to make it useless, he put it back in place and removed the spare from the box. This he put in the breast pocket of his shirt.

Turning to the younger of the two Hungarian sisters, he ordered her to get dressed. After his last encounter with Heather, he had no desire to meet with the woman face to face again. He would send the girl down to deck four with his latest gift.

Although his informant had told him that the group from the sailboat didn't plan any aggression against him or his people, Ricky was nevertheless wary about being around them. Especially Heather. She was always looking at him as if he were a bug that had invaded her space and needed to be crushed. His snitch warned him to stay away from her, that she used to be a cop and saw him as nothing but a pedophile that needed to be eliminated.

Thinking about his informant, anger flashed through Ricky as he recalled their last meeting. He was still pissed off when he found out how much his snitch had told the newcomers about him. The people from the sailboat had way too much information and it had turned them completely against him. He had planned on trying to win the people from the sailboat over with his charm, but now that they knew some of his secrets, this would be impossible.

Good thing they don't know all my secrets or they'd come after me with a vengeance, Ricky thought.

Calming himself, he considered the other news his snitch had brought him. It seemed that one of the people on deck four by the name of Randy was something of a mechanical and electrical whiz. This might fit in nicely with his plans.

When he'd grabbed power on the ship, he was looking at the short-term. With the impending loss of the Calm of the Seas though, he knew he had to look further than that in order to guarantee his continued survival. With these far reaching thoughts and ideas, he could see that he needed someone like Randy on his team. The man's knowledge would be indispensable when they reached Cozumel. Both in barter with the other people who already inhabited the island and for helping him set up his own empire when they got there. There would be much to do be done since they were starting from scratch.

The first thing I need to do is open up a church, Ricky decided, as his mind switched to the tasks confronting him when they reached land. But I'll need to alter the religion from what I preach here because it's a different situation. I need to convert those people slowly instead of banging then over the head with God. I'll quit preaching that rapture garbage too. It's getting old. It probably won't be as easy to convert the people on Cozumel as it was to fool these idiots on the ship, but all I need is a foothold. Once I get enough True Believers, this is what he decided to call his followers instead of calling them the Faithful, I'll see if it's feasible to take over the whole Island.

Having decided on a course of action, he turned to preparing a list of who would go with him - and also who wouldn't.

Sitting at his desk, the first thing he wrote was 'Get Rid of Parsons'. This was not an easy decision to come to because the man made an excellent second-in-command. The problem arose from the fact that he seemed to have aspirations to run things. Even though Parsons tried to stay blank faced and hide his ambitions, Ricky could see in his eyes how he craved power. It was a familiar look to him since it was the same one he saw every time he gazed in the mirror. He knew that it was only a matter of time before Parsons tried to take over, so it was better to nip the problem in the bud. Even if Parsons were unsuccessful in a bid for the top slot, a coup would cause a rift in the group, so he had to go.

The younger of the two sisters interrupted Ricky's train of thought when she called out that she was ready. He wanted to get his thoughts down on paper first, so he asked her to be patient with daddy and put in a DVD of the little mermaid before turning back to his list.

Now to sort out the rest of his people to see who would stay and who would go.

He admitted that Brother Seth had his uses, so his name was added to the list along with Brother William. They would be his enforcers. He'd need some muscle when he reached Cozumel. Seth had been a cop in Lee County, Florida before the dead came to life and was as dirty as they came. Brother William was a wannabe thug, but had no aspirations for the top spot, so he was safe to bring along.

Both men followed orders and had little or no imagination. This was what counted, Ricky decided. Too bad Seth didn't bring some of his fellow officers with him. To hear him tell it, the whole Lee County Sheriff's office was corrupt. I could use that kind of support, he thought.

Turning back to the matter at hand, Ricky put a number one next to each of the two Head Usher's names to indicate they could bring along one person. They could have their pick from the women who made up over half of the Faithful. Looking at where the two sisters sat watching TV, Ricky put his own name at the top of the list and penciled in a two next to it.

Now, for Brother Cal, Ricky thought. He's been loyal and is handy to have around. He knows how to fix and run generators and other pieces of equipment, but if what I'm planning comes off, I won't need him. Besides, the boat is starting to fill up. I've got to balance people versus supplies. Anyway, I won't need two guys who know how to fix a generator.

Ricky wrote down a question mark with a one next to it at the bottom of the list. Regardless of what happened, at least two more people would be coming and that made nine. Plenty, Ricky decided. It'll either be Cal or Randy that comes along and either way they'll be accompanied by one person. If it's Cal, then he's entitled to bring a companion, and if we can grab Randy, I've got a hostage in mind to threaten and assure his cooperation.

Not really a hostage though, someone who's already on my side, Ricky thought with a glee. That makes it so much easier.

Calling the younger sister over to him, Ricky handed her the box with the sextant in it and told her that on her way down to present it to the newcomers, she needed to stop at the small staff kitchen on deck eight and turn on the In Use light for the dumb waiter.

The small elevator ran through the service areas all the way from deck ten down to four. When the light was on, it alerted his informant to slip away and meet with him on deck nine.

Once the little girl was gone, Ricky lay back on the bed with her older sister and stared blankly at the cartoon while his mind drifted over his plan, searching for anything he might have missed. The people on deck four were doing their part by loading the sailboat with provisions, thinking they would use them when they departed the Calm of the Seas. Instead, Ricky gloated, it'll be me and my people who will benefit from their labor. And as for Randy, I need to set a trap and kidnap him.

As he considered how he would lure Randy away from the others, he suddenly had the answer to how he was going to get the people on deck four separated so they could pick them off in ones and twos. Ricky's mind raced as he worked out the specifics. Once I grab Randy, Steve and Heather, the rest of them will be easy to lure in different directions while they look for their missing comrades. All I have to do is cut them off from each other by sealing doors in front and behind them, and then eliminate them one by one. As soon as they realize that Randy's missing, they'll be chomping at the bit to search for him, only I'll direct the search and have my people set up to ambush them once they're separated. With a smile, Ricky planned on how he would get Heather to the Sound's Lounge and personally toss her into the crowd of dead waiting below.

That bitch is mine.

Looking at the older sister lying on the bed next to him, his mind switched track as he remembered his snitch telling him that there was a ten-year-old girl aboard the sailboat and that she was supposedly immune to the disease. Ricky smiled evilly as he thought he might be able to sell her to the government. They'd pay a fortune to have someone who they could poke and prod to try and figure out a cure for HWNW.

This thought was followed by; when I get done with her of course.

He briefly considered changing the number of people he would bring with him from a two to a three, but decided to leave it at two. The two youngest, he decided.

A huge smile broke across Ricky's face as he considered the endless possibilities.

***

Steve and Heather cautiously checked deck five as Susan and Tick-Tock covered them. They weren't as concerned about running into Ricky's people as they were about encountering the dead. Reaching the end of restaurant row and finding no signs of any Z's, they turned and made their way back. As they passed the staircase, Steve approached the doors identical to the ones on deck four which led to the cabin area beyond.

Motioning Heather to cover him, he went forward and quickly chained the doors together by their handles. Tim had told him about the watertight hatch beyond, but he wasn't going to take any chances. Fumbling one handed with the lock as he gripped the rifle his other, he half expected the doors to be pushed open by decaying hands and a flood of dead to come rushing out. His fears were unjustified as the lock closed with a secure snap. Noticing only the slight smell of funk coming from beyond, he guessed the water tight doors must be shut or it would smell as bad as it did when he drew close to the ones on deck four.

Finished with securing the doors, he gripped his M-4 in both hands and backed away. Safely by the stairs, he took one more look around and said, "No one goes into any of the restaurants that are closed until we clear them. There are plenty of open ones to choose from. Other than that, bon appetite."

With the words barely out of his mouth, the others came up from deck four and spread out to explore. As an added warning, he shouted out, "And no one goes anywhere alone."

Mary gasped and said, "Oh my god, a TGI Fridays. I love their food." Grabbing Sheila by the hand, she led her off saying, "You fix us a couple of Mojitos and I'll whip us up something to eat."

Tick-Tock headed for a British Pub before suddenly stopping. Looking at Susan, he asked, "Join Me?"

She thought about it and decided that in a world where it was unlikely she would ever have a chance to drink beer, shoot darts and eat meat pies in an authentic replica of an Olde English Pub again, she should jump on the chance. Instead, she hesitated for a few seconds.

Although she liked spending time with Tick-Tock, the thought of facing another thing about to pass from the pre- dead world depressed her. Not wanting to spoil it for everyone by pointing out that they would never see anything like this again in their lives, she forced a smile and pushed her thoughts away as she said, "I'd love to join you."

Connie and Brain stood undecided by the stairs. For them this was like a first date so, like many couples since the beginning of time, their conversation went:

Connie: What do you want to eat?
Brain: I'm fine with whatever you want.
Connie: Pick a place.
Brain: Where do you want to go?
Connie: Anywhere is fine with me.

Hearing their conversation, since he had been in similar ones before, and it could go on for days, Steve called Brain over to him. After the tech had joined him, he whispered, "Women love assertive men. Don't ask her, tell her. She doesn't care about the food anyway. She wants to spend time with you."

Brain nodded at this bit of wisdom and glanced around at the selection of restaurants. While he was doing this, Heather grabbed Steve by the hand and said, "I'm hungry for pizza. Take me now or loose me forever."

He went along willingly.

As Heather led him away, Brain looked startled at the contradiction to what he had just been told. This was until Steve called back over his shoulder, "The rule I told you about only applies until you hook up. After that, she decides where to eat for the rest of your life."

He yelped as Heather punched his shoulder and Brain laughed. Rejoining Connie he said, "Let's get some Chinese food."

Giving him a smile that made his knees weak, Connie replied, "I love Chinese, perfect choice."

Tim and Cindy looked at each other with disgust. Neither wanted to be stuck with the other, but it looked like they had no choice. Earlier, Susan had asked him to watch over Cindy. At first he had swelled with pride at being given the responsibility, but now it looked like this was going to be a drag.

In a bored voice, Tim said, "The Kidz Corner has got a bunch of video games and I can cook us up some cheeseburgers or something if you're hungry."

At this, Cindy brightened and asked, "Do they have Devious Dwarfs?"

"Oh yeah they do," Tim said enthusiastically. "That's my favorite. I love Double D."

"Me too."

"What level have you gotten to?" Tim asked.

Cindy replied, "Twenty-two."

"No way a girl got to level twenty-two. Prove it," Tim said skeptically

"Show me where the game is and I will," Cindy retorted.

Tim led her to the far end of Restaurant Row, positive that there was no way a girl had made it to level twenty-two, while Cindy thought, I'll show him, and I actually made it to level twenty-eight.

After they were gone, the deck was still for a moment.

Until Mary broke it by calling out, "Brain, how in the hell do you turn on this deep fryer?"

\*\*\*

In the red glow of the emergency lights, the dead that were locked in the engine room looked even more grotesque than the ones topside. That was, if anyone had been left alive in there to see them. Having been trapped inside the compartment for months now without any food, the figures were rail thin but still active as they staggered about looking for something to eat. It had been a long time since they had stuffed meat into their mouths to sate their cravings. They were hungry. Very hungry.

After the engine room crew had died and came back to feast on their fellow crew members trapped inside with them, the hatches of the engine room had been sealed to prevent them from escaping and wreaking more havoc on the rest of the ship. The meat sealed inside with the dead had been quickly consumed and the marrow sucked from the bones. When no new food presented itself, the bones themselves were then broken apart and devoured. This had taken three days, with the skulls of their victims' taking the longest to consume.

For this final part of their gruesome feast, the engine compartment was filled with the sounds of teeth scraping on bone.

Since then, none of the dead had eaten, but they still moved about with a purpose, to find something to feed on.

Dressed in gray coveralls, one of the crew stumbled down the stairs of a catwalk. As it neared the main deck, it slowly sank into the water that had been building up in the engine room over the past few days. With the hatches sealed, the water had nowhere to go as the compartment filled. Reaching the floor, the creature started wading through chest deep water. If the dead thing had been able to make a comparison, it would have realized that the water had only been knee deep the day before, and ankle deep the day before that.

Not noticing anything, the zombie crewman continued to slog through the water as if it wasn't there.

\*\*\*

Later that night, Reverend Ricky dismissed his informant with a flick of his hand and the warning, "The next time I summon you, I want you to come immediately. I don't care if you're eating, shitting, or playing with yourself. Lead the one named Randy to where I told you to or the consequences will be painful. Tomorrow morning, be there."

Once his snitch was gone, Ricky looked at the dials and gauges set into the consoles lining the back bulkhead of the bridge. For a moment his eyes rested on the bank of switches controlling the watertight doors before moving on. Shaking his head at the undecipherable readings on the rest of the dials, he was content that he knew enough to take care of business when the time came. He could let his dead go at anytime, anywhere. Turning to go back to his cabin and the two young girls waiting there for him, he didn't notice a row of solid red lights with labels under them that read: FLOOD WARNING; Deck One, and, FLOOD WARNING; Engine Room.

Chapter Fifteen

Russellville, Arkansas/Clarksville, Arkansas:

Major Jedidiah Cage glared through the window of his office toward the farmhouse where Doctor Lyonel Hawkins kept his research facility.

Months wasted, Cage raged to himself. All this time and not a damn thing had been accomplished. Those idiots have been screwing around trying to find the source of the disease when all they had to do was ask me. I was at the hospital where this nightmare started. Just from talking to the doctors and the nurses, I found out what was going on and how the HWNW virus got started.

Cage steamed as he recalled the meeting he'd just left.

Hours earlier, he'd been summoned from his office by Doctor Hawkins. The Doctor informed him that he had an announcement to make regarding some big advances that he and his team had made. When Cage arrived at the farmhouse, he found that besides all the officers who worked at the base, the doctor had also invited a reporter from the Army Press and someone to tape the meeting so it could be replayed over the few radio stations up and running in the Dead Free Zones.

Cage was interested in what Doctor Hawkins had to say, but scoffed at the "Press" that attended. The Army rag was nothing more than a propaganda sheet that was barely suitable as toilet paper. On top of that, the last he'd heard there was only a total of five radio stations across the country up and running. Not even enough to cover an area as big as the State of Rhode Island. Sometimes, late at night when conditions were just right, he could pick up the station out of Fort Hood while he scanned for any new stations that might have come on the air. He always spun the dial past it, since he'd listened to Fort Hood radio once and vowed never to tune in again. The broadcasts, like the Army paper, were controlled by the government and never reported anything of substance.

Arriving on time, although the meeting didn't even look close to starting, Cage was kept waiting while he tried his best to avoid conversation with the rest of those present. Finally, the great doctor himself appeared with his white lab coat flapping around him and called the meeting to order. After introductions were made, Hawkins laid out his stunning revelation about how the HWNW virus had sprung from a combined mutation of a rare disease named Prader-Willi and the H1N1 virus.

No shit Sherlock, Cage thought at hearing this. What was your first clue? Now tell us something we don't know.

Doctor Hawkins then went on for twenty minutes as he threw out a lot of medical jargon that made no sense to anyone present and explained absolutely nothing. He summed this all up by stating that he and his team were still working on a cure, and now that they had isolated the root cause of the disease, progress would speed up. He then looked at those gathered as if he'd just told them that the secret of time travel was accomplished by making a few minor adjustments to your espresso machine as he waited for his accolades. There was enthusiastic applause from all those present except Cage, who looked on in wonder.

That's it? He asked himself. That's all they've got after months of research. That information was put out days after the initial outbreak. What in the hell have you been doing over there, jerking off?

An Army reporter who asked him to stand up and join the others interrupted Cage's internal tirade. It was photo op time, which was similar to a feeding frenzy. Cage with Hawkins, Hawkins with his staff, Cage with Hawkins' staff, and once every combination had been exhausted, Cage alone. The reporter then cornered him and asked to conduct a quick interview that would appear in the next issue of the Army Times. Cage knew that no matter how he answered any of the questions, they would print what they wanted, so he replied in words of one syllable whenever possible.

He wasn't a cover your ass kind of guy, and always stood by any order he gave, but he wanted to distance himself from anything having to do with Hawkins' research. As much as the doctor seemed to be screwing around, Cage could feel an investigation coming and wanted to be known only as the Base Commander. He didn't want to be connected with the farmhouse in any way other than that he protected the compound around it.

When the interview was over, Doctor Hawkins suggested they all head over to the mess tent for refreshments. As they filed out, Cage hung back from the herd. When they rounded a corner and he was momentarily out of sight, he cut between two tents and headed for his office. He had work to do and didn't have time to waste at some kind of half-assed coffee klatch. There were supplies to order, two disciplinary reports to review, and he had to finalize plans for the most important item on his agenda; an upcoming foraging mission into the nearby town of Clarksville.

Diverting his gaze from the farmhouse framed in his office window, Major Cage leaned back in his chair and looked at the map of the city of Clarksville pinned on the wall next to him.

Since taking command of the base from Major Conway the previous day, he'd been planning this mission to look for survivors and to see what could be salvaged from the small town only twenty miles away. The former commander of the base had kept his operations limited to the nearby town of Russellville, but between the looters who had swept through before the National Guard arrived, and his own people combing through it, the town had been picked clean. The only thing left in abundance were the dead.

With supplies not arriving in a steady flow, all military commanders had standing orders to supplement their rations and equipment by foraging what they could from the surrounding areas. Since supplies in Russellville had become scarce, Cage knew it was time to look for greener pastures. There were still large amounts of food and gas, albeit in lesser quantities, scattered in the small towns surrounding Russellville and all they had to do was look for it. The problem lay in the small returns for such a big outlay in men and equipment. Most farms had their own fuel storage tanks and pantries were generally stocked with food, but they had to scrounge through so many of them to make it worth their while. This was why he wanted to go into some of the nearby towns.

Despite this temporary stop gap measure in gathering supplies to ensure they could continue operating, Cage often asked himself what was going to happen when they ran out of farms and towns to scavenge from. If the Army supply chain kept going the way it was, everything would fall apart within three months. What in the hell were they going to do next year, he asked himself?

A few days earlier, when he had been nothing but a Captain in charge of perimeter security, he had thought his job was difficult. But now...

Deciding that the burden of command really meant that you were the only one who knew how seriously fucked you were, Cage closed his eyes and leaned further back in his chair while he considered the difficulties that he and his people were likely to face in Clarksville. As he tried to focus on this, his thoughts wandered and he couldn't keep his mind off the meeting he'd just attended. He was replaying in his head what Doctor Hawkins had said when a thought came to him with enough force to make him sit upright in his chair.

Hawkins had lied.

Cage knew there was no way in hell Hawkins just figured out how the HWNW virus started, and his announcement wasn't any revelation that he and his staff had recently come up with. Hawkins was in Little Rock when the first cases were reported. He had been on the original team brought in from the University to study the disease.

Cage's thoughts drifted to Major Conway and the briefing he had given him before transferring to Fort Hood. Cage was already wondering what was really going on over at the farmhouse, but when he voiced these doubts to Conway, the Major had assured him that the scientists and doctors were working hard on the problem of the HWNW virus and trying to figure out how to turn it to our advantage.

That statement had seemed odd to Jedidiah.

Conway hadn't said, "They're working hard on a cure," he had said, "They're working on how to turn the disease to our advantage."

What advantage? He pondered as he remembered something else that Conway had said to him, or maybe had been warning him about when he told him "You don't want to know too much about what's going on over there in the lab. Just keep in mind that it's in the best interest of the country. Men like us take our orders and carry them out to the best of our ability. My job, and now your job, is to keep this compound secure. Keep in mind that everything over there is way above your pay scale."

Cage shook off his suspicions as he looked at his watch, realizing that it was time for him to walk the perimeter. This wasn't actually a job of the Base Commander, but it was something that had been his duty as a junior officer. He continued doing it because it gave him a chance to talk with his men, the people who actually worked for a living, and find out where their heads were at.

Before leaving his office, his eyes turned once more to the map of Clarksville pinned on the wall. If anyone was still left alive there, he hoped they weren't in serious danger and could hold out until tomorrow. By noon, he and his men would be all over that burg.

***

Major Cage and two platoons of his soldiers actually arrived on the outskirts of Clarksville at five minutes to ten, two hours earlier than planned. The recon team that had been sent along I-40 the previous day to scout their route had overestimated how clogged the Interstate was, so the column of four Humvees and two trucks made better time than planned. This was often the case whenever the roads were scouted, since the recon teams were under orders to only travel a mile or two in any direction before turning around. They didn't want a small group of their people getting cut off and wiped out. It was a tradeoff of safety verses information, and Cage always looked out for the safety of his men first.

He knew that regardless of the size of the town, traffic was always jammed up worse right around its edges than it was further out. This was caused by people who were fleeing from that city running into other people fleeing to that city. In the end, nowhere was safe, and it left a huge jam of abandoned vehicles and wrecks. Cage tried to plan for the blocked areas around Russellville, but since the Interstate heading toward Clarksville had never been completely scouted, he had to be ready to adjust to any situation.

In this same vein of thought, Cage considered splitting his forces and coming into Clarksville from two directions. Since one group was tasked with looking for survivors, while the other's job was to scavenge, this seemed to make the most sense. They would be able to cover a larger area. He reasoned that the timetable had been moved forward by the ease they had reached the area, so now his people would have time to reconnoiter before moving in. After considering the different scenarios, in the end he discarded the idea. Until he knew what awaited them, he didn't want to halve his firepower and risk the possibility that the roads through town were blocked and keep his forces from joining up. Erring on the side of caution, he ordered his column to keep their interval and approach as one from the south.

Although I40 was scattered with abandoned vehicles sitting on their rims, and a few cars tangled up in wrecks that had to be winched out of the way, once the force took the off-ramp onto the main drag into town, the road was clear except for a few derelict vehicles sitting in the breakdown lane.

Having travelled this section of Arkansas before, to Cage, the number of broken down cars and trucks on the side of the road wasn't even extraordinary. He marveled to himself that if it wasn't for the events of the past few months, it could be a Sunday morning with the roads deserted because everyone was at church.

This illusion was quickly shattered when the convoy crested a small ridge. Here, a line of fifty-five gallon metal drums stretched across the road to block it with railroad ties wired between each container to create a formidable barrier. Secured to the barrels were three large, hand painted, plywood signs. The first read: QUARRANTINE AREA. The second: TRESSPASSERS WILL BE SHOT IN THE HEAD. But it was the third one that disturbed Cage the most. It read: WHY HAST THOU FORSAKEN US?

Cage halted the convoy and moved from his position in the number three spot of the column to the lead. Directing his driver to advance their Humvee slowly toward the barricade, he ordered the rest of his men to face outward and hold their fire unless they were sure that their target was dead and coming toward them. At this point, he didn't want one of his people shooting a civilian who was manning the barricade or was coming to investigate their presence.

Stopping the Humvee fifteen feet from the roadblock, Cage unclipped the microphone for the radio and switched it over to PA. Speaking slowly and clearly, he said, "This is Major Cage of the United States Army. We are here to offer aid to anyone who is injured and give food, water and shelter to anyone who needs it."

His words echoed back from the bluff on the right side of the road and dissipated across the overgrown fields on his left. No one showed themselves, so he repeated his message. Still nothing. Looking around, Cage slowly stepped from his Humvee and cautiously approached the roadblock. As he glanced over the top of the barrels, he saw the scattered bones and clothing of at least two people along with what looked like a shotgun and a hunting rifle. Both weapons had been turned into rods of rust from sitting out in the elements.

Adjusting his gaze further down the road, Cage could make out the shapes of at least ten bodies and assumed they were Z's. They dotted the road in a path that led directly to where the two dead men lay.

Recreating what had occurred, Cage determined that two men had been sent to guard the roadblock and had been attacked from behind by a large group of the dead. It looked like they held their own for a few minutes, but were overcome in the end. No one had come to bury them, so he had to assume that no one else in the town's defense force had been willing or able to make it to the roadblock. It appeared to have been abandoned since then.

Cage turned back to look at his men - he had to remember to call them his people since a quarter of them were women – and found himself looking down the barrels of two fifty caliber heavy machine guns mounted on Humvees sitting abreast, which took up both lanes of the road. Beyond them, he could see three of his soldiers leaning on top of the cab of the lead truck with their M-4 assault rifles at the ready. At the rear, rifle barrels poked out of each side of the truck to cover their flanks. Seeing this, Cage was pleased that his people were so well trained. Shouting to be heard above the rumble of the idling engines, he called out, "First squad of first platoon, clear this roadblock."

The two Humvees at the front of the line pulled off to the sides of the road far enough for the lead truck to move between them so it could utilize the winch mounted on its front bumper. Six men and two women dismounted and started to dismantle the barricade with crowbars and axes while two more dragged the wreckage out of the way with the winch.

In the town of Russellville, the soldiers had come across many roadblocks erected in neighborhoods where the people had tried to isolate themselves from the virus and those infected with it. The men and women of Cage's command had gotten lots of practice clearing those, so they made short work of the one in front of them.

After they finished and mounted back up, Cage kept the lead position as they rolled slowly into the outskirts of town. Passing a few houses, he could see no sign that the living inhabited any of them. You didn't have to be a genius to figure out which buildings contained people. All you had to do was look for a big crowd of the living dead swarming around it.

A burned out motel appeared on the left and houses became more numerous. Cage stopped the column every hundred feet and made a quick announcement over the PA as to who they were since he didn't want them to be mistaken for one of the roving bands of looters that had started to pop up around the country. It would be a shame if they shot a civilian by accident, but it would be a tragedy if one of his men were killed due to mistaken identity.

Coming to the top of a steep hill, the road leveled out and he saw they were coming close to the downtown area. He knew from the maps he'd studied of the city that a large residential section lay to his right. On his left were more houses and a small college. Using the radio, he ordered second platoon to split off on the road to the right and begin searching for survivors. One truck and two of the Humvees passed him as they headed on their rescue mission.

Instead of relying on his memory, Cage checked the map and located where the combination City Hall and Police Station were situated. Radioing to the Sergeant of first platoon, he said, "We're going to start with the local cop shop. It's three blocks ahead on the right. Squads one and two will go inside with me and three and four will stay outside as security, over."

"Roger, sir, over," came the reply. They had gone over the plan numerous times, but he still liked to announce its steps as they were about to take them.

"Roll out then, over and out," Cage ordered.

The column had only travelled a hundred feet when Cage saw the first few of what quickly became a swarm of dead coming down the road. Leaning forward to try and get a better view of the force approaching him, he quickly assessed the threat and started calling out orders over the radio. "Z's, Z's, Z's, about a hundred or so at our Twelve O'clock. Humvees pull out to the left and right as far as you can and get those fifty's going in enfilade. Head shots, head shots. Pick your targets. Second platoon rejoin us. We're stopped about two blocks shy of our primary target."

As his Humvee swerved to the left to set up in position for the .50 to fire at the advancing dead from an angle, on his right, Cage could see the City Hall had a large number of Z's clustered around it. To him, the dead looked like they were undecided as to whether or not to join the mass already coming toward his position. It was like they couldn't make up their minds whether to go after the food that had suddenly appeared, or wait for the food they had trapped.

Cage assessed the situation and determined that the crowd of dead had been clustered around the City Hall building, but were attracted by the sound of his voice coming over the loudspeaker. They were on their way to investigate and see if the noise was edible when he spotted them. From above, he heard the deep, coughing boom as the .50 mounted on the roof of his Humvee opened up with its first burst. Seeing the heavy rounds impacting on the torsos of the nearest Z's, he yelled at the gunner, "Head shots, head shots. Adjust your fire."

The .50 mounted on the other Humvee opened up as it pulled to a stop on the far-right side of the two-lane road. Cage could hear assault rifles popping as his people dismounted from the truck and started to lay a withering fire on the dead.

Before jumping from the Humvee, Cage gave one last order, yelling to be heard above the noise growing around him, he screamed, "First squad, first squad. Cover our rear and watch the flanks."

Repeating himself to make sure he'd been heard, he jumped down and joined the fray.

Veterans of numerous encounters with the dead, the men and women in first squad quickly moved into position. They knew from experience that it wasn't the Z you saw that got you but the one that came out of nowhere. Covering the flanks and rear was vital to any mission. Everyone in the platoon had seen action in Little Rock, Fort Smith, or Hot Springs and had done at least one foraging trip into Russellville, so they knew they were most vulnerable when they were in tight quarters where the dead could lunge out at them from hiding. In situations like this, with the dead in the open, the soldiers had an overwhelming advantage.

It was, as one Private later called it, "Like shooting deer in a petting zoo."

A steady stream of bullets impacted the heads of the dead, blowing them apart to spray brains, chunks of skull and black puss all over the surface of the road. Some took body hits which staggered them, but the volume of outgoing fire was such that they were quickly put down. In seconds, the area in front of Cage was littered with the bodies of the dead. The volume of fire slowed and then stopped as targets were put down to never rise again.

And then the snipers took over.

Two of Cage's men had set up on the cab of the truck and started putting down the dead gathered in front of the City Hall building with scope equipped M-14's. In the silence, broken only by their firing, Cage could hear the two snipers talking to each other.

"I got the one in the overalls." Bang. "Take that farmer Brown."

"Shit, you see that chick on the right? She looks like my ex-wife." Bang. "Bye-bye, biiatch."

"See the two near the fire escape on the side of the building? I got the one on the left; you take the one on the right. In tandem, go." Bangang, the two shots almost sounded as one.

"See those three lined up one in front of the other? One shot, three kills." Bang. "Shit, I only got two of them."

Bang. "I got him for you. You suck at this."

This was followed by laughter from both men.

Cage shook his head as the firing and the chatter continued. Snipers are weird, he thought.

Hearing the whine of distant engines, he turned and saw second squad coming toward him. As they drew near, he motioned for them to stay in their vehicles as he walked over to the lead Humvee to talk with their platoon leader. In the past, only Lieutenants could command a platoon, but with the decimation of the officer corps since D-Day, Sergeants had taken their place.

Leaning down to the window of the Humvee to talk with Jones, his former driver when they were engaged in the Little Rock campaign, and now the commander of second platoon, Cage said, "Had a whole bunch of Z's clustered around City Hall so that means there's live ones inside. Since you're on S and R, I called you back. I want you and one of your squads to go with me and one of mine to check it out. We attracted a lot of attention with the gunfire, so I want the balance of the men to secure a perimeter and provide security."

"No problem, sir," Jones replied.

"I'm gonna try calling on the PA first. If no one answers, then we have to go in," Cage told him.

Jones grimaced. Clearing a structure was where they took ninety percent of their casualties. Most of the time on Search and Rescue, once the soldiers killed the Z's clustered around a house, the people trapped inside came out on their own. It was the rest of time when they didn't and you had to go inside that really sucked.

Reluctantly, Jones said, "If we have to, we have to, sir."

Despite sounding hesitant to do his duty, Cage knew Jones was solid when the shit hit the fan. Besides, who in their right mind would walk willingly into what could be a building full of flesh eating dead?

Checking his watch, he said, "We go in five minutes. Remind your guys not to get too close to any of the Z's unless they're sure they're dead. Line abreast as we advance, and give everything laying on the road a head shot."

The previous week, they had lost a man when he walked past what he thought was a dead Z lying in the street, only to have it lunge up and bite him in the calf. Before anyone could react, the soldier had shot the Z in the head and then turned his rifle on himself.

Ten minutes after giving Jones his orders, the unit formed up around the City Hall. Cage tried to hail any survivors over the PA, but received no reply. Looking at the sheets of plywood nailed up over the first floor openings, he assumed that whoever had taken shelter in the building had secured it from the outside and used the fire escape on the side of the structure leading to the second floor to get back in before locking the fire door behind them.

After considering both means of entering the building, the door at the top of the fire escape and the front doors, Cage pointed to the front doors and ordered, "Bust them out."

The fire escape would be too narrow and would only allow his people to get inside one at a time.

Two men ran forward and wrapped a steel cable around the door handles of the entrance before attaching the other end to a hook mounted on the front push bar of a Humvee. With both entry squads and two .50 calibers covering the doors, the Humvee revved its engine and started to back up. With a grinding screech, plywood, aluminum and safety glass came loose and crashed to the ground. The Humvee continued to back up as it dragged the wreckage of the doors clear, leaving a gaping six-foot wide hole in the side of the building.

Almost immediately, a dead thing wearing a blue police uniform staggered through the cloud of dust kicked up by the doors being wrenched from their frame. Three M-4's opened up on it, obliterating its head.

Except for a few scattered shots coming from the soldiers on the perimeter as they engaged the occasional Zs that showed up, the area was silent. Cage waited two minutes to see if anything else would emerge, and when nothing living or dead showed itself, waved his people forward.

As he passed by Cage, Jones said, "After this, I want to be promoted to Second Lieutenant."

"And be demoted from Sergeant?" Cage joked.

"Yeah, but the pay's better," he shot back.

Jones and his men were equipped with miner's lights attached to their Kevlar helmets as well as lights attached to the fore grips of their assault rifles. These were turned on as they approached the space where the doors had been. Beams of light crisscrossed each other as they looked for a target while they cautiously entering the building. Cage hefted his 12-gauge shotgun, and with his squad close behind him followed Jones and his team.

Although each platoon specialized in its own area, first platoon in scavenging and second platoon in search and rescue, both were well schooled in how to move around a structure suspected of containing Z's. While Jones and his people dispersed and started looking for any sign of survivors, Cage split his soldiers up into three, three person teams and told them to hold fast.

After checking the building directory in the lobby, he sent his first team to the licensing office. Two of the men carried battery packs in case they found a computer to boot up, as this would make the job of searching the city records easier. If a computer couldn't be found that could be brought back to life, the men would have to search the paper files for people who had received a permit to install an underground fuel storage tank. This was not always desirable, since they were usually kept in the basement. Not that that the dead congregated there and made it more dangerous; it was more of a psychological thing. Basements were dark, shadowy places that were cluttered and generally spooky. Once the files had been found and sorted, addresses were noted to be checked later for caches of diesel fuel. Once these were located, a squad accompanying a tanker truck equipped with an intake pump would swing by within a day to collect the liquid gold.

The job of the second team was to locate and secure any firearms and ammunition. Cage sent them in the direction of the Police Station. Finding weapons was secondary since the base had a well-stocked armory, but ammunition was getting scarce as all available supplies were being diverted to the units fighting in the dead cities. Team two would start their search at the Sheriff's Office, where they would look through the files of all the registered weapons in the county. The most important on the list being anything that fired .223 caliber, 7.62mm or 5.56mm. The logic behind this was; where there were guns, there would be ammunition.

One of the men on this team also carried breaching charges, as he was tasked with having to break into the evidence locker and the armory. The C-4 plastic explosive was strong enough to take a vault door off its hinges. While it was always nice finding an armory, most of the men were more interested in what the evidence locker contained. The wide range of items confiscated by the Police and Sheriff were of such variety that sometimes they were amazed by what they found.

For instance, when the team broke into the evidence locker in the Russellville Police Station, they came across a homemade flame thrower that was so well constructed that it put their military issue one to shame. They had tried using it on the Z's, but found all it did was create flaming dead things that continued to walk around as if nothing had happened. It took a few minutes for the brain to literally boil in their skulls and cause them to drop. The mobile units were the only ones that used this type of weapon since they could torch the dead and keep moving. Major Cage also knew that the men on this team occasionally grabbed some of the confiscated marijuana they came across, but he looked the other way at this. He did let it be known in a roundabout way though, that if they were to take something heavier, like cocaine or heroin for instance, they would be shot. So far he'd had no problems.

Team three was designated as general scavengers and Cage let them go do their thing. Three was led by a Corporal who seemed to have a knack for finding things. He would study aerial photos and maps of the neighborhood they planned on searching, and once he arrived at the designated area, would make a beeline for what was always a bonanza of supplies. In Russellville, he'd found numerous tornado shelters stocked with food they used to supplement what was served in the chow hall. He had even unearthed a hidden bunker erected by a pre-Dead Day survivalist, which yielded weapons, ammunition and the 12-gauge shotgun Cage carried as his primary weapon.

Not expecting to find much here, Cage followed team two as they headed for the Police Station. He wasn't surprised when he discovered that all the weapons and ammunition had already been taken since whoever had barricaded themselves inside the building would have picked the area clean. He did however, find a still used for making moonshine in the evidence locker. He had his men pack it up for transportation back to the base.

Thinking about how some of his people smoked pot, he justified taking the still by reasoning 'each to their own'. No matter where they went to scavenge, the only consistent thing they found was that the liquor stores were picked clean. Occasionally, a bottle of booze or a couple cases of beer turned up while searching a house, but this was rare. Due to this shortage, it had been over two weeks since he'd had a drink. He was trying to remember how to prepare corn mash when his radio buzzed.

"We found some live ones, over," Jones voice crackled from the speaker.

"Location, over," Cage asked.

"We're at the jail. It's right above the Courthouse. I need your guy who's got the C-4 because they're locked in the cell block and no one knows where the key is, over."

"How many people, over?" Cage asked.

"Twenty to thirty, over," came Jones's reply.

Twenty to thirty Cage repeated to himself. Where in the hell am I going to put them?

In the past, S and R had only come across small numbers of survivors. These people were brought back to the base where they were fed and treated for any medical problems, usually malnutrition and dehydration, before being transported to one of the refugee centers being set up in the Dead Free Zone around Fort Hood. For their short stay at the base, these refugees were quartered in two tents that had been put aside for this purpose. These temporary quarters were in no way large enough to handle thirty people though.

I'll have to figure something else out, he thought. He contacted his driver and told him to use the more powerful radio in the Humvee to contact the base and have two more trucks dispatched to their location. Escorting the man carrying the C-4, they cautiously made their way through the building back to the foyer area. From here, they took the hallway leading to the Courthouse. It was a standing order that they always moved in groups of two or more. If one of you were bit, your partner was duty bound to put a bullet in your head.

As they neared the end of the corridor where it branched off to the right, Cage heard voices coming from around the corner. Not wanting to get shot, he called out, "Two coming in."

With the point of aim changed from the center mass of the body to the center mass of the head, the number of accidental wounds caused by friendly fire had gone down.

Unfortunately, the number of deaths had gone up because of this, so it was best to be cautious.

"Advance," came the immediate reply.

Cage rounded the corner and found two men he recognized from Jones' platoon standing in front of an open door leading to a flight of stairs. On seeing their commanding officer, they both came to attention and started to salute, but Cage waved them off.

"How bad is it?" He asked. Even as the words left his mouth, the smell hit him and he knew.

The first time that he'd gone with second platoon on an S and R mission to Russellville, they had come across more than forty Z's surrounding a house that had been built up on six-foot high stilts. Constructed this way since it was near a small river that overflowed its banks at least once every few years, instead of protecting its owners against flooding, its unique architecture now protected them from the dead that besieged it.

Knowing that someone must be alive inside because the dead didn't congregate in such numbers for carrion, Cage and his men quickly dispatched the Z's and called out to those trapped inside that it was safe to come out. Not receiving an answer, and not being able to access the front door since the stairs had been cut away to keep the dead from reaching it, Cage ordered their transport truck to be pulled up next to the house so they could stand on the cab and enter that way.

Cage was the first to climb up into the bed of the truck, and before he even crossed its length the stink hit him. Feces, urine and the underlying stink of dead, rotten meat. When he pried the front door open with a crowbar, the stench was so overpowering that he had to retreat all the way back to the ground. Jones tried to take his place, but started vomiting so powerfully he almost fell off the truck bed.

The rest of the men stood around looking uneasily at each other as they wondered who would be chosen next. Cage choked back his dry heaves, wrapped a bandana around his mouth and nose, and moved forward. Breathing through his mouth, and still barely able to stand the smell, he made it to the doorway. Here, he stopped long enough to draw his pistol, turn on his flashlight, and identify himself. A weak moaning sound came to him from the rear of the house. Bolstered by the thought of actually being able to save someone, he pushed the overwhelming smell from his mind and went inside.

Listening for the moaning sound again so he could identify from which direction it came and follow it to its source, he could only hear a buzzing noise that grew louder the deeper he went into the house. Following this sound since he had a good idea what caused it, he came across a man and a woman in one of the back bedrooms.

Cage's mind flashed to pictures he had seen of people who had been liberated from World War II concentration camps. This were the only things in his life's experience he could compare to the sight in front of him.

Two living skeletons covered with open sores lay on top of a stained mattress in the center of the room. Surrounding them were dozens of empty cans, that had weeks ago held food and had been literally licked clean. Two plastic jugs, each a quarter full of rust colored water, sat on the floor. A short distance beyond these were the picked clean carcasses of what looked to have been two dogs and the skeletons of a dozen rats. Looking through an open door leading off of the room to the right, Cage could see inside a bathroom that seemed to literally swim before his eyes like a moving shadow. This was where the buzzing sound came from. It was infested with thousands of flies. Focusing again on the two people lying on the mattress, he could see that they too were beset by flies that buzzed around their sores and crawled across their bodies.

While at the same time sickened and mesmerized by the sight, it took him a minute to come to his senses. Reality finally struck him like a pool cue between the eyes and he called out for his medics to come inside on the double as he went to open the window to get some air moving through the room.

As he reached out to move the curtain aside, a barely audible voice from one of the skeletons said, "No. You'll let them in," and then started crying softly as it asked Cage if he was real.

Two medics showed up and started tending to the emaciated couple on the bed, so Cage went to search the rest of the house, knowing what it contained due to the smell that hung in the air. On the back porch he found it, the bones of a human skeleton.

Through his disgust, the thought came to him that it was ironic for people who were trying to keep from getting eaten to resort to cannibalism.

He pushed down his revulsion as he considered how to handle the situation.

Charge the couple with murder? That was impossible since courts, judges and, thank God, lawyers were a thing of the past. Even if Major Conway convened a court of law at the base, whatever verdict and punishment he handed down would never be held up if things ever went back to normal.

Handle it myself, he wondered? Martial law had been declared, so he knew he would be entirely justified in meting out punishment for any crime he came across.

But what would be the punishment?

Death?

Had the people in this house committed murder? As far as he knew, there hadn't been a situation like this in the history of the Arkansas National Guard.

Finally deciding that he would have the two people transferred back to the base and dump the problem in Major Conway's lap, he felt a modicum of relief. Not only the legal, but also the moral and ethical aspects of the situation were far beyond his scope. Plus, underlying this was the question he had to ask himself; what would I have done if I had been trapped in this house?

Standing at the bottom of the stairs in the Clarksville Courthouse, Cage tentatively sniffed the air and relaxed. While the smell of human feces and urine were thick in the air, the smell of human meat was not.

One of the soldiers saw this and said, "It's pretty bad upstairs, sir, but I don't think they've been eating each other."

The second soldier handed over the gas mask that each of the people on the S and R team carried and added, "You'll need this though. With no running water..."

The mask wouldn't completely block out the smell, but it would cut down on it considerably. He took it with a thank you.

The other soldier handed his to the man accompanying Cage, and the two started up the stairs.

When he arrived at the jail area, he saw Jones carrying on a conversation with someone through a steel door. Noticing his CO, Jones voice sounded hollow through his own gasmask as he said in greeting, "There's a total of twenty-seven, sir. Physically they're all in good shape. This used to be a civil defense shelter so they had food and water. Dysentery seems to be their biggest problem."

Rapping the steel door with his knuckles, he added, "Guy that I've been talking to told me that one of the cops who locked down in here with them got infected a couple weeks ago and started freaking out. Thought the others were going to kill him when they found out, which they were. Late that night, he grabbed all the weapons and forced everybody in here. Left them some food and water and just wandered off, sir."

"That must have been the guy we capped at the front door," one of Jones' men chimed in.

Cage studied the door and then asked his demolition man, "Can you blow this without killing everyone inside?"

Studying the lock, he answered, "Piece of cake, sir."

After moving the soldiers out of the way, and having the captives gather at the far end of the cellblock, the door was taken down with no trouble and the people inside freed. The occupants consisted mostly of county workers and their families who had taken refuge in the building. It was a bonus when Jones found that an older, rather mousy looking woman was the County Clerk. They had her escorted down to where his men were searching the records room while the rest of the group were moved outside into the parking lot and fresh air.

As the last of them filed over to where the medics waited to check them out, Cage overheard part of a conversation that Jones was having with a good looking brunette he was escorting.

"-and it seemed like something was directing them," she said.

"Directing who?" Jones asked.

"The dead. It was like something was making them move around," she replied.

Jones looked skeptical and the woman threw her hands up in the air and said mournfully, "No one believes me."

Cage spoke up, "I might. Tell me what happened."

Seeing Cage's rank, the woman clammed up. Shaking her head, she told him, "It was nothing. It only happened once anyway."

"No, really," Cage insisted. "Tell me what happened. Anything we learn about these things could end up saving the lives of my men."

Reluctantly, the woman started talking. "I was up on the roof getting some air a few weeks ago, and I thought I heard the sound of a truck engine so I started looking around. I wanted to make sure someone was really out there before I said anything. I didn't want to get everyone's hopes up for nothing. But anyway, I look down at all those things wandering around in the parking lot. There must have been a couple hundred of them. All of the sudden they kind of all started moving to the right. It wasn't anything organized or anything. They all just started moving that way."

The woman pointed to the far side of the parking lot and then pointed to the near side as she added, "Then they all moved to this side. Once they were there, they all moved back to the far side. After that, they broke up and started milling around like they normally do. It was so eerie seeing them act like that. I felt like all the hair on my body was standing on end."

Careful that she didn't see him, Cage exchanged a look of disbelief with Jones, both of them knowing that the dead were only mindless pieces of meat wandering about in search of food. While they did congregate in groups, there was nothing organized about them. Unless they had a focus, like meat on the hoof, they spent most of their pathetic existence roaming about looking for something to shove in their mouths.

Jones gave a small shake of his head and shot Cage a look. To no one's surprise, since the dead had started coming back to life, mental illness had increased proportionately. The insanity and horror that everyone lived with, combined with a lack of food and water if you were trapped, often brought on hallucinations. Both Cage and Jones had rescued people who told them of seeing Jesus, the Devil, the Loch Ness monster and aliens landing in their backyard.

Jones laid his hand on the woman's arm and guided her toward the medics, leaving Cage standing near the shattered front doors of the City Hall as he planned their next move. Forgetting the crazy tale of the synchronized dead, his mind was already looking at a mental map of the town while he planned where to have his scavengers search next.

Consumed by this task, the story that the woman told him was quickly forgotten.

Chapter Sixteen

The Dead Calm:

Tick-Tock pointed to the empty slot in the velvet-lined case and said, "That's where the spare lens is supposed to be, but it's not there. This is fucked up. I should have checked it before we came out."

Steve looked at the Calm of the Seas floating half a mile away and cursed Reverend Ricky. After receiving the sextant the previous day, he and Tick-Tock had given it a cursory inspection. Everything had appeared to be in order, and they laid plans to go out and get a fix on their position. This morning, they had taken The Usual Suspects far enough from the cruise liner so Tick-Tock could shoot the sun without interference. As soon as he held the sextant up to his eye though, he realized the lens was cracked. He assured Steve that this was not a major problem since all sextants came with a spare. Then, it had become a problem.

"That bastard's got the spare lens," Steve said vehemently. "I feel like going back and shaking it out of him. For some reason he's slow walking us and trying to keep us here."

"Maybe he thinks you're cute?" Tick-Tock suggested with a smirk.

"You're only funny to you, Tick-Tock," Steve shot back.

Looking at the empty water stretching out around them, Tick-Tock said, "Well, it's too wet to plow, and I can't dance, so unless you want to go fishing, we might as well head back. It'd be nice to know exactly where we are, but I think I've estimated our position well enough to find land. Once we hit the coast, the charts we've got are accurate enough that it shouldn't be a problem figuring out whether to go north or south."

Still angry, Steve said, "Fuck that. I'd rather carve a new lens out of Ricky's fat ass."

Tick-Tock laughed and said, "I know how you feel, but you need to take it easy. You're the steadying influence on our little group. If you go off half-cocked, then we're screwed. We have to keep our priorities straight."

Steve took a deep breath and let it out as he said, "Yeah, you're right." A thought suddenly struck him and he added, "Maybe that's what Ricky's trying to do. Provoke us into doing something so he can justify ordering his people to come down on us."

Tick-Tock thought about this as he cranked the engine over. When it had warmed up, he slowly eased the throttle forward and said, "Kind of makes sense. But what's his end game? I mean, if he wanted to try and wipe us out, he could tell his people we were sent by Satan to drag their souls down to Hell or something. He could call down some kind of half-assed Christian jihad on our ass."

Steve shook his head, "I don't know. Regardless of what Ricky wants, I think it's time we took off. We've got just about everything we can get from the ship and I'm tired of playing games. Everyone's rested up, so let's go. We can make for land and try to find Corpus Christi or some other big city and see if we can find a military unit or someone in authority we can turn Cindy over to."

Tick-Tock asked, "When do you want to leave?"

"No later than tomorrow morning," he answered. "I'd prefer taking off as soon as we can get everyone's ass on board The Usual Suspects, but there's still a few things we need to take care of."

"Like Ricky?" Tick-Tock asked.

Steve nodded. "We've got to at least warn his people that the ship's sinking. Heather wants to take Ricky out and so do I. If we get the chance, we'll go for it, but that'll be the last thing we do before we leave. Ricky definitely needs to go." Steve laughed and added, "The population's been depleted so much that it means statistically there should be fewer assholes around. If we weed some more of them out now, the human race will be better off when it rebuilds. The world doesn't need people like Ricky around."

"There will always be people like Ricky around, so why bother? Kill one and a dozen take his place," Tick-Tock pointed out.

"Don't be such a downer, Francis," Steve said with a smile.

Even though they were the only two on the boat, Tick-Tock cringed and looked around as if someone might have heard. "You promised you'd never let anyone know my real name."

Innocently, Steve said, "But I didn't tell anyone that your name is Francis, Francis. It's just us out here."

"You're an asshole."

"So, are you going to help me take Ricky out and let his people know that the ship's sinking?" Steve asked. "Or do I tell Susan that your real name is Francis Aloysius Beauregard the Third?"

"You'd stoop to blackmail?" Tick-Tock asked, to which Steve grinned and nodded maliciously. Tick-Tock laughed and said, "I would've helped anyway."

"I know," Steve replied. "But I still have to give you a ration of shit now and then, Franc-."

"Don't say it." Tick-Took warned him, "Or you're taking a swim."

The two men traded insults all the way back to the Dead Calm.

As Tick-Tock eased the sailboat up against the side of the ship, Steve had just finished telling him to learn Spanish so he could be lame in two languages when he noticed something that put a damper on their fun. Pointing at the gunwale of the sailboat, he said, "I didn't see it when we left because we were jumping down, but I see it now. The ship has settled almost two feet since we first boarded her. Remember how we had to board her from the bow of the sailboat where it curves up? Now we can practically climb in from the side."

Tick-Tock immediately saw the difference in height between the bottom of the hatch and the top of the gunwale and said, "That's not good. I'd say at the present rate, this baby's going to start taking water on in a big way in about three or four days. After that, she'll go down fast."

Looking at the hatch, Steve said, "That settles it, were not staying on board any longer than tonight. Tomorrow morning, we're out of here." Steve eyed the remaining area between the water and where it would start pouring into the Dead Calm as he considered his decision. "That doesn't look like we've got a lot of room to play with. You think it'll stay afloat until tomorrow? You said it'd take two or three days to flood. Is that a guess?"

After considering the question, Tick-Tock replied, "Based on what I know about ships, unless something drastic fails, we should be alright. These liners have dozens of safety features and hundreds of watertight compartments. Unless we hit an iceberg, we should be fine. From just looking around the parts of the ship we've been on, I've noticed that almost all the hatches are closed. That'll keep any flooding to a minimum. If we get a chance, we might want to check out the decks below four and see if they're flooded. We can't close this hatch though or we won't be able to get to the sailboat if we need to leave in a hurry."

Steve considered what he knew about ships and it concurred with what Tick-Tock said. He'd catch up with Brain later and ask him too just to be sure. As a precaution, he'd keep someone on board The Usual Suspects so they could cast off if the Dead Calm did start to go down. If the cruise liner sank, it would pull their only means of transportation with it.

Steve grabbed the case containing the sextant and went in search of Heather. He found her sitting with Mary and Sheila at one of the tables in the dining room and explained their problem. Pulling out the sextant to show her, he was interrupted by Mary who said, "What's the big deal, just grab another one. There's got to be at least a dozen of them."

Exasperated, Steve held out the instrument and asked, "Do you even know what this is? It's a sextant. These aren't just lying around everywhere."

"Maybe they're not lying around everywhere," Mary shot back in a condescending tone, "but there's a whole bunch of them in a store called the Brass Eagle. I was just in there yesterday and saw them with my own eyes."

Reciting from memory, Mary sounded like she was reading from a sales brochure, "Nautical sextant in designer display case. Sextant fashioned from solid brass with silver inlay. Hand tooled scene depicting a nineteenth century whaling ship on the cover. Nine hundred twenty-nine dollars and ninety-eight cents. U.S. Dollars."

Steve's mouth dropped open in shock. He looked at Heather, who was also awe struck, then turned back toward Mary when the ridiculousness of the situation hit him and he started to laugh. First, they were trying to get a sextant from Ricky, and then worrying about finding a lens, when of all the people on board, Mary had come across a dozen on one of her shopping sprees.

He saw Mary getting angry at his laughter, so he said, "I'm not laughing at you, Mary. I swear I'm not. In fact you just earned your keep for this entire trip."

Suddenly realizing what he'd just said, and knowing that Mary would try to take advantage of it, he added, "I mean you've earned your keep up to now."

Not exactly sure of what she'd done, but wanting full credit for it, she replied, "It wasn't easy. I work hard at what I do."

"Yeah, shopping," Steve said. "But this time it looks like it paid off."

Steve laughed again and Heather joined in. Seeing that Mary was starting to get angry again, he said, "Take me to the Brass Eagle, Mary. You da bomb, baby."

\*\*\*

Brain followed the lithe figure down the darkened hall, concerned they were getting too far away from deck four. When the person in front of him told him there was a satellite radio stowed near the bridge, he hadn't hesitated to make the journey and had dropped everything to go in pursuit of the treasure. Now, he wasn't so sure it was such a good idea. Even though there were only a hundred or so of Reverend Ricky's followers scattered about the ship, he expected to run into at least one of them by now. Instead, all the passageways were deserted. It was spooky.

Fingering the .45 caliber pistol in its holster at his hip, he realized that in his excitement they hadn't made an effort to conceal themselves, using the grand staircase instead of the elevator shaft to access the upper decks. Besides being worried about being spotted by Ricky's people, now that he thought about it, he wasn't sure if Susan and Cindy had seen them go since they were watching the stairs on deck four. Thinking about it for a second, he realized the angle was wrong. No one could have seen that they left.

Uneasy at this thought, he suddenly stopped. The figure in front of him turned and said, "What's wrong, Randy. It's just a little bit further. We're almost there. We'll grab the radio and get out before anyone knows we've been here. It's early, so the Faithful are all passed out. We still need to hurry though."

Trusting his companion, and excited at the prospect of having a radio they could use to contact the military, Brain steeled his resolve and moved forward again. They only travelled a short distance further when the person leading him stopped in front of a cabin and said, "In here," before slipping through the door. Excited at being so close to the object of their expedition, he didn't hesitate.

As Brain entered the room, rough hands grabbed him from both sides and slammed him face down onto the floor. His arms were pinned behind his back and his pistol was wrenched free of its holster. He tried to struggle, but a kick to the side of the head took the fight out of him.

Barely conscious, he heard Reverend Ricky say, "Don't hit him too hard, I need him,"

Hearing the screech of duct tape being pulled quickly from a roll, Brain felt his hands and feet bound. Once he was secure, he was lifted up and deposited into a chair where more tape was used to secure him to it. Brain shook his head to clear the cobwebs from the kick and faced his captors.

Reverend Ricky and two of his men stood in front of him. Ricky held Tim's wrists pinned behind his back. Brain felt anger rush through him at seeing Tim manhandled.

"Let him go," he said through clenched teeth. "He's just a kid."

Ricky only laughed and handed Tim to one of his men who led the boy out of the cabin. When they were gone, Ricky said, "He might be a kid, but he's my insurance policy. If you don't cooperate, I'll have one of my men start cutting his fingers off one joint at a time and send them down to his sister. Think she'd like that?"

Brain deflated at this threat. Connie loved her brother. After the loss of her parents, something like that would crush her. Not to mention Tim would be maimed for life. The situation wasn't looking good.

"You don't need to do that," Brain said calmly as he struggled to keep his anger under control. "I'm sure we can work something out. Just tell me what you want."

"That's simple," Ricky said. "I need you to accompany me and some of my men on a trip. As you know, the Calm of the Seas is sinking and it's time to move on. We're going to Cozumel. Once we're there, you'll help us start a new life."

Ricky saw the confusion on Brain's face and explained, "Cozumel is free of the dead and the perfect place to settle in until this thing blows over. But once we get there, we'll need to get things up and running. Generators and wind turbines and any number of other things will need to be set up. I have it on good authority that you're some kind of savant when it comes to machinery and electronics."

Brain stayed silent as he searched for a way out of this mess. He didn't want to be kidnapped and dragged off to Cozumel, he wanted to stay with his friends. Trying a quick con job in the hope he could get his hands and feet freed, he said, "Alright, that sounds like a good deal. I'm tired of Steve running things like a dictator. I'll go with you and help. You can let me go."

Ricky laughed and said, "I'm not stupid, Randy. Until we get on the sailboat and are well away from the Calm of the Seas, you will remain restrained. Don't try to fool me with your pathetic attempt at a con job either. You can't con a con."

Brain was prepared for his attempt to fail and wasn't surprised. He didn't react to Ricky catching on to his attempt to con him, but at the mention of the sailboat, his eyes grew wide. Seeing this, Ricky said, "Yes, we'll be taking The Usual Suspects when we go. It's the only way to reach Cozumel."

"They'll never let you take the boat," Brain said forcefully.

"They won't have any choice but to give it up after they're dead," Ricky gloated. Seeing the alarm on Brain's face, he reached down and patted his cheek as he added, "Don't worry, we don't plan on killing everyone. We'll save your little senorita for you. And if you behave, I won't have her passed around to be used by the men, but if you resist me..."

Anger and defiance welled up in him again on hearing Ricky speak of Connie like that. "Fuck you!" He spat out.

Ricky made a tsk-tsking noise, turned and called out, "Brother Seth, we need an example set."

Immediately, the sounds of slaps and blows interspersed with Tim's cries of pain came from the hallway.

"Stop it!" Brain screamed as he struggled against his bounds.

Moments later, the beating ended as quickly as it had begun, leaving no sound except Tim crying. This faded as the youngster was dragged down the hall.

Ricky tilted his head back in an arrogant posture and said, "The next time you curse at me or show any sign of rebellion, I'll tell Seth to cut off the first joint of the little finger on Tim's right hand and send it to Connie."

Knowing that any overt acts of defiance would get Tim hurt and Connie gang raped, Brain decided to act like he was beaten until he could figure out a way to escape. He let his shoulders sag and said in a dejected voice, "You win. I'll go with you, but I want your word that Connie and Tim won't be hurt."

Ricky thought about this and said, "I promise they won't come to any harm, but you need to do as I say. One deviation and..." Ricky made a scissoring motion with two fingers before walking out of the cabin followed by the other man.

Brain waited until they were gone before testing his bonds. Duct tape had been wrapped several times around his hands and feet, and several more loops were used to bind him to the chair. He knew it was futile, but he had to try. He had to get free and warn the others. The door remained open a crack, and after fifteen minutes of struggling, he heard a low murmur of voices coming down the hall. As he eyed the opening, Ricky suddenly popped his head in and said, "I know the urge to warn your friends is overwhelming, but I want you to know that Brother William will be right out here in the hallway. Don't even think about trying to escape."

He turned off the lights and shut the door, leaving Brain in the dark.

Ricky entered the bridge of the Calm of the Seas and said, "Brilliant performance, young Tim."

Standing near the wheel, Tim replied with a sob, "What do you mean, performance?" He pointed at Brother Seth and said, "He was really hitting me."

Ricky tsk-tsk'd and said, "We had to make it seem real. If your friend Randy hadn't been convinced by your act, I would have been forced to start cutting you up into little chunks. We don't want that, now do we?"

Hanging his head in shame at what he'd done, and in fear of what Ricky might do to him, Tim said, "Okay, I get it. Now I've held up my end of the bargain. You have Randy, so where's my dad?"

Dead somewhere, but you don't know that, Ricky thought. Instead of voicing this, he said, "He's safe, just like I told you, but he's going to stay with me for a while because I might need you to do one more thing for me."

"I can't!" Tim cried. "They'll know it's me if I do anything else. If they even find out what I've done so far, there's no telling what they'll do to me. Besides, we had a deal."

Ricky said sternly, "And the deal was of my making, so I can change it anytime I want. If you ever want to see your father alive again, you'll continue to do as you're told."

Tim's mind was in turmoil as he realized he was trapped. There was no way he could deny anything Ricky asked of him, especially now that he'd lured Randy up to deck ten so he could be kidnapped. He was torn by his decision to set Randy up, but he hadn't had a choice. They were holding his dad. Instead of turning his anger on Ricky though, he rued the day the people from the sailboat came on board. It was their fault he was in this mess in the first place.

He hadn't planned on being caught sneaking around the ship. It just happened. One of Ricky's men recognized him when he was up on deck nine looking around for a sextant for Steve and Tick-Tock. The man had been one of the watchers on deck five and had seen Tim with the people from the sailboat. He put two and two together and they grabbed him. At first he thought they'd kill him, but instead he'd been brought to Reverend Ricky.

Ricky recognized him from when he had seen him and Connie on deck four. He remembered that his dad was missing and his mom was dead, and he told Tim that his dad was alive and would be held hostage unless he worked as an informer. Tim was elated at the news of his father and had been more than willing to spy on the newcomers in exchange for being reunited with his dad. It had been easy at first, like playing a game. But when Ricky told him of his plan to kidnap Randy, he'd balked. Ricky threatened to have his father tortured, so he had no choice. But now that he'd delivered Randy to Ricky, the Reverend wanted something else.

When would it end? Tim's mind wailed. I'm trapped.

Ricky motioned to Brother Seth, who handed Tim a radio and a three-foot long pair of bolt cutters. Tim looked dumbly at the objects as Ricky said, "Like I told you, I may need you to do one last thing for me. Let me explain."

\*\*\*

Steve steered The Usual Suspects back toward the Dead Calm on the way back from the second trip to get a clear view of the sun.

Tick-Tock had gone below fifteen minutes earlier to use the table so he could lay out the chart and calculate their position. As Steve made a slight adjustment to their course, he came on deck and said excitedly, "I got it! I know our position."

Hearing this, Steve felt relief wash through him. He trusted that Tick-Tock could get them to land, and eventually to a port, by using dead reckoning, but being able to sail directly there without the fear of the unknown hanging over them lifted a huge burden.

"Where are we?" Steve asked.

"It's not exact, but its close. I'll need to take some more sightings at sundown and sunrise to get it perfect, but I know I'm within a couple miles," Tick-Took said.

"Where?" Steve asked again.

Tick-Tock unrolled the chart on the deck and pointed to a spot in the Gulf of Mexico. "Right here."

"Holy shit!" Steve exclaimed, as he saw how far away from Florida they were.

Tick-Tock nodded and said, "We're a long-ass way from Kansas, Toto."

Studying the chart, Steve said, "It looks like the closest port we can head to is Galveston." After a moment, he asked, "Can we even make it back to Florida? I mean, that was our original plan."

"We could make it," Tick-Tock replied, "but why bother? Texas has a shitload of Army and Air force bases where we can take Cindy. Why risk a long cruise to Florida? It's not hurricane season, but the storm that blew us out here sure felt like one. I really don't want to have to go through that again."

Steve had to agree. Although the sailboat was an excellent way to move around, their luck hadn't been too good so far. First the storm before being becalmed, and then finding the Dead Calm prompted him to decide it might be better if they got to dry land as soon as possible.

"So Galveston it is," he said and then asked, "You ever been there?"

"Nope, never," Tick-Tock replied. "But the one thing I've noticed about all port cities I've ever been to, is that very few people live down around the docks. The Z's congregate where there's food, so that means the docks should be deserted. We'll have a pretty easy time moving around when we hit land. We need to find transportation first thing when we go ashore, but that shouldn't be a problem. There're all kinds of stuff lying around out there. If I remember right, Texas declared martial law long before Florida did. Maybe we'll get lucky and come across some abandoned National Guard vehicles."

"Another MRAP?" Steve asked with a smile.

"I'd settle for a two and a half ton truck," Tick-Tock replied. "All wheel drive would be nice too."

"And we can hit the local library to find out where the nearest military bases are," Steve said.

"The hard part will be finding supplies," Tick-Tock added as Steve pulled The Usual Suspects up to the hatch at the side of the cruiser. As he did this, both men gauged the distance between the bottom of the opening and the top of the gunwale, but neither could see any change from that morning.

As they started to tie the sailboat up, Steve considered that they might be nearing the end of their trek now that they had a solid direction to go in. Out of curiosity, he asked Tick-Tock, "What do you plan on doing after we drop Cindy off?"

"Explore," he answered with a grin. "Dead or no dead, I'm going to check things out. I even thought about getting another sailboat and cruising to Europe."

Steve's brow lifted and he commented dryly, "Great, you can check out Dracula's castle while you're there."

Tick-Tock laughed. "No, I think I've seen enough scary shit to last me a lifetime. I'll skip the land of Vlad. I'm thinking of the Louvre and the British Military Museum."

"Are you going to ask Susan to come along?"

Tick-Tock shrugged, "I'll ask, but that's up to her." Then he asked, "What about you and Heather? What are you two going to do?"

"She wants to go to North Carolina," Steve replied. "She's got family up that way and she wants to check up on them. I guess I'm along for the ride. After that, who knows? North Carolina is nice. Maybe we'll stay there."

After securing the sailboat, Steve and Tick-Tock went to the kitchen in search of something to eat. As they were sitting down to fried chicken left over from the night before, Heather burst through the fire doors at the far end of the dining room. Spotting Steve, she called out, "Is Brain with you? Have you seen him? Please tell me he went with you guys."

Feeling a crisis at hand, both men rose as Steve said, "No, he stayed here because he had to watch the stairs."

Heather rushed forward as she said, "He was supposed to take over from Susan and hour ago but he never showed. She called me a half hour ago and we've been looking for him ever since."

Steve ran through the possibilities of where Brain could be. None of them were good. His first thought was that Ricky and his people had grabbed him so he asked, "Did anyone see him go to the upper decks?"

Heather nodded and said, "Susan was watching the stairs, and she said he went up to five with Tim to grab something to eat, but she didn't see them come back down. When we asked Tim, he said they both came back downstairs through the elevator shaft because they wanted to explore."

"Is everybody else here?" He asked, relieved that Ricky didn't seem to be involved. Now, they just had to find Brain in case he was hurt and laid up somewhere, and not have to take on over a hundred religious fanatics.

"Everyone's accounted for," Heather answered as she approached Steve and hugged him. "I left Susan at the stairs and got everyone else organized to search the shops. I already checked the elevator shaft and he's not there."

"Who else saw him this morning?" Tick-Tock asked.

"Connie saw him, and they made plans to get together for lunch. After that - nothing."

"Okay, we'll find him," Steve assured her. "He couldn't have gone far. Hopefully he didn't go exploring the ship on his own."

"We're almost finished searching deck four and then we planned to check five," Heather told him. "I came back here to look for him in the kitchen and the dining room."

Taking charge, Steve said, "There are three of us here now, so we'll split up. Tick-Tock and I will take the kitchen and you look here in the dining room. Before you start though, go out and tell everyone to wait when they've finished searching the shops. We'll go up to deck five as a group."

Heather rushed off as Steve and Tick-Tock each un-holstered their pistols. Even though they dreaded finding Brain injured or dead, if they found him undead, they would put him out of his misery. After a thorough search of the kitchen with no results, they re-entered the dining room to find Heather, Tim and Connie lifting table cloths to make sure Brain wasn't lying unconscious under one of the tables. Pitching in, they finished in no time. Steve noticed that Connie wore a T-shirt with the words 'I'm not as dead as you think I am' on the front. Brain had made one for everyone.

Steve thought to himself, I hope you're not as dead as I think you are, Brain. Then pushed the thought from his head. If you're alive, we'll find you, he vowed.

Moving into the Centrum, Steve heard Sheila and Mary calling out for Brain. As he approached the stairs, the shouts suddenly stopped. Thinking that the engineer had been found, he hurried forward. Instead of finding the missing tech though, he saw a man standing at the bottom of the grand staircase with Susan covering him with her rifle.

Not wanting to be interrupted in his search by one of Ricky's people, Steve asked abruptly, "What do you want?"

"Ricky sent me down to see if you needed some help," the man said. "One of our people said you were running around down here looking around and calling out for someone named Blain."

"Brain," Steve corrected.

The man nodded and smiled, "Brain then. If one of your people is missing, we can help you search for him. It happens all the time, so we've kind of got a grid system set up that covers all the accessible areas of the ship."

Steve was debating this when the man looked past him and said, "Hello Sheila. How are you?"

"You son-of-a-bitch," she spit out in reply.

Turning to Sheila, Steve said dryly, "I take it you know him."

Her face had become almost the color of her hair as she said venomously, "That's Brother Seth, one of the guys that Ricky sent to kill me."

"I beg to differ," Seth said in a sanctimonious tone. "The truth of the matter is that you killed Brother Raymond and ran off. I used to be a cop, so I could arrest you for murder if I wanted to."

"Where did you work?" Heather cut in.

"The Lee County Sherriff's office in Fort Myers, Florida," Seth said with pride.

Heather made a snorting noise. "It figures you'd be with Ricky then. You used to be one of the back shooters."

Distracted by the label she used, Steve asked, "Back shooters?"

"Every year at least three unarmed suspects are shot in the back by a Lee County Sheriff's Deputy. Somehow or another, they always convinced the Florida Department of Law Enforcement to let them investigate their own shooting. Miraculously, the officers are always cleared. They're trigger happy, and the Sherriff down there condones it and covers it up."

"Imagine that," Steve said sarcastically.

Trying to ignore the scornful looks from the group, Seth knew the conversation needed to be refocused so he said, "But that's neither here nor there. I'm down here to offer our aid in your search for Randy. We can check the upper decks for him."

Steve looked thoughtful for a moment before saying, "I accept your help. We're going to search deck five first, so give us an hour and then come back. Our people need to be in on the search of the upper decks though."

"Of course," Seth said, "we wouldn't have it any other way. We'll split it up and give you your own sections."

"And ask Ricky if he has a spare lens for the sextant he gave us. The one we have seems to have been accidentally cracked," Steve said.

"I'll pass on your request," Seth told him. Nodding to the group in front of him, he said, "I'll be back in an hour so we can plan the search. Ladies, gentleman, Sheila, stay safe until then."

After Seth was gone, Heather exchanged a knowing look with Steve and Tick-Tock. Sheila approached them and said, "Don't trust him. He's a snake, just like the rest of them. Maybe worse."

"I know," Steve told her.

Mary asked, "Then why did you agree to work with him. And why'd you ask him for the spare lens for the sextant? We've got one."

"To throw Seth off the track and make Ricky think we still need him. I want to stall them for a while," Steve answered.

"So we can search deck five?" Susan asked.

"So we can make it look like were searching deck five," Steve told her. "I'm sure they have people watching us so we have to go through the motions."

Confused, Mary asked, "What about Brain?"

"Yeah," Sheila put in. "Even though the little dweeb always wanted to talk about Star Wars and wouldn't quit looking at my boobs, I kind of liked him."

"He's not on deck five," Heather said. "Ricky's people have him."

"They kidnapped him?" Mary asked with horror. "How do you know?"

Heather answered, "Seth must have been a lousy cop. He gave himself away when he called Brain by the name Randy. Only we know him by that name. He acts like he doesn't even know Brain's name, and then he calls him Randy? What a dumbass. Seth blew it. "

Steve and Tick-Tock nodded. They'd both picked up on Seth's mistake as soon as he made it.

"What would they want a nerdy engineer for?" Mary asked.

No one said anything except for Sheila. She suddenly sat down on the planter behind her and moaned out, "Oh God, I know why. It was there the whole time, but I didn't see it."

All eyes turned to her as she told them about Cozumel.

Chapter Seventeen

Quantico, Virginia:

The Chairman of the Joint Chiefs of Staff called the meeting to order. "Gentleman, since the communication satellites have come back on line, we've been able to establish contact with the remnants of many foreign governments around the world. Two of these are China and Russia. Both were hit hard by the HWMW Virus, much harder than the United States, but they're working to eradicate the dead and rebuild. "

"How long will it take them?" The Navy Chief asked.

"Decades, but that's not the point," the Chairman answered. "The point is that one day they will again be a threat. Right now, as far as we know, no one except the United States has any kind of nuclear capability they can call upon, but that will change. We need to make sure we stay on top."

"Are you suggesting a pre-emptive strike?" The Commandant of the Marine Corp asked in astonishment. "Isn't the world screwed up enough?"

"A pre-emptive strike, yes," the Chairman said. "But not with nukes."

"But our conventional forces are tied up trying to eradicate our dead," the Marine said.

"And it's the dead that might end up being our best weapon," the Chairman told them. "I'm sending you a report on some research we've been doing in Arkansas. Take a minute to read the synopsis, I'll wait to hear your comments."

Although the civilian Internet was dead, it had been originally created so the military could have a form of secure communication in the event of a nuclear war, so the computers serving the armed forces were still humming.

After the Chiefs downloaded the file and read the report, the Navy Chief spoke first, "Incredible, but will it work?"

"They're still testing it, but so far the results are promising." The Chairman replied.

"Isn't Russellville where they're looking into a cure for the HWNW virus?" He asked. "I recall you saying something about that in an earlier briefing."

"It is, but that's not the only research they've been doing," the Chairman answered. "After you read the entire file, you'll see that finding a cure has been a slow process. Since part of the disease mutated from the H1N1 flu, it's turned into an attempt to find a cure for that along with numerous other aspects of the disease. Additionally, the lack of subjects found who are immune to HWNW has further delayed the development of an anti-virus."

"One in five-hundred million," the Commandant of the Marine Corps interjected. "That's how many people have a natural immunity."

"And of the three subjects we've studied that are resistant to HWNW, two died from other causes and the third is still being tested," the Chairman informed them. "But that isn't what I'm getting at. What I want to do is authorize Doctor Lyonel Hawkins to expand the study he's been working on into controlling the dead, to give us some solid results. This has been on the back burner, so he'll need additional resources and a free hand in his experiments. From his research, we can form a weapon that will make the United States the only world power for centuries to come."

Silence greeted this proposal. The Chairman added, "Hawkins won't go any further in his experiments until he has the go ahead from us."

The Commandant said, "But some of these experiments I'm reading about here are slightly disturbing."

"The few sacrificed for the many," the Chairman answered. "Now I'd like to put it to a vote. All those in favor of authorizing Doctor Hawkins to go forward with his test, say aye."

It was unanimous.

Russellville, Arkansas:

Doctor Hawkins looked through the shatterproof window into the room holding the test subjects and thought, hopefully today I'll get the go ahead for my new line of experiments and there'll be no more mucking around with these filthy creatures.

Lined up on the far wall in the containment room were five of the living dead, these being the object of his scrutiny. Although two technicians were also visible as they moved around the room, they were in no danger of being attacked as each of the dead was secured hand, foot and neck to the concrete wall by shackles on ten-inch chains. As further protection against them biting, each of the living dead wore a mask of heavy plastic that covered the bottom half of their face.

Despite his revulsion to the dead, Doctor Hawkins was still fascinated by certain aspects of his experiments. It was this curiosity that led him to press down on the intercom button and ask one of the men in the room to unmask the dead woman on the far right.

Carefully, the technician undid the Velcro straps and pulled the mask off with a quick jerk as he backed away. The Z lunged forward to bite, but was stopped short by its neck restraint. The dead woman looked around and gnashed her teeth at the technician who was standing well out of striking distance.

Doctor Hawkins pressed down on the intercom button again and said to the technician, "Jim, give me the statistics on that one."

Thumbing through a pile of charts, Jim selected one and opened it. After scanning through it, he flipped a few pages and started to read while adding his own comments from his knowledge of the specimen. "Forty two year old female. She was one of the first to be brought here to the facility and has been here the longest. Bite mark on her left bicep. This was what caused the initial transference of the virus. She hadn't turned when we received her from Little Rock. This was shortly before they abandoned the city. Died on October twenty-ninth at ten-forty eight AM. Came back to life on the same date at eleven-oh-one AM. Suffered convulsions before expiring. She was transferred here to Containment One where she's been kept without food and water since."

Hawkins looked at the drawn face of the subject. While she looked like she was suffering from anorexia due to the skin stretched across the bone structure of her face, she was neither lethargic nor seemed to be suffering from a lack of energy from being deprived of food. Even as he watched, the stick figure rattled its chains in fury as it tested its bonds. Whipping its head around, the dead creature banged it against the wall behind it, leaving a smear of black puss. Seeing this reminded him of something, so Hawkins asked the tech about the body fluid tests he'd ordered the day before.

Thumbing once more through the file, Jim stopped and extracted a loose page. After reading for a few seconds, he said, "No appreciable change. The alcohol base that makes up most of their body fluids and acts as a preservative is still present. There's been very little degeneration in cellular structure, and even less tissue breakdown then that of normal aging in a human subject."

Flipping the page, he added, "The new estimate based on longevity also came back. The lifespan of someone infected with the HWNW virus comes back at ninety-six years. That starts from the time of initial infection. That's plus or minus five years."

"Amazingly ironic," Hawkins commented dryly. "The secret to long life is death."

"By the way, Doctor," Jim said. "In the past month there's been no further loss of body mass. Although most of the muscle structure is gone, the subjects still function at the same physical level."

Hawkins considered this before asking, "What about the subjects that have been fed?"

Picking out another chart from the pile, Jim moved over to stand in front of the dead creature chained at the far end of the line and started to read. "Twenty-two year old male-."

"Skip that," Hawkins interrupted.

Jim found what the doctor wanted. "No nutrition was absorbed into the subject even though it consumed everything it was fed. This included sheep, pig and human entrails. They only eat to eat, doctor. They get no sustenance from it."

Hawkins was about to comment on this when the PA system beeped and informed him he had a call. Picking up a nearby phone, he listened to the message and hung up without saying a word.

Moving back to the observation port, he pressed the button for the intercom and said, "Jim, we're finished with this part of the research. Dispose of the subjects and clear this room. We'll be getting new equipment in tomorrow so I need you to start on this right away."

"What's going on, Doctor?" Jim asked.

"We're expanding research on the Malectron." Hawkins told him. "I'll also need the other three containment rooms cleared out, so you've got your work cut out for you. See if Doctor Connors needs any of our equipment for her antivirus research before you get rid of it."

"She's going to want some of our floor space," Jim warned. "She still has one test subject left in Containment Three. It's one of the people that are immune."

"She can't have any of my space," Hawkins snapped. "She has to make do with what she has, and she'll have to find somewhere else to quarter her test subject. The Malectron takes precedence over the other research at this facility. Finding a cure for the HWNW virus has now taken a backseat to more important research."

"Yes, Doctor," Jim replied.

When Hawkins was gone, Jim picked up a hand held Taser from the exam table and approached the dead creature he'd unmasked at Hawkins' bidding.

With regret, he said to her, "Sorry, Honeybun. We had a long run together, but I've got my orders."

Placing the prongs against the skin of her side, he thumbed the trigger and said, "Lights out."

Chapter Eighteen

The Dead Calm:

Steve met with Seth on deck five. Ricky's man had brought along floor plans of the ship, much like the one Tick-Tock had pried off the wall on the day they had first boarded the Dead Calm. Steve could see that the pages for decks seven and eight had been shaded with different colored pencils.

Pointing to the cabin area colored in red on deck seven, Seth said, "That's where the stinkers are locked in, so you don't have to worry about that. If your guy somehow made his way in there, you won't want him back. Next to that you've got service areas for the ship and then the Centrum. Most of those shops are sealed off, but a few might be open. You'll have to check them as you go along."

"Got it," Steve acknowledged.

"Next, you've got the Sombrero Lounge," Seth continued. "Beyond that's the main floor of the Sounds Lounge. It's not really a lounge, it's a theater for live shows. That's also full of the dead. You can't access it, nor would you want to, but-," flipping to the layout of deck eight, he continued, "You can get to the balcony through the deck above. You might want to check it out. Maybe your guy's hanging out in there. Outside the balcony area is the casino and then the Centrum again. There's not many shops and shit there. It's mostly an observation deck and a few small bars. After that, there are more cabins that are sealed off. You don't want to go in there either."

"And your people are checking the decks above this?" Steve asked.

"We've got people searching them now," Seth assured him.

Handing over the floor plans, Seth said, "You can have these. Good luck and I hope you find your guy. If we come across him and he's alive, we'll send him back to you."

After Brother Seth left, Steve unclipped his radio and removed the piece of clear tape holding the transmit button down. Keying it a few times to make sure it wasn't stuck, he pressed it and asked, "Heather, Tick-Tock, you there? Did you get all that?"

"Loud and clear," Tick-Tock replied. "I'm looking at the floor plans of the ship right now. From what I see, they're going to try and hit us in the Sombrero Lounge on seven and the casino on deck eight. Those are the best places for an ambush." Before Steve could answer, Tick-Tock came back on saying, "By the way, your other half just told me to tell you that when we're done talking we're supposed to say over, over."

"Over, over?" Steve asked.

"Say over," Tick-Tock came back.

"Over, over," Steve said, knowing it would bug Heather to no end.

"Say ov-," Tick-Tock started to say, but was cut off as Heather took the radio from him. "You two need to knock that shit off. It wasn't funny the first time."

Steve laughed and gave a chastised, "Yes, dear, over."

"Tick-Tock's going to set up to cover the Sombrero and I'm going up the casino, over." Heather told him.

Steve was about to reply, over, over but knew it was time to get serious. Tick-Tock and Heather had climbed up the elevator shaft before Steve's meeting and were waited inside by deck seven so they could have quick access to wherever Seth tried to direct the search parties.

When Seth slipped up and gave away that Ricky had Brain, his first impulse was to grab the ex-cop and find out where Brain was by beating the information out of him. He had barely restrained himself. He knew they needed to figure out what Ricky was up to first, and if need be, he could grab the man later when they met to go over the search plan. When Sheila made the connection between why they wanted Brain and told them of Ricky wanting to get to Cozumel, all the pieces of the puzzle fell into place.

Knowing that grabbing Seth and rushing the stairs before starting a search of the upper decks would result in a gun battle with Ricky's people, he decided the best way to go about freeing Brain was to first eliminate the Ushers. Ricky wanted Brain for his knowledge, and the sailboat for transportation, but the rest of them were expendable. As he considered this, it suddenly came to him what Ricky was up to. Getting the group to split up during a search would be the perfect way to take them out. This way, he got Brain and eliminated the rest of them at the same time.

Steve came up with his own plan. Ambush the ambushers. Ricky would have all his people coming after them, so they needed to turn the tables and take them out. They would try to leave one of the Head Ushers alive to find out where Brain was, but if that turned out to be impossible, they would kill them all. Without any type of effective fighting force, Ricky would have to give Brain up. Or at least they hoped so. He didn't want to get into some kind of hide and seek hostage situation on the Dead Calm. If they succeeded in taking out the Head Ushers, they would be in a much stronger position to get Brain back.

Steve explained this to the others. They decided that while it was risky, they didn't have any other options. They couldn't leave Brain, and without knowing where he was, they had no other choice but to go for it.

Keying the radio, Steve said, "I'll give you fifteen minutes to set up and scope out the area. In the meantime, I'm going to get the rest of the bait, over and out."

Clipping the radio back on his belt, he headed to deck four. Seeing Sheila standing at the bottom of the stairs, he thought to himself that from a distance she'd pass for Heather. If any of the Ushers got a good look at her though, they'd might recognize her and then we would be screwed. A lot hinged on them thinking that Sheila and Mary are Heather and Tick-Tock, so they had to be convincing.

As he approached Sheila, the first thing she did was moan, "My hair."

"It'll grow back," he promised her.

"But it's blonde," Sheila whined as she fingered it. "I look like a ditz. Blondes are all airheads. Everyone knows that."

Steve checked to make sure the transmit button on his radio wasn't pushed. If Heather had heard that comment, war with the Ushers would pale in comparison to the one between her and Sheila.

Seeing Susan hurrying toward them, Steve said to her, "Good job on Sheila. She could pass for Heather's sister."

Susan thanked him and then rolled her eyes as she said, "Wait until you see Mary. She's not a happy camper."

Susan had taken both Mary and Sheila into the Four Bells Hair Salon to alter their appearance while Steve, Connie, Tim and Cindy made a show of searching deck five in case any of Ricky's people were watching. Just then, Mary appeared and Steve had to stifle a laugh. Most of her long blonde hair had been cut off and what remained had been stuffed under a baseball cap. It was a good thing Mary didn't hear Sheila's comment about blondes either. Or maybe that's where it stemmed from, he wondered.

Steve wasn't sure what Susan had used to strap Mary's breasts down, but whatever it was had done the trick. It had taken her from about a 34C to flat-chested.

Seeing his gaze, Mary said angrily, "Quit looking at my tits, Steve."

Or lack thereof, Steve thought, but didn't dare voice. Averting his eyes, he found they'd settled on Sheila's chest for a moment. She's got bigger ones than Heather, but she'll pass, he decided.

Not wanting to micro manage a plan that had been put together on the fly by comparing boob sizes, he cleared his throat and asked, "Everyone know what to do?"

"I'm supposed to be Heather," Sheila said despondently. "I stay ten feet behind you. When the first shot is fired, I find something to hide behind."

"I'm with her," Mary said as she pointed to Susan.

"And?" Steve prompted.

"Same as Sheila, only I'm supposed to be Tick-Tock. I stay ten feet behind Susan. When the shooting starts, I find cover," Mary motioned to her legs and complained, "Why do I have to wear blue jeans? I'm already chafing."

"Because Tick-Tock does. We need to convince them that you're Tick-Took," Steve explained. "Take a little of the wiggle out of your walk too," he added. "You need to be convincing. Walk like a guy."

"I feel so butch," Mary moaned.

Steve had to cough to cover the laughter welling up in him. When he got himself under control, he turned to Susan with a raised eyebrow.

"I'm on point. I listen to the radio and follow Tick-Tock's instructions," she said, "He'll let me know where any targets are that he can't hit. I have to take them out."

"And I'll be doing the same with Heather," Steve finished. "As you all know, Connie's on The Usual Suspects with Tim and Cindy. If anything happens to us, she knows to cut loose and head west. She has enough fuel to make it to land and she knows about Cindy. She'll try to get her somewhere safe."

Checking his watch, he saw it was almost time to check in with Heather and Tick-Tock before moving out. One by one, he looked each of them in the eye to check their resolve. When he was done, he said forcefully, "Let's go get Brain."

***

As he sat in the cockpit of The Usual Suspects, Tim's mind was in turmoil. He felt trapped no matter the outcome of Steve's plan and it was tearing him apart. If Steve and the rest of them succeeded in killing Ricky's men and freeing Randy, they would surely find out his part in the kidnapping. Tim's biggest fear was what his punishment would be.

I know that treason is punishable by hanging so that's what they'll probably do to me, he thought. The words 'hung by the neck until dead', echoed through his mind.

And if Ricky wins, he wondered. Then my sister will cut the sailboat loose and head for land and I'll never see dad again. Ricky will kill dad after torturing him because I lost the sailboat. But if Ricky wins, he can force Connie to stay on the Calm of the Seas. Tim brightened at this until the thought came to him that he'd still have to live with what he'd done. Things were so messed up.

At that moment, Connie came up the ladder from below. Seeing her brother looking tense and frightened, she asked, "Are you okay, Tim?"

With guilt racking his brain, Tim glanced up at his sister. Instead of seeing her face and the concern on it though, his eyes focused on the small pistol Steve had given her for protection. His mind screamed, she knows. She knows I betrayed them all and handed her boyfriend over to Ricky. They're all after me. They know I'm a Judas.

With a cry of anguish, he bounded to his feet, his fear suddenly turning to rage at the thought of what they'd do to him. "I hate you all," he screamed. "You did this to me. It's your fault."

Stunned by her brother's outburst, Connie took a step back down the ladder. Jumping onto the gunwale of the ship, Tim found it was an easy leap through the hatch.

Connie screamed, "Tim, come back. What are you doing?" But it was too late. He'd already disappeared into the Dead Calm.

\*\*\*

Jackson Willis looked out at the casino through the steel grill protecting the cashier's cage. Glancing down at the cash drawer with its money placed neatly in its slots, he knew it was worthless, but every few seconds he would peel a one hundred dollar bill off the top of the stack and stuff it in his pocket. His left pocket was starting to fill up, so he switched his .38 revolver to his left hand and started in on his right pocket.

Curious as to when the people he was supposed to kill would show up, he considered the revolver and wished he had his own piece with him. Due to the security on the ship though, he'd left it at home.

Now that's a gun, he thought. A ghetto sweeper. My little nine-millimeter exterminator with an extended magazine. Twenty-two rounds coming out as fast as you could pull the trigger.

Jackson brought his pistol up when he heard a plinking noise as he leaned toward the security screen to get a better view. He eased back when he saw nothing and began methodically putting bills in his pocket again.

That cracker Ricky thinks he's got me fooled, Jackson thought. Telling me if I do this thing, I'll ensure my place at the right hand of God. Bullshit. The only reason I even went along with his shit in the first place was cause of all the pussy. I grew up on the streets of Overton, mother-fucking mister Reverend Ricky, I know what's what. You can snow the rest of these dumbasses with your fake-ass religion, but I got to have me mine. I'll do this thing, but then you're gonna pay and I know just what I want.

Sheila.

I seen her struttin' her fine ass around before she left your dumb ass. You can promise these other boys everlasting life, but I want to get me some of that redhead. You tell me that if I kill these people when they show up that I can have anything on the ship. Well I want to see your face when I tell you I want your ex-old lady, a lifeboat full of gas, food, water and all the booze I can carry.

Jackson chuckled softly at this.

I been dealing drugs since I was nine and I ain't never been busted. That's 'cause I always knew when to haul ass, and I see that time as soon. Too much hinky shit going down. Things is startin' to get flaky. Time to cut and run to Mexico and find me an island or somewhere there ain't no dead tryin' to eat my black ass. Just me and Red.

The plinking noise came again and Jackson finally figured out what it was. It was the sound of a coin hitting the outside of the cashier's cage. Thinking that one of the other men were screwing around, Jackson scowled and looked out to see who it was.

Probably that mother-fucker Don Parsons checkin' to see if I'm paying attention, Jackson thought. Or that ex-cop Seth. When we saw each other that first time, we didn't need no introduction or any of that bullshit. Making small talk like, "So what do you do for a living?" We knew each other on sight. Ain't much separating most cops from criminals. Some are straight, but the rest... same as me.

Looking around and not seeing the other two men looking in his direction, Jackson leaned back and continued to wait.

\*\*\*

Seth looked out from where he was lying under the blackjack table and thought; I wish they'd hurry up and get here. I'm tired of waiting for this shit. I just want to cap these people and get on my way. I never thought all this shit would come down when I took this cruise. Screw it though, I'm coming out on top no matter what.

Glancing to his right, he saw Don Parsons crouched behind a row of video poker machines and considered the swing he would need to make with his rifle to take him out. Two easy shots, he thought to himself. Put one in the chest of whoever was on the left, leave the one on the right for Jackson, let Parsons get off a few shots and then, BANG, I'm now the number two man on the totem pole according to Ricky.

Looking again at Parsons broad back, Seth thought, what the hell, it's not like I've never shot someone from behind before. The only difference is that I'm not a cop anymore and Parsons has a gun in his hand. Not that it'll do him any good, Seth gloated. He's facing the wrong way.

\*\*\*

In the Sombrero Lounge, George Day was thinking along the same lines. The Reverend Ricky himself had confided in him that this was to be Cal's last rodeo. There would be a slot open if he helped kill the man, and George could move up to the position of Head Usher. Being one of the true believers, George had jumped at the chance. Especially when the Reverend told him that Cal was a spy of Satan sent to assassinate their leader. Even if it cost him his own life, George couldn't let this happen. The plan was for him to help kill the Satanists that had invaded the Calm of the Seas and then to turn his gun on Brother Cal. But George had ideas of his own on who posed the bigger threat and should die first.

\*\*\*

Steve gave some last minute orders to Susan before they split up, "Remember that Tick-Tock will point you in the direction you need to shoot. When he opens fire on his target, you need to shoot for the center mass of yours. When I get into position upstairs, we'll wait to make sure Heather and Tick-Tock have spotted all the shooters before we move in. The casino is directly above the Sombrero Lounge, so we need to time our movements so we can reach both places at the same time. If for some reason you hear shooting from upstairs before you reach the Sombrero Lounge, listen on the radio for instructions. But if you see a threat, take it out. Just make sure it's not Tick-Tock."

Susan nodded grimly, so Steve gave her an encouraging smile. When he turned to go, she said, "Heather's lucky to have you."

Steve wasn't sure how to repl, so he smiled again and promised, "I'll see you when this is over." To Sheila, he said, "Let's go."

Poised at where the grand staircase emptied onto deck eight, Steve waited for the call on his radio from Heather telling him to move. He was impatient to get this over with, but since Heather and Tick-Tock had to go in and check the situation out before retreating a safe distance to relay what they'd seen, the initiative was theirs.

Worried that something had gone wrong, he was relieved when he heard Tick-Tock sending whispered instructions to Susan. Hearing what Tick-Tock said, he felt the urge to give Sheila a high five.

Perfect, he thought, now for Heather. Come on baby. Tell daddy some good news.

Moments later, Heather called and said she'd spotted all three of Ricky's people waiting in ambush in the casino and that there were no snipers visible on deck nine. With the three armed men that Tick-Tock had spotted, this accounted for all six weapons they knew Ricky had in his arsenal. Brain had his .45 Colt with him, but it was easy to assume that Ricky had that weapon with him.

Then Heather told Steve there was a slight problem. She only had clear shots at two of the three Head Ushers. She proposed a solution that Steve agreed would work in their favor. After exchanging I love yous, they signed off and Steve turned his full attention to what he had to do.

After giving Heather and Tick-Tock five minutes to get into position, he raised the radio to his mouth, pressed the transmit button and said, "Time to roll, Susan."

Chapter Nineteen

The Dead Calm:

The Reverend Ricky Rose tapped his foot impatiently on the deep pile carpet of the Crow's Nest Lounge as he looked at the hand held radio sitting on the bar next to him, hoping that any minute Brother Seth would call and let him know that both missions had been accomplished. That the people from the sailboat were dead, and that Don Parsons had been eliminated along with Brother Cal.

Glancing down at some movement on the pool deck far below, Ricky could see a few people begin to gather for his nightly sermon, and the rapture if it happened, which was not very fucking likely. He knew that most of them weren't there for the spiritual experience, but the party that came when it didn't happen.

Good luck, dipshits, he thought maliciously as he glanced at his watch for the tenth time in as many minutes and then took a sip from the drink sitting in front of him. Grimacing slightly, he reflected that one aspect of having his good buddy Don taken out was that he'd have to teach one of his other people how to make a decent Black Russian.

Turning to look out at the Gulf of Mexico, Ricky could see small white caps forming. Good, we've got a decent wind, he thought. Tim told me the sailboat is loaded, so all we have to do is load our things, dump whatever personal crap Steve and his people have on board, and take off. Good-bye Calm of the Seas and not a moment too soon.

Earlier that day, Ricky had gone to take a bath and found the water only trickling from the faucet. It took thirty-five minutes to fill the tub half way. When he finally lowered himself into the tepid water, the lights had started flickering and gone out. Cursing, he yelled for one of the Hungarian sisters to bring a candle and his radio. He contacted Brother Cal and asked what the problem was. After checking, Cal had called back and told him that the generator that powered deck ten, where Ricky had his cabin, had died and they couldn't get it restarted.

Ricky wondered how this would affect his plans, but couldn't see how it would hamper the ambush. The action would be on decks seven and eight, not ten. Thinking about the numerous security cameras covering the ship, he wished they were working so he could watch his plan unfold. Up until a month ago, he used the surveillance system to keep tabs on his people and to sate his voyeuristic tendencies. A power surge had blown the computer that controlled the imaging, and no matter what Brother Cal tried, he couldn't bring it back on line. Ricky briefly wondered if Randy could fix some of the malfunctioning systems aboard the ship, but sitting in the half empty tub, he was reminded that the water was running out. Screw it, it's time to move on, he decided. Randy could be put to better use building a new life for us in Cozumel than trying to keep this shit bucket afloat.

Picking up his drink from the bar, Ricky glanced at his watch again, took another sip of his Black Russian, and said to the empty lounge, "Come on, Seth."

***

Steve stood well past the landing of the grand staircase on deck eight as he looked at the upper decks of the Centrum. As they crossed the huge shopping area, he wanted it to appear like they were searching for someone so they went through the motions of testing the doors of the shops while Steve called out for Brain. From below, he could hear Susan's voice calling out the tech's name. Mary and Sheila stayed mute so they didn't give away the fact that they weren't who they were supposed to be.

When he reached a point halfway down the Centrum, Steve called Susan and asked where she was on deck seven.

"I'm about three quarters done with the observation area," she replied.

"Slow down just a bit," he told her. "You're getting close to the lounge. I don't want these guys popping off prematurely. If we can, I want to hit them at the exact same time."

"Roger that, over and out," Susan said, the words making her feel like she was in an old war movie. Clipping the radio back onto her belt, she considered what she was about to do and hoped she wouldn't fail.

Although she'd had some qualms about shooting a living person when she had first boarded the Dead Calm, those had passed when she saw how Ricky and his people ruled, yes, ruled, she thought vehemently. He didn't work for his people, he used them. It was like watching some despot dictator getting his kicks by abusing his power, and she had seen enough of that around the world to make her sick.

Her entire life, she had watched how men ruled the world. She abhorred the way most of them treated the people who were supposed to be under their care. Even in America, people were constantly being taken advantage of. To try and right the situation, she had joined protests against leaders who abused human rights. She had even gone on aid missions to Serbia and Darfur to help people displaced by civil war, but it seemed that despite her efforts, along with those of millions of others around the world, nothing ever got better. Men continued to commit war crimes and get away with it, their only punishment a strongly worded letter of condemnation from the United Nations. Peaceful protests were broken up by gunfire, dissidents were jailed or just disappeared, women were raped and abused daily by the millions, and no one gave a crap.

Hefting the M-4 rifle in her hand, she said to herself, no more will I stand by and let that happen. As the thought completed itself in her mind, in that one micro-second, she realized that a single motivated person with a weapon could get results faster than a thousand peaceful protests. In the new world that had come about as a result of the HWNW virus, guns ruled.

Excited and scared by this thought, Susan hoped it would be people like Steve or Tick-Tock who came to power. Or even herself, she thought fleetingly. This was followed by a feeling of sadness for the world that had lost so much that it could never go back. Ricky and his bunch were a microcosm of what's out there. People feeding off what's left of the old world, or setting up their own little fiefdoms where they can pick up where they left off before the dead came to life.

How will it end? She asked herself.

At this, her thoughts turned to Cindy. She decided that the little girl was their best chance to bring stability back to the world. But even then, its fate would be back in the hands of men. Shaking off this depressing thought, she forced her mind to focus on what was before her. As she gripped her automatic rifle tightly, she decided that while she didn't know how things would end out there, she knew how they would end on the Dead Calm.

I've got two targets to take out, she told herself. Behind the bar are two men who stand for everything that's wrong with the world. Two men who have no reason to live, and will just continue to feed their sick appetites if not eliminated. Two men who needed to die.

Tick-Took had told her that the third man was hiding behind some chairs grouped around a table, and that he would be his first target. The two men behind the bar were also in his line of sight, but were near a turn the bar made as it followed the back wall. If they made it around the corner, they would have cover, so it was up to Susan to shoot a full clip into the front of the bar as fast as she could from left to right, spacing her shots out every six inches to either kill them or keep them pinned down. He assured her that the high velocity bullets would blow right through the wood of the bar. Meanwhile, he would keep their heads down with suppressing fire as he moved in to finish them off.

The radio clipped to her jeans crackled to life, interrupting her reverie.

Steve's voice said, "I should be right below you now. Move out nice and easy and listen for the signal."

Either Heather or Tick-Took would send the signal by repeatedly squeezing the transmit button on their radio, causing a series of clicks to be sent to other radios. This was the five-second warning. It meant that either Steve or Susan was in position and the counter-ambush was ready to be sprung.

Heather and Tick-Took had calculated the best spot for the bait to be on each deck. For Steve, this was about twenty feet into the casino. For Susan, it was halfway through the Sombrero Lounge. Far enough back so that Ricky's men wouldn't open up on her, but close enough to bring fire onto the enemy. Susan knew when she heard the signal that she only had five seconds to get ready whether she was in the right place or not. It would be ideal for both her and Steve to be in position at the same time, but highly unlikely. The five-second warning would be a small buffer to give them time to get into place.

Susan keyed the transmit button on her radio to acknowledge Steve. Looking at Mary as she stared placidly out one of the observation windows, she wondered if she was on something. She had a glazed look in her eyes. If so, she had no problem with it other than she hoped Mary would have sense enough to duck when the time came. She almost wished she'd been teamed up with Sheila, but the redhead was too short to pass for Tick-Tock.

"Mary," Susan called out. "Are you okay?"

"Sheila gave me a Valium so I wouldn't freak," she replied vacantly.

"You remember what to do though, right?"

Mary laughed and replied, "I'm not that stoned." Sobering slightly, she said, "I'm sorry things didn't work out between us."

Susan smiled and told her, "It's okay. Things work out the way they're supposed to I guess." Looking at the thatch and bamboo of the Sombrero Lounge in the distance, she said, "Come on, it's time to go."

*\*\**

George Day looked between the chairs in front of him, spotting two people in the distance as they came toward him along the observation deck. He'd been hearing one of them call out for the past few minutes as they searched for their missing man. At their first shouted, "Brain," he'd been so startled that he almost pulled the trigger on his pistol. Now calmer, he glanced over to where Brothers William and Cal were crouched behind the bar.

First things first, he thought.

\*\*\*

Heather peeked around the jumbo slot machine at the back of the casino, marveling at its size. At least eight feet tall, and half again as wide, it provided excellent cover and gave her a decent firing position. From here, she could take out two of the three people waiting to kill Steve and Sheila.

She rehearsed in her head for the tenth time the actions she would take in just minutes. Fire around one side of the jumbo slots to take out target number one. Move quickly to its other side, fire again to take out target number two before breaking cover and moving toward the cage where the last man was hiding. If Steve hadn't killed him by them, one of them would shoot into the cage to keep him down while the other moved forward and took him out.

Piece of cake, she thought. This was quickly followed by, bullshit; a million things could go wrong. Anything can happen, especially to Steve, who'll be standing out in the open. Pushing her worries into a far corner of her mind, she ran through the possibilities of what could happen in the next few minutes. The plan was as solid as they could make it and that would have to do. Plus, if she shot accurately enough, they might even get a chance to question one of these assholes and find out where Brain is. Having never considered leaving the tech behind, she was prepared to storm the upper decks to find him.

Besides, she thought to herself, I've still got to take care of Ricky, so I'll be heading that way anyway.

\*\*\*

Steve stood near the arched entrance to the casino, wishing his stomach would stop flip-flopping. He recalled when he had been carjacked by two men carrying pistols in Detroit. They had bumped his car from behind while he was stopped at a red light, and when he got out to check the damage, both men drew weapons and started yelling at him to get down on the ground.

Without hesitation, he pulled his own pistol and opened fire, killing them both.

Back then, I didn't have time to be scared, he thought. I just reacted. Now I've got plenty of time to let my imagination run wild and it sucks. I think I liked it better in Detroit.

Swallowing hard, he pushed down his fear and stepped forward.

\*\*\*

Susan entered the Sombrero Lounge a full two minutes before Steve entered the casino. Stopping to check her surroundings, at first she worried her nervousness might betray her. Then she realized it would look unnatural to be entering a darkened area on a cruise ship full of the dead and not look like someone just goosed her.

Tables with overstuffed chairs clustered around them choked the main area of the lounge. On her left, the bar stretched along the wall for twenty feet and then turned at a forty-five degree angle before straightening to run along the back wall a short distance.

That's where they are, she thought. Behind that little ten foot long stretch of fake pinon wood and brass rails.

Glancing toward the rear of the lounge, she froze when she thought she saw movement behind one of the tables.

Damn it, Tick-Tock, she thought angrily. I wish you would have told me where you were hiding. I don't want to shoot you by mistake. Glancing behind her, she saw Mary standing outside the lounge, a good fifteen feet behind her near the entrance. Whatever calming effects the Valium might have had on her seemed to have worn off since she looked like a deer in the headlights.

Mary opened her mouth to say something, so Susan raised her hand to still her. Seeing this, Mary nodded and closed her mouth before starting to move from foot to foot like a child needing to go to the bathroom. Ignoring this, Susan turned her attention back to the bar.

Eyeing where she would place her first shot, she stepped forward.

\*\*\*

Tick-Tock crouched behind a planter thirty feet away from George Day. When he'd first arrived on deck seven, he had a hard time finding a vantage point from where he could see into the Sombrero. The trouble was that the lounge sat near the end of the Centrum on a section of deck set in front of the bank of elevators. On the lower decks, this was one big open area, but from deck seven on up, this center section had been closed off to divide the huge open space into two smaller open spaces. Directly above this was the casino, which was similarly situated. From there, gamblers could look down into the Centrum from the front and the back.

The difficulty had been in approaching the lounge. The only cover was a row of large potted plants set at ten-foot intervals along the walkway that surrounded the open section of the Centrum. Moving carefully from plant to plant, he kept checking for any of Ricky's men. He finally located the first one; a gray-haired older man crouched behind a table with a pistol in his hand.

Tick-Tock continued to look for the others, but couldn't spot them. He knew there had to be more than one. Trying to decide if he should back up and circle around from the other side to see if he could spot them, he noticed that gray hair kept glancing to his right. Moving further along the walkway, Tick-Tock spotted two men crouched behind the bar. That's when a slight problem arose since from this angle, the table on his left concealed gray hair.

Moving back along the walkway slightly, Tick-Tock found he could target all three of Ricky's men as long as the two behind the bar didn't move. This was unlikely once the shooting started.

Gray hair was the biggest threat since he would have a clear line of sight on anyone entering the bar from the front. He had to go first. Tick-Tock was sure he could get at least one of the men behind the bar, but he would need Susan's help to take out the last one. Backtracking to the elevators, he radioed his plan and then resumed his position. He spent the time waiting for Susan by listening to the creaks and groans that the Dead Calm made as she wallowed in the waves of the Gulf of Mexico, his eyes never leaving the spot where he would fire his first round.

Hearing Susan calling out for Brain long before he saw her, Tick-Tock drew a bead on the center of gray hair's back. When Susan finally came into view; he waited until she was ten feet into the lounge before he took his hand off the fore grip of his rifle and reached down to start keying his radio.

This was when Susan stopped and started looking around.

Come on, babe, Tick-Tock urged, as he waited for her to take another few steps and allow him to trigger the ambush. Seeing gray hair move slightly, his free hand flew back to his rifle. Starting to squeeze the trigger, he let up when he saw the man was only shifting his weight from one foot to another.

Susan finally took a step, so Tick-Tock reached for his radio again, hoping Steve was in position.

Then all hell broke loose.

And it wasn't Tick-Tock who started it.

Chapter Twenty

The Dead Calm:

George Day saw the woman move again and decided it was time to make his move. Knowing he was pitting himself against one of Satan's minions, and that he would have to be fast and his aim true, he flexed his legs once in preparation before popping up from behind the table.

Screaming out, "Die spawn of Satan," he saw the woman in front of him flinch in surprise at his sudden outburst. After assessing the situation in an instant, George decided that he'd made the right decision on who to shoot first. He could see that the woman's rifle was pointing away from him in the direction of the bar, and he knew this would give him time to do what he needed before killing her. Already pointing his own weapon in the right direction, George felt adrenalin surge through him as he lined Brother Cal up in the sights of his pistol and squeezed the trigger four times. Spinning back toward the woman, he steadied his aim to use the last two bullets in the pistol to send her to Hell.

***

Clusterfuck! Tick-Tock's mind screamed when he saw gray hair pop up and start yelling about Satan. He wasn't completely ready as his left hand was keying his radio's transmit button, but his right was still wrapped around the pistol grip of his M-4. Reacting instantly to the situation, he squeezed off a loosely aimed three round burst even as he heard gray hair's pistol fire four times. The thought ran through his head that he had been too slow. Way too slow. There was no way gray hair could miss hitting Susan.

But even before this thought was complete, Tick-Tock was trying to understand what he was seeing. Gray hair hadn't shot at Susan, he'd fired behind the bar. Wondering what the hell was going on, but relieved to see Susan still standing and gray hair going down from the rounds he'd fired, he jumped up to close with the enemy. Switching his aim to the bar, he opened fire as he ran.

***

George Day felt as if the wind had been knocked out of him. Then it felt like he no longer had legs supporting his body. His vision started to go black and he felt weak. It was as if his muscles had turned to water. Not understanding what had happened, but resolving to finish God's work, he focused all his energy into pulling the trigger of his pistol as he managed to fire one round at the Jezebel before he died.

***

Susan saw the man jump up and fire four rounds behind the bar before turning toward her. Trying to bring her rifle around, she knew she'd never make it in time. Her only hope was that her Kevlar vest would stop the bullets. She was tensing her body up as if it might repel the bullets that she knew were coming her way, when she saw the man aiming at her jerk as if he had been shocked. As if by magic, a red mist erupted from two spots on his chest and he started to drop. She saw a muzzle flash erupt from the barrel of his pistol even as it registered in her brain that the crazy man had been shot from behind. What she was seeing were exit wounds. Susan could see that nutso's pistol wasn't pointed at her when it had gone off, so she discarded it as a threat. Putting her mind on task, she heard Mary scream from behind her as she turned her attention back to the bar and started rapidly squeezing the trigger of her rifle.

Tick-Tock had covered half the distance to the bar before George Day's body hit the floor. He saw Susan recover quickly and open fire into the front of the bar as he triggered his own weapon in continuous three round bursts toward its back.

Wood splintered, bottles shattered and the air was filled with the smell of dozens of top shelf liquors as both Tick-Tock and Susan poured fire into the bar's front and side. Tick-Tock reached the end of the bar and emptied his rifle into two shadowy shapes lying behind it before ducking down and switching magazines. Peeking around its edge, he saw what looked like two lumps of hamburger.

Tick-Tock would never know it, but in his excitement to kill Brother Cal, George Day's first shot hit Brother William in the side of the head. His other three rounds had missed both men completely, but the fusillade of bullets from Susan and him hadn't. The damage they had done was readily apparent. Both of the Head Ushers had been hit at least a dozen times and looked like they had gone through a wood chipper face first.

Seeing that it was safe, Tick-Tock turned to Susan and asked, "Are you okay? Are you hit?"

Susan stared blankly at him, in shock from what had just occurred. Moving forward and taking her in his arms, Tick-Tock could feel her start to shake as post-battle nerves kicked in. He wanted to take some time and calm her, but knew they still had to help Steve. He couldn't hear shooting from the deck above, but with all the noise he and Susan had made, it would have been masked anyway. Unclipping his radio, he pulled slightly away from Susan and was about to raise the walkie-talkie to his mouth when he heard, "Anytime you two are done sucking face, do you think you could give me a hand? I think I got shot."

In the aftermath of the firefight, they had forgotten about Mary.

Both he and Susan rushed to where she was sitting on the floor behind one of the tables. Looking over the top, the first thing they noticed was the blood.

Lots of blood.

***

Steve was fifteen feet from what he considered the optimal place to spring their ambush when he heard a series of clicks issuing from his radio. The first three had barely sounded when he also heard muffled shots coming from below. Recognizing pistol shots instead of rifle fire, he feared for Tick-Tock, Susan and Mary as he swung into action.

From in front of him, automatic weapons fire roared as Heather opened up on her first target. Steve spun to his left as he shouldered his rifle, aiming it into the cashier's cage.

Too late, his mind screamed as he saw the inside of the cage light up from a muzzle flash, while at the same time feeling an impact on his chest as if a giant had balled up its fist and struck him. The man inside the cage had been alerted by the sound of shooting coming from below and had fired first.

Staggered by the impact of the .38 caliber bullet, Steve brought his rifle back to bear even as he heard screams of pain and more firing from his right. Squeezing the trigger, he pumped it in multiple three round bursts as he watched his bullets tearing up the security grill covering the front of cashier's cage. Another muzzle flash erupted from inside even as his first rounds hit home. This time, he felt the impact on his solar plexus. The air rushed out of him. Gasping, he realized he'd emptied his magazine, so he dropped down behind a nickel slot machine and switched it with a full one.

Crying out in pain as he levered himself back up, he squeezed the trigger on his M-4 and sent twenty-eight rounds smashing into the front of the cashier's cage. This time there was no return fire.

Only able to take little sips of air, and barely able to stand the pain, Steve cradled his wounded chest as he dropped into a fetal position and rocked back and forth on the floor. Hearing Heather calling his name, he answered weakly as he felt a little more lung capacity come back. Of all the ways to be injured, getting the wind knocked out of him was the one he hated the most. His vision was graying out as he became aware of Heather bending over him, asking where he'd been hit.

He croaked out the word, "Chest," which sent her into a flurry of motion as she ripped open his shirt and started frantically pulling at the Velcro straps that secured the Kevlar vest to his body. Pushing back on Steve's shoulder to straighten him out while lifting the front flap on the vest up, she reached down and felt for any wounds since the dim light of the casino made it difficult to see. Feeling wetness, a bolt of fear shot through her until she pulled her hand back and realized that it wasn't blood. It was sweat.

The Kevlar had stopped both bullets.

After checking the rest of Steve's body by touch, she was relieved to find no open wounds. Even in the dim light, she could see two dark bruises starting to form, one on his chest above his heart and one at his sternum. Worried about internal injuries, she told him to lay still and not to move while she took care of something.

Calling for Sheila, she made her way to where Brother Seth lay unconscious in a pool of blood. He had been her first target, but the only thing she'd been able to see of him was his feet and lower legs, so this is what she'd aimed for. She was satisfied to see that her first, three rounds burst had hit him in the left foot, almost severing it. Two rounds of her second burst had hit him in the right calf. Blood oozed around bone splinters of what was left of Seth's foot, so Heather grabbed an apron worn that had been left hanging from the back of a chair by one of the dealers and twisted it into a tourniquet. Seeing what she was doing, Sheila said venomously, "Let the pig bleed out."

"We can't let him die. He can tell us where Brain is," she replied and then said urgently. "Go find something to use on his other leg."

Sheila came back with a towel she'd found behind a service bar, and soon Seth's other leg was bound and the bleeding slowed. Heather elevated his legs on a knocked over chair and then sat back as she considered her next move.

Before she could form her thoughts, Sheila interrupted to ask, "I thought you were supposed to use direct pressure on a wound like that. I mean, I took a Red Cross class once and they told us to never use a tourniquet because it would do more harm."

In a flat voice, Heather replied, "It doesn't matter, because he won't live long enough for it to matter." Gathering her thoughts, she told Sheila, "Go collect their weapons. One's behind the video poker machine and the other one's in the cashier's cage," Pointing to the bolt-action rifle that Seth had carried, she said, "Grab that too. Stack them up on a table."

Heather was about to say more, but was interrupted by Steve gasping out from behind her, "Good shooting, Tex." Looking at the inert body, he added, "What do you know? It's our good friend, Brother Seth."

Heather saw Steve standing a few feet away and her features darkened as she yelled at him, "What in the hell are you doing up? Sit down right now or I'll knock you down. I told you to stay where you were!"

Steve eased himself into a chair and said, "I'm okay. Might have a cracked rib, but the worst was getting the wind knocked out of me. I hate that shit. First you think you're going to die, and then you wish you would." At this he laughed painfully.

"You could have internal injuries," she told him. "You could push a bone sliver into your lung by moving around like that. And then what?"

Suddenly realizing that they had gone into this without thinking about the fact that if one of them was seriously hurt they would have only rudimentary medical help available, Steve's good mood at their success went away. He imagined having to do surgery to extract a bullet, and the thought made him cringe. Not that he couldn't do it if he had to, he was finding himself capable of many things he never would have dreamed of doing before the dead came back to life, but it was the fact that he didn't know how. Making a mental note to find some first aid books, he hoped that nothing had happened to Tick-Tock, Susan or Mary down in the Sombrero Lounge.

A second later, his fears were brought to reality when Heather's radio suddenly came to life and Tick-Tock said, "Speak to me. You guys all right? Deck seven's secure and the bad guys are dead, but Mary got hurt. I'm on my way across the Centrum right now, so don't shoot me, over."

Heather replied, "We're secure here. How bad is Mary? And Connie, don't cut the boat loose. We won, over."

Down on The Usual Suspects, Connie jumped up and down with joy when she heard this. Cindy bounced up from where she'd been sitting on one of the bunks, and the two of them started dancing around the cabin in celebration.

Steve held his breath as he waited for the reply about Mary. Suddenly, Tick-Tock's voice called out loudly from the entrance to the casino. "Mary's not too bad. A stray bullet hit the table she was hiding behind and kicked up a bunch of splinters and shit. Side of her head got cut up and it bled a lot, but it's not as bad as it looks. Head wounds always bleed a lot." His voice lowering as he neared, Tick-Tock continued, "Susan's with her. There's a little aide station for the passengers on seven, so she took her there while I came up in case you needed help."

Looking down at Brother Seth, he said, "Way to go Annie Oakley. Is he the only one you let live?"

"Other two are dead," Heather answered, "What about yours?"

"Three up, three down," Tick-Tock said. "Just like baseball." Noticing Steve's pale complexion, he asked, "You okay?"

"Took two in the vest. Hurts like a bitch," he answered with a gasp.

Tick-Tock winced and said, "Be careful. Might have cracked a rib or two."

"I've heard that somewhere before," Steve replied.

Sheila went to collect the weapons while Tick-Tock related to Steve and Heather about gray hair shooting his own man. He had just come to the part about hitting the Usher in the back twice when they heard Sheila give a short yelp. All three spun around and brought their weapons up at what they thought was a new threat, but relaxed when they saw Sheila bent over near the cashier's cage, gagging and dry heaving. She had found what was left of the man inside. Despite Heather's protests, Steve rose painfully and joined Tick-Tock as he went to her.

Leaning over while propping herself against the side of the cashiers cage, Sheila spit out a wad of saliva and gasped, "That guy in there. He doesn't have a head."

Tick-Tock looked inside the cage and asked, "What did you hit this guy with, a chainsaw?"

"Two full clips," Steve answered with a twisted smile.

"A little bit of overkill, don't you think?"

Steve shrugged, wincing at the pain in his chest as he replied, "He shot me. I got a little pissed off."

"I'm not going near that mess," Sheila exclaimed as she pushed herself away from the cage and staggered over to a nearby service bar. "You're going to have to get that last gun by yourself."

Tick-Tock looked into the cage again and said, "Well buddy, you shot his ass, so I guess you get to do the honors." Steve was reluctantly reaching for the door handle when Heather interrupted by calling out, "Seth's coming to."

"Saved by the bell," he said with a grin.

The two men hurried over to find Seth rolling his head back and forth as he moaned in pain. He kept repeating, "Hurts," but no one in the group seemed to care.

Pissed off at being shot, and seeing someone to focus his anger on, Steve grunted in pain as he crouched down next to Seth and un-holstered his Glock.

"Quit moving around, Steve. You're hurt," Heather ordered him. Ignoring her, he focused only on Seth.

The Head Usher closed his eyes tightly and twisted his head away when Steve started tapping him on the forehead with the barrel of his pistol. When he saw this wasn't having the desired effect, he switched to rapping him on the bridge of the nose. At this, Seth opened his eyes slightly and rolled them around until they finally came to rest on Steve before opening wide in shock.

Seeing he had the man's undivided attention, Steve asked sharply, "Where's Brain?"

Looking at him in wonder, Seth croaked out, "I saw you take two in the chest from Jackson. You're supposed to be dead."

Sarcastically, Steve responded, "And you're supposed to be a Christian, so just think of it as a resurrection thing. Now where's Brain?"

Seth closed his lips tightly and shook his head, refusing to answer.

"The hard way then," Steve said flatly.

Pointing his pistol into the air, he fired six rapid shots into the ceiling and then locked the slide back on the Glock. Reaching down, he then pressed the burning hot barrel across Seth's lips.

Blisters rose instantly as Seth let out a cry of pain and wrenched his head away. The faint smell of burning flesh rose into the air.

"Next one goes against your right eye," Steve warned. He then told Tick-Tock to hold Seth's head as he pointed the pistol into the air again.

This was enough for Seth who blurted out, "Deck ten, room fifteen thirty-eight."

"Good answer. Now where's Ricky?" Steve growled.

"I don't know," Seth cried. "He's waiting to hear from us. He might be on the bridge."

Steve made as if to point his pistol in the air again as Seth screamed, "I don't know where he is, honest!"

Steve nodded to Tick-Tock, who released Seth's head and backed away, knowing what was coming. Standing was painful for Steve and Heather rushed forward to help him.

Seth pleaded, "You can't leave me like this. Where are you going? Please don't leave me like this."

"I won't," Steve said as he took four steps backward so he wouldn't get splashed with blood. He fired once into the center of Seth's face.

Turning toward Sheila, standing near the bar with what looked like a triple shot of whiskey, he ordered, "Lay off that stuff. We've still got things to do. Take the weapons and go down and find Mary and Susan. Stay with them."

To Tick-Tock and Heather he said simply, "Let's go."

\*\*\*

Brain heard the door bang open and a sudden light blazing through the darkened room blinded him. As he clenched his eyes against the pain, his mind flashed to the old cop shows of the black and white era when a light shined in their face disoriented suspects while they were questioned. Thinking that Ricky or his men had come to interrogate him about his friends, he steeled himself to resist. Waiting to be beaten with a rubber hose, or to have his fingernails pulled out one by one, he was surprised to hear Tick-Tock's voice say, "What the fuck, Pork Chop. How do you rate a grand suite while I sleep on a mattress on the floor?"

Brain's eyes flew open, and he saw his friend standing a few feet away.

Unsheathing his K-bar, Tick-Tock said, "Don't worry, I'll have you free in a second."

Tick-Tock sliced the tape and helped him stand, his hours of being bound having caused his legs to cramp up. Tears of gratitude and relief poured from Brain, and it was a few minutes before he could speak.

Finally, in a choked voice he said, "Thank you. I owe you a big one. Now we have to save Tim? Did you see him anywhere?"

Tick-Tock gave him an odd look and replied, "He's with Connie on The Usual Suspects."

"Good, good," Brain said. "He must have gotten away then. I tried to escape, but they had me taped up too tight. Is everyone else okay?"

Wondering what Brain was talking about when he mentioned Tim getting away, Tick-Tock replied, "We had a go with Ricky's Head Ushers. Steve and Mary got a little banged up, but no one's hurt bad. Steve took two in the chest, but his vest stopped the bullets. Mary just got hit by some splinters and shit."

"What about Ricky's people?" He asked.

Tick-Tock gave him an evil smile and replied, "As we used to say in the Marine Corps; the enemy has suffered grievous losses."

Filling Brain in on the events of the day, Tick-Tock led him down the passageway. When they reached the doors leading to the Centrum, he finished by saying, "Steve and Heather went to check the bridge for Reverend Ricky. I checked the cabins before I cut you loose, but no one was there." Looking at his ultra-posh surroundings, he compared them to his own accommodations and added, "I guess you either have to be an asshole like Ricky or dead to get a nice room on this tub."

Tick-Tock and Brain waited at the stairs for Heather and Steve. After they joined them, Brain gave them each a big hug, in Steve's case a gentle one due to his injuries, and thanked them profusely for saving him. When his gratitude had run its course, Brain turned his attention to who had kidnapped him and said, "Now let's find Ricky. I want his ass."

Tick-Tock laughed and said, "Get some, Pork Chop."

"Won't do any good looking," Heather informed him. "Steve and I were talking about it and decided we'd be wasting our time. The ship's too big and there's only the four of us. Five if we include Susan. Ricky can slip past us too easily with all the passageways and decks we'd have to cover. We need more people to do a real search."

Hearing what Heather said about not having enough people suddenly gave Steve an idea. Surprised that he hadn't thought of it before, but cutting himself some slack since it wasn't every day he got shot twice in the chest, he called Susan on the radio. After giving her the good news about Brain being freed, and getting an update on Mary; the splinters had been removed, the wounds dressed and Sheila had given her another Valium, he told her to send Sheila up to deck ten on the double.

Securing his radio, he said to the others with a smile, "I know where we can find over a hundred people to help us search. Once we tell them what's really been going on with this ship, they'll look like a mob of villagers going after the Frankenstein monster."

Chapter Twenty-One

The Dead Calm:

Ricky considered his future as he looked down from the Crow's Nest Lounge at his followers milling restlessly about on decks eleven and twelve. Something had gone terribly wrong with his plan, and now he didn't know which way to turn. For over an hour, he'd tried to reach Brother Seth or Brother William, but his calls on the two-way had gone unanswered. He'd been told not to use the radio lest his calling give the people waiting in ambush away, but it had been too long since he'd heard from anyone and he was getting more nervous by the second.

When at first he couldn't reach his men, Ricky had considered the possibility that his Head Ushers and Steve's people had wiped each other out. Overjoyed at the idea, he realized that if this was the case, then he could waltz on down to the pool deck, promote a few of his Ushers to the status of Head Usher, take the sailboat and go. But that would also mean leaving the security of the Crow's Nest armed only with the .45 he'd taken off Randy, and he wasn't quite prepared to do that just yet. Until he could be assured that it was safe, he knew he couldn't expose himself. The people from the sailboat knew what he looked like, and if any of them had a weapon, they would shoot him on sight.

In that same vein, if Brother Cal or Don Parsons had survived their respective assassins, they would also be looking for him since it wouldn't be hard to figure out who had ordered their assassinations. But this in itself was something that made Ricky believe his Head Ushers had been wiped out. Whether it was to kill him or kiss his ring, none of his people had contacted him. He hadn't told any of them where he would be waiting during the ambush, but it would be easy to narrow it down to the ship's bridge, his cabin or here at the Crow's Nest.

And what if they all survived, Ricky wondered. His brow furrowed as the thought of Steve's people, Cal and Don Parsons coming after him made him shiver. With a sudden rush of fear, his thoughts started running away from him. In a flash, he was convinced that the men and women who he wanted killed had survived. This was followed by the immediate belief that they were on the hunt for him. He even started to imagine they were just outside the closed doors of the Crow's Nest Lounge, waiting for him to open it so they could shoot him down in cold blood.

His eyes grew wide at the thought as he found the idea utterly terrifying. Initially, this had only been a slim possibility, but now it was looking more like a reality. Besides the paranoia and fear that the threat of death brought up, being hated was something that Ricky found hard to stomach. He had spent months being adored by his followers. He was the king, and all those around him were his subjects. All of them prepared to satisfy his slightest whim.

How have become so hated and hunted? He lamented.

Tears sprang to his eyes as he looked around the dark, empty lounge for someone to assure him that everything would be all right. Seeing nothing except his own reflection in the mirror behind the bar, he was suddenly struck by another bolt of fear when he realized he was all alone. This hadn't happened in months. Normally he had at least one person with him, whether it was one of the Hungarian sisters or one of his Ushers, so this was an entirely new experience.

The feeling of abandonment that came to him was almost overwhelming in its intensity. Between this and the fear of a nasty death at the hands of whoever was waiting outside the door, Ricky considered dropping down onto the carpet and crawling into a corner to hide. The thought of failure had never crossed his mind before, but now....

What can I do? He whined to himself. Who can I turn to? I'm all alone. Everyone who I can count on has either taken off like Sheila - Ricky conveniently forgot that she ran away because he was trying to have her killed. Or been killed by the people who invaded the ship - Ricky also neglected to admit the fact that he had sent his people to kill them and take their sailboat. Or like Cal and Don, who turned and are stalking me – ignoring that he had set them up to be ambushed and slaughtered in the first place.

Ricky's mind spun as he tried to deal with the situation that he suddenly found himself in. He was starting to sink to the carpet when suddenly he stopped. Standing upright to his full five foot nine inch height, his body went rigid as he came up with a solution.

You idiot, he scolded himself. You thought of what you could do just a minute ago when you were hoping everyone had gotten killed. You need to quit thinking like a peon and consider the situation on a bigger scale. You've got all the people you need, and not just replace Seth and the rest of the Head Ushers. You've got over a hundred men and woman who will do whatever you ask if you put the right spin on it.

But what's the right spin? He asked himself.

Pirates, the idea popped into Ricky's mind. That's the threat I'll use. The people who came aboard are really pirates who want to rape and pillage the Calm of the Seas. They tried to kill me and take the ship and now we have to kill them before they kill everyone like they did my Head Ushers when they murdered them in an ambush. I'll make myself the victim, and the Faithful will rally behind me. A realistic threat like this will even get those who don't believe in the rapture to support an all-out assault on the lower decks, if only to protect themselves. And if we find the people from the sailboat dead when we get below, then we've won. And if they're still alive, they'll be overwhelmed by my shock troops. I can also tell the Faithful that Brother Cal and Don Parsons joined up with the pirates and need to be killed on sight. That way I'm protected from all threats.

This idea coalesced with another thought. I'll have my Faithful hide their weapons as they approach the lower decks and then pull them out when it's time to attack. This way, the people from the sailboat will hesitate to shoot. Those people down there are too civilized to kill unarmed people, and that's why they'll lose.

Rejoicing at the prospect of coming out on top of the mess that had befallen him, and too arrogant to admit that he'd been the cause it, Ricky rushed to the front of the Crow's Nest overlooking the pool area. He wanted to make sure his people were still there since he was long overdue to for his nightly sermon. Confidently thinking that the Faithful would rally around him once he got them worked up, this was replaced by; I am so screwed, as he looked down.

At the far end of the pool area were Steve, Heather, Randy and worst of all... Sheila.

\*\*\*

With his M-4 held at port arms, Steve walked up to the startled man sitting in the DJ's booth. Stopping in front of him, he waved his rifle at the equipment stacked inside and asked, "You got a PA system hooked up to this?"

The man looked at him in shock and wonder, surprised to be suddenly confronted by this assault rifle-wielding stranger. Moving his mouth like a fish out of water, he only managed to make a slight squeaking noise.

Seeing this, Brain said, "I got it," before going around the soundboard and gently easing the man from his chair. He sat down and scanned the controls in front of him before flipping a few switches.

Twenty feet away, a brief whine of feedback came through the amps mounted on both sides of a small stage set up for when the cruise directors hosted activities by the pool.

Steve told Brain, "Turn it down. Remember when we were at the rock climbing wall and it almost blew our eardrums out."

Brain nodded and adjusted some dials. "You're all set," he told Steve and then turned to the DJ and said in a low voice, "If you touch anything, I'll cut your fingers off and feed them to a Z while you watch."

The man nodded vigorously at this and retreated from the soundboard until his back hit the rear wall of the booth. There had been rumors going around about people coming on board, but beyond that, no one knew if they were friendly or hostile. After his first encounter with them, he decided they were hostile.

Steve climbed onto the stage and had a brief sense of déjà vu from the times he worked as a disc jockey and had introduced the band at a live show. Standing in front of the microphone, a feeling of giddiness washed through him and he was overcome with the desire to grab the mic and say, 'And now, live and in concert, presented by KLAM Music Radio, BLUE-OYSTER-CULT, but lost this urge when he saw the faces of the Faithful looking at him with a mixture of fear, curiosity and hostility.

Tighten up, he told himself.

Speaking into the microphone, he said, "My name is Steve Wendell. My friends and I came aboard the Calm of the Seas a few days ago. We came in peace."

Steve almost laughed at this. I come in Peace. I sound like an alien. But instead of 'Take me to your leader', it's going to be 'Bring your leader to me so we can kill his ass.'

Steve cleared his throat and related to those gathered how they had come across Connie and Tim. He told briefly about how the two young people had to go into hiding because of Reverend Ricky. After telling them how Sheila had appeared, he related some of what she'd told them about the things Ricky was up to. How he preyed on the trust and fears of those around him while using the HWNW virus and the dead to keep them terrified. As he spoke, he noticed that the Faithful at least seemed to be paying attention. When he mentioned Sheila, he saw some of those in the front rows recognize her and pointed to where she stood nearby.

Then Steve hit the Faithful with the bombshells. Ricky had conned them. There was no rapture and the ship was sinking. He informed them that Ricky was the one who controlled where and when the dead were released on the ship and that he was preparing to abandon his people on the sinking ship. He tried to go on about how Ricky planned to kill him and his people and steal their sailboat, but his words were met with open hostility as some of the Faithful tried to shout him down. Knowing this might happen, he waved Sheila on stage and turned the microphone over to her. She was his ace in the hole to get the Faithful to believe him. She had been one of them and had been with Ricky from the beginning.

The crowd grew silent as Sheila took the stage. This was someone they knew and could trust and the boos and catcalls fell off. A few people even called out greetings to the redhead. This was until she started to talk.

Beginning with what she knew of Ricky's past, that he was nothing but a fast talking con-man who worked as a promoter, craved power and wanted nothing more than to wallow in sexual self-gratification, she laid out in detail how Ricky had conned them by using their fears and gullibility. She knew everything Ricky had been up to, like his pedophilia that many had turned a blind eye to, and she pulled no punches in talking about his other activities, including his having sex with some of the dead women locked up in the Sounds Lounge. By the time she finished vouching for Steve and telling the Faithful that everything he had said to them was the truth, the crowd was completely silent.

The Faithful were shocked at the revelation that they had been taken. Despite a few catcalls from the group, with so much evidence laid out in front of them, they had no choice but to believe her. For quite a few, it blossomed into awareness with ease since hadn't this been what that little voice in the back of their minds had been telling them all along?

The Faithful now believed, but not in the rapture. Sad, embarrassed faces looked up at the stage as if to ask, how could this have happened? What did I do to deserve this?

Suddenly, the mood changed as a man's voice called out sharply, "You were one of them, Sheila. You helped Ricky do this. If we got conned, you're one of the people who did it."

The crowd turned angry at the accusation as hundreds of voices shouted out in agreement. Thankful at finding someone to vent their frustration and embarrassment on, since it was easier to blame somebody else than to believe themselves fools, in no time, heated voices were calling out, "Whore," and "Kill Ricky's slut."

Steve stood by patiently as he waited for the uproar to die down. Instead, it grew louder. He looked at Sheila and saw that she had hung her head in shame, the microphone dangling loosely in her hand. He felt a moment of compassion for her. He turned back toward the Faithful and was about to tell them to shut the hell up, when to his amazement, he saw that the crowd had turned into a mob and were actually pushing toward the stage to get to Sheila. In their humiliation, they had found a target to take their frustration out on.

What in the hell is wrong with these people? Steve asked himself. Don't these morons realize they only have themselves to blame?

Anger replaced his confusion, and in a flash, he un-slung his M-4 and shouldered it as he saw Heather do the same from the corner of his eye. Brain pointed Steve's Glock at the nearest people in the crowd. Sheila had backed away as the mob moved forward, the microphone still in her hand. In two steps Steve reached her and stripped it from her. Holding it up to his mouth, his words cut across the pool deck as he yelled out harshly, "Anyone who touches her dies. Back off! You fucking idiots brought this on yourselves. She's not to blame for your stupidity. You are."

Hearing these words booming across the deck like the voice of God himself, and seeing the weapons and the determination on the faces of the Steve and his crew, the crowd stopped with a jerk and started to back up. At the rear of the mass of people, a few of the Faithful broke and ran.

As he watched this, Steve thought, ain't no fun when the rabbit's got the gun.

He stepped protectively in front of Sheila, trying to reassure her by saying, "Don't worry, no one's going to touch one red... well... currently blonde, hair on your head. If they do, they die."

Until now, Sheila had been nothing more than a hanger on, almost a camp follower. Except for Mary, none of the group had much to do with her, nor wanted to. This had changed when she walked into the casino and risked her life to help get Brain back.

Standing with his rifle pointed at the crowd, Steve realized that good, bad or indifferent, and despite her morals or lack thereof, Sheila was one of them now. She was part of their group, and anyone who screwed with one of them would feel the wrath of them all.

"Calm down and shut up," Steve ordered as the crowd backed up.

They began to comply, so he lowered his rifle, but kept it held at the ready as he started speaking into the microphone again, finishing his account of the events that had occurred since his group set foot on the Dead Calm. Just by looking at their faces as he spoke, Steve knew that the crowd was his and they would band together to search for Ricky. But when he reached the part about Ricky's Head Ushers being wiped out, and that Ricky was hiding somewhere on the ship, he was surprised at the ferocity of the crowd as they screamed for the Reverend's head to be cut off and displayed on a spike.

Now you've got someone to really focus on, he thought.

Steve let them rage on for a few minutes. When they had quieted down to a dull roar, he started giving orders on how they should split up and search the ship for the Reverend Ricky Rose.

\*\*\*

As soon as Ricky saw Steve take the stage, he knew his reign on the Calm of the Seas was over. Instead of crumpling to the floor like he had almost done earlier, a new resolve came over him as he spun from the window.

If it was over, then he had nothing left to lose.

With a purposeful stride, he walked to the elevators and pressed the call button, his irrational fear of someone waiting for him beyond the doors a thing of the past. He knew what he was up against now. Since the people from the sailboat seemed to have taken control, this meant his men were dead and it was just him against the world. But, he'd grown stronger due to his near breakdown and could deal with this.

With everyone on the pool deck, Ricky had no problem making his way to deck eight and cutting across to the grand staircase. Huffing and puffing as he climbed, by the time he reached his cabin, he was out of breath. Opening the door, he saw that the Hungarian sisters were gone and felt a moment of mixed anger and relief. Anger that they were gone, but relieved that he didn't have to drag them along with him since they might end up getting in the way of what he planned next.

With this resolved, Ricky made his way to the bridge.

As he approached the heavy security door, he noticed that it was slightly ajar and that the locking mechanism had been shot out. At first it troubled him that he couldn't secure the door, but this worry went away when he realized that it wouldn't matter anyway. He didn't plan on staying for any length of time. He would be here just long enough to insure that the ship went down with its Captain.

Looking at the switches that controlled the watertight doors, Ricky hesitated as his mind flashed to the one person on the ship who could be an ally. The one person that could help make sure that no one escaped his final farewell to the Calm of the Seas.

Bringing the two-way radio to his mouth, Ricky pushed the transmit button and said in a firm, steady voice, "Tim, are you there? We need to talk about your father."

\*\*\*

As Steve jumped down off the stage, the jolt sent a shock of pain through his chest. Heather saw him wince and in a firm voice commanded, "That's it, buddy. You're through. You're benched. And if you try to fight me on this, I'm going to get some of the Faithful and have them carry you down to deck four and sit on you."

"I'm fine," Steve protested and smiled. "Besides, it looks like the Faithful are following me now, so they won't listen to a mere mortal such as yourself. I'm their new leader. All hail Reverend Steve, leader of the Church of Cosmic Reality."

Heather smiled at the weak joke, but it had a ring of truth to it. Steve had a charisma that seemed to make people want to do his bidding, the Faithful being no exception. They had gotten organized into groups of four under Steve's direction and were now filtering down to the lower decks in search of Ricky. Heather decided that if Steve asked them to storm the forward cabins and fight the dead bare handed, they would obey without question.

But that's them, Heather thought. There are two people on this ship that are completely immune to my man's charms. One is Mary, and the other is me. And I'm done fooling around.

Giving Steve a twisted smile, she said, "Alright Reverend Steve. You want to play tough guy and keep running around until you really hurt yourself, then it's time for me to pull out the big guns. If you don't get down to deck four and get your ass into bed, then you're cut off. No more nookie, no more lovey-dovey, no more nothing."

Steve deflated visibly at this and said dejectedly, "No more feather?"

"Separate beds," Heather threatened.

Holding his hands up in surrender, he said, "Okay, you win. I'll be good, I'll go peacefully."

"I thought you'd see it my way," Heather said with a smirk.

Looking around at the pool deck, where only a few of the Faithful still loitered, he nonetheless tried to stall by saying, "What about the lifeboats? We need to get everyone up to speed on how to pilot them."

"But you won't be here to do it," Heather shot him down. "Tick-Tock and I will take care of it."

Steve looked at his second in command for help, urging him with his eyes to say they needed him.

Instead of coming to his aid, Tick-Tock said, "Go downstairs and lay down. Heather dropped the big one and it's over. Go peacefully."

Steve opened his mouth to try and find another excuse, but just then, a sharp pain hit his solar plexus. Finally admitting defeat, he gave in. He knew he had to get some rest and let his body heal. Besides, everything is moving along smoothly now, he placated himself. They'd find Ricky, throw him to the sharks, evacuate the boat, and sail off into the sunset. Ricky and his Ushers would be nothing more than a bad memory.

He decided to be satisfied with the successes of the day and give in - and on top of that, the threat of getting cut off really hit home – so he kissed Heather and turned to head for the stairs leading to the lower decks. Once he was out of sight, he planned on cutting over to deck seven to check on Mary and then going back to the Sombrero to collect the weapons left by the Head Ushers. He might be slightly incapacitated, but he could still do his part as he went to convalesce.

Before he could make it two steps, he heard Heather call to Brain, "You and Sheila go with him and make sure he heads straight for deck four. No detours. And Brain, if I find out that you let him make any side trips, I'll talk to Connie about cutting you off from any more kissy-huggy."

Brain opened his mouth to protest that he wasn't the one who was causing all the trouble, but Tick-Tock cut him off by saying, "Don't argue, Brain. Chicks do that kind of thing for each other. She's not bluffing."

"Whose side are you on?" Brain asked accusingly.

"My own. Now unless you want to spend your foreseeable future alone, I suggest you do like you're told."

Brain took his advice, and with Steve and Sheila in tow left to go below.

Once they were gone, Heather turned to Tick-Tock and said, "Now let's go find Ricky. I'll check deck ten again and you work on nine."

Despite Heather's threat, Steve managed to convince Brain to stop off at deck seven so he could look in on Mary. He knew that Heather had nothing to coerce Sheila with since Mary would disregard anything she was told to do, especially when it came to when she had sex. And besides that, after Steve saved Sheila's ass on the stage, she owed him one so he wasn't concerned with her ratting him out. Knowing they would be at the aid station for a few minutes, Steve sent Brain to collect the weapons left in the Sombrero Lounge.

*At least I got a few things done,* he consoled himself.

After the tech was gone, Sheila stopped before they entered the aid station and said, "Thank you for standing up for me with the crowd. For a second there, I thought they were going to come after me."

Steve gave her a strange smile and replied, "No problem. We stick up for our own."

Sheila turned to go, but was stopped when Steve said in a low voice, "And by the way, now that you're part of the group, one thing you need to keep in mind is that if you ever put any of our lives in jeopardy, you'll wish I had let that mob tear you apart compared to what I'll do to you."

Without another word, he entered the aid station.

Shocked and angry at the threat, but then remembering what Steve had done to Brother Seth and the offhand way he had killed him, Sheila made a mental note to never cross Steve.

Looking at Mary as she slept on one of the padded examination tables, Steve tried to determine how bad the wound was. Around the bandages, all he could see was that her cropped hair had been cut even further away to dress her wounds. Susan joined him and said quietly, "She's in pretty good shape considering how many splinters I pulled out of her. I gave her some Ibuprofen for the pain and Sheila gave her a Valium."

Sheila entered, so Steve moved away from Mary's side to the far corner of the room where he beckoned for both of them to join him. In a whispered voice, he said, "Sheila, you stay with Mary. Don't give her anything besides some Advil when she wakes up. She might have a concussion. Watch her for vomiting too."

To Susan, he said, "You go below with me. I'm going to need you to check on Connie and the kids and then come back and watch the stairs."

Steve then explained everything that had happened up on the pool deck so she would be up to date. He didn't think Ricky would try to make a grab for the sailboat now that everyone was turned against him, but anything was possible. He told her to keep a sharp look out, and if Ricky did show up, he would be in the Captain's Clothes Store.

When he was done briefing her, she insisted on examining his wounds. After he removed his shirt, she gently prodded the areas where he had been shot, and told him that to the best of her knowledge, nothing seemed to be broken. His ribs were bruised, but that was to be expected after taking two bullets at close range. Both discolored spots where the bullets had hit were about the size of a silver dollar and had turned black at their center. This color flowed outward to a dark purple and then to yellow.

As Steve was putting his shirt back on, Brain entered to let him know he had retrieved the dead Ushers' weapons. With everything seemingly under control, they headed to the grand staircase. On the way down to deck four, Steve checked in with Heather and Tick-Tock to see if they had found Ricky. When she asked where he was, he assured her he was calling from deck four, and after a suspiciously long pause, she told them there was no news on Ricky. She promised to call and let him know the minute he was spotted. Then she told him that he better be on deck four, because if she caught him out of bed, he knew the consequences.

Hurrying down the stairs was painful for Steve, so it was a relief to finally reach deck four. Standing at the base of the grand staircase, he was trying to think of anything he might have missed when Connie called out to him from down the Centrum, "Have you seen Tim? He's really upset about something and he ran off. I don't know what got into him. I didn't want to bother you all with it because you already had so much going on, and I was sure he'd come back, but he hasn't."

In the dim light, it took her a moment to see Brain standing there. When she did, she let out a cry of delight and rushed forward to hug him. Speaking in a rush of words, she said, "Oh, Randy, I'm so glad you're all right. I was so worried. No one knew where you were." Backing away slightly, she ran her hands along his arms and chest asking, "Are you hurt? Did they hurt you?"

Slightly embarrassed at the attention, Brain tried to deflect it by asking Connie about her brother, "How's Tim? They didn't hurt him, did they? After what he went through, it's no surprise he's upset. He's going to have to tell me how he got away because Ricky had me taped up like you wouldn't believe."

Seeing Connie, Susan and Steve giving him an odd look, Brain said in explanation, "They grabbed us both. They stuck me in the room where Tick-Tock found me, and then one of them starting beating Tim as an example of what would happen if I didn't cooperate. When I acted like I was going to help them, they took Tim away and told me they'd keep him around to make sure I did what they wanted."

Things had been moving so fast that this was the first time Steve had listened to Brain's story about being abducted. The tech had mentioned a few things in passing as they waited for Sheila to join them, but no real details of how he'd been captured.

"Tim's been with us the whole time," Steve informed him.

Brain shook his head and asked, "How? They had us both."

The question hung in the air as Brain took a deep breath and then tried to make sense of what was going on by describing the details of his kidnapping. Only partially paying attention, Steve already had an idea about what had really happened. Tim had set Brain up, although he didn't voice his theory in front of Connie.

As it turned out, he didn't have to. When Brain got to the part about Tim being beaten, she said forcefully, "That little shit. He told me he tripped and that's where he got that bruise on his cheek. When I find him, I'm going to beat him myself. Why would he hand you over to Reverend Ricky? Why is he working with that sick freak?"

A sudden thought occurred to her. Turning to Steve, she pleaded, "Please, don't hurt Tim when he shows up. He's a little boy. There's got to be a reason for what he did. I know he betrayed Randy, but..." Suddenly switching back to being mad, she added, "But whatever reason he thought he had, it's not good enough. I'm going to personally strangle him."

Steve held up his hand for her to be silent and said, "Calm down. We don't know all the details yet, but it doesn't look good for Tim. For whatever reason, he set Brain up and he could have gotten us killed. He did get Mary and I hurt, so we'll have to do something about it."

I just don't know what, he said to himself.

Connie started to cry so he added, "I doubt Tim helped Ricky willingly. That'll go in his favor. We need to find him though."

Calling Heather and Tick-Tock, Steve filled them in on this new development and told them to keep an eye out for Tim. Angered at the betrayal, Tick-Tock threatened to shoot the youngster, which sent Connie into tears again. After making Tick-Took promise to bring him in alive, Steve signed off.

Just when I thought things were settling down, I've got another crisis to deal with, Steve lamented. My chest hurts, I'm dead tired, there are still a dozen details that need to be dealt with, and now we've got to find Tim, who it seems, screwed us over.

Sorting through the priorities, he said to Connie and Brain, "Go up and grab the rest of the weapons that Sheila collected from the Ushers in the casino." He shook his head rapidly to clear it and added. "I forgot where she put them, so stop by on seven and ask her. Susan, you stay here. Watch the stairs and don't let any of the Faithful down here. They'll be wandering around looking for Ricky, but I don't want them on deck four."

Turning back to Brain and Connie, he said, "When you get back, start loading everything on The Usual Suspects. We aren't staying here any longer then we have to. Get ready for a quick exit."

At this, Connie gasped and said, "I know Tim did a horrible thing but I hope you're not thinking of leaving him. We can't just abandon him."

"We're not leaving yet," Steve assured her. "I just want to be ready." He then reminded them that the ship had settled two feet since they first came on board. He stressed that either Brain or Connie needed to be on The Usual Suspects at all times in case they had to make a hasty exit.

"What about Tim?" Connie asked.

"I think he's done all the damage he can do, so I'm not worried about him pulling any other shitty stunts tonight. Keep an eye out for him in case he shows up, but if he doesn't, we'll all look for him in the morning. Hopefully by then, the Faithful will have found Ricky so we can get them looking for Tim, too."

A coughing fit seized Steve that almost doubled him over from the pain. When it passed, he spit onto the deck and was relieved it came out clear. No blood. Despite this good sign, he knew he had to lie down for a little while. They were shorthanded and he planned on starting the search for Tim himself, but knew it was out of the question tonight. He wouldn't last more than five minutes before he collapsed. It would have to be tomorrow.

As the others moved off to carry out their orders, he went to the Captain's Clothes Store and gingerly lowered himself onto the mattress he and Heather shared. Most men would have had a hard time falling asleep as the memory of almost being killed by two bullets fired into their chest from close range bounced around in their heads. But in a world where the dead had come back to life to feed on the living, this paled in comparison to existing on a daily basis in one of the middle levels of Hell.

In two minutes, Steve was asleep.

\*\*\*

Tim watched as the group in front of the stairs broke up and went in separate directions, relieved that Susan was left to guard access to deck four. He didn't want Steve to be there since he was always too aware at what was going on around him. Steve would make what he had to do all the more difficult. With Susan guarding the stairs though, she would watch the stairs. If Steve or Tick-Tock were guarding the stairs, they could be counted on to watch everything around them. From helping Steve and the others, he'd learned much about their strengths and weaknesses and he used that knowledge against them now without any qualms.

Glancing down at his watch, the watch his father had given him on his last birthday, Tim saw he still had forty minutes until it was time for him to act on Reverend Ricky's last order. He had been surprised when he heard the Reverend's voice calling to him on the two-way radio, but in the back of his mind he knew it was inevitable that they interact one last time.

After running away from Connie, he'd gone to the back room of a shop that specialized in making stuffed animals. Months ago, he had set up his own little hide-a-way that he never told his sister about. It was here that he stored his treasures. Some old playboy magazines, a few t-shirts with funny sayings that he'd made up in the Shirt Shack, an old brass compass that he found on one of his scavenging trips, and after Ricky had given him them, the radio and the bolt cutters.

As he sat on top of a flattened pile of dolphins that would never be stuffed and cuddled by a child, he calmed down enough to think clearly and knew he had to come up with a solution to the jam he'd gotten himself into. Like any pre-teen who didn't know enough about how people thought and acted, he first reasoned that everybody in the whole world was against him. No one would understand that he'd been doing what he did to save his dad, and they would want to punish him for it.

As he thought along these lines, Tim became angrier with Steve and the people from the sailboat. They were the ones who would hang him if they caught him. They seemed so nice at first but then had turned on him and wanted to kill him. At this thought, he decided he hadn't betrayed them, they had betrayed him.

And Ricky had betrayed him too, he realized. He's got my dad and won't let him go. We had a deal and he broke it. And after all I did for him, that fat fucker.

Tim smiled at his use of the curse word.

If Steve and the rest of them had never come aboard, none of this would have happened. They're fuckers too. All of them. Ricky would have never taken dad if I hadn't been caught sneaking around trying to help Steve, he thought vehemently.

His anger turned to sadness at the thought of everything he'd lost and he started to cry. He saw no way out of the dilemma. Curling up in a ball, the emotional strain caught up with him and soon he was sobbing loudly. His tears eventually tuned to sniffles. Worn out from his internal struggle and emotional trials, the tears dried on his face as he drifted off to sleep.

When the voice called out his name, waking him from his restless nap, he jerked upright and started to defend himself. His first thought was that Steve had found him and was going to drag him up on deck to hang him from the yardarm. Looking around blearily, he saw that he was alone. Tim decided he must have been dreaming and lowered himself back onto the soft pile of deflated dolphins. He had just gotten comfortable when the voice came again. This time he recognized it and knew it wasn't a dream. It was a nightmare.

From the radio's speaker, Ricky's voice said, "I know that you're listening Tim. I know that you can hear me. You need to answer me or it's going to be very painful for your father."

Tim snatched the radio from where it lay on a nearby sewing machine and said angrily, "What do you want? Haven't you done enough? Let my dad go."

"Ah, young Tim, so good to hear from you," Ricky purred.

"Let my dad go," Tim repeated.

"In good time, in good time," Ricky intoned. His voice growing stern, he said, "But you need to do one last thing for me before you're reunited with your father. The thing I told you about when you were up on the bridge."

Feeling hope burst in his chest, Tim asked, "And then you'll let my dad go?"

"Do what I told you to do at exactly ten o'clock tonight, and you'll be with him soon."

In hell, Ricky thought, but didn't say. Instead, he asked, "Do you have a watch?"

Looking down at the present from his dad, he said, "Yes."

"What time does it say, young Tim?"

Tim told him and Ricky had him advance it by eight minutes.

"Just like in the movies, we're synchronizing our watches, young Tim."

'When do I see my dad?" Tim asked.

"I'll be watching to make sure you do what I told you to. Your father will be with me and I'll have a gun to his head. When I see that you've completed this last task for me, I'll let him go."

Tim steeled himself as he considered what was being asked of him.

"Do we have a deal?" Ricky asked.

"Yes, yes" he cried. "It's their fault anyway. They deserve whatever happens."

"Good boy. At exactly ten o'clock, cut the lock on the doors to the cabins on deck four and open them. Then I'll release your father. You have my word."

With an amused tone in his voice, Ricky added, "And one more thing, Tim. After you've opened the doors, you better run."

Chapter Twenty-Two

The Dead Calm:

Steve's bladder woke him, and for a minute he lay on his back, wondering if he could ignore it and go back to sleep. He decided that it the urge wouldn't go away through will alone so he started to sit up before the pain in his ribs stopped him. Cursing, he cautiously rolled onto his side and then on to all fours. Slowly levering himself into a standing position, he noticed that it only hurt when he moved, breathed, or stood still.

With the Head Ushers dead and Ricky in hiding, the time for sneaking around and using the rear corridors had passed, so Steve grabbed his M-4 and went out through the front door of the Captain's Clothes Store. Noticing with satisfaction that Susan sat in such a way that she could see the stairs, and down the Centrum, with just a turn of her head, he waved to her and said, "Bathroom break."

Slowly, he made his way to the public restroom halfway down the Centrum. When he was finished, he saw that the toilet wouldn't flush. When he went to wash his hands, he noted with frustration that no water came out of the faucet either. Steve thought back to how they had filled the Usual Suspect's water tank by pouring gallon jugs one at a time through the filler near the bow, but to do that on the Dead Calm would take a year if they could even find that much water.

Tomorrow, we help the passengers get the lifeboats ready and then it's time to go, he resolved. No more screwing around here. It's time to haul ass. The accommodations are really starting to suck.

As he returned to where Susan sat, he was surprised to see Cindy with her. He hadn't noticed the little girl before because she had been curled up asleep on a bench behind Susan. Pointing to her, he raised his eyebrows in question.

"She got lonely," Susan explained in a whisper. "Brain brought her up here about an hour ago and she talked my ear off for fifteen minutes before she crashed."

"Brain and Connie are on The Usual Suspects?" Steve asked quietly.

Susan nodded and said, "You didn't rest for very long."

"When you gotta go..."

Susan smiled and asked, "Can you do me a favor? Can you go into the Ship's Store and grab me a bottle of water?"

Realizing he had put Susan out here with no one to relieve her, he apologized for not being more on the ball.

"You can't think of everything," she assured him.

He replied, as he left to get her water, "But I still have to try."

\*\*\*

A jolt of fear shooting through him, Tim froze and when he saw Steve come out of a store.

Don't let him spot me, he prayed as he willed himself to be invisible.

He had managed to slip behind Susan and had made it all the way past the stairs to the registration desk that dealt with people who wanted to book activities at one of the ship's ports of call. Here, he waited for his watch to show one minute to ten o'clock. Sadly, he remembered his dad standing at this very same desk when he signed the family up to go horseback riding on the beach. With a flash of anger, he also remembered seeing Steve here for the first time as he tapped his rifle on the counter to see if any dead were behind it.

Hoping the shadows would conceal him like they did when he cut the chain used to secure the cabin doors on deck five, Tim crouched and backed up until he felt his tail bone hit the front of the desk. His heart pounding in his throat, he barely dared breathe lest he give himself away.

I'm so close, he thought. Please don't let them spot me now.

Tim looked around for a direction to run if they noticed him, and then watched with relief as Steve turned away and headed down the Centrum while Susan followed his progress. He used this distraction to slip over the desk, freezing when he accidentally knocked the bolt cutters against the counter top. As he looked back to where Susan stood, he saw her interest was still taken by Steve. With a quiet sigh, and a, "Thank you," muttered under his breath, he continued on. Once on the other side, he found himself in complete darkness. Pressing a button on the side of his watch, he saw by the glow that it was ten minutes to ten.

More than enough time, he thought with relief. In a crouch, he went to the far end of the counter and slipped back over. The nearest emergency light was twenty feet away, leaving the area in darkness. The doors to the cabin area were only a few quick steps away.

***

Heather glanced at the group of Faithful making their way down the Centrum as they prowled through the rows of high-end shops on deck ten. She had just finished searching each of the royal suites and was exhausted. There hadn't been any sign of Ricky, but she was relieved when she came across the two Hungarian girls trying on clothes in a boutique. She escorted them up to the pool deck, so Ricky wouldn't come across them too, and left them with two older women. After explaining the situation to them, they assured her that the two girls would be looked after until she returned. Heather would have to tell Steve that the sisters would be staying with them, and he was now a foster dad, but she knew he wouldn't object since it was the right thing to do.

Resuming her search of the high-end cabins reserved for Ricky and his Head Ushers, Heather was repulsed at how dirty everything was. Soiled clothes and half eaten food lay scattered around most of the rooms, and they all had an underlying odor of dried sweat and body waste.

Now, breathing the semi-fresh air of the Centrum, she decided to call it a night. Checking her watch, she saw it was a few minutes to ten. Unclipping her radio, she pressed the transmit button and asked, "Tick-Tock, where are you? Over."

"Deck six, over," came his reply.

"I'm calling it a night," Heather told him. "I want to check on Steve anyway, and then I need to go up to the pool deck and do something, over." Heather didn't want to get into explaining about the new additions to their group until she had to.

Tick-Tock replied, "I'm almost done with deck six and then I'm going to go through seven real quick. Shouldn't be more than an hour. I'll see you downstairs, over."

"Over and out," Heather acknowledged.

Securing her radio, she slowly headed for the stairs thinking, as much as I've gone up and down these damn things, I should have the butt of an eighteen year old.

***

The Reverend Ricky Rose had a sudden change of heart as he looked down at the switches that controlled the watertight doors. He still planned on flooding the ship with the living dead, only now he decided he didn't want to die after doing it.

Considering the layout of the ship for a moment, he quickly came up with an escape route. He wasn't too worried about his Faithful trying to stop him since, with what he had planned for the ship, they would be too busy trying to save their own lives to bother. Ditto with the people from the sailboat. All he had to do was set his final plan into motion.

Ricky looked at his watch and saw it was one minute to show time.

***

Steve handed the bottle of water to Susan, who opened it and took a long drink. Eyeing him, she asked, "Aren't you supposed to be in bed? You're looking a little rough. And besides, I just heard Heather say on the radio that she's on her way."

Steve nodded, the thought of bed sounded enticing. While he felt like he still had a million details to go over, the idea of lying back on the mattress and relaxing was almost overwhelming. Combined with the fact that his other half would kill him if she found him up, he decided it would be in his best interests not be standing around when she showed up. He had gotten up to answer the call of nature, and figured that while he was awake, he would take care of a few things, but as he looked around, he realized that there wasn't anything that couldn't wait. Heather would be back in a little while and she could sort out who would watch the stairs. Together, they could gather up their belongings so they could leave the Dead Calm the next day.

Steve nodded again to Susan, and was about to agree with her, when a metallic rattling sound coming from the area by the doors to the cabins stopped him. In the silence of the Centrum, the noise seemed deafening.

Instantly alert, he motioned for Susan to stay where she was as he brought his rifle off his shoulder, holding it ready at waist height.

Crouching slightly, he went to investigate.

\*\*\*

Tim cursed under his breath as he looked down at the discarded spray-paint cans he'd kicked. He thought he was home free as he moved toward the cabin doors to cut the chain off, but with his first step, he'd blown it by kicking one of the canisters left lying on the carpet by whoever had painted the crosses on the doors. He knew the noise would alert Steve, so he had to move fast.

He took another quickstep forward, opened the bolt cutters and closed them around the lock holding the chain together.

\*\*\*

Steve circled the grand staircase, instantly spotted the shadowy figure standing in front of the doors leading to the cabin area. At first he thought it was Ricky and raised his rifle, then realized that the shape of the person was wrong. It was shorter then Ricky and this person was slim where Ricky was fat.

In a flash, he realized who it was. Holding his fire, but not lowering his rifle, he barked out, "Whatever the fuck it is you're doing, Tim, you need to stop."

Then, the chain around the door handles rattled and Steve knew exactly what he was doing. At first he didn't believe it, but when Tim turned slightly, he saw the bolt cutters as the youngster pushed their handles together.

The chain parted.

\*\*\*

Quite a few of the dead in the cabin area on deck four were attracted to the doors leading into the Centrum because they could sense food on the other side. With the scent of fresh meat being so strong for the past few days, the short hallway that led to these doors was now packed wall to wall with the living dead. They milled about, with the ones in the front constantly switching places with those at the back. Occasionally, when the urge struck one of the creatures, it would reach out and move the push bar to see if it could free itself and it could get at the food waiting beyond.

Up until now, the chain had always restrained them, but after hearing something rattling against the doors and the sound of a voice calling out, one of them tried again.

This time the doors opened.

\*\*\*

Ricky's hands moved quickly as he activated the switches that opened the watertight doors on every level of the ship. He had originally planned on just opening the doors to decks five through nine but in the end flipped all the switches. Looking down at the rows of green lights that showed across the console, indicating that all sections of the ship were now open, he barely felt the slight lurch as the Calm of the Seas settled at the stern.

The excitement of what he had just done bubbled up in him, causing insane laughter to burst from his throat, Ricky quickly spun around and ran for the door leading from the bridge.

\*\*\*

The engine compartment and deck one had flooded completely, leaving those dead inside to float weightlessly, trapped in a liquid prison. With the watertight doors shut, there was a benefit to the living on the ship that they were unaware of besides keeping the dead locked in. No more water could enter the ship because the pressure had equalized, effectively stopping the Dead Calm from sinking. Although this circumstance was only temporary, and with the pumps out, eventually the ship would sink into the Gulf of Mexico, it gave the living on board at least two more weeks before they had to abandon the cruise liner.

That was until Reverend Ricky opened the watertight doors.

With a pop and a roar, water rushed out from these flooded compartments at the rate of hundreds of thousands of gallons per second. The sudden change of pressure also caused the seals on the screws and the pumps to blow, letting in more water to add to that already flooding the ship.

As the water surged in from below, the hatches on the upper decks that kept the dead imprisoned in the cabin areas parted or swung open.

At first, only those zombies near the openings went through. Then, the smell of human meat flowed into the cabin areas and the rest rushed forward.

Water and the dead quickly flooded the Calm of the Seas.

*** 

Tim heard Steve's warning as he cut the lock. Turning around, he saw that he was trapped. Steve stood with his rifle at the ready, blocking any chance of escape. Tim's eyes darted around, looking for a place to hide, but he saw it was fruitless. There was nowhere to run. Behind him, he heard the chain as it pulled through the handles, right before the door banged open.

Dirty hands reached out and grabbed him. Tim's last coherent thought before pain blotted everything out was, I did what Ricky wanted so at least now he'll let my dad go.

This thought mollified him for only a second before the first set of teeth bit into the back of his neck. He twisted his body around and broke free for a moment. Looking up in terror and confusion, Tim saw who had bitten him.

He could only squeak out, "Mom?" before she fell on him.

***

Steve watched as the doors to the cabin area burst open and the dead pushed through. Instinctively, he fired at the first of the figures that came into the Centrum even as he watched Tim pulled down and torn apart.

Too many, his mind screamed, as he saw dozens of the dead stagger forward with more crowding behind. Hearing rifle fire on his left, he turned his head slightly and saw that Susan had joined him and was shooting into the throng of dead. Maybe they could hold them, he thought as he resumed firing, but immediately saw that it was hopeless. The area between the cabins and the grand staircase already held over fifty of the dead with more pouring through the doors by the second.

For as long as he could remember, Steve had had the ability to consider numerous aspects of any situation and come up with a solution within a split second. Even as he fired a shot into the head of the zombie nearest him, his mind flashed to the last known location of all of his people. It was like he had the ship's layout in front of him and he could see where Heather, Tick-Tock, Mary and Sheila were. He then flashed on Brain and Connie being in the sailboat and Cindy behind him. He instantly cataloged everything at their disposal that they needed to get out of this deadly mess. In a split second, the solution to how they could escape came to him.

Firing into the head of a zombie, he shouted to Susan, "Give me your radio, mine's in the clothes store."

She unclipped the two-way from the waistband of her jeans and handed it over as Steve started giving out orders, "Get Cindy and head for the sailboat. Cast off and tell Brain to watch for us."

Susan fired twice, taking off half the cranium of one of the dead coming toward her as she shouted, "We're not leaving you."

"You won't be," Steve yelled back, his ears ringing from the noise of the rifle fire. "Tell Brain to sit off the stern of the ship and watch for us. We'll be coming down that way."

Susan started to open her mouth to object, when the deck shuddered under her feet. Wide-eyed, she looked to Steve for an explanation, but he was as clueless as she was. He had no idea what could make an almost one hundred thousand ton ship shake like that. The one thing he did know was that whatever it was couldn't be good.

Having been pushed back to the rear of the grand staircase by the oncoming waves of dead, Steve knew he would have to break off or he'd be trapped on deck four. He had to get to the upper decks before he was cut off. He knew he had to reassure Susan or she would never leave, so between firing into the heads of any zombie that got too close, he briefly laid out his plan. By the time he was done, they had been pushed to the front of the grand staircase. He yelled at her to grab Cindy and haul ass as he started up to deck five, taking the stairs two at a time.

Susan fired into the center of the face of a snarling gray-faced woman that had gotten to within ten feet of her and then turned and ran to where Cindy had been laying on the bench. Circling a planter that hid it from view, she hoped the little girl hadn't run off to hide. She really didn't have time to search for her.

Relieved when she found Cindy huddled by the end of the bench, she saw that the sounds of gunfire and the screeching of the dead had terrorized her.

Forcing a smile to reassure her, Susan crouched down and said, "Come on, we've got to go."

As she looked at Cindy, she saw the girl's eyes get wider as they shifted from focusing on her face to something behind her. Cindy's mouth opened to scream even as Susan spun around.

The dead thing wore a red T-shirt, signifying that it had once been one of Ricky's original gang of Ushers. Most of its neck had been torn away, causing its head to flop at strange angles as it lurched forward and grabbed Susan with both hands. Still in a crouch, she had no leverage to work with as she felt herself being pushed back. She let the M-4 fall from her hands as she reached for the pistol holstered at her hip. Bringing it up with lightning speed, she placed the muzzle under the dead things chin and squeezed the trigger.

Blinded by the torrent of black pus and brain matter that sprayed her face as the bullet blew the dead thing's head apart, Susan pushed the body off her as she spit chunks of rotten flesh from her mouth. The reality of what had just happened, and its consequences, struck her like a physical blow. She fought the urge to pass out as she felt her body freeze up as the knowledge washed through her that she was now infected.

Distantly, she heard Cindy scream and focused on the sound. The thought that the little girl was in trouble energized her into action. Wiping slime from her eyes, she blinked rapidly to clear them.

Susan saw at once that a group of a dozen dead were advancing on them, the closest only a few feet away. Using her pistol, she fired as she lifted her body into a sitting position and put one hand down to heave herself to her feet. Blowing air out her nose to clear it of the black puss that blocked it, she continued to fire as she reached down and picked up her M-4. Emptying her .45 as she did this, she holstered it and opened fire with the assault rifle.

Without even turning her head, she screamed, "Move, Cindy, go! Head for the sailboat."

She backed up and fired the final round from the magazine in her rifle then ejected it. Fumbling in the cargo pocket of her pants, she found her last remaining one and slapped it home. As she let the bolt slam forward, she saw that she had cleared some space in front of her. She took the respite to quickly check on Cindy, but saw that the little girl hadn't run for the boat. She had started to, but then stopped and was standing only twenty feet behind her.

Fear that Cindy would be killed turned to anger as Susan screamed at her, "Run, goddammit!"

Equally scared, Cindy screamed back, "Not without you."

Understanding that if she stayed to cover them that Cindy wouldn't leave her, Susan said, "Then we both go," and ran to the little girl, grabbed her by the hand and literally lifted her off her feet as she headed down the Centrum, the dead only feet behind them.

As they raced for the safety of The Usual Suspects, Susan contemplated her own death and how she would handle it. They had made it halfway down the Centrum when she settled on how she would die. Then, she noticed the water coming toward them. It was only a few inches deep, but it was coming fast.

Susan realized that the ship was sinking, and it took her mind off the fact that she had been infected with the HWNW Virus. She sped up, urging Cindy on. Glancing behind her, she saw they had outrun the dead. The question now was if they could outrun the water pouring into the ship?

It seemed to be coming in fast, and she knew they had to make it to the hatch before it was submerged. With the dead behind them, they couldn't go back. She tried to judge how fast the water was rising as she ran through the passageway.

We'll either make it or we won't, she thought in a fatalistic way. And if we don't, I'll come up with another idea. I won't give up on Cindy until I'm dead.

By the time they reached the dining room, the water was calf deep. It slowed them as they tried alternately high stepping and wading through it. From the flow, Susan calculated they should make the sailboat before the hatch was under water.

Finally reaching the watercraft storage room, she wadded through thigh deep water as she literally dragged Cindy behind her. Filling her lungs with the scent of sea air pouring through the open hatch, Susan realized that this was something she wouldn't get to enjoy much longer. She would either be dead, or... No, she told herself as she reached the spot where The Usual Suspects was tied up. I won't let myself become one of them. I'll be dead. I've already made up my mind on that.

Reaching the hatch and looking through it, she expected to see the sailboat waiting to take Cindy to safety, feeling her heart drop when she saw that the boat was gone. Nothing could be seen except the dark water flooding into the Dead Calm.

Of course, she thought, Brain would have seen that the Dead Calm was sinking and cut the sailboat loose.

She looked behind her at where the jet skis were stored, trying to calculate how long it would take her to free one from its cradle, when suddenly the hatchway was bathed in light. Shielding her eyes, she squinted out at its source. Through the blinding light, not thirty feet away, she could see The Usual Suspects.

"Susan," Brain yelled to her. "What's going on? What's happening? Where is everyone?"

She replied, "Come and get Cindy. We don't have much time. Things got fucked up fast."

Brain maneuvered that sailboat next to the hatch as Susan quickly filled him in on the dead getting loose on the ship. She told him about Steve's plan, but didn't bother to state the obvious.

The Calm of the Seas was sinking.

When the sailboat was butting up against the hull of the cruise ship, Connie reached down over the gunwale to hoist Cindy up and over it as Susan fought to push the little girl forward against the rush of water coming through the hatch. Connie managed to grab Cindy's wrist and, with a grunt, pulled her on board. She reached out to help Susan, but she shook her head no then pointed to her face. It was then that Brain and Connie noticed the streaks of black goo running across it.

Connie didn't understand, but Brain did. They had found out from people calling into the radio station that if you had any contact with infected body fluid, if it got in your mouth, or nose, or eyes, it was a death sentence. You were infected.

Brain moaned, "Oh shit..."

Susan handed her M-4 up to Connie and said quietly, "Take Cindy below." To Cindy, she called out in as much of an even voice as she could muster, "Go with Connie, sweetheart. I'll be there in a minute. I've got one more thing to do."

When they were gone, Susan pulled the .45 from its holster and said, "You've got the M-4. Before this is all over, I'm sure you'll need it, but I need the pistol one more time. Please tell Cindy that I love her, and try to explain this to her. Tell Tick-Tock I'll miss him."

Speechless, Brain nodded, understanding what Susan was about to do. He turned his head for a second to give himself a chance to gather his thoughts and to find something to say in farewell, but when he turned back, the hatch was empty.

She had retreated into the Dead Calm.

Susan waded through the dining hall and into the Centrum, studying her surroundings in the dim glow of the emergency lights. Her heart ached for all that she had lost in a world that had passed on, and for all she would never have. She prayed that the rest of the group made it to safety and that the dead would go back to whatever hell had spawned them so the survivors could live in peace.

Gratefull, she saw nothing of the dead. They seemed to have lost track of her and Cindy when they outran them and had gone in search of easier prey.

That's good, Susan thought, since she only had one magazine left for the .45. And besides, I can use a little peace.

A quarter of the way down the Centrum, she came across a statue of Neptune and decided that this was the spot. Sitting on one of the benches that faced it, she realized she didn't feel any fear at what she was about to do. In fact, she was calm, cool and collected about it.

Mechanically, she raised the pistol, switching out the empty clip for a full one before cocking the weapon and placing the barrel in her mouth.

I've done good and bad in my life, she thought as her finger tightened on the trigger. I just hope the good outweighs the bad. God forgive me for what I have to do.

He did.

Chapter Twenty-Three

The Dead Calm:

Steve was halfway up the stairs to deck five when he tried to call Heather on the two-way radio. Receiving nothing, he realized that either the device was dead or the batteries had run down. After clipping it to his belt, he increased his pace. Now he had to find everyone the hard way.

On reaching the landing that led onto deck five, he immediately saw a large group of the dead coming toward him from the cabin area. He estimated there were at least thirty. Not as many as below, but too many to shoot. Remembering what Susan had told him about Heather coming back down to deck four, he by-passed five and continued to head upwards in the hope he would run into her.

His initial adrenalin rush had worn off by the time he reached deck six, and now he could feel the pain from his injuries. Every time he inhaled, it felt like someone was jabbing a hot needle deep into his ribs, and every time he exhaled, it felt like the same was being done to his solar plexus. Steve pushed the pain down as he drove himself on with the need to find Heather.

When he passed deck six, he was moving so fast that he almost ran right into two dead crew members that were coming down the stairs from seven. Realizing that Ricky had opened all the watertight doors that keeping the Zs contained, while his cohort Tim took care of the chains on decks five and four, Steve cursed when he saw that he might be cut off.

No time to stop now, he told himself.

Instead of slowing and shooting the two Z's, Steve thought of Heather being in danger and increased his pace, taking the stairs three at a time. Ducking slightly, he dodged the dead man on the left as it reached out to grab him while butt stroking the one on the right in the face with his M-4. The zombie was knocked back and landed with a thud. Steve looked up and saw at least twenty of the dead staggering down the stairs between decks seven and eight, and decided that it might be in his best interests to exit on deck seven. Here, he could warn Sheila and Mary before making his way to the exterior staircase at the back of the ship. Those should be clear, he assured himself. Ricky let the dead go from where they were locked in cabin areas at the forward sections of the ship and it'll take the Z's a few minutes to get to the rear.

At this, another thought struck him. The Faithful. They would either fight to protect themselves and kill the dead, or run off and lead them away. If they ran away, he knew that people being chased instinctively headed for higher ground, so they would lead the Z's upward. Steve's final destination was deck twelve, and he hoped he could find the others and make it there before the dead did. He slowed as he reached the landing for deck seven, but found himself confronted by three of the dead that looked like business men who had died and then come back while on vacation. Each of them wore loud Hawaiian shirts, Bermuda shorts and sandals with black socks. Sickened more by their fashion sense than their torn, puss leaking faces, he shot each of them in the forehead.

Passing them before the last body hit the ground, he dodged a pre-teen girl in a bathing suit with her lower chest ripped open to reveal her ribs. She screeched as he dodged her. He could see a few of the dead scattered on the walkway in front of him and knew he could easily take them out. When he saw what they were doing though, he suddenly felt sick to his stomach.

They were huddled in two groups over struggling bodies as they fed.

Looking toward the first aid station thirty feet beyond them, his heart dropped when he saw that the door was open. They had gotten to Sheila and Mary before he could warn them.

Steve stopped and looked behind him to make sure he had time to do what he needed, seeing only ten of the dead heading toward him from the far side of the grand staircase. He wondered at this small amount of flesh eaters compared to the hundreds flooding the other decks, then saw the reason why deck seven wasn't overflowing with the dead. The watertight doors leading to the cabin area had jammed after only opening a foot. As he watched, he saw four or five of the creatures fighting each other to squeeze through the narrow opening.

Bathing suit girl caught his attention as the only immediate threat, so he shot her once between the eyes, spraying the carpet behind her with black goo, white skull and gray brains.

He turned back to where the dead were feeding and began methodically shooting each of them in the head, stopping only once to insert a fresh magazine in his M-4. He noticed both of the zombies' victims were still alive, so he stepped forward to get clean shots to put them out of their misery. This was when he saw that one of them was a man. It was one of the Faithful he remembered from the pool deck. One of the men who had cursed Sheila out.

Relief flooded through him as he realized it wasn't Mary or Sheila. Glancing over at the other body, he noted that despite having its face chewed away, it was an older lady with gray hair.

Taking aim at the man's head, Steve wondered what had happened to Mary and Sheila. After firing two quick shots, he took off at a run for the stern of the ship.

\*\*\*

Heather had just passed deck eight when she heard cries of, "There he is, get him," from above her. Her heart sped up as she realized that someone had spotted Reverend Ricky.

"You're mine, you sick fuck," Heather vowed as she started running up the grand staircase.

She cautiously looked around as she reached deck nine before mounting the last few steps. No sense popping up and giving him an easy target, she thought.

Peeking over the edge of the landing, she looked down the Centrum and saw some of the Faithful pointing up to deck ten while others ran toward the stairs. They were all in hot pursuit of what could only be Reverend Ricky.

"I'm on your trail now, asshole," Heather said out loud.

She was about to continue up to deck ten when she was surprised to see the people coming toward her stop dead in their tracks. One man even went as far as to drop down like he was sliding into home plate before spinning onto all fours and scrabbling away on hands and knees as he tried to get his feet under him.

Screams of, "Stinkers," filled the air.

Perplexed, at first Heather thought the Faithful had gotten her confused with one of the Z's that occasionally got loose. This was until she looked over her shoulder when a high-pitched keening noise caught her attention. Sixty to seventy of the dead had already flooded through the doors from the cabin area to her right with more coming behind them. Staggering, limping, crawling and pulling themselves along by their arms, they were intent on the people running away until they spotted her. The noise they made got louder as they sped up and headed in her direction.

"Oh, shit," she breathed as she mentally booted herself in the ass to get moving.

Running as fast as her feet would take her, she continued upward. She knew they would have to abandon the Dead Calm, but she had to make sure Ricky got what was coming first. She worried about Steve, but this was interrupted when she reached deck ten and heard a boom she recognized as a .45 caliber pistol followed by screams.

Repeating the same cautious approach she had used on deck nine, Heather spotted a young woman crouched behind a planter not far from the stairs leading onto deck ten.

Heather waved to get her attention, and then asked in a quiet voice, "Is it Ricky?"

The woman started babbling at the top of her voice, causing Heather to worry that she'd give their position away. "It's Ricky. I couldn't believe it when I saw him. A bunch of us started chasing him. He made it all the way to the rear of the Centrum. That fat-ass can really run. Then he shot at us, so I turned around and came back here. If you hurry, you can catch him. He's probably heading for the stairs at the back of the boat."

Heather took this all in while she cautiously advanced and said to the woman, "I'll get Ricky, but you can't stay here. There's Z's on deck nine, too many to deal with, so you have to make your way to the lifeboats on seven. You need to warn the others to do the same. Find as many people as you can and spread the word."

The shrieking of the dead came from below, causing the woman's eyes to go wide and her body to freeze in shock.

Seeing that she wasn't going to move, Heather approached her and grabbed her by the arm, lifting her to her feet, she yelled, "Go on! Warn the others. Go through the upper decks and warn anyone you see. Then cut back and use the rear stairs to get to the lifeboats. It's time to get the hell off this ship!"

Giving the woman a shove to get her moving, Heather started down the Centrum as she repeated her evacuation instructions to everyone she came across.

After exiting at the rear of the super structure, she approached the exterior stairs, taking every precaution while moving as fast as she could. As her foot settled on the first step, her radio crackled to life, "Steve, Heather, Susan. It's Tick-Tock. Speak to me. I've got an ass-load of dead coming onto deck six. I'm on seven now and they're here too. What's the plan, over?"

Heather frowned, disappointed in herself that she'd been so caught up in catching Ricky that she'd forgotten about the others.

Stepping out of the line of any possible gunfire from below, she spoke into her radio, "It's me, Heather. I'm on deck ten. We got a shit load of Z's coming onto nine too. Ricky must have popped the doors and now he's heading in your direction to try and grab a lifeboat, over."

There was silence for a moment, and then she heard the faint sound of an M-4 being fired from somewhere in the ship. She counted to thirty, and was about to call Tick-Tock again, when his voice came over the speaker, "I heard shooting and went to go see who it was. It's Steve. He's on his way, over."

Shots that seemed to come from just below her snuffed out Heather's joy at hearing that Steve was okay. She listened for a moment and could hear the deep boom of a .45 interspersed with the sharp cracks of two M-4s.

Then, Heather smiled evilly as she realized what had happened. Ricky had run into Tick-Tock and Steve.

She started rapidly descending the steps to deck nine. Here she paused briefly as she drank in the cool night air.

The sound of gunfire had ceased, so she took a chance and called Tick-Tock on the radio. Steve answered. After assuring each other they were okay, he filled her in on his plan to exit the Dead Calm and told her he had seen Ricky leave the stairs at deck nine. He and Tick-Tock would come to her and they would head up to deck twelve together.

"Negative," Heather replied, hearing the voices of the Faithful above her as they started to descend the stairs. "I've got people coming down to seven to get on the lifeboats. We've got to deal with Ricky so that I can get them past deck eight, over."

Brain's voice broke into the conversation saying, "There's something else you need to know, over."

"Brain, where are you?" Steve asked.

"Holding position off the stern," he replied. "Susan told me that's where you wanted me, over." There was a pause and then Brain added, "Susan didn't make it."

Heather's heart felt sick at this news. She thought to herself, poor Tick-Tock, poor Susan. Her mind flitted briefly to Marcia, Jonny G and Meat, who had all been killed when the radio station was overrun by the dead.

So many gone, she lamented. And so much pain for the survivors.

Switching mental gears, rage flooded through her as she thought that so many good people were dead, and that a scumbag like Ricky was still walking around sucking air. This shit ends here, she vowed.

Keying the transmit button on the radio she said, "I'm going after Ricky. I'm coming down from deck nine. Steve, you and Tick-Tock work your way up from seven. We'll make sure Ricky doesn't screw with the people trying to evacuate the ship, over."

Brain cut in saying, "Then you need to hurry. The ship's starting to sink. The water's already covered the outer hatch on deck four, over."

"Watch for us at the stern," Steve told Brain. "We'll be on deck twelve. Heather, we move out when you call it, over."

"Then I call it," she said. "Move out."

She clipped the radio to her belt and moved in a crouch as she descended the stairs. The rear of the ship was only thirty feet or so to her right, and the area was wide open except for a few deck chairs. Ricky was too fat to hide behind any of them, so she knew it was clear. To her left was the superstructure of the ship, but there were no doors as this would be the back wall of the Sounds Lounge. The only way to get into the ship was to go along the twenty-foot wide walkway that ran the length of the superstructure on its port and starboard sides.

Reaching deck eight, she saw movement on the stairs below and recognized Steve. Tick-Tock appeared moments later. After they joined up, Heather said quietly to Tick-Tock, "I'm sorry about Susan."

Tick-Tock nodded but kept his feelings to himself. "We'll grieve later," he told her. "Right now, we need to take care of Ricky and get the hell off this ship."

Heather wanted to say something to console him, but was silenced by his blank faced expression. Instead, she turned to Steve and said, "You guys take the starboard side and I'll take port. If I remember correctly, we have to go a couple hundred feet before we get to a door. With the Z's coming from the forward sections and us from the rear, we'll trap Ricky in between. It shouldn't be hard to find him."

Steve nodded his assent to the plan. Before heading off with Tick-Tock, he gave Heather a kiss and told her to be careful. She told him to do the same. Parting, they turned their full attention to the task at hand while a steady stream of the Faithful went down the stairs to the lifeboats.

Heather, Steve and Tick-Tock entered the Dead Calm for the final time.

*\*\**

The Reverend Ricky Rose left the bridge and ran through deck ten out into the Centrum. Here, he saw a few of his former Faithful going in and out of stores as they searched for him, so he kept to the outside of the walkway as he raced past. Ready to shoot anyone who barred his way, to his surprise, he made it halfway down the Centrum before being spotted.

As the first cry of alarm went out, Ricky held the .45 out in plain view as a deterrent to anyone trying to stop him. The few Faithful who were still in his path quickly moved out of the way upon seeing the gun, so he had a clear path to the doors that led out onto the stern of the ship.

Once there, he paused to catch his breath. As he panted like a dog, he turned and saw about twenty of the former members of his congregation coming toward him. Raising his pistol, he fired a single shot in their direction as he started moving again. Not stopping to see if he hit anyone, he went outside and waddled quickly down the stairs to deck seven before having to stop again to rest. He was feeling nauseated from running, and for a few seconds thought he might pass out. Steadying himself on the handrail, the waves of sickness washing through his overtaxed body finally faded.

It was at that moment that he ran into the people from the sailboat. Firing blindly to try and keep them away, Ricky saw that his path to the lifeboats was blocked. He had to find another way. He headed back up to deck eight, planning on cutting through the Centrum and using the grand staircase to descend to deck seven.

The only problem was, he'd forgotten about the dead he had released.

He barely made it to the casino before he saw thirty of the creatures coming toward him from the front of the ship. A few stopped to fight over pieces of some of his Faithful who had been brought down, but most were heading in his direction.

Cursing his luck, he headed back the way he had come. As he neared the sliding glass door leading to the portside exterior walkway, he stopped again when he saw Heather cautiously look through the very door he was going to use to escape. Rage at this woman overcame Ricky's common sense, and from thirty feet away he fired an un-aimed shot in her direction. She ducked back and fired a few return shots that shattered the glass panel of the door, but otherwise did no damage.

Then, Ricky got an even bigger surprise. More bullets came at him from the doors set in the starboard side of Centrum. Without thinking, he spun in that direction and started squeezing the trigger of his pistol as rapidly as he could. Three times it fired before the slide locked back. It was empty.

Squealing in rage, he flung the empty pistol down and looked around wildly for somewhere to hide. There was a door in front of him, and without thinking he ran through it.

Entering the balcony above the Sounds Lounge, Ricky heard the keening noises coming from the dead below as they sensed him. Seeing no other way out, he hid behind the last row of seats near the rail of the balcony. Looking around at where he'd ended up, he cursed the fact that the dead he had let loose were the very reason he was now trapped.

\*\*\*

Heather picked up the discarded pistol and handed it to Steve. Without a word, she walked purposefully to the doors leading to the balcony of the Sounds Lounge. Although Ricky was unarmed, she still used caution entering. Once inside, she stopped for a moment to let her eyes adjust. With her rifle at the ready, she moved down the center aisle as she checked each row for Ricky. She had seen him duck inside and knew he was here. Behind her, Steve and Tick-Tock covered the Centrum, occasionally shooting any of the dead who approached their position.

Heather was closing in on the last row next to the balcony rail when she heard someone crying softly.

Stopping, she called, "Come on out Ricky. I promise I won't shoot you."

I've got another idea on how to deal with your fat ass, she thought.

The sobbing grew louder, so Heather said, "If I have to come get you, I'm going to shoot you in both your knees and drag you out into the Centrum for the stinkers to eat. Now show yourself."

From behind the last row of seats, two hands poked up followed by Ricky's fat, red face. His crying stopped and he opened his mouth to speak, but Heather ordered, "If you say one word, I'll shoot you in the nuts."

Ricky shut his mouth with a snap.

Heather ordered, "Move over to the aisle and stop."

Ricky obeyed and was quickly standing with his back to the railing, the main floor of the lounge spread out behind him. Heather advanced until she was only feet away, never moving the barrel of her rifle from where it was aimed at Ricky's crotch.

He opened his mouth to speak again, but Heather cut him off by saying, "You make me sick. When I was a cop, I used to see perverts like you all the time. We'd lock them up, but after ten years or so, they'd get out and go right back to chasing little girls and boys."

Ricky looked uncomfortable as Heather went on, "One of the little girls you molested on this ship was twelve years old. You're a sick freak. You manipulated her and her sister along with all the rest of your Faithful."

Ricky remained silent as he pushed himself further back over the balcony rail, trying to put as much distance as he could between himself and Heather. Behind him, he could hear the whining of the dead.

"So you like screwing little girls?" Heather accused, as she advanced on Ricky in four quick steps. "So you like getting fucked?"

Snapping out with the butt end of her rifle, Heather drove it into the center of Ricky's face to send him reeling backwards off the balcony.

Above his scream of terror, she yelled, "Now you're fucked!"

The Reverend Ricky Rose bounced off a seat in the main gallery of the Sounds Lounge before coming to land in a crumpled pile on the deck. Knowing where he was and that he had to run, he tried to get his feet under him. As soon as he moved his right leg, he screamed in agony. When he looked down, he saw it was bent at an unnatural angle halfway between his knee and ankle. He inhaled blood and started choking as he tried to draw a breath through his shattered nose.

As he rolled over, coughing and sputtering while trying to blow out the blood so he could get some air, a shape blocked out the emergency lights, casting a shadow over him. He looked up to see what it was and all he could do was issue a barely whispered, "No."

Standing in front of him, still wearing the same torn Miami Dolphins jersey, was the dead woman who had gotten him sexually aroused months earlier on his first trip to the Sounds Lounge.

The same woman who he'd had hoisted up and strapped down so he could see what it was like to have sex with the dead.

The same woman who now lunged down to bite him as the hundreds of other flesh eating dead that populated the Sounds Lounge fell on him for what they could tear off his body and devour.

Heather turned away as Ricky's screams echoed through the compartment. For her, justice had been served.

Chapter Twenty-Four

The Dead Calm/The Gulf of Mexico:

Tick-Tock yelled down to Brain from the rear of deck twelve, "Hold it steady, Pork Chop. Heather's coming down." Looking at the sailboat below her, Heather adjusted the rope trailing down that they had taken from the rock-climbing wall.

"This is too much like the bank building," she said. "I think I'm getting déjà vu."

"If you throw up, do you call it déjà food?" Steve tried to joke, following up with, "Can you get déjà vu all over again?"

Heather chuckled, but stopped abruptly when she looked at Tick-Tock standing nearby, solemn faced and silent. Suddenly, the pain of losing Susan hit her harder than before and she felt the anger build up inside her. She wasn't mad at Steve for his dumb joke, she was pissed off at the loss of a friend, angry that there was nothing she could do to make it better for Tick-Tock or herself.

Looking over the stern of the Dead Calm, Tick-Tock said, "He's in position, Heather. Wait until your feet are on the deck before you let the rope go from the D-ring."

Heather nodded. Before lowering herself over the side, she said, "It'll get better, Tick-Tock."

He nodded once and motioned for her to go. As she started to descend, she heard him say, "Maybe, maybe not."

Once the three of them were on The Usual Suspects, Steve told Brain to start cruising from lifeboat to lifeboat to search for Mary and Sheila. After Heather had taken care of Ricky, they had attempted to look for the two women, but by then the dead had swarmed over the ship in such numbers that it was impossible. After making their way to deck twelve, they saw dozens of lifeboats holding the remnants of the Faithful floating on both sides of the Dead Calm. This gave them hope that somehow Heather and Sheila had made it into one of them.

As they checked each lifeboat, they gave its occupants directions on how to start the engines and showed them how to use the compass to keep them headed west toward land. Some of the boats with more experienced people on them had already started to head for shore. Heather was sad to find out that the one holding the two Hungarian sisters had already taken off, but was glad the two young girls had made it to safety. She silently wished them luck. They, however, had no luck finding Sheila and Mary until they came to the final lifeboat.

Here, an older man told them about how he'd been searching for Reverend Ricky on deck seven when the dead started coming out of the cabin area at the front of the ship. He'd been talking to Sheila, and when the dead showed up, she had taken off into the aide station. Seconds later, she came out helping some butch looking woman - at this description of Mary, Tick-Tock gave a quick, hard laugh before falling again into silence - and together, the two of them went to one of the lifeboats, climbed in and lowered it down to the water. Sheila's last words to him had been, "Haul ass, Pops. That bastard Ricky must have opened all the hatches. In about ten minutes you're going to be up to your balls in stinkers."

Steve thanked the man and told Tick-Tock to take the wheel.

"Which way?" His friend asked. "They could have gone in any direction."

Steve gave him a skeptical look and said, "There's no way either of those two could figure out how to start a boat, much less how to steer or navigate it, so we need to look -"

"Down current," Tick-Tock finished.

As they motored away, neither turned to look as the Dead Calm settled at the stern. Already, deck eight was submerged.

They were well away when it slipped completely beneath the waves.

*** 

Mary and Sheila watched the sunrise with dread. In their rush to escape the Calm of the Seas, they had taken one of the few open lifeboats in the ship's compliment. Now that the sun was rising, they knew they would pay for it as they were exposed to its harsh rays. The night had been cool, so they had huddled together for warmth, but despite it being February, they could already feel the air warming up as the morning wore on.

"Maybe I should try the engine again," Sheila said.

"You tried to start it for two hours and didn't get so much as a pop," Mary replied. "Besides, where are we going to go?" She asked as she waved her hands at the empty expanse of the Gulf of Mexico.

"Steve said we're not far away from Texas" Sheila replied. "We could make it there by heading west."

"And then what?" Mary asked.

Sheila shrugged. She hadn't thought that far ahead. They had a little food and some water, but all they had for a weapon was the knife that came with the survival kit on the lifeboat.

Looking at the oars stowed along the gunwale, Sheila decided that she wasn't going to just sit and let herself die of exposure and thirst. As she started to unfasten them, Mary watched what she was doing for a minute before turning and looking out over the Gulf, not looking forward to manual labor. Suddenly, she spotted something. Not believing her eyes, she blinked rapidly to clear them and it was still there. Standing, she said to Sheila, "Don't bother with those."

"I'm not going to just sit here and rot," Sheila snarled back. "We're going to row for shore and you're going to help," She'd already made up her mind that if Mary didn't help her, she was going to tie her to one of the oars and whip her if need be.

"No, Honey," Mary said in an exasperated voice. "We don't need to, look."

Sheila saw that Mary was pointing off in the distance. As her eyes followed in that direction, she saw the mast of a sailboat. After watching in silence for a moment, she could make out the boat itself and saw that it was heading toward them.

"We don't need to." Mary repeated before adding brightly, "Here comes Steve."

*** 

Steve lowered the binoculars from his eyes and said to Tick-Took, "It's Mary and Sheila. Let's go pick them up."

Tick-Tock sighed and said something that gave Steve hope that his friend was starting to come out of his depression. Looking at him with one raised eyebrow, he replied, "Do we really have to?"


Watch for:
DEAD WEIGHT; Book Three of The Dead Series (Now available)
DEAD END; Book Four of The Dead Series (Now available)

Made in United States
Orlando, FL
10 December 2022